Also by Molly Harper

Never Been Witched

MOLLY HARPER

sourcebooks
casablanca

For my kids, the real Josh and Mina

Published by Sourcebooks Casablanca, an imprint of Sourcebooks
P.O. Box 4410, Naperville, Illinois 60567-4410
(630) 961-3900
sourcebooks.com

Originally published in 2024 as an audiobook by Audible Originals.

Cataloging-in-Publication Data is on file with the Library of Congress.

Printed and bound in the United States of America.
VP 10 9 8 7 6 5 4 3 2 1

Chapter 1

Alice

STARFALL POINT, MICHIGAN

ALICE SEASTAIRS GREW UP IN a household where having her hands slapped away from rare antiques was an expected occurrence, but no one expected to have their hands slapped by a ghost. No one.

Such was life as Starfall Point's least relevant witch-slash-ghost-wrangler.

Her morning had started off so normally. Well, normal for Alice. She'd barely slipped on her sensible gray blazer when a maple cabinet just sort of materialized at Superior Antiques' front door. Her grandparents hadn't seen fit to tell her that they'd secured several pieces from the estate of Matilda Thigpen. They didn't bother to tell her the pieces were scheduled for delivery before the island's late-summer tourist crowds besieged the cobblestone streets. Mitt Sherzinger and his veritable train of pedal-wagon drivers were delivering it before her grandparents' usual morning call from Boca Raton.

Sherman Thigpen had the good grace to look embarrassed,

being caught peering through her front-door glass as she descended from her apartment above the shop. "Sorry, I thought the lawyer would have called you, the one who's handling my grandmother's estate?"

Alice sipped her blessedly hot, life-giving coffee while Sherman explained that her grandparents had liked several of Matilda's pieces so much that they'd purchased them from her estate for a prepaid price. Matilda was able to keep her beloved antiques until she passed, while using her newly acquired pocket money for several trips to Vegas and a week in Antigua. It seemed like a strangely patient, altruistic move from Franklin and Marilyn Proctor—who tended to be, well, neither.

"Mitt and his crew were willing to get up extra early to help me move this stuff...but I am paying them by the hour," Sherman said, nodding to the yawning college kids.

Mitt, whose muscular bicycle-pushing thighs were legendary on a tiny island that restricted the use of motor vehicles, grinned and waved. "Morning, Alice!"

Alice lifted her hand awkwardly, turning to Sherman. "Was Clark Graves your grandma's lawyer?"

Sherman smiled. "Yeah, how did you know?"

Alice tried so hard not to let her annoyance show, because she was unwilling to explain why exactly Clark Graves would want to complicate her morning by sending a client by the shop before she'd had an appropriate amount of caffeine. She preferred to tell herself that it was something to do with the letter opener her coven-mate Riley Denton-Everett had telekinetically flung at Clark's... legal briefs.

"Small town. Not many options." Alice sighed. Despite the fact that they hadn't bothered to warn her about this "shipment," she was sure her grandparents would expect to see each of these pieces displayed to their best advantage when they arrived. Whenever that would be.

It took an hour and considerable sweat equity from all involved to get the dozen or so pieces situated in era-appropriate clusters with the current stock. Alice's dove-gray suit—which looked pretty much like every other article of clothing in her wardrobe—was a dusty shambles by the time they were done, but she was happy with the overall effect of blending Matilda's things into the showroom. The trick was to make the room look like little conversational clusters of furnishings, so customers didn't feel like they were crashing through their grandma's garage sale.

Swiping at her wrinkled blazer, Alice supposed she was lucky Clark didn't come along to oversee the delivery and watch her squirm in discomfort. Frankly, she was surprised he had passed up the opportunity.

She stepped in front of the most formidable piece in Matilda's collection. The tall maple armoire was basically elegant, freestanding towel storage. Alice doused a soft cleaning cloth in her own custom polish blend, a beeswax base that left wood surfaces bright and smelling of lemon. Her grandparents preferred an older brand that left the entire showroom reeking of synthetic flowers, but she was allowed some secrets.

Rubbing down the cabinet's gleaming front panels with the cloth, Alice wondered what she was going to do about the Clark situation. She'd betrayed her sisters, her coven, in so many ways, big and small. She'd lied, by omission and outright. She could have told them so many times about so many things, and she'd chosen not to. And now she was in so deep, she wasn't sure they'd ever forgive her, even if she confessed everything. Grace was a gift she wasn't familiar with, on several levels. She dragged a hand through her thick coppery hair, gone slightly wavy thanks to her early-morning exertions. Nope, she definitely hadn't drunk enough coffee to think about Clark.

Alice tugged at the deep storage drawers, but they appeared to be wedged shut, which wasn't entirely uncommon with pieces this old. Wood swelled over time, with temperature and humidity. Or sometimes, extremely old internal metal bits just decided they didn't want to do their jobs anymore. Over the years, Alice had quietly become an expert in how to coax those old bits out of their retirement.

Besides, she *had* to search the cabinet thoroughly before she officially put it up for sale. It wouldn't do to sell a piece that could contain Matilda's belongings—old quilts, financial records, vintage erotica. She'd seen enough of that to want to avoid the screaming phone calls from upset clients at either end of the transaction. She pulled carefully at the drawer, listening for the telltale squeak of distressed hardware. No sound came forth, because the drawer refused to budge.

"Come on," she whispered, wrenching the drawer pulls just a little harder, nudging the drawer back and forth. She sighed in satisfaction when she managed to open the drawer just an inch.

"Get your grubby hands off my Bessie!" a voice shouted directly into her ear just as cold, insubstantial hands slapped her own. She jumped, as much from the noise as from the unsettling pins-and-needles sensation of a ghost touching her.

Alice tumbled back, knocking into a side table as she sprawled on the imitation Aubusson carpet. Hissing, she rubbed her elbow where it had smacked into a lower shelf. The ghost, standing over her in all his silvery-gray transparent glory, was dressed in a workingman's version of Charles Mulworth's clothes: loose lawn shirt, homespun breeches, leather work apron. Though Shaddow House's resident Regency-era ghost gentleman would never wear something so coarse and vulgar as sportswear, she supposed.

Stop. Breathe. Think, she commanded herself. Considering that she worked in a store full of other people's cherished furnishings, it was shocking she didn't see more "attachment objects"—items that held so much significance in a person's life, or sometimes in their death, that the person's ghost stayed connected to them rather than move on to the afterlife. Still, she'd never encountered a ghost without her coven before; at least, not a hostile one.

How would Riley approach this?

Alice pasted on her best customer-service smile. "Hello. How can I help you?"

"You can tell me what you think you're doing, yanking at me drawers like that!" the ghost yelled.

Caroline Wilton would have laughed at such an obvious and unintended double entendre. Also, Caroline would have done it silently, but Alice lacked the ability to effectively snicker under her breath. This spirit had an East London accent as rough and hardened as his hands. He would not appreciate being condescended to.

Alice wiped the shopkeeper's smile from her face and held her hands up as if to shield herself. "I'm sorry. I meant no offense."

"You can see me?" he asked, eyeing her suspiciously. "It's been ages since anyone has been able to *truly* see me. Normally, I'm just a shadow or a cold draft. When I want to make contact, I give people a good smack and they think it's static or some such thing. Makes 'em uncomfortable enough to leave my Bessie alone."

Alice was weirdly charmed at the tumble of words coming out of his thin lips. She replied, "Yes, sir, I can see you."

The ghost scoffed. "'Sir' is for fancy lords and snobs. My name is Arthur. I must be rusty at this ghosting bit. Matilda hasn't paid attention to me in years."

Alice conceded, "I'm a witch, with magical skills that allow me to communicate with you. In most cases, ghosts have to choose for people to see them, but my magic—well, my coven's magic—lets us work around those rules. Most of the time, at least. Your lovely piece has been purchased by this antique shop, and I have to open the drawer so I can make sure the previous owner didn't leave anything inside," she explained, careful to keep her tone polite as she pushed to her feet. The carpet was disheveled by her fall, revealing the much-preferred wooden floors underneath.

"The previous owner," Arthur scoffed, imitating Alice's formal tone. "Awful woman. Spent her entire life harping at her husband about their equally stupid children. Never had enough money to suit her. Of course, holding on to money wasn't a skill any of the Thigpens had a knack for."

Alice considered that for a moment. Art and Matilda Thigpen were known spendthrifts, which might have been why Matilda felt compelled to sell her furniture. The couple were known for taking expensive vacations every winter "to get away from the gloom," and for frequently redecorating their large home, which was just down the street from Riley in Shaddow House. Frankly, it was a miracle they'd held on to so many nice pieces over the generations. And this ghost held the cabinet so dear that he'd named it Bessie.

OK, then.

"I think the Thigpens' grandson has learned from the error of their ways," Alice said. "He's going to rent the house out when he can't spend time there himself. That seems pretty sensible."

Arthur harrumphed. "I'll believe it when I see it with my own eyes. Little sneak never stopped trying to pry open my Bessie so he could search through her. Kept insisting there had to be treasure hidden inside her, because she was *so shiny*. Of course, she's shiny. Didn't I spend weeks sanding her with my own two hands? Bessie is my masterpiece. American red maple. Do you have any idea how difficult it was to get that in my time? I worked too bloody"— Arthur stopped himself and glanced guiltily at Alice—"too hard on her to let some scamp ransack her."

"How did you prevent that?" Alice asked, letting a laugh escape. Plover, the ghost of a very proper British butler who oversaw the many ghosts haunting Shaddow House, appreciated being asked questions. He enjoyed instructing "his ladies" in the ways of keeping Shaddow House safe. She hoped that Arthur would relax under the same treatment, or at least stop the ghostly hand-slapping.

"By holding the drawers shut," Arthur said proudly, making Alice laugh. Ghosts could only physically interact with their own attachment objects...and people—obviously they could slap people.

Clearly, Arthur held Bessie very dear indeed. "I did it off and on for decades. One year, they could store their precious blankets behind Bessie's doors, and the next, she wouldn't budge."

"Why?" Alice asked.

"Because it was funny to give them false hope," Arthur replied. "I'm dead, aren't I? How else am I going to occupy myself?"

"Good point," Alice conceded, pinching her lips shut to prevent another laugh from escaping. But she couldn't, and soon Arthur was chuckling too. "How long have you been holding them closed, at last count?"

"The drawers?" He considered it for a moment. "The top, three years. The bottom, a hundred fifty years, give or take. The cabinet doors? I don't hold them as much. I couldn't have them getting rid of Bessie because she was unusable. As it was, they stuck her in one of the guest rooms, where hardly anybody could see her."

"You could have just opened all of the drawers and doors all at once," Alice noted.

Arthur shot her an incredulous look. "Where would the fun be in that?"

Behind her, the phone rang. Alice huffed, checking her watch as she turned toward the checkout counter. She'd let time get away from her. Her grandparents were a bit late with their call this morning. Every single morning, they called to make sure the shop was "properly prepared" for the day, and those calls had gotten more contentious as their annual summer "inspection" had been delayed. She grabbed her coffee cup where she'd set it aside and took a fortifying swig.

In the summers, Alice's grandparents came back and lived

in their family home, Proctor House. In fact, they'd planned to come back earlier than usual this year, but Grandfather Franklin's doctor had declared him unable to travel without surgery on his hip. Frankly, Alice was surprised that the Proctors hadn't demanded that she come down to Florida to take care of him while he was infirm.

"Bah, those infernal talking machines. Matilda used hers to distraction, always jawing to this neighbor or that," Arthur grumbled as the phone continued to ring. "Never had a nice thing to say."

Alice turned back toward Arthur and shrieked at the sight of yet another man, standing on the other side of the front door, peering in at her. This one was alive—how strange to have to make that pulse-based distinction—and waving at her. Alice stepped back, wincing at the grating noise her low-heeled shoes made on the hardwood. Grandfather Franklin hated it when she walked too loudly.

The confusion had her bobbling her coffee, nearly splashing it on the expensive surfaces around her.

"What is *wrong with me* today?" Alice whispered, setting the cup aside and walking to the door. She opened it and gawked. She had no excuse for her undignified response, other than the fact that the man at her door was…lickable, but Alice would never have the confidence to say it out loud.

Behind her, the phone was still ringing.

The stranger had a lean and hungry look. Alice never really understood that Shakespearean sentiment before now, but there he was in all his glory, his eyes blue-gray pools of appetite. His lips made her think…things. His well-defined jaw gave his suntanned face a long, angular shape. His hair was wavy and the sort of dark brown she'd only seen in highly polished hickory finishes.

She had to stop thinking about people in terms of furniture...

He was tan and tall, and his suit... Alice knew enough about clothes to know that she'd never seen its like before. This was not an off-the-rack selection from a department store. This man had stood patiently waiting while a tailor chalked lines on the charcoal-gray pants.

Why was she thinking about this man's pants?!

She wanted to *rumple* him, climb on his lap and unbutton that shirt while disheveling the hell out of him. And she wanted it badly.

"I know it's early, but I saw you through the window—are you open?" he greeted her in a smooth tone. Her cheeks flushed red and she barely—*barely*—resisted the urge to fan her face with the nearest file folder.

"Um, yes, only just," Alice said, running a hand over her mussed hair. Of course, a man who turned her knees to jelly would walk through the door when she was as unkempt as a Dickensian street urchin. The phone, which had briefly stopped ringing, renewed its wailing.

"I was looking at that letter opener," he replied, nodding to a display of smaller items Alice had arranged in the window. Curating the front window displays was one of the few areas of the shop where she got away with some creativity. The "hand-sized" collectibles tended to sell much faster, particularly in the tourist season—pocket watches, ceramics, even desk accessories. The stock rotated so quickly, her grandparents didn't have time to complain about her arrangements.

"When I was younger, my dad had something like it," he said. "It caught my eye as I was walking past and I... Did you need to get that?"

He pointed at the ringing phone on the counter. The motion brought the scent of him closer to her face, the smell of a warm summer breeze blowing from the ocean through a citrus grove. Yep, it was entirely possible she was losing her mind.

"Oh, no, the machine can get it," Alice assured him.

"Are you unwell, miss?" Arthur asked, gesturing his transparent hand at his cheeks. "You're going a little bit flushed, there."

Alice turned toward Arthur, grimacing.

"Oh, no, he can't see me," Arthur informed her cheerfully, sliding behind the cabinet as if he was hiding. He peeked out with an impish expression. "Because I don't want him to. It's much more fun this way. Oh, I think I'm going to find this very amusing indeed."

"Shh," she hissed at him.

The customer's eyebrows arched. "Beg pardon?"

"Oh, just warding off a sneeze," Alice lied, waving a hand in front of her face. "You know, antique shops, they get so dusty."

"That was a terrible lie," Arthur snickered. When Alice shot him a scathing look, he added, "And you can't even shush me again! This is brilliant. And I was afraid this place was gonna be boring!"

The man glanced around, unaware of Arthur's cackling. Between the lack of caffeine, the ghostly laughter, and the phone—which had started to ring *again*—a stabbing headache was starting to develop right behind Alice's eyes.

"I don't see any dust in here," said the customer. "You keep this place impressively clean. It's a little crowded, maybe. You know, I normally don't like antique shops. They always seem to smell like mildew and broken dreams, but this one is…nice."

She laughed. "Must be the floral air freshener."

"No, now that you mention it." He wrinkled his nose. "It's a bit strong, isn't it?"

The floral air freshener was the same brand as her grandparents' favorite polish, and they used so much of it that the smell lingered on everything, no matter how Alice tried to air the place out.

"The owners insist on it," she told him. "They think it makes the place smell like an English garden."

Arthur gasped, clearly insulted.

"I have been in multiple English gardens, and I can tell you they are way off the mark," the newcomer told her. "Is it possible your employers are smell-blind?"

"Anything is possible," Alice said.

"What the bloody hell is 'smell-blind'? Is this what passes for flirtation in this modern era?" Arthur groused. Alice shook her head slightly at him.

The stranger frowned at her. "Is everything all right? Are you sure you don't need to get that phone?"

"No, it's just—my grandparents call every morning to, uh, check on me. They own the shop," Alice admitted. She tried not to clench her eyes shut in regret. *Why* did she just admit to working for her grandparents? Why not slap on a name tag that read "UNEMPLOYABLE LOSER" to go with her bedraggled suit?

"Oh... So I just called your grandparents' olfactory senses into question?" the man said, wincing.

"Yes, but you're not the first one to do that," Alice assured him. "A very dear friend of mine compared it to air freshener in a funeral home restroom."

The man threw his head back and laughed, while Arthur made

a disgusted sniffing noise. "It's a wonder the human species has continued, if this is what you call wooing."

Alice frowned at him, shaking her head. She would not shush him again.

"Well, I guess 'smell-blind' is nicer than 'air freshener of the living dead,'" the man hooted, extending his hand. "Collin Bancroft."

"Alice Seastairs," she replied, gripping fingers that were long, tapered, and warm against her skin. The name sounded familiar, but she wasn't sure from where. "And I don't think that's exactly what I said."

Collin chuckled. "I took poetic license."

"That was *not* poetic," Arthur insisted, from behind Collin. "That was pitiful."

"Would you like to see the letter opener?" Alice asked, ignoring their historical heckler.

"Please." Collin grinned at her, and the jellification of her knees only worsened. It was such a smile. Warm. *Kind*, even. The sort of smile that launched movie careers and melted a thousand hearts. And it didn't matter what this man's price range was; she was going to make sure he walked out of the shop with the letter opener. It was worth it, if it put that expression on his face. She would put the difference in the till out of her own pocket.

"My dad always swore it was a narwhal horn," Collin told her as she pulled the blade from its green velvet display box. The polished steel blade was set in a spiral-shaped handle made of some sort of bone or horn material. Honestly, it looked like something one would buy in one of those fantasy shops in a mall that sold twenty-sided dice and pewter wizard figurines. But Alice had liked the way it felt in her hand when she'd seen it in an estate sale. It had felt *significant*, like it was going to be important to her life.

"I can't guarantee that this is narwhal, as, oddly enough, I don't have a lot of narwhal samples to compare it to," Alice told him, making him laugh—a pleasant, low rumble that sang across her nerve endings like a cello player's bow. "It's most likely a ram's horn, or a goat. I have a list of experts you could contact for testing if that sort of thing is important to you. But I can date the maker's mark on the hilt to Danbury's, an English artisan who operated in Bath in the early nineteenth century. It wasn't a particularly prestigious workshop, but they created some interesting pieces."

"I like it," Collin said, balancing the blade in his hand. "Reminds me of hanging out in my father's office, waiting for him to finish work, pretending I was a pirate."

Though it sounded like a happy memory, the look on Collin's face was so sad in that moment, Alice's heart lurched. Forget the letter opener. She was in very serious danger of giving this man her grandparents' whole shop.

Oh, dear. This was inconvenient.

"I'll take it," he informed her. "No need to wrap it."

He hadn't even checked the price. She didn't know whether that was a positive sign. But given that he didn't balk when she handed him the velvet case that came with the blade (and the price tag), she proceeded with the sale.

"So, have you lived on the island long?" he asked as the phone rang again. She tried very hard not to let the distress show on her face, knowing that she was going to pay for ignoring her grandparents' calls. Even if she explained that she'd been with a customer, they wouldn't be appeased. Alice knew this wasn't a smart play. She just needed this conversation to last a little longer.

"Most of my life," Alice replied as he handed her his credit card. To her surprise, Collin frowned at that. "Really?"

And because she needed just a little more chaos in her life, three members of the Shaddow House Ghost and Friday Night Euchre Club (Riley and Caroline were still arguing about the coven's name) chose that moment to burst through the door. Mina was at the head of the pack, of course, as "she who could not be contained." Also, despite being a teenager, she was considerably taller than both Riley and Caroline, so her legs were longer and cardio took less effort.

Mina had stopped at the door long enough to hitch heart-shaped aqua sunglasses into her messy chestnut bun, so Caroline crashed into her back.

"Oof, no sudden stops, sweetie," Caroline said, rubbing her nose, which had smashed between Mina's shoulder blades. Riley was a little faster on her feet and had sidestepped the collision, but seemed as shocked as Alice to find a customer in the shop before eight a.m.

"Alice, uh, we were just heading over to Starfall Grounds for rugalach... Everything OK?" Riley asked. She barely gave Collin a glance as she tried to subtly sidle between Alice and Arthur. She was getting better and better at that.

They'd become a coven unintentionally, which seemed apparent in their affectionately dubbing themselves the Shaddow House Ghost and Friday Night Euchre Club. Riley's hereditary magic had chosen Alice and Caroline to be her "witch support," assisting the last of the Dentons in managing Shaddow House and its hundreds of ghostly residents. Then Mina and her brother, Josh, had been appointed, well, junior members, with Mina gaining telekinetic magic similar to Riley's. Josh was the victim of matrilineal magic sexism, getting a more passive "listening" ability, more like Caroline's ability to communicate with even the most recalcitrant of ghosts. Alice still hadn't figured out exactly what her particular magical talent was, or who would want to share in it. So far, the most significant development she'd experienced was a sort of magical Bat-Signal, being able to sense when either Riley or Caroline was in distress from across the island.

"Yes, Collin here was just purchasing this lovely letter opener. What brings you here so early in the morning?" Alice asked, cutting her eyes toward Arthur.

Riley shook her head.

"Don't bother. They can't see me either," Arthur chortled.

Mina responded to this by turning, behind Collin's back, and pointing two fingers at her own eyes and then the same fingers at Arthur. The cabinetmaker gasped, as if deeply offended. "They can see me?"

"If I can, they can," Alice told Arthur.

"'Can' what?" Collin asked.

"Um, get up this early in the morning," Alice replied, smiling sweetly, even as lying to him made her feel an icy twinge of guilt. "As a friend group, we're all trying to be a little more cheerful in the mornings. Did you need something, Riley?"

"Oh, nothing *specific*," Riley said, tilting her head toward Arthur. "Judith was walking past the shop earlier and told us she saw you having quite an animated conversation. We thought we'd stop in, see how your day was shaping up."

Riley gave Arthur a pointed look, which probably meant that Judith Kim, one of the cornerstone members of Nana Grapevine, had seen her talking to herself through the shop window. If that was the case, within the hour every woman in town over the age of fifty-five would know that Alice had been seen talking to herself through the shop window. Great.

"I told her you were probably just talking to your grandparents on speakerphone," Caroline assured her.

"Thank you," Alice told her. "You are a very good friend."

"Nana Grapevine, *neutralized*," Riley said solemnly.

"I still can't believe they see me," Arthur grumbled. "After I specifically set out for them *not* to see me, so I could laugh at their expense. I suppose they can hear me too."

Now it was Caroline's turn to wave a hand at her ear, behind Collin's back, and then point to Arthur. His ghostly mouth dropped open. "How rude!"

"They're a little more talented than the average person," Alice muttered quietly. "You weren't prepared for it."

"I'm sure they are," Collin said, blinking at her. "Should I just come back at another time?"

Oh, this was becoming complicated.

Suddenly, Caroline's eyes narrowed, and a smile of recognition bloomed on her face. "Wait, Collin! Collin Bancroft? Good to see you again."

Alice frowned as Caroline threw her arms around Collin's besuited middle. Collin startled at Caroline's casual affection—which was, honestly, something Alice had had to adjust to, herself—and then he chuckled, patting Caroline's back and managing to back out of the hug without a single wrinkle to his shirt. Alice was pretty sure she'd never seen Collin in her life. Why was Caroline hugging him?

"I know, it's been a while," Collin said. "I was trying to avoid unpleasant family scenes. You know how it goes."

"Yes, I do. Collin's family owns Forsythia Manor. He just purchased the Duchess," Caroline supplied helpfully. "And he holds the record for failed beer-ordering attempts at The Wilted Rose."

"With your brothers serving at the bar, I had some chance," Collin muttered. "It was a numbers game."

"He's not wrong," Caroline conceded.

"Collin Bancroft, as in *those* Bancrofts," Alice said. "Ah."

Her grandparents had warned her about the Bancroft family. Repeatedly. The Bancrofts were greedy and hateful. The Bancrofts were selfish and couldn't be trusted. The Bancrofts didn't care who they stepped on to reach their own goals. Then again, they'd also warned her about the Denton family and the Wilton family.

The Bancrofts were summer people. They didn't even live on the island full-time. Alice had learned to take her grandparents' warnings with a grain of salt. Besides, they'd never really elaborated on *why* they thought the Bancrofts were pure, unadulterated evil. As usual, they just expected Alice to take their pronouncements as law.

Alice worked to keep her face impassive. It was very good that she hadn't answered her grandparents' calls, because they would have been furious to know a Bancroft was in the shop, even if he was spending several hundred dollars on an arguably very ugly desk piece.

"Yeah, those Bancrofts. I swear, I'm nothing like my aunt and uncle, if you've met them," Collin told her, pursing his lips.

Alice wanted to bite his lips.

What was *wrong* with her?

"By the way, this is Riley Denton-Everett, Nora's niece," Caroline told him.

"Really?" Collin clearly recognized the name and reached out to shake Riley's hand. "Nice to meet you. When I wasn't trying to illegally obtain alcohol, I pestered your aunt incessantly to let me inside Shaddow House. She was very skilled at telling me where to quote 'park my entitled little ass'—which always seemed to be elsewhere."

"Sounds about right," Riley said.

"I wasn't the most likeable kid," he admitted.

"And this is Mina Hoult," Caroline added.

Collin looked truly discomposed for the first time since entering the shop.

"Hoult? As in Ben Hoult? So, you and Ben?" Collin asked, his dark brows arched, as he looked between Caroline and Mina as if he was searching for shared features.

"No, no," Caroline said, shaking her head. "I'm not her biological mom. Ben went away for college and only moved back last year. I serve in more of a mentor-slash-unofficial-stepmom-slash-boss capacity."

"And she *loves* me," Mina sighed, wrapping her arm around Caroline and grinning at her. "Way more than Josh."

Caroline rolled her eyes. "She's right. I do. It's super annoying."

Mina sighed, contented.

"Except for the Josh part. Don't think I didn't catch you there, because that was mean," Caroline told her. Mina shrugged off the criticism with a saccharine smile. "Josh is Mina's little brother."

Shaking her head, Riley asked, "Wait, so you and Alice never met?"

Collin frowned. "Oh…"

"Alice was usually working," Caroline reminded Riley. "Here at the shop."

Riley grimaced, as she so often did when Alice's grandparents were mentioned. "Right, sorry."

"How am I being ignored here?" Arthur demanded. "I'm a *ghost* in a room full of people who can see me, for the first time in centuries, and I might as well be that hideous vase over there."

Mina snickered. "Well, we're used to it, so it's not really a novelty for us."

Collin eyed Mina speculatively. "What's not a novelty?"

For one so young, Mina demonstrated an absolutely alarming ability to think on her feet and lie. "Alice, working her tail off, being great at sales and a generally awesome business lady that I strive to pattern myself after as an adult."

Alice swallowed a little lump gathering in her throat as she handed Collin's card back. Casual praise from her coven was something else she was getting used to, along with unexpected hugs and birthday presents.

Arthur grumbled. "Watch out. That one wants something."

Caroline, who was clearly taking way too much pleasure in Alice's discomfort, interjected, "Speaking of business-lady things, we will leave you to your sales, Alice, as long as you're OK."

"Everything is fine," Alice promised.

"Well, we don't want to interrupt your, uh, transaction," Caroline said. "We'll see you later."

"You don't have to make 'transaction' sound so dirty," Alice muttered.

"Yes, I do." Caroline waggled her eyebrows at Alice before adding, "Collin, good to see you again."

"I'll come by the Rose soon, to see if I can get *someone* to serve me *something*," he said, making her laugh. "Riley and Mina, nice to meet you both."

Mina gave a passable curtsy, making Riley roll her eyes and drag the teenager toward the door. Caroline gave Arthur a significant look. Alice shook her head. Caroline shrugged and followed the other two outside. Collin watched this mime with very little response.

"So... Those are my friends," Alice said, before biting her lip.

"It's good to have interesting friends," he told her. "I can't believe we've never met before."

"Like Caroline said, I worked quite a bit during the summers," she replied as Collin's receipt printed.

"Now that I think about it, my family didn't exactly encourage me to come by the antique shops on the island," he said, frowning. "I always thought it was because they didn't want me to destroy expensive things. I was a teenager, so I didn't see the appeal anyway. I only bothered Miss Denton about Shaddow House because she was one of the few adults outside my family who told me no and meant it. I found it fascinating. Now that I think about it, nothing I just said paints me in the most positive light. Can we go back and pretend I didn't say that?"

As Alice chuckled, Arthur rolled his eyes. "This is painful to watch."

Alice dropped the receipt into Collin's maroon Superior Antiques shopping bag. "You recognized that it wasn't flattering, which is a good sign. Thank you for your patronage. We hope to see you again soon."

"Oh, I think you will," Collin told her, giving her a smile that had Alice propping herself against the counter for support. *That was just unfair.* "It was lovely to meet you, Alice."

Alice nodded. And it was the best she could do, in terms of responses. Collin turned on his heel and gave her the gift of letting her watch him walk out. This time, she *did* grab the nearest file folder and fan her face. The man could fill out a suit.

And the phone began ringing again.

Well, in for a penny, in for a pound of her grandparents lecturing her about her irresponsibility. She crossed the room and watched Collin walk down the street toward Main Square. Because apparently, she had no dignity left in her body.

"I'm assuming it has been a while for you, then, since you've had a gentleman caller?" Arthur asked, appearing to her left. Unlike the ghosts of Shaddow House, Arthur could leave the cabinet temporarily. He would just be uncomfortable until he returned to his "Bessie."

"That's none of your business," Alice told him, backing away from the window. "Also, that seems like a very direct question for someone who was embarrassed to curse in front of me a few minutes ago."

"No reason to be prim," he told her, watching the summer

crowd begin to filter into the street. "It's a natural thing, and your generation has the right of it. It's one of the few things I admire about this new age."

It had, in fact, been a while for her—almost a *year*. For a practitioner of magic, all that bottled-up energy could be dangerous. And while certain parties had made it clear that they would be happy to help her release some of that energy, she couldn't walk back into that particular trap after her eyes had been opened. She would not be fooled again.

"Is that really what you lot consider outerwear in this day and time?" Arthur asked, watching a woman walk past in denim shorts. "That wouldn't have even passed for drawers in my time."

Drawers. Right. Alice used this moment of Arthur's shorts-based distraction to yank at the drawer pulls in a series of sharp tugs, finally opening the bottom drawer of the cabinet with a shriek of hinges.

Wow, even she wasn't prepared for that to work. She tried not to make any triumphant noises as she realized she was the first person to open it in more than a century. Inside, she found…the ugliest candelabra she'd ever seen. She eased it out of the drawer just as Arthur whipped his head around.

"Ooh, you got that one past me," Arthur said. His eyes were narrowed at her, but he was laughing. "But it's my own fault for being so distracted by a woman's bared thighs."

"We are a wily and devious bunch," Alice told him absently as she dropped the candelabra on a nearby sofa. She held her hands up and shook them, as if she could rid them of the negative energy she felt coming off the truly hideous copper monstrosity shaped into nine connected loops, large enough to take up most of the deep drawer. Each loop was indented with a little cup shape, not quite deep enough to hold a candle. It was cold—not the normal cold of a bare metal object in Michigan, but a bitter temperature drop that radiated a malevolent energy. This object had a will of its own, and it did not want good things for Alice. It reminded her of—oh, no, something about the angry-looking runes etched into the candelabra's loops reminded her of the Welling locks. The locks themselves, which were made up of three circles that interlocked around empty space, resembled nuclear symbols. And they were etched with runes that seemed to match the ones in front of her.

Now that she was looking closely at the object, she realized that each little "eggcup" was just about the right size to hold one of the locks. The whole thing was like an ugly accompaniment to the Welling locks from Hell's Hideous Home Accessories catalogue.

"Oh, yes, that thing." Arthur sniffed. "Shocking, isn't it? Some cousin of the family, several generations back, hid it away in my Bessie during a visit and then slunk off to who knows where. As much as I hated to store such a thing in her, I didn't want that cretin having access to whatever it is. So I kept it shut away, until now. Gave me the creeping dread, that did."

Alice's gaze bounced between the candelabra and Arthur, then back again. This was a major development in her work with the coven, and it had just been shoved in a linen cabinet somewhere on the island, to be discovered by sheer dumb luck? What if Sherman had decided to keep the cabinet? What if he'd sold it off-island? What if the Thigpens had had a house fire?

Then Alice used language she'd never uttered in her grandparents' shop—or presence—before. "*What the fuck?*"

Chapter 2
Collin

IT WAS UNSETTLING, THE WAY Starfall Pointers stopped talking the moment Collin entered a room. He supposed there was a certain amount that was expected when you entered a room full of your employees, most of whom who had only known you as their boss for about two days. Still, the sudden cessation of whispering sort of stung, like he was too stupid to realize they were talking about him.

Still, they could have changed the subject and talked nonsense about something. The foliage. The weather. Football. Michiganders loved to talk about football. Anything to prevent this stifling cloud of conversational awkwardness.

Collin thought of the enchanting Alice Seastairs and her friends. During his strange encounter with them at the antique shop, they were *clearly* talking about something not immediately obvious to Collin—Alice with her "more talented" comment and Mina's references to "novelty." But they'd been kind enough to pretend it was part of the conversation they were having *with* him.

It had been a categorically odd morning, he decided as he walked up the elegant staircase that defined the lobby of the Duchess Hotel.

When his family built the hotel, workmen had carved the staircase from walnut imported all the way from England; it had served as the focal point for many a dramatic entrance. Debutantes and brides, politicians and celebrities, the famous and infamous had retreated for restorative, occasionally scandalous, summers at the Duchess from the moment it opened on the shore of Lake Huron in 1902.

Adorned in pristine white clapboard, the Duchess was square and blockish, emphasizing the real treasure of the property, which was the view. The Duchess stood on a small peninsula, giving it much-desired waterfront views from the lobby section that faced the lake broadside *and* two guest wings flexing back toward Main Square. Each room on its second and third stories had its own little balcony and a stunning view. The roof tiles were a distinctive brick red that looked like feathers flared back. The building gave an over-all impression of a sturdy, if slightly ostentatious, seabird ready to take flight.

Back then, the Bancroft family had a single focus: providing five-star accommodations off the beaten path for the well-off seeking a little privacy with their opulence. Generations of Bancrofts had made their money in shipping lines, mining, newspapers, and mysterious military contracts that probably weren't entirely consci-entious. They'd wanted somewhere they could retreat that wasn't already populated by other financial luminaries they saw in their daily lives, like Newport and Denver were.

The family legend went that Forsythe Bancroft III saw enough of his robber baron contemporaries in New York City on a daily basis, so when he escaped, he wanted to *escape*. He had been a rare titan of industry who had genuinely doted on his wife and children, and he had wanted his time with them to be free of scheming social climbers and business meetings disguised as friendly morning calls.

First, Forsythe constructed Forsythia Manor, the family's sumptuous "beach shack." In the early spring, the yard was ablaze in yellow from the bushes for which he'd named the house—a clever twist on his own name. Then, Forsythe realized that there was money to be made in Starfall Point. He could enjoy the pastimes the hotel had to offer—boating, beaches, croquet, pastry chefs who would sneak him sweets when his wife wasn't looking—while watching it make him money, which was his *favorite* pastime. And when he wanted, he could retreat to his own exclusive family space.

Construction of the Duchess Hotel had been careful and deliberate, resulting in a building that was comfortable and luxurious, but sturdy enough that it had been used as a storm shelter for the island's entire population on multiple occasions over the years. At the time, there were some rampant rumors that the hotel was being built for a duchess—no one was sure who or from where—who was planning a visit to Starfall Point for reasons unknown. For his own amusement, Forsythe chose to name the hotel after the gossip, since the family vacation home was named after himself.

Despite this initial enthusiasm, Forsythe sold the hotel to a family friend—another robber baron type—a few years after it was completed. Collin's parents told him that the project had simply demanded too much attention from an industrialist with extensive business interests, but Forsythe had kept the manor house for the family's use. The hotel had exchanged hands multiple times over the years, between family owners and corporate chains, before the Gilford Family Hotel Group gifted the Duchess to their youngest daughter, Aura. The Instagram-conscious socialite-slash-aspiring-lifestyle-guru spent most of the early 2000s trying to turn the Duchess into the Michigan version of an ultramodern luxury boutique hotel. She even tried to change the name to The Hotel D.

It didn't go well.

But somehow—most likely because Forsythia Manor stood so close to the hotel—the island's residents still seemed to think of the hotel as belonging to the Bancrofts. It had been odd, growing up so closely associated with something he had no real connection with or power over. Collin's parents only inherited a share of Forsythia Manor because the family tree had dwindled down to a handful of (extremely wealthy) people by the time Collin was born. He'd spent childhood summers staring up at the hotel from the manor house lawn, wondering how their family had let such a gem slip out of their hands. Not only that, but the family had largely avoided the property. They didn't sleep there. His parents didn't eat at the hotel restaurant or use the pool or any of the other amenities. It felt like a waste.

Purchasing the Duchess a few months earlier had been the culmination of Collin's lifetime dream, including years spent learning the hotel business from the ground up, careful investments of his late parents' resources, and making his move when Aura was looking to off-load a property that wasn't as profitable as it once had been. And, yes, maybe he had taken advantage of their tenuous, friend-of-a-friend, "grew up in the same circle" acquaintance, but his offer had been for fair market value. The market just wasn't great at the moment.

Even now, the lobby was not as crowded as Collin would like.

At this time of year, they should have been enjoying late-summer crowds eager to make the most of Michigan's last balmy, humidity-free days before the school year started. He couldn't get his general manager, Robert, to show him what the actual occupancy rate was, but Collin could tell that it was way below what it should have been.

He turned right and paused at the entrance of the second-floor office suite, pricking his ears as lobby conversation rekindled. He shook his head, smiling to himself despite the dilemma of what to do about Robert, who considered himself an indispensable fixture of the hotel. Collin had kept Robert on as manager on a probationary basis in an attempt to maintain some continuity of operation and comfort for the staff. Robert, who was currently sitting in Collin's chair with his feet up on Collin's oversize antique walnut desk.

Collin made plenty of noise while entering the office, thinking to give Robert an opportunity to rectify his error. To his surprise, Robert didn't seem remotely embarrassed by his posture and didn't move to take his shoes off the shining wooden surface. In fact, Robert's smart blue suit jacket was hanging on a brass clotheshorse in the corner, near the dark fireplace. He looked very comfortable.

Collin supposed he couldn't blame Robert for wanting to use this office, to keep his own award plaques and yuppie executive toys on a desk that was no longer his. Collin could only be grateful that Aura hadn't liked the "vibe" of the space and had elected not to remake it in the bright orange tones she'd splashed all over the rest of the hotel.

The owners, over the years, seemed to have respected the original elegance of this office, with its dark-wood floor-to-ceiling bookshelves over every wall not covered in navy-and-cream watered-silk wallpaper. It also offered a beautiful view of the water, had lots of space, and housed a ridiculously oversize sailboat in a bottle that had apparently belonged to Forsythe Bancroft III himself.

"Collin, my boy, how's your morning going?" Robert asked, his florid face peering over his copy of the *Detroit Free Press*. "So glad to have you bringing your expertise to the hotel after all this time."

Collin paused to force his jaw to relax. He'd be without tooth enamel within a week if he kept this up. Insincere toadying aside, Robert seemed to enjoy calling Collin "my boy" just a little too much. Collin supposed it was to be expected, as Robert had started working at the hotel as a bellhop when Collin was just a kid.

"That's my desk," Collin noted, staring pointedly at Robert's shoes.

Robert dodged this comment with a cheerful shrug. "Well, I've been using it for so long, I really didn't see much point in changing now. I believe it's appropriate for me to use this workspace for my daily duties. And I'm very comfortable here."

Collin kept his expression neutral. It wouldn't do to let Robert know how much his blithe attitude irked him. "While I agree that this office is *very* comfortable, it's never been your desk. This is not the general manager's office. This is the owner's office, and my desk now, so I'm going to need you to take your feet off it. There's an office off the front desk area, designed specifically for your use."

Robert wrinkled his nose as if he didn't agree with any of these points. "Well, I've always found this office much more convenient."

Right. Collin resisted the urge to clench his jaw.

"It's more convenient for the general manager to be located two floors away from the front desk and all its functions?" Collin asked, setting the bag from Superior Antiques on the corner of the desk. "Robert, when I took possession of the hotel, we discussed the change in your duties and the fact that I'm going to be running the day-to-day operations of the hotel."

"Well, I don't see how things really need to change in the long term. The last 'owner-operator' was fairly hands off, and I think it's best to let that continue. It's not as if you're going to…"

Collin decided the time for a neutral expression had ended. "It's not as if I'm going to what?"

They both knew where that sentence was headed, because Collin had heard it from nearly every friend and colleague back on the mainland when he'd decided to move his life to Starfall Point. *It's not as if you're going be there long term.* With dire predictions of Collin running to the nearest major metropolitan area before the end of his first winter. No one in his life seemed to believe he could live with the snow, the cold, the short days, the isolation, the lack of luxury brands.

Robert hitched his suit pants over the beginnings of a paunch. "Well—"

"Please stop starting all your sentences with 'well,'" Collin said.

"Aura never had a problem with how I did things," Robert told him, his voice flat.

Right. Collin sighed internally. Aura, who'd gotten bored once she'd hosed the entire hotel down in orange, launched a disastrous rebrand, and left everything in Robert's control.

"That was then, this is now," Collin shot back.

Julie Teagan, a longtime desk clerk, walked in with a poster-sized occupancy board, a practically prehistoric method of keeping track of room reservations for a given week. Her shoulder-length amber-colored hair fell over her pale heart-shaped face as she struggled to fit the board through the door. Collin had known Julie since they were teenagers. She was a local, a hard worker. The last time he'd seen her, she had been a waitress at the hotel restaurant.

"Julie, good to see you," he said, nodding politely.

Her dark-blue eyes darted between Collin and Robert, assessing. "I can come back."

"No, please come in. I was hoping to speak to you," Robert said.

"Actually, we were in the middle of something, Julie. Would you excuse us, please?" Collin asked.

"No, Julie, stay," Robert insisted.

Despite the pleasant smile he was plastering to his face, Collin felt a flush of guilt, because clearly, this was the last thing Julie wanted: to be trapped between her old boss and the new boss. Collin didn't know what Robert hoped to gain from this show of "dominance" over his employer.

"Um, with all due respect, I don't think I need to be here for this," Julie told Robert. "I would be happy to talk to both or either of you when you two sort this out."

With that, Julie backed out of the office with a poise Collin couldn't help but admire. And she took her board with her.

"Please clear all of your personal effects out of my office and use the front desk manager's office downstairs," Collin told Robert, making a sweeping gesture toward the door. "I'll give you time to pack."

Collin had hoped to extend Robert some grace, or at least allow him a little dignity, by not hovering while Robert boxed up his belongings. But apparently, Robert had exchanged that dignity for the sake of storming after him, out of the office, down the stairs. The sheer orange-ness of the lobby knocked Collin back a few steps, after just a few minutes' absence.

Ten years before, Aura's spiritual adviser had promised her the hotel would prosper if everything was done in bright oranges and yellows. Aura combined that with a postmillennial Scandinavian motif with (of course, orange) plastic chairs that looked like unfolded paper clips. It didn't exactly go with the rest of the island's cozy cottage ambience. Collin could only be grateful that the threat of an injunction from the local historical society kept Aura from altering the large wooden front desk and the staircase.

No one touched the staircase of the Duchess. No one.

"What do you expect me to do, if you're taking over all of my duties?" Robert demanded, following him down the stairs into the lobby.

All motion and sound seemed to stop at their descent. Of course, the lobby was considerably more crowded than it had been just a few minutes before—with five whole guests. The staff was also silent, immobilized by the sight of their manager having what could only be described as a temper tantrum on the stairs.

Yet another dramatic entrance was being staged on the famed Duchess staircase.

"There are other positions in the hotel suited to your talents: front desk manager, kitchen manager—hell, housekeeping supervisor," Collin told him quietly, even as guests and employees alike strained to hear what he was saying. "But, for all intents and purposes, yes, I will be taking over your job. Your salary will not change. That wouldn't be fair to you."

Robert bellowed, "Who do you think you are, telling me that you're just going to do *my* job? Demoting me? You think you deserve this somehow, just because you have the right name? You didn't earn this. You're just going to piss it all away! All this history! All the work of all the people who came before you, the people who poured their blood and their sweat into this hotel because they loved it. And fuck you for thinking your spoiled Manhattan ass can even begin to understand that."

"We're done here," Collin told him, walking toward the desk as calmly as he could manage. Robert had hit several nerves, but he couldn't show it. He couldn't flinch.

"I know all about you," Robert barked, even as the people around them stared. "You think you're Teflon, but I've heard the stories. And I didn't spend thirty years kissing ass and working my fingers to the bone just to have you waltz in here like the crown prince of spoiled dipshits and take my job."

Even as rage welled up in his throat, demanding to be let loose on Robert, Collin had to remind himself that this wasn't personal. It was just business. And Robert's shouting obscenities at Collin in a lobby occupied by his employees was disrespect Collin couldn't allow to stand. Collin may not have been familiar with this particular hotel, but he knew if his employees saw Robert talk to him like that and get away with it, they would think Collin was afraid. He would lose what control he had over the place within a month.

So, Robert had to go.

"Robert, I appreciate your many years of service here at the hotel, but I'm afraid that it's time for you to move on," Collin told him, in a crisp, even tone. "You will, of course, receive a generous severance package and a reference letter, if that's what you want. But I'm afraid you cannot continue your employment after this gross insubordination."

"You can't fire me. I quit!" Robert yelled.

"All right, then, forget the generous severance," Collin said, smiling. "Please submit your resignation in writing by the end of the day."

Robert looked like he couldn't decide between punching Collin or smacking him with one of the angular chrome vases that looked... sharp. Why were the vases *sharp*? That had to be some sort of liability. Dammit, Aura.

Collin filed it away for future consideration.

"Fuck you, Bancroft! Fuck your whole damn family." Robert bared his teeth and threw his hands up. He stomped off toward his actual office. Collin turned back to the lobby. Suddenly, staff and guests alike were moving again, as if a great cosmic hand had just pressed Play.

Collin approached the front desk. "Julie, can I speak to you now, please?"

"Well, at this point, I don't think I can say no," Julie replied.

"That's not—you're not ever obligated... Can we please start over?" he asked. He made a welcoming gesture toward the staircase and hoped it didn't come across as imperious.

Julie began, "Again, I don't know if—"

"You can say no," he told her. She gave a slight eye roll, but followed him up the stairs to his office. He waved toward the leather club chair opposite his desk and took his own seat.

"How would you like to be promoted to front desk manager?" Collin asked.

She smirked, taking a seat. "Purely based on spite toward Robert?"

"Not *purely*," he assured her. "You've worked here full-time for eight years. Your work history is commendable—spotless, even. Your performance reviews are practically perfect. You never take vacation or sick days, which I think we should change right away because that's not healthy. In fact, Robert was stupid enough to leave several proposals you'd written for policy changes and new programs behind in your employee file, like they are indictments of your character, when I find them to be intriguing."

"I always thought he just threw those away," she muttered.

"No, he willfully ignored what are some very solid suggestions. I'm not sure if it was fear for his job, sexism, or good old-fashioned incompetence," Collin said.

"Maybe a combination of all three," she replied.

"Are you really filling out an occupancy chart by hand? We have more than three hundred and fifty rooms," Collin marveled.

"Yeah, but we're only at thirty percent capacity," she replied with a shrug. "Mostly because Aura refused to book rooms through travel apps—with Robert's full support—because more guests meant more work."

Collin sighed, pinching his lips together. Aura also hadn't liked the "vibe" of modern advances like travel apps, computerization, and the hotel having a website.

"I have a plan for that," he told her. "I've purchased new computer equipment, new software. By the end of the month, you'll be able to track which rooms are booked, which ones have been cleaned, how many tiny shampoo bottles we have, the works. Thirty percent, huh? I knew the numbers were down, but I had no idea things were this bad."

She nodded sympathetically. "They are this bad, and they have been for a while."

"So, can you see why I need a competent manager who's not going to call me a dipshit in front of all my employees?" Collin asked.

"Technically, he called you the 'crown prince of *spoiled* dip-shits,'" Julie said.

"Yes, I know," Collin shot back, even as he smirked.

Julie's lips twitched. "I can see why you need me. But I have to ask you: Are you here to change everything, fire longtime employees, and streamline just to make the hotel attractive to a big buyer? Because I'm not willing to help you flip a hotel."

"Good," he sighed, relaxing back into his seat. "Because I'm here to stay. And I think we're going to work well together, Julie. Honesty, I can deal with. Mutiny in the lobby? Not so much."

"I can respect that," she said, nodding. "And I can promise not to foment a mutiny in the lobby."

"Thank you. I would expect that of my new front desk manager," he replied. "Which leads to my official offer to hire you for the position. I was hoping to promote you eventually, but Robert's tantrum moves up my timeline. I have a whole prospectus prepared on why you should take the job."

She grinned. "You have a whole PowerPoint presentation, don't you?"

"The slides are set to inspirational orchestral music," he told her, nodding solemnly. Julie buried her face in her hands and laughed. For the next hour, Collin and Julie went over his extensive plans for the property. The problem was that as a hotel, the Duchess was confused. The myriad of owners over the years had tried to change with the times, adding features like a yoga room, miniature golf, a golf simulator, *a miniature golf simulator*, float tanks, an indoor infinity pool—Collin still wasn't sure how that was supposed to work. And it hadn't helped. Bookings slowly dried up, summer after summer, to the point where the hotel just about broke even.

Adding to that was the orange of it all.

Now that Collin had officially taken the helm, he knew the Duchess needed to take advantage of what few other hotels had: the history. He wanted to wipe the slate clean and start over, shoring up the older sections of the hotel for structural safety and redecorating pretty much every square inch of the hotel except for his office. In a normal hotel that was open year-round, that would have to happen in phases and could take years. But, because the Duchess shut down entirely for four months when the lake froze over in winter, Collin hoped that they would be able to complete most of the changes before next summer's vacation season.

It would mean closing to guests a little earlier in the year than usual, and the construction crews would have to stay on the island and ship all the materials before the lake froze, but with an oversize crew and a bit of luck and focus, they could at least get the main wings redone in time. And the good thing about the insular nature of the island was that there wouldn't be much to distract the workmen. He just had to keep them from going full *The Shining* on each other.

By the time Collin was done outlining his plans, he and Julie were devouring cheeseburger platters from the hotel restaurant, looking over the blueprints sprawled across his desk. Just from hearing Julie's responses to his plans, he knew he'd made the right choice in promoting her. She had a realistic understanding of what was happening at the hotel, and unlike nearly every other employee he'd talked to—who had sugarcoated, downplayed, and lied to him, even—she was candid with him.

"You're really going to stay here? Year-round?" Julie asked, chewing on an onion ring. "Permanently?"

He drank from his bottle of mineral water. "Why is that so hard to believe?"

She wrinkled her nose. "You've never seen a winter here. Every Michigan winter has its own character, its own challenges. I know New Yorkers are tough and all, but—"

"I'm not saying it's going to be easy," he protested. "But the house is comfortable and I'm sort of interested in seeing if it's really as bad as people say it is."

"I'll remind you that you said that when you have half a ton of blue ice rolling up from the lake, blocking your front door," she muttered.

"Blue ice?" Collin asked.

"I'll explain later," she promised. Sipping her Coke, she pointed at the Superior Antiques shopping bag on his desk. "You took the time to go antiquing before overthrowing Bob the Terrible?"

He took the letter opener out of the maroon bag and showed it to her. "It reminded me of something my father used to keep around his office. What do you think?"

"Have we officially reached the stage of our professional relationship where I can tell you what I really think?" she asked.

Collin chuckled. "I think I've made it clear that I prefer it."

She grimaced. "It's pretty hideous."

"Well, I guess beauty is in the eye of the beholder, with this sort of thing," he said, chuckling and turning it over in his hands.

"If it makes you happy, I'm happy for you," she said. "I'm just surprised that you went into that *particular* antique shop."

Collin blinked at her. "Why?"

Julie made a helpless gesture with her hands. "The Bancrofts and the Proctors have always had…well, what most people would probably call 'beef.' But not you, because I'm guessing that you attended a private school where you had to wear a tie to class. You would probably call it 'filet mignon.'"

"You would be correct in assuming that I attended several of those schools. Any idea why the two families had 'beef'?" Collin asked.

She grinned. "It pained you to say that, didn't it?"

"A little bit," he acknowledged. "How did my family even have time to create a feud? They barely spent enough time on the island to socialize."

Julie pondered that. "I don't know… I just remember my parents saying things casually in conversation. 'The Bancrofts had never had any use for the Proctors' or 'The Proctors would never set foot in the Duchess.' As if I was just supposed to understand that was reality, like the lake freezing over or a drunk tourist ending up naked on Main Square at some point every July."

"And you don't know why?" Collin asked.

She shrugged. "Well, when people go on vacation, they tend

to get drunk, and they think tourist destinations don't have, like, *laws—*"

"No. Not the naked-tourist thing," he exclaimed, making her laugh. He was glad that she seemed to have relaxed over the course of their impromptu lunch. He was going to need Julie's support over the next few months, and that could create resentment unless they could build a comfortable working relationship. "The family-feud thing. Did one of your family members mention to you *why* the 'Bancrofts never had any use for the Proctors'?"

"Nope." She chewed her lip. "Now that you mention it, they did not. Did anybody in your family ever say anything to you?"

"My family tended to gloss over unpleasantness," he said, helping himself to one last fry. The chef made them just the way he remembered from when he was a kid: crispy, with just a little bit of sugar mixed in with the salt. As a precocious nine-year-old with considerable allowance, he'd had to sneak over to the restaurant for his fry fix. He'd spent quite a bit of his summertime sneaking around the hotel, learning about it, getting to know the staff. He'd swum in the pool, played on the putting green, made a game of memorizing the restaurant menu. He'd even requested increasingly complicated and somewhat gross sandwich combinations to see if the chef, André, would comply. And the chef very pointedly put the sandwich on the menu and named it after Collin.

Collin didn't realize it at the time, but the employees largely put up with it because he was a Bancroft, and therefore bonded to the hotel, no matter how tenuously. Unfortunately, after the sandwich thing, his parents caught wind of his adventures and were *mortified* that he'd caused trouble for people who were just trying to earn a living. He'd been "grounded" from the hotel, which just made him better at sneaking over there.

Collin hummed. "In a weird way, my father would have considered it bad form to speak poorly of a family that had less than we did. He had an old-fashioned sense of honor about that kind of thing."

Julie smiled. "I think I remember him a little, from when I was a kid, coming into Starfall Scoops and dropping twenties in the tip jar when he thought no one was looking. He always seemed like a good guy."

"He was, and he was a man who appreciated Regina's frozen-treat artistry," Collin said, the corner of his mouth lifting. Like most of the Bancrofts, Collin's father had been good at making money. He'd spent his life amassing and selling commercial real estate across the country, and he believed that spreading that money around was a great way to spend his time. It was why Collin chose to believe his parents would approve of his buying the Duchess. They'd wanted their son to be happy, productive.

Collin chose his next words very carefully. "Alice Seastairs didn't seem...put off by having me walk into her store."

"Well, she did sell you that extremely ugly knife, which does demonstrate a certain amount of hostility," Julie replied, making him snicker. "Besides, Alice wouldn't dream of being rude to a customer. She's too...civilized, I guess, is the word. Even if you'd set fire to one of those god-awful credenzas her grandparents stock, she'd just show you politely to the door. And she'd probably ask you to come back when your arson phase was over."

Collin nodded. It was an exercise in his hard-earned self-control to not demand a dozen answers from Julie about Alice: what she liked, where she spent her time, why they'd never met before. Instead, he just asked, "Do you know her well?"

"No, no one does," Julie scoffed. "Well, that's not true now, I suppose. She spends a lot of time with her friends Caroline and Riley. And their partners, Ben and Edison, by extension. And Ben's kids."

"Why wouldn't anyone spend time with Alice?" Collin asked.

"Oh, not because of Alice. She's really nice. Her grandparents are, well, *difficult* is the nice way of putting it," Julie said. "Alice's parents met when they were in college, had her a little too young, got married, and then both died, also way too young, leaving her to live with her maternal grandparents. The Proctors kept her at the store all the time, from the minute she was old enough to work there—probably a bit before, legally speaking. They're just mean people, spiteful. They always gave my mom a bad feeling, especially when they started homeschooling Alice—like they were afraid to let people talk to her. They told everybody Alice was too smart for regular school with the rest of us kids and needed special attention. And it's obvious that Alice *is* really smart, so it was believable."

Julie frowned then and swallowed heavily. Collin wondered exactly how bad things had been for Alice when she was young, to make Julie look so sad. There was a sweetness to Alice, an honesty that he found intriguing. When people found out who his family was, he could usually almost see the calculations behind their eyes, but Alice had just smiled at him as if she understood what it was like to come from complicated people. And her eyes, the endless, fathomless sea green of them—

No. After the pointless, frustrating saga of his last relationship, he didn't have the right to think about Alice like that.

"But she seems to have made some good friends now," Julie said, brightening considerably. "I'm really happy for her."

"I met Riley earlier. She seems very friendly," Collin replied, contenting himself with what Julie had revealed about Alice so far, because pushing felt...wrong.

Julie considered it for a moment. "She's interesting. Not what I expected."

Collin put his water bottle aside. "How so?"

"Well, for one, Riley had no idea she was even from Starfall Point," Julie said. "You know the Dentons have always lived here, since, like, the 1700s. Her mom took off, never to return. It was a big deal because there have always been Dentons watching over Shaddow House. But I guess her mom never even talked about the island or her family or anything. Riley only found out she had family here when her Aunt Nora died and Clark's office contacted her about the will. And now she runs Shaddow House."

Collin grimaced. He'd met Clark Graves in passing over the years. The guy seemed like the kind of smarmy douche who would hit on your date while you were in the men's room just to prove he could get her number if he wanted to.

"Everybody kind of expected Riley to be like Nora—you know, reclusive, protective of Shaddow House, a loner—but she's super friendly. Caroline and Alice are over at the house all the time. Hell, Riley's boyfriend Edison moved in earlier this year."

"The librarian?" Collin's brows rose. "She hasn't opened up Shaddow House to the public, has she?"

"Nope, only a select few get past Riley. The Shaddow family's incredibly restrictive visitor policy remains intact, which is fine with me. Place still gives me the creeps," Julie said with a shudder.

"And I don't suppose any member of the Shaddow family has actually shown up on the island in the years I've been gone?" he asked.

"Nope." Julie folded her orange linen napkin and put it on her tray. "The Shaddows are still jet-setting across who knows where, far too busy and important to visit little old Starfall Point."

"Hmmm," he said. Then there was an awkward silence. "So, the naked-tourist thing—that's still going on?"

"Every year." She nodded.

He sighed, his gaze landing on the ship in a bottle again. Collin could have taken a position at his father's company. He could have made more money, increasing the already substantial family fortune, but there were other, better-qualified people on the board who could do that. The Duchess was something he could build, something he could *save*. He wanted a life here. Starfall Point represented what he hadn't had in his life since his parents died: a home. He could have peace, contentment, and acceptance here.

Now he just had to figure out how the hell he was going to accomplish that.

Chapter 3
Alice

ALICE DIDN'T CONSIDER HERSELF A person who "scurried." But, after flipping the BACK IN 30 MINUTES sign on the shop door, she was definitely moving across Main Square with a quickness that might have communicated "person fleeing from an exploding volcano" to the casual observer.

It was possible that she was just trying to put that horrific phone call behind her. Franklin and Marilyn had been highly displeased that she'd ignored not just one but *four* of their morning phone calls, and they did not accept "early customer" as a reasonable excuse to not pick up. The only thing that kept the sour little knot in her belly from growing was the fact that her grandparents would have been just as upset if she'd answered the phone in the middle of a transaction, potentially offending a customer. Of course, she hadn't told them that the customer was a Bancroft, but that was neither here nor there.

In her rush, she didn't even pause in front of Shaddow House to admire it, something that would have been impossible just months ago, before she'd been welcomed into its secrets. It wasn't the world's most attractive home, due in part to being a mishmash of architectural styles and details added as the Dentons tried to confound the less agreeable ghosts who resided there with perpetual construction. In the end, it was a large semi-Victorian house sided in a dreamy cornflower blue with huge windows, turrets, and an honest-to-God stone folly attached to the back of the house that had never been finished—which was the point of calling it a folly, really.

While Caroline favored the gazebo, the folly had always been Alice's favorite feature of Shaddow House, a sort of half-finished tower that only people who had been in the backyard knew about—like a secret treasure. It was one of many weird quirks of the house meant to confuse the ghosts there.

As she had every time she'd visited these past few months, Alice worried that the doors of Shaddow House might not swing open for her in a gesture of sympathetic magic that she and the coven still hadn't figured out. The house didn't communicate with them directly, but it seemed to *know* things and had opinions. Every time she approached, for just a split second, she worried that the doors would stay sealed shut and she would know—finally—that the house had decided she was unworthy.

She would be deemed unfit because of her mistakes, because of how she'd betrayed her sisters, because she—didn't have to wait for this dilemma to be decided, because Edison was currently hurrying out the door, slinging his sport coat around his shoulders...and wearing a giant purple top hat. With rabbit ears attached.

"Everything OK, Edison?" she asked, trying not to stare at the big violet accessory. It definitely did not mesh with his usual "West Coast academic" vibe. "Are you late for a very important date?"

"Margaret called in sick," he said, frowning. Riley and Caroline approached the door from inside, stretching their arms out to welcome Alice into the house. Josh appeared behind them, shoving blueberry rugalach into his mouth. He needed all calories available to fuel what seemed to be *another* growth spurt.

Edison struggled with his jacket, turning in circles until Riley gently stopped and slid the sleeve onto his arm. He huffed. "Margaret never calls in sick. And now I've got to go handle story hour at the last minute."

"She's been having some health problems lately. Ned said something about her maybe stepping down as lead volunteer at the library," Caroline told him.

Alice frowned. "Really? It's kind of sad that she's spent all this time at the library trying to get hired on as librarian, but never managed it. Even with her husband sitting on the library board."

Edison shot Alice an incredulous look, which wasn't surprising considering that she'd just said it was sad he couldn't be replaced at his job. She grimaced. "Sorry, Edison."

Riley quickly changed the subject. "So, Collin Bancroft was cute."

"Cute, and way out of my league, I think," Alice replied. "Who was it that said the rich are not like us?"

"Rich people are just people with money," Riley huffed. "He seemed really nice."

"Says the rich person," Caroline noted.

Riley, a lifetime paycheck-to-paycheck girl who was still getting used to the concept of having a trust fund, began to protest, "I'm not—"

"You have a butler," Alice reminded her, nodding inside to the ghost of a pale, gaunt man looking absolutely dapper in his three-piece "service" suit and high collar.

Riley blew a raspberry sound. "A ghost butler."

"Miss Alice." Standing at Josh's elbow, Plover bowed his head to her. "We've missed you. You're such a *calming* influence on the living and dead residents of Shaddow House."

There were times that she considered it very sad indeed that her longest-running supportive father figure was the ghost of a World War I–era Englishman, but Plover loved them all so much. He had no idea how much she needed absolute approval from an older authority figure. It probably wasn't healthy, but it was what she had. Plover was everything she could have asked for in a champion.

"Still counts," Alice insisted.

"Collin Bancroft is basically a unicorn," Caroline told them. "A funny, cute, wealthy guy who's *actually* nice… Oh, shoot. No offense, Edison. Sometimes I forget you also have money."

"No offense taken," Edison said. "This is what happens when I neglect to wear my monocle. Wait, Collin Bancroft? As in the New York Bancrofts? Yikes."

"Why 'yikes'?" Riley asked. "Wait, do all rich people know each other? Is there like a secret social media platform the 'normies' don't know about?"

Edison waggled his hand back and forth. "My family is *comfortable* and nouveau riche by comparison. The Bancrofts are well beyond that. They own a little bit of everything and have done for generations. Real estate, tech, mineral rights. I think they bought part of Antarctica once, just to prove they could. If Collin is who I think he is, my grandfather was intimidated by his grandfather, and my grandfather was rarely intimidated."

"Your brow is pretty heavily furrowed there, hon," Riley noted.

Edison shook his head. "It's just that Collin and I are around the same age. When I was in school, my parents warned me not to hang out with him if we ever crossed paths."

"Why?" Alice asked.

Edison frowned. "I only saw him a few times growing up, and he seemed fine. Good guy. But I guess he went through a wild period when he hit college. The rumor was that it got so bad, his guardians threatened to disown him—which would have taken considerable legal maneuvering."

"Did anything happen while he was in college?" Alice asked.

"No...oh...*oh*," Edison gasped, looking stricken. "His parents died when he was in high school. I never made that connection. I know this sounds bad, but I barely knew the guy. I was getting these updates from my parents at intervals."

"Also, your parents aren't great at making connections via human emotion," Riley said, patting his arm.

"I would say you're wrong, but they do occasionally ask how my girlfriend, 'Miley,' is doing," he conceded. He kissed Riley soundly. "I'll text you, let you know when I'll be home."

"How very domestic," Caroline teased her as Edison practically ran down the square, purple hat catching the wind.

"I'm not going to take any shit from someone who made smiley-face pancakes for her kids this morning," Riley replied.

"It's not like I did it in heels and pearls!" Caroline shot back. "Besides, they're Josh's favorite!"

"She makes them with love," Josh said. "And shit tons of sugar."

"Language," Caroline retorted, then clapped her hands over her mouth. "Oh, good grief, I sounded just like my mother just then. It just slipped out. What are you kids doing to me?"

When Riley smirked and opened her mouth to reply, Caroline pointed a finger in her face. "If you answer, I'll show you how I cleared that lacrosse team out of the Rose last Memorial Day weekend."

Riley cackled. Caroline groaned. "Thank goodness Mina is working lunch shift at the bar right now, or she'd have a field day."

"Miss Alice, would you care to join us inside?" Plover asked. "There are crowds milling about on the sidewalk. The less they can see into the environs, the better."

Alice glanced at the large Superior Antiques shopping bag in her hands. In general, it wasn't a great idea to introduce antiques into Shaddow House without vetting them. Because of the nature of the house and the power of the Welling locks, bringing a haunted object within the walls could result in the ghost attached to that object getting trapped inside with the coven. And given the creepy ceiling ghost, that could be very unpleasant.

"Yeah, maybe we could adjourn to the backyard?" Alice suggested, waggling the bag.

"Aw, man, when you do that, we miss out on so much!" exclaimed Natalie, a smartly dressed brunette office worker who haunted the dry-erase board in the kitchen. Like Plover, she couldn't travel beyond the walls of Shaddow House.

"We'll leave the door open," Josh promised her as he followed the coven into the backyard. It was sort of a miracle, Natalie not only appearing but communicating directly with them instead of using the board, which had been her preferred method for years. Josh had that sort of effect on the ghosts. He had a gift for listening.

The bag seemed heavier as Alice carried it through the house, and she wasn't sure if it was her imagination or if this hideous object was responding to the house. The locks were ritual items that the Dentons' magical rivals, the Wellings, had hidden in Shaddow House when it was just a stone footprint.

The Dentons eventually uncovered the plot and drove the Wellings away, but the locks remained hidden in the house like little supernatural time bombs. Riley's family created the fake narrative of the Shaddow family as benevolent but remote owners of the house to misdirect attention away from the Dentons, who spent decades searching the house for them and trying to figure out their purpose.

Even with all their magical experience, the Dentons had only managed to find one lock before Riley arrived. The coven had managed to find six more in the past year or so. Well, technically, fewer than six, because some of them had been located by people sent by the Wellings to confuse, attack, and otherwise sabotage the coven's search.

The Wellings wanted their locks back to do... Well, the coven still hadn't figured that out. At first, Riley and the coven were sure they were supposed to destroy the locks, but as they'd found more of them, they'd realized the locks did more than what the Dentons originally had thought. They didn't just lock ghosts in place (literally), or enthrall ghosts to the user's will. The locks opened doorways into the next spiritual plane, and one of those doorways opened onto something on the other side: some enormous, silent, formless void that still occasionally showed up in Alice's nightmares, like cold storage for ghosts that had tried to murder them.

Also, the coven had tried to destroy the locks in a few different ways, but nothing had worked, so there was that too.

Josh opened the kitchen door, where Plover and Natalie were waiting, looking like the ghostly version of *American Gothic*. Josh made a sweeping gesture toward the yard.

"Thank you, young sir," Plover intoned.

Caroline pulled her phone out of her pocket. "Hold on, let me turn off Ben's backyard cameras."

Riley turned to her. "We're sharing app access now?"

"Do you *want* Ben recording secret magic rituals in your backyard on his home security system?" Caroline asked, her brows arched as she tapped her phone.

"I do not," Riley replied.

"And yet, Mina and I suggesting that you and Dad get married is somehow crossing a line," Josh said.

"We're taking things slow," Caroline reminded him. Josh sighed with all the disappointment of a matchmaking auntie, making Alice chuckle.

It was strange, now that Caroline and Ben were settling into their lives, moving in together, and talking about marriage in the abstract. Now that Caroline and Riley were both paired up, Alice often felt like a third wheel. Riley and Caroline had clearly defined magical powers—telekinesis and communication—and the kids' gifts were growing stronger. They could all work their magic without Alice, and that was a particularly difficult feeling for her because her grandparents had always made her feel much the same way:

like a hanger-on, a parasite sucking away their precious time and resources.

She knew the coven was entirely different. But it still hurt that they didn't need her either. Then again, she supposed it wasn't so bad. Alice wasn't like Caroline, who couldn't leave the island up until last year without the threat of death. Alice could go freely. The only thing that kept her tied to the island was the coven itself. These were the only people who had loved her in a way that didn't hurt, but she was hurting *them*, even if she didn't mean to.

"Besides, engagements tend to go…not great in this group, so I don't think we want to run the risk after the whole 'I survived my family's centuries-long curse' thing," Caroline reminded him. She turned to Alice, snapping her out of her meandering thoughts. "You OK?"

"Hmm? Oh, yes, that's sensible," Alice conceded.

"You sure?" Riley asked. "Is whatever's in that bag distressing you in some way?"

"Maybe?" Alice took the candelabra out of the bag and set it on the grass. It felt unsafe, somehow, to put it on the flagstones leading to the house. "I found this in the drawer of Arthur's cabinet. Arthur is the cabinetmaking ghost who was all indignant this morning about us not paying attention to him. He's amused himself for the last few centuries by randomly holding the drawers closed, meaning whoever put it in there hasn't been able to access it."

"Which I also find kind of amusing," Josh said. "That's just mean enough, without being awful."

"When you look at it, what does it remind you of?" Alice asked.

Caroline suggested, "A rejected remainder from Pier 1 Imports?"

Riley got on her knees to inspect the copper arms. "The markings look like the runes on the locks."

"What's Pier 1 Imports?" Josh asked, as she looked the object over.

"Josh, I don't want to smack a minor, but I will," Riley told him, standing up.

"You'll only hit my shoulder," Josh scoffed as she peered up at him, even at her full height. "Possibly under my shoulder."

"Not if I wait 'til you're sitting down," Riley shot back, narrowing her eyes in an exaggerated manner. Josh patted her on the top of her head affectionately, making her scowl.

"I think it's like a display for the locks?" Alice suggested. "Look at all the little depressions."

"I see it," Caroline said. "Well, that's interesting. I never considered that it was all part of a puzzle."

"A very ugly puzzle," Riley added, pursing her lips. "Plover, Nat, any weird 'ghostly apocalypse-type feelings'?"

"No more than what we normally feel when the locks are around," Natalie replied.

Plover shook his head. "I feel no significant distress. I suspect it will be as safe to house this…fascinating item as it is to keep the locks here."

Josh's head whipped toward the house. He frowned. "Oh, no, not this guy."

The others turned toward the house to see an oily dark shape moving along the kitchen ceiling. Alice took an instinctive step back. Nothing good ever came of the ceiling ghost showing up. A part of Alice felt bad for rejecting this ghost so overtly when she'd been open to most of the ghosts at Shaddow House. But the ceiling ghost had no backstory, no personality. It had never given any indication that it wanted anything good for the coven. Josh's theory was that it was a sort of poltergeist, the will of the Wellings personified. It was the personality of the family's magic and, in his words, "it was real shitty."

Plover threatened to have the "young sir's" mouth washed with soap for that one.

The ceiling ghost darted toward the back door like a particularly lithe sea predator. Plover pulled Natalie out of harm's way. The ceiling ghost threw itself at the barrier of the open door.

Alice had to admit it was a relief to see the ghost all smooshed up as an amorphous blob against the magical boundary like a jellyfish pressed against an aquarium wall. It sort of took some of its scary mystique away. The ceiling ghost seemed to be straining toward the candelabra. It had lurked menacingly around the locks before, but this intense, creepy interest was something new.

Then it got angry and threw itself against the barrier over and over, making a sort of screaming-roaring-shrieking noise.

Nope, it was scary again.

Huffing out a breath, Riley grabbed a silver garden gazing ball meant to serve as a hide-a-key safe. It folded back to reveal a baggie full of herbed salt, which she opened and slung toward the open door. The salt sizzled as it struck the ghost's oily surface. The ghost let out one last guttural howl and dissipated, leaving an irritated Plover in its wake.

"That particular being is becoming very forward," he muttered.

"The ceiling ghost wants the candelabra," Caroline said. "What does that mean?"

"Well, we need to be pretty careful about warding it, wherever we put it," Riley told her.

"Plover, any chance we could stash it in one of the scary red storage rooms downstairs we don't talk about?"

Plover shot a guilty look at Natalie. "I'm sorry, Miss, but those are full."

Riley nodded. "Awesome."

"It's never gone after anything like that," Natalie observed. "It's never gone near any of the doors."

"Huh. Well, this is pretty significant, in terms of progress," Riley said, looking up at Alice, her expression anxious.

"So why do you look so unhappy?" Alice asked. "For the first time, we might actually know how many locks there are for sure. Nine depressions, nine locks…probably. Most likely."

"I'm *concerned*," Riley said carefully, taking her arm. As usual, an electric flutter ran up Alice's torso, registering the presence of Riley's magic nudging hers. "Because every other time we've had a development, we've all felt it from each other, this surge of energy—or, you know, panic. The psychic Bat-Signal. And this time, when you found this significant thing on your own, we felt nothing."

Alice frowned. "Nothing?"

Riley and Caroline exchanged a concerned look, then Riley said carefully, "Something just feels off in your magic."

"It's like there's a hole in it," Caroline added. "Does that make any sense?"

Alice swallowed the molten lump gathering in her throat. It did make sense, because she was hiding something from them. Magic didn't tolerate, well, bullshit. It wasn't a particularly flowery senti-ment, but she'd found it to be true.

"It doesn't feel different to me, but I'm not as sensitive as the others," Josh told them. "But you seem stressed out, Alice. Like more than normal."

"I'm fine," Alice assured them. "It's just my grandparents and running the store and apparently, I have a new haunted armoire to contend with. It's a lot."

"Are you sure?" Riley asked. "It feels like you've been distant lately."

"There have been so many changes," Alice insisted. "Good changes, you know. You and Edison living together. Ben and Caroline making a family. We're all so busy."

"I would make a joke about finally getting a baby brother, but this feels like a significant moment," Josh mused.

"We're never too busy for you," Riley assured Alice.

"You're our sister," Caroline told her. "We love you."

"I also love you," Josh told her. "Even though I just joined up."

Alice nodded, smiling weakly. It was all too much.

"Well, I've got to get back to the shop," she said. "I'll trust you to find a way to store it safely."

Caroline blinked at her, startled. "Really?"

"Tourist season," Alice said, shrugging. "I can't leave the shop without a clerk for hours at a time. Plus, I don't know what Arthur is capable of. That cabinet is sizable."

"OK, well, come by after work or something," Riley said, frowning. "We can look through Aunt Nora's journals, see if we can find anything mentioning an evil candleholder."

Alice edged toward the gate. "I don't think it's *pure* evil. I'm not even sure the locks are entirely evil. I think it's how you use them."

Josh shivered. "They still give me the creeps."

"Alice, are you sure—" But Riley's question was lost to warm winds blowing in over Lake Huron as Alice bolted back toward Superior Antiques. She took the long way around Main Square to avoid the law offices of Tanner, Moscovitz, and Graves.

———

For two days, Alice took the coward's way out. She told herself it was the increased summer traffic keeping her in the shop, not direct efforts to avoid anyone and everyone. She worked. She answered her grandparents' calls on the first ring. She read the group coven text chain—a thing she never thought she'd be a part of—without responding. Then again, she at least opened those texts. More hostile messages—from burner phones a certain party used to get around the block she'd put on his number—were deleted unread.

How had she reached the point in her life where she was dodging texts from burner phones?

Arthur was a perfectly nice roommate, all things considered. He stayed on the first floor without her having to place a circle of charmed salt and herbs around the cabinet to contain him. He greeted her warmly and kept her apprised of any "suspicious characters" he saw lurking near the windows while she slept. (Squirrels, mostly.) He was pleasant company while she was alone in the shop, and he'd at least stopped heckling her while she was working with customers, which was a nice gesture. He had no interest in moving on to whatever constituted the next plane. And frankly, the idea of selling the cabinet and losing this comfortable new friendship when she needed one... Well, if she hid the price tag and claimed it was a "display only" piece, that was her business.

Her grandparents would probably argue with her on that point, she thought as she sold a set of Saltykov enamel scent bottles to a perfectly lovely couple from Missouri. She bid them goodbye at the door, telling them to enjoy the rest of their honeymoon.

"Wouldn't you hope they would enjoy their honeymoon whether you told them to or not?" Arthur asked her.

"It's just something you say, because 'have a nice day' is overdone. And customers like it when you demonstrate that you remembered something they told you in passing in conversation. It encourages them to come back and patronize the shop again, if not on this trip, then the next. Giving you their money becomes a cherished vacation tradition," Alice said.

Arthur's expression was amused. "Ah, a secretly mercenary soul, then."

"Money makes the world—" she started to reply, when a tall, sandy-haired figure walking through the crowded cobblestone streets caught her attention. It was the determined set of his shoulders, the angry energy of Clark's steps, that was so different from the people around him. She'd always thought of him as handsome, with his big brown eyes and square jaw. She'd thought the ruddy cheeks gave him a boyish appearance, but Riley hadn't quite trusted him from their first meeting.

Rightly so, Alice supposed.

And he was heading right for the shop door.

Alice flipped the door sign to CLOSED. Moving quickly across the polished wooden floor, she reached the sales desk in seconds. She clicked a button under the register that allowed her to lock the door remotely. It was recently installed and one of the few security measures she'd suggested that her grandparents had actually taken seriously.

"Isn't that one of those customers you love so much?" Arthur asked, frowning as she switched off the shop lights.

"No, it's not," she told him.

"Why are you hiding from him? Has he hurt you?" he said, suddenly hostile and turning toward the door. Snagging her key ring from under the register, Alice ducked out of sight behind the heavy damask curtain that separated the supply room from the showroom. Her phone and her purse were upstairs, where she'd left them—to avoid calls and texts. And if she wanted to go upstairs, she would have to go back out to the showroom where Clark could see her.

"Why aren't you answering?" Arthur yelled as a fist began to beat against the glass panels. Alice stood absolutely still as she listened to Clark hammer at the door. Her breathing felt like hot, jagged glass piercing her chest, and she wondered if the coven would pick up on this.

A few seconds of silence passed and she counted them, forcing herself to breathe deeply and slowly.

Clark couldn't yell, she realized, because a raised familiar voice might attract the attention of locals. To the tourists, he just looked like an impatient customer, pissed off that she was taking a lunch break.

"Alice?" Arthur had rematerialized in the supply room with her. "Are you all right?"

"I'm not sure. But I don't want to talk to that man. I'm going to leave and come back later," Alice said.

"Who is he? You're a witch. You commune with the dead like you're chatting over tea. Why are you so scared of a nitwit in a necktie?" Arthur asked.

"I have my reasons, and I'm going out the back," she told him. "Be back later."

Arthur tried to call questions after her, but she was already out the back door, using her enormous ring of keys to secure it before dashing along the alleyway behind the other stores on the square: the fudge shop, the T-shirt store, the other fudge shop, Manley's Finer Antiques. She made it to the end of the row and realized she was out of cover.

How was she going to make it across the square to Shaddow House without Clark seeing her and making a scene? Was she in actual physical danger? Had things between them escalated that far? Could she defend herself if necessary? She crept around the street side of Manley's, searching for comfort in the familiar, warm, sweet, buttery-sugar smell of bubbling fudge. She supposed she could duck across the street to the snow globe emporium and run until she reached the dock. It would take longer, but it might give her a better chance at reaching Shaddow House without being seen. Why weren't Riley and Caroline picking up on her distress? Every time they'd been in danger she'd felt it, and she'd gone running. And now, she was all alone…because of her relationship with Clark.

It had been a matter of convenience at first, really. Comfort. They'd gone on a few dates and while they weren't particularly compatible *emotionally*, their physical chemistry was undeniable.

He knew when she needed him to be rough, and when she needed him to be slower, deeper. She'd enjoyed lovers before—kinder men, more sincere—but it was Clark who never left her unsatisfied. He'd teased her, telling her how shocked everyone on the island would be to see such a "good girl" as Alice Seastairs behaving as she did, taking what she wanted.

Eventually, they'd done away with the pretense of dates, meeting in secret, coming to a sort of "friends with benefits" arrangement. And that was fine. She didn't have to pretend that his inability to feign interest in her life was acceptable or that there was a possibility of anything more. It was simpler that way, less stressful.

Until Alice met Riley. The new Denton's arrival on the island had clearly thrown Clark off, making their meetings less about satisfaction and more about grilling Alice over her relationship with the island's latest resident. He tried to be subtle about his questions: What was Riley like? How did she spend her time? Was she planning on leaving the house any time soon? Alice told herself it was just professional curiosity, considering that Riley's aunt had been his client. He was just trying to make sure that Riley had everything she needed after the settling of Nora's will.

Alice had lied to herself, right up until the moment Riley figured out that Clark had paid a young man named Kyle to terrorize her and break into Shaddow House to steal the locks and that Clark worked for the Wellings. Alice still didn't know how she'd held it together around her sisters, how she'd hidden her shame and regret from them for so long. She remembered standing in the parlor at Shaddow House, acid boiling up in her throat as she realized what she'd done, even accidentally, remembered inadvertently giving

Clark information that he had used against them. She'd pushed all that panic down until she could breathe again, until it was squashed into a little box hidden under her heart. Heaven knew she had enough room for several. Maybe that was the beginning of the "holes" in her magic—locking those secrets away from the coven and pretending everything was OK.

And now, she was hiding in an alley behind a snow globe shop. She was miles away from OK.

Her awareness of what Clark was doing didn't stop him from seeking her out, trying to get more information out of her, telling her to be that "good girl" and give him what he wanted. He was fully aware of the leverage he had on her. It was a sort of mutually assured destruction. She didn't want her coven to find out what she'd been doing. But at the same time, she could go tell the whole island that he'd taken advantage of a confused, motherless boy to spy on Riley. Clark had been subtle before, sort of floating in her periphery. But lately, he was becoming more menacing. He was pursuing her with more fervor than he had before, because Clark Graves was a man who didn't tolerate being told "no."

Alice moved closer, seeking the safety and noise of the crowd. Somehow, over the din of footsteps and happy chatter, she could hear a familiar voice. It wasn't Clark's; it was Collin Bancroft.

She zeroed in on that warm and comforting voice. It settled something in her chest, even if he was saying, "Are you sure that's a fair price?"

She cocked her head. She heard that phrase all day, every day. She had a special antenna for it, and that antenna told her that Collin wasn't trying to haggle. He sounded truly clueless as to whether he'd just been quoted a fair cost for a green-patinaed iron bench cast to look as it was formed from seashells and fronds of kelp.

"Absolutely, Mr. Bancroft. You will not find a finer example of the Coalbrookdale Company's work in any store in the state, definitely not on the island," Nick Manley was telling him. Alice glanced around the corner of Manley's Finer Antiques.

Now, Alice liked Nick. He was a nice person, even if Franklin Proctor did consider him his personal nemesis. (Probably because Nick put the word "finer" in his store name. Franklin considered that a personal affront.)

"Alice?" Nick's voice startled her. He was a short, stocky man with sunburned cheeks who dressed for comfort at work—khakis and a collared shirt—because he spent a lot of time moving furniture around. That was probably another reason her grandfather looked down on him. "Are you all right? You look a little flushed."

Collin's gray-blue eyes narrowed at her, his brow crinkled with disquiet. Another tailored suit today, making Alice wonder if he slept in them.

"I'm fine," she insisted, forcing a smile onto her face. "I was just trying to escape over to Petra's for a pastry."

"She's trying a lemon rugalach for the summer. It's causing quite a stir," Nick said, nodding sagely as he gestured at the bench displayed just outside his shop door. "Mr. Bancroft here is considering this beautiful Coalbrookdale bench. It's in wonderful condition for something made in the Victorian period, don't you agree?"

Alice glanced up at Collin, who was looking at her, not the bench. He seemed...upset, and she wasn't sure why. Was it the bench? Did he know that Nick was trying to sell him a fake?

Nick had always been very sweet to Alice, but he had a terrible eye. He couldn't tell a Stickley from an IKEA flatpack. He thought every item that sellers brought him was the genuine article. And while Alice valued that sort of optimism, it devalued the stock of his store, including this perfectly nice cast-iron garden bench Collin was inspecting.

It simply wasn't a Coalbrookdale bench. And the price Nick just quoted Collin would be outrageous, even if the surface had been visited by Queen Victoria's royal bottom. Collin seemed financially comfortable, but Alice's conscience wouldn't let her allow him to be duped like that.

She glanced down the street at Clark, who was still knocking on her shop door. If she was smart, she would run across the square and up the hill while Clark wasn't looking. But it felt better here, close to Collin, which made no sense, because she knew nothing about him. He could be crueler than Clark, as far as she knew. But the warmth radiating from his lanky frame and the clean citrus-and-ocean smell felt like something she should hover close to. Also, she was wearing heels.

"It's a lovely piece," Alice said carefully. "And it looks very comfortable. But, I'm sorry, it's not a Coalbrookdale."

"How do you know?" Collin asked, and the question wasn't a pointed challenge of her expertise. He was genuinely curious. He leaned closer and Alice's breathing hitched for entirely different reasons. Sensation returned to her fingertips and toes, the fear bleeding out of her system.

"Well, Coalbrookdale pieces tend toward more botanical designs, flowers and leaves, that sort of thing." Alice ran her fingers

over the molded seashell pattern. "This piece has more of an...
oceanic feel? Also, it's been treated with chemicals to give it the
distressed effect. You wouldn't have to do that on a hundred-and-
seventy-year-old iron piece. It would just be there."

"You can tell?" Collin asked.

"You can see the splash patterns if you look closely enough,"
she said, casting a glance toward Nick, who seemed more annoyed
than angry. "And it was made in Alabama, not England. Probably
about ten years ago. I remember seeing it in mail-order catalogues."

"You're kidding!" Nick exclaimed. Annoyance had given way
to interest as she shifted the bench forward until they could see the
bottom slats. The stamp for McMurtree Creek Iron Works was
punched into the bottom of the seat.

"Huh, I'll be darned. I never thought to look there," Nick
mused. "Maureen Laughlin swore her grandmother brought it over
from England after the Great War."

Alice wondered why Nick believed someone's ancestor would
prioritize patio furniture when they were fleeing war-torn Europe,
but she decided to keep her mouth shut. She didn't feel good about
moving this sale out of Nick's reach.

"McMurtree's an excellent company," Alice assured them.
"They make nice sturdy pieces that could definitely last more than
one Michigan winter, but it's not worth hundreds of dollars."

"Thank you, Alice," Collin said. "You saved me a bit of trouble
there."

"I–I'm so sorry, Mr. Bancroft," Nick stammered. "Please believe
me, I would never cheat a customer."

"Of course not. Everybody knows that about you, Nick. Now,

that hand-carved oak letter box you have in the display in there? The one with little deer leaping across the lid?" Alice noted, pointing to a glass case just inside the shop. Even from the door, she could see the price tag listing an amount that was considerably higher than the price on the bench. She'd always admired Nick's insistence on pricing items in an obvious manner, so customers wouldn't be surprised. The virtue of honesty outweighed the potential negative impact of sticker shock, in Nick's mind, and she appreciated that in his character. She turned to Collin. "It's authentic and well worth the price. It might go nicely with your letter opener."

Nick flashed her a grateful grin. She winked at him as Collin peered into the shop. "I like it. Can you put it on my account?"

"Absolutely," Nick said. "Just let me wrap it for you."

"You've already established an account?" she asked Collin as Nick rushed into the shop.

"I plan on establishing accounts at all the antique stores on the island for a project at the hotel." Collin lowered his voice to ask, "Should I worry about shopping here?"

"Oh, no, Nick means well," Alice assured him. "But he believes every story that comes through his door. He's the kid who wants the pirate treasure map to be real. I choose to think of it as charming."

Collin smiled at her in a way that made little crinkles form around his eyes, softening the intense gray. It was adorable. "That's kind of you."

"Alice!"

Her head whipped toward the sharp voice, and she saw Clark striding up the sidewalk toward them. He had a smile on his face—or, at least, his teeth were showing, but it didn't reach his eyes.

Dammit.

Her brain had been so desperate to think of anything other than her Clark situation that she'd let herself be distracted. Alice reached out in that moment and grabbed Collin's arm. She wasn't sure what she was grasping for—anchoring, assurance, something to keep her from stumbling onto her butt on a public sidewalk. But Collin reached up with his free hand and wrapped those long fingers around hers, squeezing them tight. Rather than the electric buzz of her magic when meeting a fellow witch, she felt a sort of slow-spreading glow, like the sun shining through a bottle of honey. She wanted to bathe in that light.

Her eyes locked on Collin's face, and she knew that he'd felt it too. What did *that* mean? Did Collin have magic? He didn't seem frightened or surprised, but it struck her that he'd probably learned to hide his emotional responses in the corporate world.

Interesting.

"Alice!" Clark called again, sounding less friendly this time. Locals and tourists alike turned to watch his progress along the sidewalk.

"Do you want to talk to him?" Collin murmured.

"Definitely not," Alice said, twining her fingers through his.

"Right." Collin nodded sharply and looped her arm through his as if they were out for a Sunday promenade.

"Here you go." Nick appeared behind them, carrying Collin's shopping bag out of the shop. He brightened upon seeing another potential customer. "Clark, how are you?"

"I'm just fine, Nick," Clark said, a thin smile plastered across his face. It looked like his skin was stretched too tight across his blandly handsome face, and there was something off about his complexion. He was…gray, not quite the luminous silver-gray of a ghost, but certainly not his usual suntanned health. And there were large, bruise-like smudges under his eyes. He looked desperate and ill. Rather than sparking empathy, it only made Alice step closer to Collin. "I was hoping to chat with Alice for a minute."

"No, thank you," she said. But Clark was reaching for her arm, as if she hadn't uttered a word.

"Oh, I'm afraid Alice and I have lunch plans," Collin lied smoothly. "I'm making some changes to the restaurant's menu, and I need someone with her discerning palate."

Alice fought to keep her expression neutral, not to show even a flicker of surprise.

"I certainly understand that. Everybody knows what a *good girl* Alice is to have on your side, but I really need her at the moment," Clark insisted.

Alice managed not to recoil at the words "good girl," but it was a near thing. "No, Clark, we can talk later. I don't want to be rude to Mr. Bancroft."

"Um, is everything all right?" Nick asked, his gaze moving between Alice and Clark.

"I insist," Clark said, reaching for her free hand. Alice flexed her fingers, preparing to… Well, she wasn't really sure what. Throw him off? Punch him in the throat? At this point, she was so tired of Clark that both options seemed reasonable. Collin interceded smoothly, reaching out to shake Clark's hand.

"Collin Bancroft. We've met before, I believe," he said. "Nice to see you again."

"Of course," Clark seethed. "If I could just borrow Alice for—"

"You don't 'borrow' a person," Collin told him, his expression perfectly civil, even if his voice was fog rolling over a dark, icy road—dangerous and full of hidden threats. "And I'm afraid *I* insist that we leave now. Nick, I'm sure Clark would love to hear about this lovely Coalbrookdale bench."

Nick frowned and opened his mouth to object, but saw Alice's subtle shake of the head. He smirked. Hmm. Alice wondered if Nick wasn't all that fond of Clark either.

Clark shook his head. "I really don't have time."

"Well, use the time you would have used to 'chat' with Alice," Collin told him, all dismissal as he turned, gently pulling Alice away. "Thanks, Nick. Tell Clark all about Ms. Laughlin's grandmother."

"Sure thing," Nick said, waving affably.

As they walked away, Alice heard Nick ask, "Clark, you're in the market for unique outdoor seating?"

"How far away do you need to get?" Collin asked softly as they strode smoothly away. She vaguely heard Clark huff that he didn't need *any* outdoor seating. Collin didn't drop her hand as they walked away. He still held it in that perfectly proper "strolling" position, even as he stroked warm, comforting fingertips over the back of her hand.

"I was going to try to get to Shaddow House," Alice whispered.

"Are you expected? Would you be safe there?"

She shot him a curious look.

"You don't reach out to another human being, like you did just now, if you feel safe," Collin told her. She opened her mouth, but couldn't seem to produce an answer. He added, "You don't have to tell me anything. I just want to make sure you feel secure. But, if you don't have plans, why don't you join me at the hotel for lunch? I know it sounds like a line, but I'd like to make you an offer."

"I'm not expected, and that really does sound like a line," she noted.

"But an entirely sincere one. If you join me for lunch, I'll know you're OK. It's minimal investment for you, and knowing that you're OK is a priority for me at the moment," Collin said.

Her cheeks went so hot, she actually had to look down at the ground. This was embarrassing.

But... If she went to Shaddow House right now, she would have to explain her lack of contact for the last two days. She would have to admit to her coven what she'd been doing with Clark. She would have to explain why there were holes in her magic that had kept them from feeling today's distress. And as much as Alice hated to admit it, this felt better, spending time with someone who didn't know about her "ghost problems" and the questionable decisions she'd made. "Is it true there's a grilled-cheese sandwich named after you at the restaurant?"

"Yes, there is," Collin insisted, glancing over his shoulder. When he didn't seem alarmed by what he saw, she relaxed ever so slightly into the long line of his torso. Through his jacket pocket, she felt his cell phone buzz against her elbow.

"Does it really have peanut butter and bacon on it?" she asked.

"I was seven when I came up with it, and it was sort of a sarcastic gift from the chef," he muttered. "How did you know about that, anyway?"

"Caroline told me. She said there's sprinkles on it too." Then

Alice smiled sincerely for the first time since bailing out of her shop.

Collin reminded her, "I was *seven*."

———————

Alice had never stepped inside the majestic Duchess Hotel, but she'd expected the interior to match the sweeping elegance of the rear exterior. But the lobby was some sort of mod eclectic nightmare. She'd never seen so many mismatched finishes and styles and old beautiful pieces mixed with chrome. Why did chrome vases exist?

And why were they *sharp*?

"It's so…orange," she marveled. Vaguely, she could hear his phone buzz again in his pocket.

"I have a plan for that," he told her, nodding toward the crews that were carefully taking down a massive wall accent piece made of shining aluminum panels. It seemed like a bad idea to Alice, since there were still *some* guests milling around the lobby, but given the sharp-looking edges on the panels, she wasn't sure how safe it was to leave it. At least the lady dressed in a floor-length cotton pique tennis dress and flat straw hat wasn't at risk. She'd probably died right after the hotel was completed in 1900.

Alice had all sorts of questions about why the woman was dressed in Edwardian sportswear. Had she died in her tennis clothes? Had she suffered an accident caused by the giant puffy sleeves? But randomly yelling questions at dead people wasn't exactly how one maintained a reputation for sanity over the long term. Also, this wasn't the only ghost in the lobby at the moment. Alice could spot at least three more, in various outfits from across history.

She was suddenly glad she'd never stayed here. Imagine not knowing that the dead were watching you sleep. She shuddered.

Collin motioned toward an archway marked with an old-fashioned standing brass sign that read Forsythia Dining Room. She hoped the first change Collin's decorators made was repainting, because even in this vaulted, open space with its stunning views of the lake, the constant battering of tangelo was starting to hurt her retinas.

Collin's phone buzzed again from his pocket. He ignored it, and didn't wait for them to be seated by the staff. He chose one of the many available four-top tables, one closest to the window.

"Would you mind if we sat outside?" Alice asked him, nodding through the floor-to-ceiling windows at the (definitely not Coalbrookdale, but comfortable-looking) cast-iron tables on the flagstone waterfront patio. "I think I could use some fresh air."

"The orange?" Collin asked. She nodded. He didn't get annoyed, simply opened the nearest door and gestured her through. It struck her as odd that there were so many tables available during what should be the lunch rush on a summer day. The exhaustion of dealing with Clark, the fresh air, and the smells drifting out of the kitchen were making her stomach rumble. The streets were crowded with tourists. This place should have been packed.

He pulled a seat out for her, somehow managing to do it without making the iron legs screech on the stone. While the breeze coming off the glittering silver water was lovely, she had the urge to tie her scarf around her hair. Like most items in her wardrobe, her suit was gray, but she'd tried to "spice it up" as Caroline kept insisting she do by knotting red-and-gold silk around her throat. Would preserving her hair make her look like she was trying too hard?

Sure, this was definitely the time to mentally overanalyze her accessories, she told herself.

"Do you want to talk about what just happened with Clark?" he asked as his phone buzzed. He pulled the latest-model smartphone from his jacket pocket and frowned.

"No, I do not," she said. "Do you need to answer that?"

"No." Collin shook his head as he tucked it away unopened. "No, I do not."

"So, you have plans?" she prompted him as Henry Melton, an ancient waiter who had worked at the hotel restaurant since the 1960s, shuffled forward.

"Can I take your order?" he asked, his voice quavering slightly, as if the effort to speak cost too much of his current oxygen supply. But his crisply pressed, shin-length white apron was immaculate, and his gaze was piercing as Alice looked over the menu.

"Still no order pad, Henry?" Collin asked.

Henry tapped his temple, near a fall of snow-white hair. "Still sharp as a tack, Mr. Bancroft. Haven't forgotten an order since you were running around the hallways blindfolded."

When Alice's brows rose, he told her, "I was trying to memorize them."

He looked at Henry. "I thought I asked you to call me Collin," he noted. "You've known me for too long for formality."

"And I thought I told you that I wouldn't be doing that," Henry shot back, a wry grin on his face.

"Fair enough. I'll have the Michigan salad and a mineral water, please," Collin replied.

"I'll have the Collin sandwich," she told Henry, whose eyes went wide.

Collin's full lips twitched. "Really?"

"What if you change the menu?" she said, pressing her mouth into a thin line to keep her smile at bay. "I might miss my chance."

"Would you like strawberry or grape jelly?" Henry asked without missing a beat.

Suddenly, Alice wondered if she was putting Henry in an awkward position with his boss—ordering the sandwich "to Collin's face." But Collin didn't seem offended. If anything, he was amused, and Alice appreciated that. For someone who clearly had so much, to be able to laugh at himself—it was refreshing. She could do with a little more of that kind of humor in her life.

"Can I get strawberry jelly on the side?" she asked.

"Absolutely," Henry said. "Would you like the sliced banana on the side too?"

Alice sent an astonished look across the table.

"I was a real pain in the chef's ass," Collin admitted. "I made a nuisance of myself."

"On the side, please," Alice said, laughing.

Henry promised speedy delivery of their lunches and disappeared.

"I would say I'm sorry, but I'm not," she told him.

"I would rather you poke at me a little bit than fawning all over me." He squinted one eye shut as he absorbed the full weight of his own words. "That sounded incredibly arrogant, didn't it?"

"Well, it didn't sound humble," she conceded. "But I suppose you weren't raised to be humble, were you?"

"There's no good way for me to answer that," he told her. "And I'm not going to make *that* many changes to the menu, by the way... OK, I'm going to make changes to the menu, but I wouldn't take the sandwich off. It's the first mark I ever made on the hotel, even if I did it by being an annoying kid who had absolutely no business here—at the time."

"OK." She nodded. "On that note, you cannot get rid of Henry."

His brow furrowed. "Why would I fire Henry?"

"He's a seventy-seven-year-old waiter?" Alice guessed. "Some business types might not consider that the height of efficiency."

"He's an institution around here," Collin insisted. "There are customers who show up just to see him."

"Oh," Alice said, sitting back in her chair. "That is exactly the point I was going to make to you."

"There's no reason to sound so surprised," Collin told her.

She turned her hands up in a sort of shrug. "From what Caroline tells me, the only thing that kept your predecessors from firing Henry was the potential age-discrimination lawsuit. I thought maybe you would find some way around it."

Collin snorted. "Henry's great-nieces have been trying to get him to retire for years. I've offered him increasingly attractive retirement packages. But if he doesn't want to leave, and he's doing his job, who am I to tell him he has to go?"

She beamed at him. "Exactly."

He smiled back and it was like sliding into that honeyed sunbeam again, all radiant warmth and sweetness. She gripped the (orange) napkin in her lap, willing herself to keep a neutral, non-starstruck expression. It would not do to scare a new business acquaintance with her face.

Collin cleared his throat. "I have a proposition…proposal. It's a proposal. I'm not propositioning you. I clearly don't know how to identify appropriate sentences to say aloud *or* antiques. I don't know what I'm looking at and whether it's worth the price asked. And that's a problem because I'm planning a major makeover of the suites on the top floor, including some era-appropriate antiques to make it feel authentic, sumptuous."

"I'm not a decorator," Alice told him.

"I don't expect you to be," he assured her. "I don't need you to decorate. I've hired interior designers who have come up with a lovely non-orange, *neutral* scheme for the other, more reasonably priced rooms in the hotel. But they're not antiques experts. And I want to make the suites something special. That's what the hotel used to be known for: luxury, comfort, something more than the ordinary. I want all our guests to have a taste of that, but I want the suites to be an experience beyond, a conversation piece."

"I don't know if the shops on the island have the kind of things you're looking for—at least, not the quality you're talking about," she said.

Collin was undeterred. "So, source them from reputable shops off-island. Have them shipped here. I'll make arrangements with one of the ferry lines."

"I couldn't let it interfere with my duties at the shop," Alice told him.

Collin shrugged. "Roll it into your duties at the shop. As far as I'm concerned, working in your shop is scouting for the hotel. I'll work up a contract for you as a private consultant, pay you a retainer."

Alice blinked at him. She was so used to fighting her grandparents at every step, for every scrap of cooperation, she wasn't sure how to handle someone assuring her that problems weren't really problems. Or, at least, they were problems that could be solved with money, which was also a nice, novel response.

"Why me?" she asked.

"Because you obviously have a good eye and a passion for antiques, and you're honest," he said. "I like that in people."

"Oh, I don't know if I have a passion for antiques," she demurred. "I know a lot about them because I've worked with them for so long, but I don't know if they're my *passion*."

He leaned closer. "What is your passion?"

The very question sent a pleasant little shiver down her spine. She thought about the potential answers: spending time with her friends in a haunted house, talking to ghosts, psychically inspecting haunted bric-a-brac. Instead of telling him any of that, she frowned and said, "I'm not sure."

"OK, fine, not your passion, then," he conceded. "I just have a good feeling about you. I don't get that feeling very often, so I think I should pay attention to it."

She blushed then and looked down at the linen napkin in her lap. Despite herself, she liked Collin Bancroft. She knew it couldn't—and shouldn't—go anywhere, but she was enjoying her time with him. And lately, it was more difficult to find bright spots like this in her life.

"Are the suites also very orange?" she asked, wrinkling her nose.

"Oh, yes," he said, nodding. "It's a shade of orange that, under previous management, would cost you about two hundred dollars more a night."

They shared a laugh and she thought she saw something in his eyes that she was probably going to write off as professional respect. She doubted very much it could be anything else.

"All right," she told him. "I'd like to work for you."

Just then, Henry arrived with not only their drinks but also their meals, which she supposed was the benefit of lunch with the owner. Her sandwich was an enormous three-stack of Texas toast griddled to a golden brown, with melty Swiss cheese and peanut butter oozing over thick-sliced bacon at the corners. As promised, jelly and banana slices were served in little silver cups on her plate. The crusts were dipped in a rainbow of tiny nonpareil sprinkles more suited to topping a cupcake, yet here they were...on her sandwich.

She hummed, wondering how to best attack this plate.

"I can order you something else," he said quickly.

"Are you doubting my resolve?" She arched her brows, using the provided steak knife to slice the bread into a manageable bite. Liquid peanut butter oozed into a puddle over the plate.

He shook his head as she forked a bite into her mouth. "Never."

It was a strange combination of tastes and textures, salty-sweet peanut coating salty-savory bacon and perfectly buttered bread—then the dry tang of cheese. And while she wasn't exactly enjoying the experience, she wasn't about to let that show on her face.

"So... You went with round sprinkles and not oblong?" she asked Collin.

Collin sighed. "I was *seven*."

Chapter 4
Collin

COLLIN WAS IN REAL TROUBLE with Alice Seastairs.

Alice was a consummate professional, knowledgeable, occasionally a little bit of a pain in the ass. And completely charming.

Alice seemed to know something about everything: history, art, carpentry, geography. How did she keep track of it all? If it was anyone else, he would suspect her of googling behind his back or making it up as she went along, but Alice didn't flatter him, even when it would have been better for her. She didn't try to work him.

She was artless.

That didn't mean she moved without grace. She clearly didn't enjoy that awful grilled-cheese sandwich, but she'd managed to hide that, eat the whole thing, and thank him for lunch. Honestly, he'd only "invented it" as a kid to see if Chef André would do it, and she'd eaten it not to be polite, but out of stubbornness.

When she'd asked him if he was doubting her resolve, something shifted in his gut and he knew...yep. He was in trouble.

There were probably better uses for his time than seeking out old furniture for a fairly minor aspect of a big project. His days seemed to be a never-ending to-do list of little chores to close the empty hotel for the summer and start the construction. And yet, he kept being drawn back to Alice.

Alice, who was all calm, steady, obstinate humor. Alice, who seemed content to roam the unoccupied floor of suites to get a better feel for the space, even if the sheer orange-ness of the decor should have been enough to send her running back to her shop. Alice, who was smiling up at him with those big green eyes, because she didn't know what a mess he really was.

"This is the Cowslip Suite," he told her days after their lunch, as they walked into what would have probably been considered the honeymoon suite in most hotels. They were greeted by a huge bedroom with fantastic lake views opening onto a bathroom almost overtaken by a huge whirlpool tub.

"We're going to name the suites for flowers native to Michigan. Cowslip, Apple Blossom, Dwarf Lake Iris, which doesn't really roll off the tongue. Not exactly inspired, I know," he said. "But it's returning to the names Forsythe used when the place was built."

"Better than Bloodroot or Bladderwort," she replied. "All species found in Michigan are not particularly romantic, I suppose, but—oh, my God."

She stood on the bright carmine carpet and averted her eyes from the horror. The walls were coated in a shade of ginger that belonged on the heads of 1950s starlets. The big overstuffed couch and chaise lounge were black leather, paired with chrome accent tables and a gray rubberized chair that looked like if you sat in it wrong, it would launch you out the window.

"I need to ask you a serious question," Alice said. "Is this a prank? Haha, get the uptight girl to buy antiques for the sex room? Because I am not OK with that."

"No, I promise." He burst out laughing and covered his mouth. He cleared his throat. "This is very, very real."

"How did people sleep in here?" she asked, slipping her sunglasses out of her jacket pocket and onto her nose. It only made her more adorable. "It would be like camping on Mars."

"The previous owner was vulnerable to decorating advice based on soul-candling?" he said, shrugging. "I'm not sure what that means."

"And impractical modernism, it would seem," Alice mused, staring at the spring-loaded chairs.

"Online reviewers have complained of orange-related headaches," he sighed, making her snort. "We're going to wipe this slate clean—the whole hotel, really. You have carte blanche."

"Are you sure you want to put real antiques in a hotel room? You're going to have to do a lot to make them safe for guests to use. And don't people usually treat hotel rooms like garbage?" she asked as she used a laser gadget to measure the wall where the bed was located. Then she measured the space between the far wall and the french door as well as the length of the wall that led to the bathroom. "Wouldn't reproductions make more sense?"

He opened his phone to show her photos of the designers' sketches and samples of the furniture they'd selected. "The decorators have already selected reproductions for the widely available rooms. While the rooms will be the best possible imitation of the suites, they'll be able to hold up under a whole soccer team and still look clean and unscathed."

"You're actively working not to call them the 'regular rooms' for the regular people, aren't you?" she asked, smirking at him.

"No, as there are more than three hundred of them, they are widely available," he said. "But the nightly rate we're going to charge on the suites will discourage most 'disposable treatment.' And the guest agreement makes it clear how expensive it will be for them to mess around. They don't want to 'find out,' as the kids say."

She nodded as he scrolled through the images. "You've got a sort of simplified art nouveau. Rich finishes. Long, curving lines, scrollwork everywhere, slender table legs that are a lot more stable than they have a right to be. Nice job."

Despite not knowing anything about what she was talking about, Collin nodded. "Mm-hm. The hotel sort of peaked after World War I. I want to recapture that elegance. I want people to feel like they're walking into an Agatha Christie story."

"Didn't people get murdered in those stories?" Alice reminded him. "At hotels?"

"An Agatha Christie story, minus the murder," he amended.

When she stared up at him, all skeptical smiles, he added, "OK, that sounds like a really boring murder mystery. I just want guests to feel they're somewhere special, the kind of trip they'll talk about for the rest of their lives—or, if we're lucky, they'll make us a part of their lives and we'll see them over and over. That's what I want to return this place to: a monument to our guests' enjoyment."

She was staring at him again. "You are an enigma."

His brows rose. "How so?"

"You dress like the scariest businessman in the room, but you're just a big old ball of sentimental schmaltz."

"I am ruthless," he insisted, making her giggle. Oh, that sound and what it was doing to his chest. "Coldhearted and unfeeling, absolutely relentless in my pursuit of the almighty dollar. Don't you ever forget it."

"Yes, you're clearly a business ogre," she said, shaking her head.

After showing Alice some of the equally orange suites, where she took more measurements, they took a walk around the island—the prohibition of motor vehicles in certain historic areas of the island being something Collin was still getting used to—looking at some of the stock at local stores.

Collin had never been much for shopping for the sake of shopping. But with Alice, he enjoyed himself, even if she did seem very tense every time they were out on the sidewalk. Her eyes darted nervously around the crowded streets, even with the warmth of summer sunlight on her cheeks.

"Do people really travel to an island to go antiquing?" he asked, trying to distract her. "As a tourist, I would think it would be difficult to get the furniture home on the ferry."

"Most people buying furniture from us are decorating homes on the island," she said as she opened the door to Tremont's Treasures. "But we do occasionally sell to tourists. We have some sweetheart deals with the Perkins ferry line to help offset the shipping costs. Not that my grandparents pass those savings along to the customer."

While Collin had trained himself to accept the orangescape of the hotel's interior, the chaos of Tremont's made his brain jam for a few seconds. There was simply stuff *everywhere*: large stained-glass panels that looked like they belonged in church windows, rusty tricycles hanging from the ceiling by piano wire, silverware, moldering ladies' hats, costume jewelry, dented musical instruments.

"Willard Tremont thinks his 'styling' of the store dazzles the eye. It's more of a punch to the optical nerve." She murmured as she took his hand and squeezed. "Breathe. It will pass in a second."

"What's that smell?" he asked of the sweet-moldy scent that invaded his nostrils.

"Old stuff," she said. "Willard is a bit of a pack rat, but he has a much better eye for authentic pieces than Nick."

She paused as her eye seemed to land on a waxy-looking imitation fruit pie displayed on glass cake stand. "And I kind of owe him a favor. Willard! I brought you a customer!"

Over the next hour, Mr. Tremont was thrilled to point out several dressers that might fit the hotel's needs. All of those dressers were currently being used to display figurines in every medium. Alice took note of each one, unwilling to negotiate pricing until they had a place to store the pieces. She measured them, inspected them for scratches and, at one point, she pulled open the top drawer of a particularly handsome specimen, cocking her head so...she could listen to how smoothly it opened? Alice reached into the back of the drawer, tapping and frowning at the noise she heard.

She stretched her arm farther into the dresser, until she was almost shoulder deep in the drawer. He couldn't see what she was doing, but a couple of seconds later, he heard a pop, and she pulled out a thin board the full length of the dresser.

"Did you break it?" he asked quietly.

"It's a false back," she told him. "You find it sometimes in pieces like this. People didn't always trust banks after the crash. And they didn't have the document storage options we have today. Not a lot of space in this one, considering the size of the drawer, just big enough to...wow."

She pulled a small gold ring out of the dresser and held it up to the light. He didn't know a lot about jewelry, but it looked like a small sapphire surrounded by tiny diamond chips, set in dulled gold.

"Probably late nineteenth century," she murmured. "Stone's not exactly showy, but respectable and nice clarity considering the age and the fact that it's probably been back there a while." Alice glanced up at him and blushed at her own rambling. "Sorry, occupational hazard."

So much trouble.

She tilted the ring back and forth. "There's an inscription inside the band. 'V & S.' You know, Riley and Caroline and I found a ring sort of like this once. There was a big mix-up over the inscri—" She was smiling when she suddenly paused and glanced up. "Never mind."

"I'd like to hear the rest of that story," he told her.

"It's a long one." She slipped the ring onto her finger and beamed, even though it was a loose fit. He wanted to offer to buy it for her, right that second, just to keep that smile on her face. But she probably wouldn't have appreciated that. She'd stuck to the bounds of employer-employee propriety so far. Collin didn't want to ruin that.

"Hey, Willard!" she called, carefully putting the false drawer back in its place. "How much for this?"

"Did you find something, Alice?" Willard asked, sounding pleased as he peeked around a marble statue of a dryad.

"Yeah, at the back of the drawer," she said, handing the ring over. "It's not marked, but I want to give you a fair price."

"Oooh, drawer treasure, that's the best kind," Willard hummed. He looked at the ring and glanced at Collin.

"Where did the dresser come from?" Collin asked. Alice beamed at him as if he'd said exactly the right thing. He'd never understood the phrase about one's heart leaping in one's chest, but his did. He had to prop his hands against a glass display case to keep his knees from giving out.

Pull it together, man.

"Oh...that dresser? Don't tell your grandparents," Willard said, leaning to conspiratorially whisper to Alice. "But one of your grand-pa's third cousins sold it to me."

"Cousin Avery?" she asked quietly. "He and Franklin haven't spoken since Cousin Avery's mother died a few years back. I think it was because Franklin expected Avery to hand over anything inherited from the 'family line' the minute Avery's mother was buried. Avery expected to be able to mourn his beloved mother, who was a really nice lady."

Collin wondered why none of these reasonable-sounding relatives stepped in on Alice's behalf when she was a child, but figured the answer was something like, "because her grandparents were horrible human beings." According to the comments he'd heard about the Proctors, the couple were difficult at best, "raging ass-holes" at worst.

That last one came from Caroline.

"I won't say anything," Alice promised. "Avery was free to sell his furniture to whoever he wanted. Back to the ring. What do you want for it?"

Willard held the ring up to the light. "Not exactly the Hope Diamond, but a nice little piece. And you did bring in a pretty significant bit of business for me today, Alice. Plus, since it was technically found in a dresser belonging to your extended family, why don't we consider it a finder's fee?"

"I couldn't do that," she said, her eyes falling back to the waxy pie thing again.

Collin wondered, what was with the waxy pie thing?

"And Avery was a third cousin pretty far removed," Alice added. "We weren't even invited to their reunions."

"Wasn't it just your birthday?" Willard asked, peering over his glasses at her.

"Four months ago," Alice objected.

Willard placed the ring in her hand. "Besides, you'll have to pay to have it resized."

"I have to pay you *something*, for my conscience's sake," she told him.

Willard named a price that was less than what Collin paid for an average lunch. He immediately liked Willard and pledged to give him all the business he could. The ring, Collin noticed, was already on Alice's finger, and for some reason, that made him very happy. Alice searched through her handbag to pay in cash, and when she put it down on the register counter, she dislodged a stack of what looked like glossy furniture magazines.

She apologized quickly, but Willard only grinned at her. "Brand-new auction catalogues, fresh from the East Coast. I'm glad you came in today so you could see them."

"Anything interesting?" Alice asked.

He hummed. "Oh, the usual landfill fodder posing as Fabergé, but a few nice ones. Mollerson's has some nice Steiff pieces."

Collin hoped one day he would understand what any of that meant. Alice paid and began leafing through the catalogues. She seemed to freeze as her hands touched a particularly colorful page. She breathed out, "Oh, my."

At first, Collin thought he was looking at a close-up photo of a painted shoe, which showed how much he knew. It was a bowl, maybe, made from stained glass. The rounded panels were cut from shell-pink glass with beds of roses, violets, and pansies blooming from the base up. Each petal was divided by black leaded iron, with a border of sunshine yellow around the lip.

"Wow," she said, her hands running across the page.

"Wait." Collin cocked his head and placed his hand on the paper, his fingers brushing against hers. "Is that a stained-glass *tub*?"

She snatched her hand away and smiled shyly up at him.

"Yeah, I've never seen anything like it." She squinted down at the description. "I've never even heard of the manufacturer. Canton Glassworks? I know it's incredibly impractical and will probably explode in a shower of water and glass when filled... But it's the most beautiful thing I've ever seen."

And the way her face looked when she touched the page, he knew he would find a way to give it to her. Yes, he'd resisted the urge to buy the ring, but a stained-glass bathtub was an appropriate birthday present from a friend...ly...business acquaintance, right?

So. Much. Trouble.

"It probably graced the bathroom of a very happy mistress for one of history's most indulgent political figures," Willard told her. "Who didn't care if said bathroom was flooded."

"How dare you. It looks more like something a fairy queen would take bubble baths in," she snipped back, even while her eyes were alight with glee.

"Is that a reasonable reserve for a stained-glass bathtub?" Collin asked, noting the very bold, very *red* number on the bottom of the page.

"I have no idea," she admitted, shaking her head. "I would have to do some research."

"I finally found something you don't know," Collin said. "I didn't realize that was possible."

She gave him a half-hearted glare. "Well, you could enjoy it less."

"No." He shook his head. "I don't think I could."

After bidding Willard goodbye, they worked their way down the street. Alice kept twisting the ring around her finger, occasionally stopping to smile down at her hand.

"I really should get back to the shop," she murmured, grinning up at him. "But I can't remember when I've enjoyed myself so much. And I'm just going to call this 'professional research'—scouting out the competition."

"I'm flattered you're willing to bend the strictest description of your duties for me," he told her as they moved through the crowd. A lot of locals stopped Collin to say hello and welcome him back to the island. At first, it was kind of nice, but when it took them almost an hour to make it up one block, it became a little embarrassing. While those same locals were perfectly polite to Alice, there was a distance there, a reserve that wasn't present when she was with Riley or Caroline. Strange.

"It's like spending the day with a politician," she teased him as they walked away from a conversation with Betty Cortez, who ran Starfall Point Pages.

"Bite your tongue," he told her. "I think my Grandpa Fort had long-term plans for me."

"People missed you, that's nice," she assured him. "And they're a little curious, which is natural. You were away for a while, from what I understand."

He nodded. "College and life and everything else kept me away. I studied business, which I needed. I paid my dues, working every position from night-desk clerk on up to GM. I shadowed some of the best hotel managers in the business. Eventually, I was able to consult for other hotels, telling them how they should run things," he said. "It was better, learning the hard way. Unfortunately, that's how I learn best."

She nodded. "I get that."

There was a moment of silence as they walked together on the crowded street, the color and energy of other people's cheer surrounding them, and he had the strangest, almost compulsive urge to fill it. And even though what he was about to say might make her think less of him, he wanted her to know *him*, the truth behind the rumors and the polished veneer.

"The stories that a lot of rich kids tell you about emotionally distant parents who handed them off to the staff and went on their merry jet-setting ways? That wasn't my parents," he told her. "They let me know every day how much they loved me, how grateful they were to have me. They were the model of what a good, loving relationship is supposed to be.

"I was fourteen when they died. Normally, my parents didn't travel without me. But it was their twentieth anniversary and I didn't want to hang around, watching them being all googly-eyed at each other. I wanted them to go have fun. They were driving around Monaco in a convertible, took a turn too quickly. I want to think they were happy in those last moments, Mom looking all glamorous with a scarf tied around her hair and Dad in those aviator sunglasses that he swore once belonged to Paul Newman. I like to think they weren't in pain at the end, and that it was good, that they were together." Collin let out a slow breath.

She took his hand and while he felt that same low hum of electricity along his skin, the moment the sapphire ring brushed against his knuckle, he felt a sort of punch to his chest that made his feet stop mid-step. It was the familiar strike against the heart he always felt when talking about his parents—regret, loss, *grief.* And now it felt so much worse. Was it being home? Being touched while his heart was so exposed?

Alice simply squeezed his hand, and he found the air to say, "My Aunt Cynthia and Uncle Lawrence stepped in and declared they were taking custody of me. It wasn't what my parents had outlined in their will, but everybody in the extended family was too shell-shocked to say anything, I think. Dad had never let Lawrence near his business dealings and the board was far less sentimental when Lawrence tried to 'insist' he take Dad's place. The pair of them had their own interests, none of which were particularly profitable. I believe my uncle tried to start his own smooth-jazz record label, and

Cynthia bought a vineyard in New Jersey. Which is probably why they wanted custody of me: the money that came along with me.

"Anyway, Lawrence and Cynthia had always 'meant well,' so what was left of my extended family just went along with it for about a year," Collin told her. "It became very uncomfortable, very quickly. They spent a lot of time trying to get me to sign papers regarding control of my parents' estate, my dad's shares of various companies. Lawrence had all the same advantages my dad had growing up, but he just didn't have my dad's gifts of choosing the right idea at the right time. He'd run through most of his inheritance by the time my parents died. Hell, my dad bought him out of his share of the manor house when I was nine to keep him from losing a house. The estate papers wouldn't have held up in court as I was a minor—a grieving minor who couldn't function. It took my *Aunt Christine's* lawyer threatening them to get them to back off."

"Aunt Christine?" she said, tilting her head. "I don't think I've ever heard of a Christine Bancroft."

"She was a VanWyck, my mother's sister," he told her as they started to walk again. "She removed me from their custody, which *was* what my parents wanted, moved me back to her farm in Vermont. She *actually did* mean well, but she didn't know how to handle a kid who was angry and confused and sort of drowning in unprocessed rage at the world in general. She tried to get me help. She thought about pulling me from my prep school, but I think she was afraid that would take away what little familiarity I had. I'd almost had enough therapy to make a little dent by the time I went away to college. I didn't want to go to school, but I did because that was what my parents wanted. I had a healthy college fund and

Bancrofts had attended Dartmouth for generations. I shouldn't have struck out on my own. I wasn't ready. And I was still just so angry at...everything. My girlfriend at the time, Paige, decided she would go there too. And by then, I was as dependent on her as anything else."

"I'm sorry to ask an obvious and intrusive question but... Are you alluding to drugs?" There was no judgment in her voice, just a need to know him. And as much as it pained him to tell her this, he felt the stone settled on his chest wiggle a little. He wanted her to know him, even if it scared her away.

"I'm not going to lie. I dabbled," he admitted. "A little weed, some pills here and there, but I never really fell in too deep because that would have disappointed my parents. I know that doesn't make any sense, but in my head, I made the emotional math work. I would get just inebriated enough to do something stupid and give the most pointless middle finger possible to the universe. It was like I was daring it to take me too. You know that story about the frat bro who tried to ride a Jet Ski down the stairs at Gray Fern Cottage?"

He paused and pointed a finger at his own chest.

She stopped walking and stared at him, mouth agape. "Really?"

He nodded. "Cost me fifteen thousand dollars out of my own pocket to fix it, which I deserved. I was in a lot of pain and I just couldn't figure out a way to live without my parents. I was completely reckless. The riskier the behavior, the better. I was destructive and stupid, and I was trying to prove to God or the universe or whatever that I didn't need this life. And if I put people around me in danger, well, I could only hope that they figured out to stay clear of me. Eventually they learned to stay away. Paige never did."

He swallowed heavily. His history with Paige LaGravenesse was so tangled and toxic, he didn't know how to explain it. Paige had seen him at his worst, and she wasn't above reminding him of that. Her version of a fun lunch out was reminiscing about the "good old days": retelling long-winded stories of his humiliating antics from their youth, only to conclude with something like, "I'm so glad no one knows that story but me" or "I'm so glad your parents didn't see you doing something like that." She left out the fact that most of their travels were based on some whim of hers, where they would meet friends of her friends, end up at a club where they had no business going, where she would order round after round of shots for a huge group on *his* credit card, cheering him on while he did increasingly risky stupid shit, making suggestions for even more stupid shit. And while he was a willing, if drunken, participant, the worst part was waking up to Paige's complaints the next morning, how she couldn't *believe* he'd done those things in front of all her friends, and what would his family think if they found out? Then she'd list the ways she'd protected him from himself: taking him out of clubs before it was "too late," preventing people from taking photos, getting him in and out of the ER quietly. And what would his poor parents think if they'd lived to see this? The shame of it would make him repeat the cycle harder.

Hell, she'd none-too-subtly reminded him of all that in the recent string of texts he'd been ignoring; how she was "just check-ing in" and "wanted to make sure he wasn't regretting his choice" to live in Starfall Point, because she knew how "self-destructive" he could become when he was bored. It was bait. And he wasn't going to fall for it.

"Is that when your guardians threatened to disown you? The Jet Ski thing?" she asked. When he frowned, she added, "Small town, Nana Grapevine. And Edison."

He shook his head. "No, Aunt Christine would never do that. At one point, my Uncle Lawrence and Aunt Cynthia threatened to take conservatorship of my assets until I was sober, which was more than the wake-up call that I needed, because Christine's lawyers informed me that they might actually have a case. The idea of either of them having control of something my father loved was enough to get me to pull my head out of my ass. I got into treatment—well, I took treatment more seriously—got sober, went to work."

She nodded. "Wait, why were you renting Gray Fern Cottage? You have a house right here on the island."

He burst out laughing. "Really? That was your question?"

"Oh, no, I have plenty of questions," she countered. "But you just shared a whole lot and it wouldn't be kind to poke at you for more details."

"I wasn't renting Gray Fern. I was there for a party, looking for the guy I usually bought weed from." He paused and frowned. "Also, I don't know if Ben is aware I'm the Jet Ski guy who half-destroyed his house."

"Ben's not the type to hold that against you," Alice assured him. "And the repairmen did a great job."

They walked again, their hands still joined, though he was careful to avoid contact with the ring. They made it to the front door of Superior Antiques.

"To be clear, you are not obligated to buy anything from our stock," she told him. "I have set aside a few pieces that might work, but the whole point is finding what *will* work. And I don't care where that comes from, as long as you're happy with the outcome."

"I don't know if that makes you a bad salesperson or an excellent consultant," he told her, leaning so close that he could smell the faintly peach-scented lip gloss that made her lips so shiny and tempting.

"Either way…" She grinned at him as she moved to unlock the front door. The knob twisted freely and the door popped open. The smile evaporated from her face. "I know I locked that before I left."

Collin nodded, pushing Alice gently behind him. The lights were on and the showroom seemed to be undisturbed in the seconds they had to process before someone shouted, "Alice Penelope Seastairs!"

Alice startled and distantly, Collin heard the plink of metal hitting the floor. Collin threw his arm in front of her as if to shield her from the diminutive older woman in tailored white linen storming across the polished wood floors.

"Where have you been?" she demanded, her cloud of carefully styled blond hair barely quivering as she moved swiftly across the floor.

"Grandmother," Alice whispered, her voice so shaky that Collin's head whipped toward her, his mouth turned downward. "I didn't know you'd come back to town."

An older man stood near the register, glaring, his arms stiff at his sides as he balanced himself on a carved ebony walking stick. Dressed in pastel madras, he looked like the silver-haired villain in a wacky 1980s class-struggle comedy. But there was nothing remotely funny about him. Collin doubted there ever had been.

So, this was the infamous Marilyn and Franklin Proctor—yelling at their granddaughter in front of a complete stranger. Collin was not impressed.

"Well, obviously. If you'd had any idea, I doubt you would have left our business unattended while you gallivanted off to God-knows-where with this hoodlum!" Marilyn sniffed. "Explain yourself, young lady!"

"Hoodlum?" Collin asked dryly.

Alice's voice was shaky as she tried to cling to some semblance of a normal business interaction. "Franklin and Marilyn Proctor, this is Collin Bancroft. He owns the Duchess Hotel, and I've been assisting him in finding antiques for the hotel's soon-to-be remodeled suites."

"I know exactly who he is," Marilyn seethed, her face going the same puce as the paisley in her Aigner scarf. "I can't believe you would let him into our shop, after all we've told you about the Bancrofts over the years. We knew your judgment was defective at best, Alice, but honestly, this can only be classified as a betrayal."

"I *beg your pardon*?" Alice cried. "All you've ever told me was that I was to stay away from the hotel. I thought it was because you didn't want me getting into trouble for breaking something."

"We thought you were intelligent enough to make the inference," Marilyn hissed. "Clearly, that was a mistake."

Alice began, "How on earth was I supposed to—"

"Don't speak to your grandmother in that tone!" Franklin thundered.

"Don't speak *your granddaughter* like that!" Collin shouted. Franklin, who seemed unaccustomed to this sort of defiance from anyone, took a step back. "What's wrong with the pair of you? Alice has only ever protected your interests here—"

"Who do you think you are, speaking to us like that in our own establishment?" Marilyn cried. "Leave at once, or I will call the authorities."

Collin pressed his lips together and turned to Alice. "I'm not comfortable leaving you here with them. Would you come with me?"

Marilyn gasped. "How dare you suggest—"

"I'm not speaking to you," Collin told her.

"I don't think that's—" Alice began, only to have her grandmother interject.

"Alice, we expect you to face up to your mistakes like an adult and explain yourself. Not to go slinking off with this *boy*."

"Ma'am, I am thirty-five years old," Collin told her. Old enough to know he didn't want to leave Alice with them. He'd faced this sort of reptilian disdain in conference rooms across the world, but he'd never seen it coming from a *family member*, not even Cynthia and Lawrence. The cold rage radiating off these two was enough to make Collin want to give Alice permanent residence at the hotel. He did not want her anywhere near these people.

"You're old enough to know how easily we could charge you with trespassing," Franklin told him.

"All right, all right," Alice said, turning and gingerly pushing Collin back out the door. "I'll be fine, Collin, honestly. They're just upset because I left the shop in the middle of the day. It's not normal for me to do that, and it scared them."

"They don't seem upset," Collin retorted, glaring over her shoulder through the glass shop door. "They seem unhinged."

"Their whole routine has been disrupted for the summer, after my grandfather's surgery," she told him, fully aware of the excuses she could hear in her own voice. "It's got them all off-kilter."

Collin was aware that his face, normally difficult to read, was the very image of skeptical.

"I'll be fine," she promised him. "You know how it is with families."

"I don't think I would call those people 'family.' They're more like a pack of wolves. Or an unkindness of ravens. Or whatever you call a group of sharks." She stared up at him through her eyelashes, frowning slightly. He sighed. "Call me if you need anything at all. In fact, call me anyway, just so I know that you're all right."

"I will," she promised before closing the door in his face.

Collin did not feel good about leaving her behind. But Alice knew her family better than he did, and he wouldn't have appreciated anyone telling him how to handle things with his aunt and uncle. Still, he walked back toward the Duchess with his phone in his hand, just in case she called.

Chapter 5
Alice

EVEN AS EVERYTHING SCREAMED AT her to follow Collin out the door, Alice took a fortifying breath and prepared to deal with the storm brewing behind her. She turned around, finding her grandmother standing approximately six inches from her face.

"We know what you did!" Marilyn shrieked. The noise and proximity had anxiety creeping up Alice's throat, sending waves of magic throbbing toward her hands, aching to become *something*—most likely posing a great risk to the precious items that surrounded them on all sides. Alice took a deep breath, doing her best to keep her expression neutral. She would not make every fragile object in this shop explode—even if it would be extremely gratifying. Grandmother Marilyn had started arguments in this manner before, trying to entrap Alice into confessing some unknown offense. The screaming was a little over-the-top for her, though. *Hmm.*

"I don't understand what you mean," Alice said. Now that the angry panic was starting to ebb a tiny bit, the sour burn of humiliation rose in Alice's chest. She couldn't believe they'd spoken to her like this in *front* of someone. Normally, they liked to keep this sort of "performance review" private, behind closed doors. Why were they starting this interaction at what Josh would call "a hundred"? She knew that people of Starfall Point didn't see her as petted and doted upon, but having her grandparents' absolute disdain for her laid bare like this? It was insupportable.

"We saw you, Alice. We *saw you* remove stock through the *front door*, blatantly stealing from the store. From us!" Marilyn shouted, crossing to the far wall. Absently, Alice wondered how her grandmother had mastered the art of walking without moving her upper body. Maybe it was a finishing-school thing?

"I beg your pardon?" Alice blinked at her. She rubbed her thumb along her finger, where she expected to find her recently purchased ring—how had that become a habit so quickly?

The ring wasn't there. She couldn't even register distress that she'd apparently lost it. The room was just too loud.

"Don't you try to play innocent with us, young lady. We have cameras!" Marilyn cried, pointing at the corner of the showroom. Alice's eyes followed the motion and as she moved closer, she saw a tiny pinhole in the crown molding. It was almost hidden behind the raised cornice of a wardrobe, so unless one was looking for it, there was no way to see it. Hell, she hadn't seen it, despite spending hours in that room every day.

"As soon as we saw the footage, we knew we had to make the trip immediately, even if it did pain your poor grandfather," Marilyn said. "He shouldn't be traveling in his condition. We shouldn't be traveling at all! We shouldn't have to check up on you every summer! We should be able to trust our employee to run this store competently!"

Silently, Grandfather Franklin pointed to another pinhole just above the register, which would have recorded every transaction Alice made. Her brain felt like it was short-circuiting. Her grandparents had fought against the idea of interior cameras in the store for years, claiming they were "gauche" and communicated distrust to the customers. And somehow, they'd managed to install them in the store without her knowledge? How had they managed to do it without her seeing it? She *lived upstairs*. It wasn't like they could sneak a workman in without her noticing.

Wait.

Alice recalled a recent weekend when Marilyn and Franklin *insisted* that she take a few days off; during the busy season, no less. They asked her to visit a contact of theirs in Canada who specialized in Staffordshire ceramics. They told her they wanted to install the remote door locks, triggered by a button under the register. They said she should consider the "time off" their present to her for her birthday. They must have had the cameras installed then. She was particularly hurt, as she'd thought for once they were doing something nice for her. She'd been such a fool. She'd been grateful for the time away, even if it was months after her actual birthday.

Then they'd used security measures against *her*. The one thing she'd asked them to do that they'd followed through with, something that would make her feel safe, and they'd weaponized it.

Arthur materialized by his cabinet, shaking his head sadly. "Are you all right, miss? These two seem like right bast—rude people."

Alice shook her head because she was *not* all right. She'd done everything they'd ever demanded of her and more, and it was never good enough. They'd rewarded hard work and earnest effort with scorn and secret cameras.

Meanwhile, Marilyn was still screeching—apparently unable to see Arthur because he didn't want her to. "We knew it would come to this. We *knew* nothing good could come of you spending time with that girl up at Shaddow House. We knew it was going to give you ideas, ideas like stealing from your grandparents, who spent the best years of their lives investing their time and attention in you."

Time and attention, but not love.

Investment, but not love.

Through the scorching prickle of rage, Alice was struck by a sudden sadness for her mother. If Felicity Seastairs had lived, Marilyn and Franklin would have treated her exactly the same. Even if Alice's parents had lived a long happy life together with a houseful of children, the Proctors would have lamented the ruin of Felicity's life and all their plans for her. Felicity could have chased their approval until they died, and she never would have gotten it.

The worst part was, the Proctors' behavior wasn't rooted in love. It wasn't the grief of losing their only child that made them act this way. It was a pervasive dissatisfaction with life. And Alice might feel sorry for them if they weren't such absolute—

Would it really be so bad, to be disowned by her grandparents?

No, that was wrong, she corrected herself, as that fire in her gut was banked by the more familiar guilt. She took another deep breath to steady her nerves. And she recalled how her grandparents had made considerable sacrifices to raise her. They'd never planned on raising a baby in their golden years and it would be ungrateful to abandon them when they were just starting to enjoy their lives.

Alice commanded her brain to slow down, to consider what was happening around her. What was the real damage here? Given the angle, the camera couldn't have recorded what she'd taken from Arthur's drawer. The camera had been pointed at the back of his armoire.

The burning anxiety melted away and all she could feel was the indignity of it all.

"You don't know what I took out of the shop in that bag," she said. "It could have been my laundry, for all you know."

Marilyn sniffed. "I doubt that very much. Whatever it was, we insist you bring it back this instant."

Alice felt her magic dig somewhere deep within her chest, to where that tiny ember of rage flared. She tilted her head and smiled sweetly. "No. It doesn't belong to you."

Her grandmother's head reared back as if she'd been slapped— which was a bit outrageous, considering the difference in their approaches. Alice hadn't just screamed at *Marilyn.*

To Alice's surprise, it was Franklin who responded. "Don't make us take more drastic measures, Alice. You know what we *did* capture on camera? You, standing in this room, talking to yourself. That's more than enough evidence to have you sent away somewhere—somewhere you can't cause so much trouble."

Alice blinked at him. This was a surprise, coming from Franklin. Her grandfather wasn't exactly the soft touch. But he was distant and withholding, rather than confrontational. In general, he simply stood behind her grandmother, glaring, the enforcer. She knew it could have been much worse, but she'd never pushed back hard enough for him to get involved. One of her homeschooling assignments in high school had been on the perils of the foster-care system. At the time, her grandparents thought her gratitude was waning. Now, Alice supposed they thought that gratitude was nonexistent.

"It wouldn't be difficult to convince everyone on this island it's the best thing for you," Marilyn added, apparently recovered from the awful assault of being told no. "Your mother had her problems, you know."

Alice's jaw ached from clenching her teeth. She was... She was *pissed*. Yes, even though she was hearing the curse words in *Caroline's* voice in her head—she was pissed off, pissed right the fuck off. The little flame of anger flashed, and somehow, she managed to bite out, "No one's ever said anything like that to me."

Marilyn huffed, rolling her eyes. "We've tried to protect you from the talk, but we can't do that if you keep behaving like her. All you have to do is be a good girl and do what little we ask."

Good girl.

Alice nearly stumbled back a step. It hurt, hearing Clark's words thrown in her face. All she could feel was pain, a soul-deep scar of guilt that might never close. Why wasn't her coven feeling this? Why were they leaving her all alone?

Fuck this, the angry internal voice told her. *Run.*

She had to get out of there. She had to move. She wasn't scurrying. She was *bolting*, like a rabbit on the run from wolves. She didn't remember touching the shop door. She wasn't sure how she was doing it in heels, but she didn't even feel her feet hitting the ground. She needed to get to Shaddow House. Nowhere else was safe.

She could hear someone behind her, yelling her name. But she didn't stop as she tore through the waning early-autumn crowd, planning her dodges three and four moves ahead. Why couldn't the others feel her? What if she got to Shaddow House and couldn't open the door? The panic of that thought spurred her on even faster. She felt one of her shoes stick in the grass of Ben's yard as she cut the corner and ran up the steps. To her relief, Riley opened the door and her arms, catching Alice as she stumbled over the threshold.

"Sweetie, what's wrong?" she demanded, wrapping her arms around Alice. As soon as she crossed the boundary into the house, Alice could breathe.

"Grandparents," Alice told her, struggling to keep her voice steady. She sucked in a huge breath. Oxygen flooded into her lungs, and she could feel her hands and her feet again. Behind Riley, Plover had materialized, wringing his hands. Mina and Josh were standing with Caroline, Josh seeking out the protective curve of Caroline's arm even as he stood nearly a foot taller. Mina was holding something in her hand, the fused copper loops of a Welling lock.

Why was she holding that out in the open? Had they just found it? She nodded toward the lock. Josh reluctantly broke away and ran to the kitchen for a glass of water. Mina stepped forward to show it to her as Caroline knelt to help them off the floor.

"We just found it," Mina said. "Under the corner of the atrium. Apparently, it was originally supposed to be the back half of the house. We were in here talking, and you know, we've never really spent time in here together as a group, just being together. There's usually some sort of crisis happening or we're in the parlor or something. But we could all feel it pinging from under the floor, which was different. We had to break a few of the slate tiles to get to it. Eloise is taking the whole thing very personally."

Alice heard a burbling noise from the atrium, where Eloise, the French ghost who died during an attempted elopement, peered sullenly over the lip of her Persephone-themed fountain. Alice was oddly hurt that they'd found a lock without her, even though they'd found previous locks one at a time, without the presence of the whole group. Maybe this was a sign of things to come. Maybe as a group, the coven would be better off without her. They were operating as a unit and she was just a distraction, crashing into the house with her drama and tears.

If anything, she was a vulnerability to the group, dangerous. Maybe she should just leave the island altogether. The coven was the only thing holding her here. She could start fresh somewhere else. At the shop, she made enough to cover her food costs and clothes, but very little else. Fortunately, she had few other expenses on the island. She didn't go out. She didn't take vacations. She had a little bit of savings that could help her make a new start, but not enough to sustain her if there was any sort of emergency. She was sure that her grandparents wouldn't help her if she needed it, and that was sadder than she could even fathom. She hadn't even considered life off the island before. And even now, it hurt to think about leaving. She didn't want to live anywhere else. She loved it here. She'd built a family here, more of a family than she'd ever known. But she'd lied to them. This was the cost.

"Wait, so your grandparents just showed up?" Caroline demanded as she and Mina knelt close to her. "I thought they were supposed to stay in Florida for a few more months."

"They put cameras in the shop," Alice said, taking Josh's offered water and sipping it slowly. Calm, she had to stay calm. "They saw me leaving with the candelabra thing. They thought I was stealing."

"Well, that's ridiculous," Plover insisted. "You would never do such a thing."

"Alice, are you all right?" Collin asked, following her through the door. "I saw you running across Main Square, but I got stuck behind Mitt with his pedal-bike and a dozen people and—"

Everything in the room seemed to stop at once. All the living people just froze and stared at the newcomer. The ghosts were similarly caught off guard. People didn't just *walk into* Shaddow House. Alice doubted that Collin could see the ghosts, since *they* controlled that sort of thing. But, given the look on his face, he knew *something* wasn't right. He glanced around the room, even as he moved closer to her.

Mina, having more presence of mind than the rest of the people in the room—as usual—hid the lock behind her back like an illicit cigarette.

"Alice," Collin began as he knelt next to her.

Suddenly, there was a ghost crouched in front of Collin, screaming in his face. Well, Alice's face too. It was a collective face-screaming, really. Alice was getting tired of having her face used as a screaming target.

"*Where is he?*" the ghost wailed.

The ghost had probably been pretty once, in a delicate, almost elfin way, before she died. But now her lips were peeled back from her teeth in a permanent grimace. Her eyes had once crinkled with mischief, but now they were just shadowed pools of anguish. She was wearing a sky-blue "visiting dress" from the late 1890s, the high silk neckline stained with blood and the hem dirty and torn. A brooch dangled from the neck of the gown, as if it had been partially torn from her. The large ruby was set in a Byzantine gold setting made to look like a flaming sun.

This wasn't a woman accustomed to disarray in life. But now, her hair was a wild dark tangle, hanging over her pallid gray face. She wasn't like Eloise, who seemed to be made of sadness. This woman was *suffering*.

"Where is he?" the woman howled in Alice's face. "I can smell him on you! You've been near him!"

It took all of Alice's previous experience with ghosts, combined with her exhaustion from the day, not to panic. Collin, however, was clutching on to her as if he could haul her out of harm's way. She patted his arm. "I'm all right."

Plover sighed. "Really, Miss Victoria, this display is unseemly. And Miss Alice is already distressed. Could this not wait?"

Apparently, Plover had made himself visible to Collin in that moment, because Collin hauled Alice off the floor into his lap and used his long legs to push them away from Plover. "What the?"

"*Where is he?*" the woman screamed again, louder this time. Alice could almost feel the ghost's long curls dragging over her own hands. Alice raised those hands and with a force born in the depths of her belly, pushed them forward in a "warding off" gesture. It wasn't quite a spell, but it was an instinctual measure to protect herself and Collin. "Miss Victoria" practically slid across the floor, like she was dragged on a string.

"You'll find that yelling in my face is something that I'm quite accustomed to, so it doesn't affect me," Alice replied, her voice icy and smooth as Victoria blinked in shock. "Now, who are you asking me about?"

"*Bring him to me!*" the ghost roared and then disappeared.

Collin fell back against the wall and pulled Alice's weight against him. He took a deep, shaking breath through his nostrils.

"Are you OK?" he demanded as he wrapped his arms around her. He seemed to be checking her over for wounds and bruises, counting all her appendages. "What in the hell was that?"

Alice turned to Riley. Shaddow House was her legacy, her family secret to protect. Alice couldn't be the one to reveal it. Riley was staring at Collin, as if trying to determine whether he could be trusted. And then, of course, Plover decided to break the tension and decide for them, kneeling into Collin's line of sight and announcing, "That, sir, was a ghost."

Collin's eyes went somehow wider, and he yelled, "*What the fuck?*"

Step one was getting everybody off the floor. Step two was pouring heaping helpings of brandy for Collin and Alice as they collapsed on the couch in the parlor. Collin politely declined his and asked for water.

Alice felt a strange flush of guilt for not catching that, after Collin's being so open about his past struggles. Collin always seemed so polished and perfect; hearing that he'd had a more complex past made him more human. Approachable. Less intimidating.

She was in very real danger of developing devastating feelings for Collin Bancroft.

"Your first ghost sighting can be a lot," Riley told Collin even as Plover tsked over the wasted double of "Miss Nora's favorite." Caroline happily sipped it to appease him. Riley brought them a pot of spiced apple cinnamon tea and a plate of fruit, warning them of the potential post-adrenaline blood-sugar crash.

"I also feel shaken up by the appearance of an unknown and aggressive ghost," Josh said, all guileless brown eyes and innocence as he nodded toward the brandy bottle. Riley simply stared at him. Josh bit his lip and looked away. "It was worth a shot."

"That was such a pathetic attempt, it's like you don't even *want* to try alcohol," Mina sighed, shaking her head. When Caroline's brows rose, she added hastily, "Not that I have, obviously."

"OK. One issue at a time," Riley said, taking a seat near the huge stone fireplace.

Lilah, the ghost of a little girl attached to the brass match cloche on the mantel, appeared with a hopeful expression on her face. Riley shook her head. "It's still too warm for a fire, honey."

"Fine." Lilah sighed and wiggled her fingers in greeting at Collin. "I'm going into the kitchen with Miss Natalie."

The pink that had returned to Collin's cheeks faded. "Um, how many ghosts are haunting this house, exactly?"

"That's a pretty long story, my guy," Josh told him solemnly as he flopped onto the couch next to Alice. "And as funny as I think it would be to count how many ghosts you can't see in this room, I think we're supposed to be talking about you and Alice having a collectively shitty day."

Caroline shot him a warning look, her hands in the air. Josh shrugged. "Tell me I'm wrong."

Plover looked down his long ghostly nose at Josh, making the teenager sigh, "Pardon my foul language, please, ladies. Anyway, ghosts are real. There's an afterlife. These women are witches who can work magic on ghosts and haunted objects. And I'm sort of magic-adjacent. I mostly listen. Also, the house is full of hundreds of ghosts attached to basically every antique object you see in the house, so be careful of what you pick up—particularly the toaster in the kitchen. It bites."

Collin took a deep breath as he absorbed the CliffsNotes version of Hauntings 101. "OK, then."

Mina's dark brows lifted. "Really?"

"No! Clearly, I have hundreds of questions, but I'm trying to play it cool so I don't melt down," he shot back, making Mina laugh. He chuckled. Alice took his hand, finding comfort in that low-key electrical pulse. He frowned down at her hand. "Where did the ring go?"

Alice shook her head. "It was so loose on my finger, it must have slipped off. I was distracted by my grandparents back at the shop. I barely noticed. I just ran."

"Can we go back to what happened at the shop?" Caroline asked Alice. "What made you run over here?"

"My grandparents *hid cameras* in the shop while I was out of town," Alice said, taking a deep drink from her own brandy snifter. Collin squeezed her hand.

"Raging assholes, both of them," Caroline marveled, shaking her head.

Josh looked to Plover to admonish Caroline, but the ghost butler shrugged. "She's an adult. And correct."

"They traveled all the way up here to demand that I return to them whatever I took out of the shop. The camera wasn't angled to their advantage, so they don't know what it was."

"How much have they seen with those cameras?" Riley asked.

"Well, they didn't mention having footage of ghosts, so I guess not much," Alice muttered into her glass. "They think I was talking to myself on the videos. They threatened to have me institutionalized."

"We wouldn't let that happen," Caroline told her.

Alice shook her head. "It's an empty threat. It's just that they started saying things about my mother, and it was too much."

"They're the freaking worst," Riley said. "Maybe it's time to think about finding other employment."

"Already done. She's doing private consulting for me," Collin replied. "I am willing to increase your retainer considerably, Alice."

"And it's maybe time to move out of the shop apartment, considering that they're hiding cameras uncomfortably near your living space without telling you," Caroline added.

"Oh, no… I hadn't even considered my apartment," Alice said, her mouth dropping open.

"You don't have to stay there," Riley told her. "We have plenty of room. Most of the guest rooms are charmed to keep the ghosts out and give you privacy."

"Most of them?" Collin asked. Riley shrugged.

"No," Alice said, her voice firmer than it had sounded since she fell through the door. She couldn't stay with Riley after what she'd done. And staying at Shaddow House might give Clark more of a reason to show up there. "You and Edison have enough…additional people staying with you."

The expression on Riley's face was hurt, but Alice couldn't "help" by taking it back.

Alice insisted, "I won't be a burden. I'll figure something out."

"I would offer to let you stay in my old place, but Wally's moved in there," Caroline said. "Mom and Dad are actually pretty thrilled to have their whole house to themselves."

"I'll figure it out," Alice told them.

"We still have tourists taking up all the rentals," Caroline replied.

"It doesn't make sense," Mina insisted.

"Labor Day is this weekend. This is when the tourists have their last big hoo-ha," Josh told her. "What's the big mystery?"

"No." Mina rolled her eyes in the way only an older sister could. "And it's 'hurrah,' not 'hoo-ha.' I mean, we haven't brought in any new haunted items recently. Alice has been inside this house hundreds of times. Why would this ghost lady, Victoria, suddenly show up and scream in her face? What's new?"

"Other than Collin?" Riley asked. "She said she could 'smell him' on Alice."

"The ring," Alice said. She looked at Collin. "I was wearing it before I walked into the house. The inscription on the band was 'V & S.' The ghost's name was Victoria. Plover, do you know anything about her?"

"Miss Victoria is one of the more reticent residents of the house," Plover told Riley. "I believe she was brought into the house sometime in the 1940s, without commentary from your great-grandfather. She appears every decade or so, but doesn't interact with the other residents."

"You think the ring could be her attachment object?" Riley asked. "How would that work if it's outside the house?"

"We found it at the back of a drawer in Tremont's Treasures," Collin said.

"A drawer from a dresser belonging to a distant cousin of mine." Alice nodded.

"You think there's a family connection there?" Caroline asked her.

"I don't know," Alice admitted. "My grandparents never mentioned anything about particularly tragic deaths in the family, or anyone named Victoria. I could talk to Willard."

"Where does that leave us?" Collin asked.

Alice shrugged. "Sometimes, a ghost just needs someone to talk to about their trauma, some action that will resolve the unfinished business that's keeping them attached to the earthly plane. And sometimes, they're a little less cooperative and we give them a little...nudge. That's where our magic comes in."

"And with everything you have going on, you think that talking to Willard is a good use of your time?" Collin asked.

"Victoria's in a lot of pain," Alice said. "I don't like the idea of leaving her in here, in that state, with people I care about. For that matter, I don't like the idea of leaving Arthur alone with my grandparents in the shop. Poor Arthur."

"Well, I don't think your grandparents would be willing to sell his cabinet to anyone present right now," Riley speculated. "I don't think I'm supposed to go back into the shop. Legally speaking. I've said a lot of things to your grandparents that could be construed as threat by some people."

"*Boring* people," Mina muttered.

"That counts as 'some people,'" Riley added.

Alice blew out a breath. "Good point."

It took some time for Collin to work through his various questions about their magic and the history of Shaddow House and how it all worked. All things considered, he was handling the transition from nonbeliever to believer pretty well. But finally, Edison and Ben came home from work. Ben presented Alice with her shoe, which had apparently been in his yard this whole time.

Alice realized she was imposing on the kids' evening routine and dinner. Edison looked exhausted, which made sense, considering that he'd lost his key volunteer at the library. Margaret Flanders's health issues were still keeping her at home.

"I should go," Alice said, standing suddenly. She was a little wobbly, hardly surprising considering the amount of brandy she'd consumed. Also, she was only wearing one shoe. She slid the other one on.

Collin stood and offered her his hand. "I'll walk you out."

"To where?" Riley asked. "Where are you going to go?"

"I'll figure it out," Alice assured her. "I have to at least go back and grab a bag of my stuff from the shop. You have other things to worry about, like the fact that you found a lock this afternoon."

"Oh, yeah. I kind of forgot in all the hubbub," Riley said, frowning. "Mina, has it been in your pocket this whole time?"

"No, I stuck it in the couch cushions," Mina said, holding it up.

Riley pinched the bridge of her nose.

"You did what, now?" Edison asked.

"I'm going to leave you with that," Alice told her, patting Riley's shoulder. "Good night, Plover. Natalie. Eloise. Various ghosts."

"Good night, Miss." Plover materialized by the door. Alice wondered if he did it specifically to startle Collin, who only nodded politely at the butler.

"What's a lock?" Collin asked as they walked out the door.

"That is information you don't need heaped on you right now," she sighed as she clipped her way down the stairs. She paused at the gate of Shaddow House, wondering how the hell she was going to go home.

What if her grandparents were waiting for her at the shop? Normally, she went to Proctor House to deep-clean it a week before they arrived for their "summer inspection." But since they hadn't given her warning of their arrival, they would have to accept that dust existed in their house. Hell, they might be waiting for her at the shop just to berate her for *that*.

"I don't think you should go back there," he told her.

Alice chuckled. "Yes, I think you've made that clear."

"I think you're forgetting that I own a hotel," he told her. "I literally have more than three hundred guest rooms. We could consider temporary residency part of your compensation as my consultant."

"Oh," she said, frowning. "I hadn't thought of that."

Collin laughed. "And thanks to an archaic booking system, I happen to know that a lot of those rooms are available. And none of them are haunted."

Alice's lips pulled back in a grimace.

Collin's jaw dropped. "Are some of them haunted?"

She walked away without answering.

Collin cried, "Oh, come on!"

To Alice's relief, the code to the shop's back door had not been changed when she returned. She didn't know where else her grandparents might have set up cameras, so she was careful as she made her way up the back stairs to her apartment. She wanted to go look in the shop for the lost ring, but she didn't want the cameras to capture her "break-in." She left Collin outside this time, so he wasn't seen breaking in with her.

It took a sadly short amount of time to pack her clothes and a handful of personal items into a few bags. How had she collected so few things in life, working in a shop where she sold items to people to fill their own homes?

Arthur appeared at the foot of her bed as she tucked personal papers into her laptop bag.

"I'm sorry," she told him. "For that awful scene and for my grandparents."

"No, miss, that... I've never seen anything like that. What was that?"

Alice shook her head. "There's a lot of history there."

"The way they spoke of you after you left," he said, frowning. "They want you back here. They don't want *you* to know that. They want you to think they've cut you out forever. They want you to sweat over it. But they know they can't run this place without you, especially not when things are busy. They just want to bring you to heel."

"Is that what they said?" Alice asked.

"No," Arthur replied, looking distinctly uncomfortable. "I'm putting it kindly."

She frowned. "*That* was kindly?"

"Don't come back here, Alice," Arthur said. "You're a sweet girl. You deserve better."

"I'm not sleeping here, at least, I know that," Alice said. "There are reasons I need to come back. Besides, I don't want to leave you here either."

"I don't suppose I can stray too far from Bessie, can I?" he mused. She shook her head.

"Well, I don't like it. But I want you to be protected. That's more important. Your young man is out back, isn't he?"

Alice replied, "I didn't want to include him in this particular bit of breaking and entering. And he's not *my* young man."

"Tell him that," Arthur snorted. "I'm withholding my judgment on him. If he proves that he's good to you, I'll let him see me. Your grandparents? Unless it's to scare them into apoplexy, they can get—"

"Understood," she said, cutting him off. "It's like the ghost cut direct."

Arthur beamed at her. "Precisely."

Collin was surprised to see how few bags she was carrying when she emerged from the shop's back door. "Do we need to come back later?"

"Would you believe I'm a minimalist?" she asked as he shouldered her largest duffel bag. When he answered with the lift of a brow, she added, "OK, fine, I'm not. But I like to keep things simple."

They took a long, circuitous route around Main Square to avoid Clark's law office.

"Has he given you any more trouble?" Collin asked, nodding to the window marked TANNER, MOSCOVITZ, AND GRAVES.

"No, he has been eerily quiet," she muttered. "I'm hoping maybe he realizes he went too far, chasing me down the street like he did, in public. The problem is that he's probably regrouping to come up with something worse."

"Are you ever going to tell me what was going on there?" Collin asked.

"I think you've been privy to enough of my secrets for one day," she said.

He considered it for a moment. "That's fair."

They remained quiet for the rest of the walk back to the hotel. She'd expected them to walk into the front entrance of the hotel, but to her surprise, he walked her through the rose garden on the north lawn, past a gazebo frequently used for weddings, and through a door marked STAFF ONLY. While there was an entrance to the hotel kitchen on the left, opening a door on the right led them into...a house?

"What in the what?" Alice marveled at the comfortable den area with sturdy oatmeal-colored canvas furniture and a large flat-screen TV. A dining table for six occupied a space just off a completely modern kitchen. It was basically a single-family home tucked away in the hotel. "How did I not know this was here?"

He nodded toward the staircase central to the room. "Well, when the hotel was built, the architect who designed it stayed here on-site with some of the construction foremen, and sort of built the hotel around it. And then, when my ancestors took on management and weren't quite sure how to run things here and maintain some sense of family life, a lot of them stayed here in the 'guesthouse,'" he said, carrying her bag upstairs. "Now we're going to maintain it for long-term on-site employees, such as yourself, or special guests. You would be welcome at the manor house, but I didn't think you would be totally comfortable staying with me. You'll have privacy here, and security. And housekeeping services. And complimentary room service, if you want it."

Oh, she wanted it. While the "Collin sandwich" had been an abomination, she'd been thinking about the accompanying fries since their lunch.

"Thanks," she told him.

He shrugged. "Towels, sheets, the good snacks from the minibar cart. Anything you need, I'm here to see to it... That sounded dirtier than I meant it to."

Alice chuckled. It was a novel feeling, being catered to—something that had been missing from her last three or four "entanglements," including Clark. Alice remembered waking up to one particular partner who asked if she wanted breakfast, only to tell her where the closest grocery store was located and how he liked his eggs. She'd immediately walked out and blocked his number.

"This is just temporary until I figure something else out," she promised. He opened the door to a guest room and she knew she'd just lied.

The walls were a lovely shade of pale yellow, matching the stripe of the seersucker bedspread on the king-sized bed. Everything, from the throw pillows to the cherrywood desk to the chocolate leather club chair positioned next to the window, was designed for rest and comfort. If she'd designed a room, this was what it would look like.

But all she could manage to say was, "It's not orange."

"Aura didn't like the energy in here," he told her. He carefully set her bags near the desk and stepped closer to her. "So, um, there are no ghosts in this room, right?"

"No," she said. She looked down at her hands, somehow missing the weight of a ring she'd only worn for an hour. Maybe it was cursed, instead of haunted? What else would make her feel this way? "And you're not going to be seeing them all the time now, unless they choose to show themselves, the way the Shaddow House ghosts approached you."

He took her hands, turning them over as if he was searching for wounds. "But if you need to keep them out of here, you can do that?"

"Yes," she said, nodding.

"That scene earlier with your grandparents, is that...typical?" Collin asked.

"They're usually far more passive-aggressive than whatever *that* was. My parents died young and my dad's family wanted me, but diseases and accidents seemed to pick them off one by one. By the time I was nine, the Proctors were all I had left. They have made it clear that I'm... I don't know anything about my mother. I only know what other people have told me over the years. My grandparents didn't keep anything of hers. I mean, there are pictures, most of which they put away. But no toys, no report cards, nothing. It's like they took her away so I wouldn't know whether they were telling me the truth about her. And they've used that to shape this narrative of her life, and I never know if they're doing that because they're trying to get me to learn from her mistakes, or because doing that is to their advantage. Maybe both," Alice said.

Collin asked, "What mistakes?"

"She made one impulsive decision to leave a party with a boy and it threw her whole life off-track. She was supposed to finish college and move away from here. Regina, down at the ice cream shop, told me once. They were friends back before…back when she could have gotten away from them."

"I doubt she saw you as a mistake," Collin said.

Alice hummed absently as he rubbed his hand over her wrist. She could feel his sympathy wrapping around her like a warm blanket, sliding over her skin, making her chest ache a little less. Was this real…or some sort of magical quirk caused by Collin's extraordinary empathy?

"Well, what have other people told you about her?" Collin asked.

"A lot of platitudes about how we have the same hair color and the same smile," she said, rolling her eyes a bit. "She loved chunky peanut butter and black jelly beans, which makes me think she was a little bit of a contrarian. She hated jazz music. I mean, *really* hated it, used to get mad if it came on the radio. That's something we have in common."

There was a silence, but it wasn't awkward. He folded his long fingers over hers and pulled her gently forward until her forearms were tucked against the warmth of his chest.

"How am I supposed to leave you?" he asked softly. "My whole worldview has been turned on its ear in one day. You're central to it all… How do I leave you?"

She tilted her forehead against his chin, sighing deeply. "I think maybe we've been through too much together in the past twenty-four hours, between the scene with my grandparents and you chasing me across the island and a ghost screaming in your face and finding out I'm a witch. It's probably something akin to trauma bonding."

"And yet, here I stand, unable to walk away from you." He slipped one hand under her chin, rubbing his thumb along her jaw until she was looking up at him. "You're right, this isn't a good idea," he said, his breath feathering over her lips. "We're emotionally and physically exhausted. And I'm technically your boss."

"Mm-hm," she murmured, even as her lips inched closer to his. "Those are all very sensible reasons not to kiss you. And I'm going to do it anyway."

Collin huffed out a relieved breath. "Oh, thank God."

She pulled his shirt down until his lips were crushed against hers. Together, their mouths tasted of cinnamon, sweet heat, and sin. He moaned softly into her mouth, sliding his free hand down her back and pressing her closer. With the other hand, he still held hers close to his heart. She could feel it pounding against her knuckles.

His tongue slid tentatively against her bottom lip, and she opened up to him, inviting it in to dance with hers. She wanted to drag him toward the bed, to burn away the hurts of today against his skin. But she didn't want to do that to Collin. He was someone who felt things deeply, and she didn't want to use him to make herself feel better. She'd done that with Clark, and obviously that hadn't turned out well.

But from the very moment they'd met, whatever she had with

Collin was different. There was premeditated gentleness in him that was so different than her dynamic with Clark that she wanted to burrow into him and stay there. Collin made her feel secure, desired. And she *wanted* in return, so much that it physically hurt her not to be tucked closer against his body.

Reluctantly, she pulled away, and his mouth followed hers. For a moment, he looked down at her, dazed, and Alice was weirdly proud of herself. She craned her neck up and kissed him again, pushing him very gently but deliberately toward the door.

"You're right," he sighed, opening the door. "This probably wasn't a good idea."

"And yet, I'm not going to apologize," she said, kissing him one last time. "And I apologize to everyone. Ask anybody."

"One more." He was nodding and laughing as he backed out the door. He pressed his lips to hers. "Good night."

"Good night," She took a step back before she did something very foolish.

He shook his head as if fighting through a fog. "If you need anything, I'm just down the way at the house. Press four on the phone and it dials directly to the line in my room."

"Pressing four isn't going to give me what I need," she told him, smirking ever so slightly.

And in a feat of human superstrength, she closed the door in his gobsmacked face.

Chapter 6
Collin

IN HIS DREAM, COLLIN WAS running…in high heels.

This wasn't the sort of dream in which he was in a situation so out of the ordinary that it was obvious he was dreaming. He felt like a passenger in this body. He was living out someone else's memory.

Collin ran down the hall of the hotel's north service wing. He knew these walls, but they were different, covered in a sickly yellow paint he didn't recognize. The wooden floors felt alien against his feet. Looking down, he realized that he was wearing old-fashioned shin-high lady shoes. His hand, small and dainty, was tangled in the skirt of a long sky-blue dress with lacy cuffs at the wrists, holding it up so he could run. On a chain around his neck, he saw the ring Alice found in Tremont's.

What in the hell…

The thoughts of the body he was occupying crashed against his own like rogue marbles, making his head a noisy mess. Why was he running down a dark hallway in the Duchess at night inside this smaller, shorter body? And he was afraid. It wasn't a feeling he was accustomed to, and he didn't like it. He dropped his skirts and turned. He didn't know why he was running, but a woman in this sort of dress didn't run down dark hallways at night for fun.

"Victoria!" A shadow fell across the end of the hallway, tall and thin, but somehow so intimidating, even in that slim silhouette.

Collin bolted away, but toward what? The nearest exit was the back garden, down two short flights of stairs, and he was in heels he couldn't take off without special equipment. He was lucky he hadn't tripped and fallen on his face already.

No. He knew this hotel better than anybody, and that Slenderman motherfucker wasn't about to take him on his home turf.

That thought, Collin knew, was his own.

He didn't bother rattling the doorknobs of the storage rooms around him. He didn't want to hide inside a room and wait for whoever was behind him to bust through the door. He wanted to be outside. There were no people to scream for. He could *feel* the thunder of footsteps on the floor behind him as he reached the stairs, and then—

Agony seized the base of his skull and exploded into a shower of stars behind his eyes.

He'd never had long hair before. The pain of having it pulled from behind by angry hands was *blinding*. His body was thrown back onto the wooden floor, the breath stolen from his lungs as the boards seemed to punch him in the back. *Everything hurt.* He could barely think. He was powerless, helpless. He'd never been so frightened. He couldn't even *move*.

Long legs clad in dark tailored pants emerged from the darkness, standing over him. He opened his mouth to scream.

Collin awoke mid-shout, standing in the hallway of the north wing. He looked down and saw that he was wearing sweatpants and a Dartmouth T-shirt—and no shoes at all.

He whirled around, half-expecting the tall shadow figure to be lurking somewhere, but all he could see were orange walls lit by the red emergency-exit lights—which was honestly creepy enough on its own. The hallway was empty, as were the guest rooms upstairs. The last of the guests had left earlier this week during the shutdown process for the season, and construction.

In the dark, Collin stumbled over to a bench and collapsed. He propped his elbows against his knees and forced air into his lungs. He was himself again. He was OK. He supposed that he should be grateful he didn't sleep naked.

He was just one door away from the guesthouse. Desperately, he wanted to go to Alice, to tell her what had just happened to him, but she had enough on her plate. In addition to some magical powers he still didn't fully understand, she was dealing with her grandparents and·their epic assholery. He'd never seen two grown people treat someone they were supposed to love the way the Proctors had treated Alice. What was *wrong* with the two of them? Even Cynthia and Lawrence never had the nerve to openly berate him in front of other people. And with all that, Alice shouldn't have to prop up a frantic grown man at—he glanced at the clock on the wall—*argh, two a.m.* because he had a nightmare.

Collin had never been a sleepwalker—to his knowledge. Had he done this before, wandering around the hotel in his sleep? He was pretty sure that was the sort of thing guests would complain about. He padded down the hall toward the exit that Victoria had been running for in the dream. Had she known her way around the hotel like he did? Or were those his own thoughts entirely? He'd never felt fear like that before—like a freezing, frantic living thing burrowing in his chest, taking up space—but he supposed that was normal, having never been a woman walking around a public space in the dark.

He stood, shaking his head. No, that wasn't right. Victoria had been scared, but not for herself—at least, not at first. She'd been scared for someone else. And somehow, she'd felt familiar. Had he occupied the ghost of the woman who'd screamed at him and Alice in Shaddow House? He'd been wearing that ring on a chain, and it seemed like too much of a coincidence that he'd been wearing a blue dress and was called "Victoria."

Then again, the whole thing could have been a dream. Maybe sleepwalking was some new symptom of unprocessed trauma, which was being triggered by returning to his family's space after all these years. Not to mention the shocking realization that ghosts were real. It felt like his whole brain had changed somehow.

In the days following the revelation at Shaddow House, he was seeing not full-form apparitions around the hotel, but shadows seemed to be more meaningful. He could see shapes out of the corners of his eyes, there and then suddenly not. There was a particularly dark presence that he could feel near the entrance of his second-floor office—a place where he had always felt content as a kid. Shouldn't he have felt something then, if there was something to be afraid of? He thought kids were supposed to be more sensitive to this sort of thing.

He stopped, his head still slightly fuzzy from sleep. He could swear he heard footsteps at the far end of the hall. Small, hurried feet were striking hardwood floors that were no longer there.

Collin murmured, "What the…"

A shadow separated from the tangerine depths of the hallway. It was a small feminine outline in a long dress, hair piled on top of her head. She was running, looking behind her as she was being chased.

Collin froze.

Another shadow formed behind the first, a long-limbed male silhouette, shoulders set in angry lines. In his head, Collin could hear the rumble of an angry voice, but not actual words. Maybe Collin wasn't ready to hear it yet? The smaller shadow person ran toward him, becoming more and more solid the closer she got. He could hear her breathing.

"Victoria, wait!" Collin yelled.

But instead of turning toward his voice, the figure kept running, as if she didn't even register him there. He felt a cold draft as she passed him. The taller figure stormed closer, arm outstretched, and Collin's head ached in the moment that the man's ghostly hand caught her around the hair.

"Stop!" Collin yelled.

The man yanked her backward, and the two shadows faded back into the orange recesses of the stairway. Unlike the ghosts at Shaddow House, they hadn't interacted with him at all.

Collin breathed shakily. "What the hell?"

If he sat back down, he wasn't sure he would ever get up again. He had to keep moving. He shuffled toward the stairs and realized he was walking toward the "guesthouse" portion of the hotel, where Alice was staying. Was that where Victoria had been heading? Who was she? Had she worked in the hotel? Her clothes seemed to be from a time just after the hotel opened. Anything was possible.

It would be so easy for him to walk into the guesthouse and knock on Alice's door, tell her all about this.

No. He slowly and deliberately aimed his footsteps away from Alice and toward the staff exit nearest Forsythia Manor. Unfortunately, Sleepwalking Collin had not thought to put on shoes, so he walked along the stony beach path barefoot. Alice was going through enough. And he'd already blurred the employee-employer boundaries enough by moving her within the hotel's walls. And then kissing her.

He tried to muster up some guilt about kissing Alice, but he couldn't feel bad about it. Was it unprofessional, potentially unethical, and a huge legal liability? Yes. But she'd kissed him back. Enthusiastically.

The cool air blowing in from the lake helped wake him up, forced some sense into his head. He hadn't been in a relationship in... He wasn't sure he'd had a real relationship since Paige. He'd met some lovely women. He'd dated. But he hadn't allowed himself to get truly close to anyone—not because he didn't trust them, but because he didn't trust himself.

And Alice had trusted him with possibly the biggest secret in the known universe. Sure, it hadn't been entirely intentional, considering he'd stormed into Shaddow House uninvited like a big idiot. But once he knew, she hadn't panicked, and there was a kindness in that. He was confident that he hadn't been offered that kind of trust so casually...probably ever.

And while "interested" was a massive understatement for how

he felt about Alice, he didn't know if he was a grown enough man for a woman like her. Besides being breathtakingly beautiful, she was smart and cultured and sweet. She saw *ghosts*. Hell, she had magic. It made sense now, that uncanny energy sizzling along his skin every time he touched her. Literally, every little thing she did was magic.

Magic was real. Ghosts were real. And, according to the coven, there was some turf war over magical "locks" that gave witches more power in interacting with those ghosts. The house being named "Shaddow House" suddenly made much more sense. Talk about hiding in plain sight. Collin felt stupid for having been fooled for so long.

Somehow the world was a more interesting place to be in, knowing that there was more out there. Of course, the something more seemed to be waking him up in the middle of the night to wander around the hallways of a hotel, which wasn't going to be safe during renovations, but he supposed it was a fair trade.

Sleepwalking Collin had not had the consideration to lock the door behind him, which he supposed was good news, since he didn't have a key on him. The second bit of good news was that no one seemed to have broken into his house while he was out. Wait, had he forgotten to set the alarm, or had Sleepwalking Collin taken the time to deactivate the alarm system?

Sleepwalking Collin was kind of a dick.

He locked the door behind him, unsure of whether he wanted to go back to bed or make coffee and call a moratorium on sleep for the night. He paused, taking in the cozy environs of Forsythia Manor. While less overtly opulent than the hotel, it was still lushly comfortable.

He was still adjusting to the idea that he lived here. This place had a sort of fairy-tale mysticism in his memory. Every image in his mind was warm and soft. He loved it here. He was loved. He was happy.

Over the years, his dad had bought out his relatives' shares of the manor house until his little family of three were the sole owners. His mother had redone the place in a sort of nautical theme with white and navy stripes, brass accents, and pops of turquoise here and there. The furniture was durable enough to hold up under marauding kids, uncles who went comatose during baseball games, and aunts who never quite learned how to not spill chardonnay. It was a home built in optimism for a big family and their messes…but somehow, all that was left was him. A singular mess on a lot of levels.

Overhead, he heard the ding of a text notification coming through on his phone.

Collin frowned. Who would be texting him at this hour?

He padded up the stairs, cursing shoe-skipping Sleepwalking Collin, and followed the noise into the primary suite. It had been difficult moving into this room, like he was admitting with absolute finality that his family was gone. His phone lay on the cherry Federalist-style nightstand, charging. He could see on the screen that there were several text notifications piled up, all from Paige.

He sighed. Apparently, they'd reached that stage of the cycle again. He'd made a mistake, ignoring her earlier texts. She'd seen it as a challenge.

Hi

Sorry to text you so late.

You know how I am with time zones.

Planning to come visit you sometime this month.

Been too long.

Collin swallowed a heavy lump of dread. He had ghosts and a potentially inappropriate romantic interest to deal with. He couldn't deal with Paige too.

Paige wrote in staccato bursts.

I think it's time we talk about us, don't you?

I've spent too long waiting for you to make up your mind,
    Collin

when you know this is what you want.

This is what our families want.

We have too much history together to just throw away what
    we have.

There's no point in putting off the inevitable.

He flopped back on his bed, feeling all the adrenaline that had carried him after the dream ebb from his body. His nearly lifelong relationship had started off so sweetly when they were kids. She was his first girlfriend, the first real friendship he'd built at their socially chilly prep school. She'd been his first everything. She'd been there for him when he'd lost his parents. Now it was so messy and noxious, it was barely recognizable as a friendship, much less a romance. But Paige had never responded well to being told "no." And it was way too late to deal with the repercussions of raising her ire. He wasn't sure his phone had enough battery for that, even fully charged.

He set his phone aside, thinking of all the things he had to do the next day for the renovation—and how he was going to use all of them to avoid texting Paige back.

Yeah, he was definitely not emotionally mature enough to try to date Alice.

———————

The next morning, Collin sat at his desk, thinking about his nightmare, pretending to review the binder of pieces Alice had scouted from her contacts. She'd suggested dividing the various suites into different looks from the art nouveau movement, and then she started talking about different "schools"—"Nancy" and "Glasgow" and some guy named Mackintosh. Collin wasn't sure what any of it meant, but it was beautiful and exactly what he was looking for—classic, airy, but still comfortable, even if the guests might be a little afraid to sit on the chairs. It was exactly the sort of elegance people expected when they visited the Duchess.

Was it the work on the hotel that had Victoria running down the hallway from an unseen threat? Now that he knew ghosts existed, he'd done some reading. The "highly reliable" ghost-hunting websites he'd read (and then immediately cleared from his browser history) stated that sometimes changes to a house stirred up ghost activity. Changing their environment confused them.

He wondered if that was why there always seemed to be renovations happening at Shaddow House when he was a kid, to keep the ghosts subdued. Apparently, there were hundreds of them over there. How much havoc could hundreds of ghosts cause?

Collin shook his head and tried to focus on the work Alice had done for him. The moment she'd presented him with the binder—all pretty and pink-cheeked in her sensible gray suit before she'd run off to her actual job at Superior Antiques—he'd wanted to blurt out the whole story about the nightmare and his sleepwalking. But she just looked so busy and hurried that he didn't have the heart to lay something else on her shoulders.

He was really going to have to do something about his feelings for Alice.

On his desk, his phone dinged with a text notification from Paige. He'd successfully avoided dealing with the previous texts by focusing on other things. He wasn't about to lose focus now.

Nope.

Paige had texted several times that morning. Most of the texts boiled down to, Miss you. Can't believe you left for the summer and didn't say goodbye! and When are we going to catch up? He sighed, pinching the bridge of his nose. He had too much going on right now for a Paige visit. But if he ignored her, it was like leaving a toddler unsupervised with a can of spray paint. You didn't know how it was going to turn out, but it wasn't going to make you smile.

He dialed her number and after a few rings, he'd hoped that maybe he was going to get the opportunity to leave a voicemail without an awkward conversation. But on ring four, no such luck.

"Darling, how are you?" Paige cooed. "Is the cell signal terrible there? You haven't been responding to my texts."

In the background, he could hear the click-clack of her heels on hardwood floors. An art gallery? Paige never walked through galleries slowly, appreciating the art. She moved like she was on a mission: find the best art, buy it, move on to the next gallery. *Terminate.* Her parents appreciated it. She'd put together a very nice collection for their various homes.

"I'm fine. Still settling in here," he told her without addressing the surprisingly robust cell signal on the island.

"I know," she sighed, as if he'd told her he was almost done with this round of rash medication. "I was thinking of coming to visit."

"Oh, I don't think that's a good idea, Paige," he protested. "The island isn't really what you're used to."

"Don't be silly. I used to come there during the summers to visit you."

"You stayed in my house, which is, uh, under renovation, and the hotels just aren't up to your—"

"You know, if I didn't know any better, I would think you were trying to put me off," Paige said, her pout smacking him in the ear.

Thank goodness, there was a knock at his office door. For a second, he wondered if it was a real knock or a ghost knock. Wasn't that how ghosts were supposed to communicate in seances?

The knock sounded again.

"I have to go." Frowning, Collin hung up without another word to Paige and crossed his office to find Clark Graves standing there in his doorway. Collin tried not to let his distaste show. He didn't know what to make of Clark Graves and the way he'd approached Alice on the sidewalk, all possessive and weird. Alice had been frightened that day. The way she'd reached for Collin—she'd needed help in that moment. But then she'd shrugged it off. Even now, she was...skittish. There were times when Collin thought Alice was comfortable around him, but then she'd pull back. It was like she'd built an impenetrable force field around herself and no one could get through. Was it an unresolved relationship with Clark? Clark and his stupid handsome face?

And why the hell was that stupid handsome face in Collin's office? This couldn't be good.

"Clark, uh, come in," he said, making a welcoming gesture. "Can I get you some coffee or something?"

"No, I won't be here long." Clark flipped a sheaf of stapled papers upward like a fucking sleight-of-hand magician. He smirked as he pressed the thick manila paper into Collin's hand.

Collin's brows lifted. "What's this?"

The smirk on Clark's face twisted into something uglier, gleeful. "You've been served."

Shit.

Clark waited, as if he wanted to see Collin's reaction to the legal papers he'd just pressed into his hand. Honestly, this was embarrassing. Collin should have known better, getting served like that. Years in the corporate world had taught him never to accept an envelope from someone he wasn't expecting mail from. Rookie mistake.

"This isn't from your law firm," Collin noted, keeping his expression impassive as he looked the papers over. Simply put, his aunt and uncle were trying to claim that as his former legal guardians, they had spent "considerable resources" on him in the brief time he was in their custody. Their care and the family money had ultimately placed Collin in the position to be successful in life. And therefore, they had rights to the Duchess. The fact that Collin had purchased it independently, without "family money," seemed to escape them. He was more annoyed than anything else. His lawyers would turn this into legal confetti.

"I'm doing it as a favor for a friend who does work for their firm," Clark said.

"Do you always serve papers for clients personally?" Collin asked.

"Only for special cases. Anyone in your family is considered a special case," Clark announced with a little too much authority.

"Look, I don't have time to deal with you. I'll have my lawyers call you to explain why this is a pointless exercise."

"Will do." Clark's smile was joyless. "Look, practicing law isn't personal. It's not like, let's say, Alice Seastairs, and the care and *attention* she gives every customer at the antique shop."

Collin frowned at him. That was a weird thing to say. "Have you seen the door?" he asked, nodding to the exit. "There's the door."

Instead, Clark flopped into the chair across from Collin's desk, as if they were old buddies casually discussing golf. He seemed disappointed that Collin wasn't taking the bait. Well, Clark had never spent Thanksgiving with Aunt Cynthia.

"Please, make yourself comfortable," Collin drawled, taking his own chair.

"I couldn't help but notice you're spending time with our Alice," Clark said. When Collin simply stared at him, Clark continued. "She's a great girl, isn't she?"

While Collin wanted to agree that of course, Alice was a great girl, he didn't want to feed into whatever the hell was going on in Clark's head. And he didn't want to say anything that might give Clark a clue that Alice was staying at the Duchess, so he just continued to stare.

"We've been on *intimate* terms for years," Clark continued, putting an emphasis on the word "intimate" that made Collin distinctly uncomfortable. "But Alice, she's, uh, complicated. Doesn't know what she wants, gets confused sometimes. That's why I needed to talk to her the other day, to make sure there were no misunderstandings about the last time we talked. She can just be so stubborn sometimes when she gets an idea into her head. She fixates. You know how irrational women can get, overemotional."

For the first time, Collin let his frustration show. He could feel it, in the faintest twitch of his cheek muscle. Alice wasn't stubborn. She wasn't confused. She certainly wasn't overemotional. She might fixate, but it was usually about something that would help someone, like tracking down the perfect lamp for Collin, or the stained-glass bathtub. Alice wouldn't do anything to hurt Clark. She was trying to *avoid* Clark.

How many people had Clark spewed this sort of lie to on the island? How many people had heard tales of Alice being an unstable, emotional wreck? After what she'd already put up with from her grandparents? Fury rose in Collin's chest, burning away the last wisps of fear clinging from last night's episode.

"Get out of my office," Collin told him, his voice glacial. "Now."

"No reason to get touchy," Clark said, raising his hands. His smile had changed into a more self-satisfied one.

Collin rose, not even moving his hands. Clark practically slithered out of his chair, moving across to the door.

"Be careful of that one, Collin," Clark told him. "Once she sinks her little teeth into you, it's hard to shake her off."

Clark didn't even do Collin the courtesy of closing his door as he left. Collin clenched his fists.

Fucker.

Alice didn't want to cling to Clark. She was trying to shake *him* off. What was this guy's *deal*? And how was Collin supposed to approach Alice about it? Because he was concerned for her on a very personal level, but this seemed like the kind of thing he wasn't supposed to ask an employee about... Yeah, this was why you weren't supposed to kiss employees.

He sank into his chair and dropped his head to his desk. He barely resisted the urge to smack his forehead against the surface of the wood, over and over.

Right next to his ear, his phone rang, making him flinch. Knowing his luck, it was probably Paige, video-calling to demand his reasons for hanging up on her. To his surprise, it was Uncle Lawrence's number on his screen.

"Oh, for the love of—come on," Collin sighed. His aunt and uncle appeared on the screen. And even while he was massively irritated with both of them, they were the only family he had left, and it was a little painful to see their aging faces after so long. Uncle Lawrence had the Bancroft gray eyes and a thick head of dark-gray hair, swept back to show the startling white at the temples. Aunt Cynthia's strategically tightened face was surrounded by a cloud of carefully coiffed platinum curls. Both of them looked almost haggard beneath their tans. Collin wondered if it was financial strain adding the webs of lines around their mouths.

"What, did Clark send you a text notification of delivery?" Collin asked by way of greeting.

Cynthia nodded but Lawrence cut her off.

"Now, Collin, we understand you're upset," he said, using a condescending tone, as if Collin was a toddler demanding ice cream. "But with all the changes you've been making, we felt we simply had to step in and remind you of what we're owed as Bancrofts."

"I cannot wait to hear this," Collin muttered.

"Collin, the hotel is a *family* business, and we have the right to have input in this renovation process," Cynthia protested. "You know how much the Duchess means to the Bancrofts. Surely, that grants us some ownership. If not legally, then emotionally."

"There's no such thing as 'emotional' ownership of a building." Collin shook his head. "And the 'family' hasn't owned the hotel in almost a hundred years."

A light knock sounded at his doorframe. Julie poked her head into his office. When she saw that he was on the phone, she grimaced and was about to retreat, when Collin used his free hand to motion her in.

"And yet, we still feel the loss of the property," Lawrence intoned. "It's our birthright, Collin, and it would be wrong to keep it to yourself. To make all these changes to the building without our guidance, it's nonsensical."

"The most disturbing of which is firing poor Robert," Cynthia added. "Robert is an institution at that hotel. It's ridiculous that your misunderstanding has gone on this long. We assumed you'd just had a minor disagreement, and soon after, you'd realize your mistake and put him back in his rightful place."

Julie, who had taken a seat in one of Collin's chairs, full-on winced. Collin didn't roll his eyes like a teenager, but it was a near thing. How would his aunt and uncle even know who Robert was? Was Robert in contact with them, like some sort of mole? Was he hoping to leverage that somehow to get his job back? The last Collin had heard, Robert was lurking around The Wilted Rose, complaining that he was ill-used. But because he'd never bothered drinking at the Rose when he was manager of the hotel, he had difficulty finding a sympathetic audience.

"How do you even know Robert?" Collin asked. "You haven't been back on the island in years—"

"That's beside the point. Surely, you have to see how these drastic changes can only cause chaos at the hotel," Lawrence insisted just as Cynthia interjected, "Robert brings a nice sense of continuity for the employees."

Collin shot back, "Robert brought a sense of delegating his job to other people."

Julie covered her mouth to keep them from hearing her snort. It made him feel better to have Julie in the room. She felt the same way he did about Robert. It meant a lot, that someone he deemed as reasonable agreed with him. He needed the validation, down to his soul. Weird.

"If this legal paperwork was a misguided attempt to help Robert get his job back, in some weird bribery quid pro quo, it is not going to work," Collin told them. "I bought this hotel, free and clear."

"With money you inherited from your family," Lawrence insisted. "So the hotel should be under *family* control again."

"No," Collin told them.

"Collin, we *raised you*," Cynthia cried. "We gave you the best years of our lives."

"Year," Collin replied. "You gave me a *year*. And while I appreciate that—"

"Well, you have a ludicrous way of showing it." Lawrence snorted.

"We *need* this," Cynthia told him. "You don't know what it's like, having to *economize*."

"Cynthia," Lawrence barked. "That's enough."

Collin drew a breath through his nose. "Now, as a former employee, Robert's not welcome on the grounds. Please understand, you're only welcome on the grounds as paying guests."

Julie's eyes went wide, but she only mouthed the word, "Wow."

Cynthia gasped and clutched at the chunky peridot beads at her neck. "You wouldn't do that to family."

"Watch me," Collin shot back. Julie rose and crossed to what used to be a wet bar in his grandfather's day, hidden behind a sliding wooden panel. In the interest of good decisions, Collin had refitted the space as a coffee bar, with a very expensive digital espresso machine and all the flavored syrups and milk options a caffeine enthusiast could want.

Lawrence looked disturbed for a moment. "You would do that? Embarrass the family that way, instead of giving us our due?"

"I think I've made it clear I would," Collin retorted as Julie poured them both cups of coffee. "Until this legal situation is straightened out, I think we should let the lawyers handle any communication between us. Good luck to you."

Collin ended the call with a decisive beep.

"Remind me never to piss you off in a legal fashion," Julie muttered, handing him his coffee. "Or an illegal fashion, for that matter."

They shared an easy laugh, and that cold tension in Collin's chest eased. Julie had proven over and over that he'd made the right choice in hiring her. She'd taken off running with the computer equipment and programs he'd purchased for the hotel, completing her training in a week and turning around to train the front desk staff herself. She had great suggestions and better instincts, and she was not shy about telling him when he was making a bad call. In his summers on the island, he'd had plenty of acquaintances, but very few real friendships. He hoped he was on the way to having that with Julie.

Of course, it would be a friendship in which he could never, ever talk to her about ghosts or haunted objects or sleepwalking in the hotel hallways, but he would take what he could get.

"Are they really going to try to get 'partial custody' of a hotel you bought with your own money?" she asked as he doctored his coffee with almond milk.

"I don't think my aunt and uncle have the resources for that. I don't think they really want the hotel," he said. "They just want to play the victim over it, complain to whoever will listen about ungrateful I am, and maybe squeeze a little money out of me to hold off whomever they owe."

Julie wrinkled her nose. "Well, I don't want to rub salt in the family wound, but…yeah, that tracks."

"So did you come up here to make sure I hadn't pitched Clark's legal papers out the window?"

"No, I just wanted some decent coffee," she scoffed, sipping from her cup.

"The employee lounge doesn't have decent coffee?" he asked, frowning.

"Not like this," she said, shaking her head.

"Please purchase all the supplies you'll need for the staff to have 'decent coffee' in every staff break room. Landscaping crew to café waitstaff to housekeeping," he replied, toasting her with his cup. "I hereby appoint you 'hotel coffee czar.'"

"Do you mean 'decent coffee' or the kind of coffee you're making for yourself in here?" she asked, brows lifted.

Collin silently pointed at his coffeemaker. Julie broke out the little notebook she kept for tasks like this and started scribbling. "Have I mentioned how much I like working for you?"

"Coffee fuels our business," he said. "Also, I'm not sure I would survive the aforementioned staff mutiny. Some of those ladies who work in the gift shop look like they would throw elbows."

"They would," she assured him. "And they have extremely bony elbows. Item two on the 'checking on you' agenda—do you really have Alice staying in the guesthouse?"

Collin nodded, while sipping his coffee. "Is that a problem?"

"Absolutely not," she assured him. "Alice is a dream guest. Makes her own bed, for goodness's sake. Besides, we're already keeping housekeeping and kitchen staff on to take care of the construction crews staying here, which is going a long way to building you some goodwill with the locals, providing work during the slow season. And this is good for Alice. She needs to be away from her grandparents. Far, far away."

"I met them. Do they always talk to her like she's a disappointing employee?" Collin asked.

Julie sighed. "I've never seen it myself, but I've heard stories. I'm glad she has you, someone who will give her other options."

"Speaking of other options." Collin cleared his throat. "Do you know anything about her relationship with Clark?"

"Graves?" Julie's brows lifted. "I wasn't aware that they had one beyond nodding at each other at the grocery. And frankly, with the Nana Grapevine, it would be almost impossible for them to have one without me hearing about it."

"So why would he chase her down the sidewalk and scare her?" Collin mused.

"That sounds like a question for Alice," Julie told him. "To be fair, Alice is someone who frequently seems frightened. Or, at least, she was until Riley came around."

Collin made a mental note to spend more time around Riley. Anyone who made Alice's life better was worth knowing.

"Well, unlike your family, I come bearing helpful papers," she said, flipping open her notebook to a page heavily occupied by scribbles. "What would you think of making more changes? Centered on the hotel's new, more historically accurate look? Curated tours, now that the halls have been de-oranged. Special themed afternoons, where we have reenactors demonstrating proper high tea. That sort of thing."

"I think that would be a great idea," he replied. "How would we organize all that?"

"I don't know," Julie said. "I was always more of a math person than a history person."

Collin grinned. "I think I might know the person for the job."

Chapter 7
Alice

SITTING IN THE STARFALL POINT Historical Society's reading room, Alice yawned over a book of birth records. It had been a rough day already and it wasn't even noon.

It was Sunday and technically her day off. Usually, she would spend the day puttering around the shop, organizing, but since she'd spent the last few weeks establishing new expectations with her grandparents, she needed somewhere to go. The Proctors had put on a big show of demanding an apology, even though she knew—thanks to Arthur—that they were secretly panicked over her departure. And Alice decided to use that to her advantage. Ruthlessly.

Oh, she'd put on a show of a sincere, heartfelt mea culpa for her behavior, complete with a perfectly nice Lewis Foreman Day mantel clock Collin insisted she take from his house. He told her to claim it was the thing she'd supposedly smuggled out of the shop, which was plausible, given that her grandparents didn't fully understand the shop's computerized inventory system. He just gave her a three-hundred-dollar clock like it was couch change.

She didn't care what Riley said. Rich people *were* different.

Alice told her grandparents that she'd found the clock in the cabinet and taken it to Barber's Watch Repair Shop on the mainland. She'd claimed she'd been reluctant to tell them because they'd previously vowed never to speak to Mr. Barber. They swore he charged them more than other customers, and Alice couldn't find a way to tell them that their tabs included "pain in the ass" surcharge without a resulting explosion.

After putting up a token protest, the Proctors graciously "allowed" Alice to return to work. She did not put in her usual effort to sell or even clean. She stuck to her purpose—checking in on Arthur and searching for Victoria's lost ring. Unfortunately, Arthur hadn't spotted the ring in his meanderings about the shop, which would have solved a lot of problems.

Manipulating her grandparents was possibly the most Proctor-ish thing she'd ever done, and the similarities made her uncomfortable. But subterfuge was allowing her to find better work-life balance. She was leaving precisely at closing time every day. And she'd drawn the line when they none too gently suggested that she might come to Proctor House to "help" them straighten it up, since it hadn't been prepared for their arrival. Spending time in her childhood home always put Alice in a touchy mood—which was ironic because the house was filled with furniture labeled with "don't touch" signs, plus taxidermized animals and porcelain plates with creepily ornate moth-themed patterns.

Her grandparents were still unhappy that she'd moved out of her apartment, and even less so that she refused to tell them where she was staying. They grumbled about "putting on airs" and getting ideas from spending too much time at Shaddow House. But they were also so desperate to eventually access the house's famed collection of antiques through her relationship with Riley that, for once, they held their tongues.

Alice knew it wasn't a good idea to put herself back under her grandparents' authority, even under false pretenses, but she *needed* to find Victoria's ring. The little sapphire had been stuck in Alice's mind since the minute she'd found it. She wasn't accustomed to losing valuable antiques, so it was a bit of a blow to her professional pride.

At the same time, she'd never had such circular thought patterns relating to one item like she had with this ring. If her mind wasn't actively engaged in something else, it felt like it was constantly wandering back to the ring—how it had felt on her hand, the promise of it, even though it wasn't the most elaborate or expensive of settings. There was an uncomfortable Gollum feeling to it, but Alice refused to give *that* too much thought. It was natural, she supposed, considering that Victoria might be a member of her family. She still didn't know how to process that one. And honestly, Victoria had been no help. Despite her initial interest, the very vocal ghost had not made another appearance during Alice's subsequent visits to Shaddow House. But honestly, Alice was used to this sort of mercurial communication style from family members, so it didn't throw her off.

Edison hadn't been able to find any information about a Victoria Proctor in the public library or in the Shaddow House collection. So Alice was here at the Society, housed in Beach Glass Cottage, sitting at an uncomfortable donated desk, poring over the names and birthdates for every citizen born on the island. The white clapboard two-story house just off Main Square was unremarkable aside from blue-and-green windows made entirely from bottle glass supposedly salvaged from beaches along Lake Huron. Donated to the town in the 1970s, it was a sort of genealogical archive and museum—and it was normally closed on Sundays. But Alice happened to know that volunteers spent Sunday afternoons re-shelving and updating the materials, so she managed to sneak in under the good graces of Norma Oviette, a museum volunteer and founding member of the Nana Grapevine.

The problem was that, like Edison, Alice couldn't find a single mention of a Victoria Proctor in the birth records from the period about twenty years before Alice guessed she might have been born, based on her dress. She'd found plenty of Proctors, far more than she'd expected given the current size of their family, but no Victoria.

Maybe she hadn't been born on the island? Alice wasn't about to call her grandparents and ask them about it.

"You're wearing an awfully big frown for someone who's supposed to be doing genealogical research for fun," a husky voice said from the foyer. Norma was an absolutely lovely older lady who landed on the wiser side as opposed to displaying the judgmental tendencies Alice had experienced with the other Grapevine members. But Norma had also worked as Clark's legal secretary for years, and Alice didn't know where her loyalties lay. Would Norma mention to Clark that she'd seen Alice here? Was that a bad thing? It felt like giving Clark any information about her habits was a bad thing.

But honestly, what was Clark going to do with demographic details about one of Alice's dead relatives? He wouldn't even know what to do with it. And she wasn't even sure there was anything he *could* do with it.

"I'm just having a little trouble tracking down the person I was looking into," Alice said.

"And that would be?" Norma asked.

"Victoria Proctor?" Alice said, still unsure she was doing the right thing.

Norma frowned at that, her rich sepia-brown skin crinkling into unfamiliar lines. "Not a name I've heard before. Any idea of birth date and death date?"

"Late 1800s?"

Norma chuckled. "So, it's one of those vague and unhelpful searches with no parameters, hmm?"

"I really thought my grandparents would have kept more of a record," Alice replied, careful not to let her annoyance show. For all their posturing about preserving history through antiquities, they didn't have a journal or even a family Bible around the house to track their family's story.

"Can you tell me anything else?" Norma asked.

"She liked to wear a ruby brooch that looked like a flaming sun?" Alice said, shrugging. "I figure it had to be important, or at least genuine, because it didn't go with her outfit at all. *I* would only do that with an important piece of jewelry."

"You've seen a picture of her?" Norma asked.

"Mm-hm." She nodded. "Er, my grandparents wouldn't let me take it out of the house."

Norma bit her lip, mulling it over. "Are you sure it was a Proctor ancestor?"

Alice blinked at her. She wasn't sure she *was* related to Victoria. She'd just assumed, based on Victoria's response and the ring having been found in one of her family member's dressers. "Now that you mention it...no."

Norma grin became downright brilliant. "Then there's a collection of letters I think you'll find very helpful."

Norma clipped across the wooden floors in her sensible heels, took a leather-bound book from one of the shelves, and returned. "A few years back, that nutty Bancroft woman with the blond helmet hair donated this to the Society with a bunch of other documents."

Norma sat next to Alice and opened the book to reveal stationery protected behind peeling acetate covers. The ink was so old, it was bleeding purple onto the ancient pages. "She took entire boxes from the attic at Forsythia Manor. Told us they were 'just taking up space,' and left it out on our front porch. In the *rain*."

Alice's mouth dropped open. "She did what?"

"Yes, I know," Norma said, shaking her head. As she moved, Alice noticed a bronze lapel pin near the collar of Norma's coral tweed jacket. It was a small shield with a capital "J" etched inside. Alice had never seen anything like it. "It was bad enough that we couldn't keep that awful Aura creature from doing the inside of the hotel in orange and chrome, but this was actual abuse of historical materials."

"I am genuinely horrified," Alice whispered. Journals and letters had always been an invaluable resource for their coven. From the diaries left behind by previous Stewards of Shaddow House to the retellings of Caroline's deadly ancestor and her reign of social terrorism on the island, firsthand accounts were always more informative than other, more "official" sources.

So Cynthia Bancroft had donated Collin's family history to the Society? Did Collin know?

"I believe Collin's parents were off-island with him at the time, doing some sort of school interview," Norma said. "And this was a motivator for buying Lawrence and Cynthia out of the beach house, rather forcefully."

"They had it coming," Alice grumbled.

"We were careful to mark them inconspicuously, just in case the family ever asked for them back," Norma assured her. "These are letters from Collin Bancroft's great-great-great-aunt, I believe. Gladiola Bancroft describes a very eventful summer on Starfall Point to her sister-in-law, who lived in New York. In 1898, there was an engagement between a young man named Stanford Newlin and a Victoria *Bancroft*. Stanford was the son of a wealthy New York family, nouveau riche, just one generation away from working for a *living* instead of *entertainment*, but respectable. He'd taken an interest in the hotel project and spent time with the family on Starfall Point. And, next thing you know, Stanford has designed the hotel in its entirety and managed to affiance himself to Victoria."

"That's a good word, *affiance*," Alice mused.

"Yes, that's why I used it. Now, pay attention," Norma told her, carefully turning the pages until they reached a photo of a beautiful young woman in early-1900s garb. She had the piercing eyes typical of the Bancroft family, delicate features, and full lips twisted into a playful smile. Her dark hair was piled into a Gibson-girl style on top of her head. Alice had been right. Victoria had been beautiful before death and rage had taken hold of her soul.

"So...not my ancestor. Collin's," Alice said, absorbing the information. She was oddly hurt that Victoria hadn't been yelling at her, seeking connection with *her*. Then again, she'd only appeared when

Collin entered the house. She'd wanted *Collin*. So... Who was the "he" that Victoria had been screaming about? Was it Stanford, the fiancé?

"The inscription read 'V & S,'" Alice murmured.

Norma paused to gingerly open a very old journal bound in lilac linen. "This is a diary kept by Victoria's younger sister, Lillibet, during the construction of the hotel. Lillibet made it clear that *she* and her brothers did not like Stanford, whom she also occasionally refers to as *S*. She says she doesn't like his eyes, but it sounds to me like it was a case of a baby sister who was used to having Victoria's attention not liking the change in the family dynamic. But there are several pages dedicated to speculating about Victoria's feelings for 'S.' *Victoria lights up when she's speaking to S. Victoria spends hours discussing music and literature with S.* So at least, Victoria had warm feelings for 'S.' Lillibet wasn't a terribly organized writer, but her penmanship is lovely for one so young."

A photo slipped out of Lillibet's journal, another sitting portrait of Victoria in another high-necked dress, formal. She was so young, hopeful, sweet. Just under Victoria's lacy neckline, a sun-shaped pin hung so heavy that it made the silky fabric of her dress bunch.

"The year before her engagement, on her sixteenth birthday, Victoria had been given her first important piece of jewelry, a pigeon's blood ruby brooch called the Ceylon Sun Fire. At the time, it was worth several hundred dollars. Now? Much more, obviously. And she was known for wearing it most days."

"I'm going to assume from your tone of voice that Victoria's story didn't have a fairy-tale ending," Alice said, as if she didn't know.

· "Victoria died in 1900," Norma told her. "Her body was found on the far end of the island, on a quickly emptying lot where wood was being cleared for the hotel. Her neck had been broken."

Norma hopped up with considerable spryness for a woman in her seventies and grabbed more books.

"She's a *murder* victim? That's awful." Alice gaped at her. Another woman found dead on Starfall Point. Another tragedy. Why were there so many stories like this on such a small island? And why hadn't she heard more about this? There were so many ghost stories attached to the Duchess, but she didn't remember one about a murdered girl, which in itself was surprising.

Alice gasped. "Wait, is the brooch important? Was it lost when she died? Did the killer rob her for the brooch?"

Was Alice about to be sent on a treasure hunt for a ghost's lost ruby? Yes, she had more important things to worry about, but she'd always wanted to Indiana Jones her way across the island. It might be just the distraction she needed.

"No, it was found near her body," Norma said, rolling her eyes at Alice's antics. "I don't think robbery was a motive. I believe the family sold the Sun Fire and started a literacy charity in Victoria's name, back in New York. Victoria was passionate about equal access to education. The murder was never officially solved."

"Oh," Alice huffed, slumping down in her chair. What was wrong with her? She was acting like this was a particularly juicy *Dateline* episode. This was Collin's relative she was talking about here—a relative she'd *met*, ever so briefly.

"The day before Victoria's body was found, a local man named Samuel Proctor disappeared. I don't know if you know this, but your family made caskets and cabinets at the time, in their workshop. Samuel delivered a load of wine racks to the hotel and disappeared."

"Caskets?" Alice burst out laughing. She covered her mouth with her hands. "My family made *caskets*?"

Norma spared her a wink. "Well, cabinets, too, but mostly caskets. It was too expensive to ship anything across the lake, so they had plenty of business here on the island. That, and the lumber mill."

Her grandparents constantly talked about the fact that Superior Antiques had been open for more than a century, even though the family only bought it in the 1960s. They'd always said with a lofty air that they had "roots in the furniture business." But caskets and lumberjacks?

And… Alice realized she was laughing in the middle of a murder story. That couldn't be good in terms of her character development. She nodded slowly. "So, people thought that Samuel killed her?"

Alice chewed her lip. That might explain the feud between their two families. An unsolved murder, in which the Bancrofts suspected the Proctors of hurting one of their own. If she'd lived back then, she probably wouldn't have wanted to spend much time around the Bancrofts if they thought a relative of hers was a murderer. And over time, that sort of thing festered and here they were, two families who resented each other for reasons even they didn't fully understand.

Norma showed her a sheaf of newspaper clippings, including tintype photos of a young man in a high collar, dark hair parted ruthlessly in the middle. "Well, the speculation was that he was in love with her, obsessed, and he killed her when he realized that she would never leave her successful fiancé. He'd been spending too much time around the hotel, chatting with Victoria in a way that was considered highly inappropriate, given the time frame. Her family had complained to his parents several times and threatened to cancel the cabinetry contract if he didn't leave her alone. He wasn't present at the workshop when the police arrived, demanding to know his whereabouts on the day of Victoria's murder. He was never seen again.

"The family continued the construction, but I don't think Forsythe's heart was in running it anymore," Norma told her. "He sold it to the Frickes, who sold it to the Drewes, who sold it to the next owner and the next. But the Bancrofts' reasons for loving the island were the same. And they felt closer to their lost daughter here. Plus, it gave them the opportunity to prod local law enforcement about catching the killer. Or, at least, catching up to Samuel. If anything, they spent *more* time here after Victoria's death,"

Alice sat back in her chair. How was she going to tell Collin about any of this? How could she tell him that a member of her family was probably responsible for hurting a member of his? That his however-many-times-great-aunt had probably been begging him to help her find her fiancé?

"What happened to the fiancé?" Alice asked.

Norma shook her head sadly. "Poor Stanford. The stress of Victoria's death, combined with what was considered advanced age at the time—"

"Wasn't he in his thirties?" Alice asked.

Norma gave her a pointed look. "At the time."

Alice raised her hands in defeat.

"In the weeks after Victoria's death, he took to strolling around the island at night, told people the quiet let him concentrate on the good times spent with her," Norma said. "He was found on the Main Square one morning, dead as a doornail. It was probably a heart attack or some very common ailment that could have been treated today."

"How sad," Alice mused, looking at the photo of Samuel. He just didn't look like the murdering type. The kind of guy you would have to give the "let's just be friends" speech to more than once, maybe, but not a murderer.

"So." Norma reached out and patted her hand. "You seem to be spending a lot of time with Collin."

Alice nodded. "I'm helping him with some projects at the hotel."

"This young man, is he good to you?" Norma asked.

Alice thought about it and answered, "Yes."

"Good, you deserve that," Norma said, patting her hand again. "Clark Graves is a decent employer, but I don't think I would want him dating any daughter of mine. There's a warmth that's missing in him. When I realized that you two seemed to have ended your... arrangement, I was relieved for you. You should have someone who's going to give you the affection you deserve."

"Oh, Clark and I never—" Alice began.

Norma arched a graying eyebrow at her. "Sweetheart, I run his office. I know things."

"Thank you, Norma." Alice pressed her lips together.

Norma stood.

"Could you do me a favor?" Alice asked. "Don't mention to Clark that I was here? Or anything that we talked about?"

Norma waved a dismissive hand. "I don't see why he would ask, but I won't say anything. Historical Society business is different than law-firm business."

"Thank you," Alice said.

"Now, put everything back where I found it," Norma told her, walking back to the welcome desk.

Alice's lips twitched. "Yes, ma'am."

After Alice put her research materials back *exactly* where they belonged, she packed up her bag, walked toward the door, and called, "Thank you for all your help!" before opening the door and nearly running into Margaret Flanders.

"Oh!" Alice cried. "I'm so sorry, Margaret!"

"That's all right, dear, no harm done," Margaret told her. Small and spry with thick gray hair piled on top of her head, Margaret hopped back before any damage could be done to either of them. But... Margaret seemed fine. She looked a little tired around her periwinkle-blue eyes, but not ill. Oh, no, Alice hoped it wasn't some unseen ailment requiring surgery or something.

Margaret was a fixture on Starfall Point. She'd been unfailingly sweet to Alice since she was a child, always inviting her to the Saturday Storytime with Mother Goose she hosted as one of the chief volunteers at the public library. Alice had always found Margaret's grandmotherly energy a little cloying, but she was aware that she had her issues with grandparent figures.

Alice cleared her throat. "I was just doing a little research."

"Strange way for a young person to spend their weekend," Margaret said. "A pretty girl like you should have someone to spend Sunday mornings with, Alice."

Alice chuckled. "Oh, I don't know. I find Norma's company highly entertaining."

"I'm a laugh riot," Norma commented dryly from her desk without looking up. "Why don't you close that door and start your volunteer shift, Margaret? The utility bill doesn't pay itself."

Margaret rolled her eyes and grinned conspiratorially at Alice, closing the door behind her and enclosing Alice in the Historical Society building. She lowered her voice so Norma couldn't hear. "Alice, dear, are you trying to find a way to avoid going home?"

Alice blinked at her. "Why do you ask?"

Margaret looked uncomfortable for a moment. "Well, I know that Franklin and Marilyn aren't exactly…easy to live with. I don't like to speak ill of people, but I could see why you wouldn't want to spend your free time at the apartment with them being home for the season."

For a second, the warmth of a blanket seemed to slide around Alice's shoulders. Someone else saw it—or, at least, someone who was her grandparents' peer saw that they were unreasonable and difficult to live with. Her eyes didn't exactly well up with gratitude, but it helped. "I'm not staying at the apartment anymore, Margaret. Thanks, but don't worry about me."

Margaret frowned. "Well, where are you staying, then?"

Alice's lips clamped together. She was not about to tell one of the most active members of the Nana Grapevine that she was staying in Collin's guesthouse. "I've gotta go. Thank you, Norma!"

"Alice, wait!" Margaret called as Alice scurried out the front door.

"I will not be featured news on the Nana Grapevine. No,

ma'am," Alice muttered, hurrying down the street toward the hotel. Then, when she realized that Margaret could be watching her through the window, she turned toward Shaddow House.

The next day, Alice was walking through the rain, grateful for the lack of traffic on Starfall Point streets because she was texting and walking as she returned from an "errand" at Clark's law office. As a thank-you for Norma's help, Alice had dropped off a framed postcard from the early 1900s, showing one of the first Perkins ferries to operate on the island. And if Alice happened to use the opportunity to drop some disinformation for Clark, confusing him into wasting his time and staying away from the coven? Well, that was simply icing on the revenge cake.

Meanwhile, she needed this time to catch up on non-work-related phone use. She had a huge backlog of emails from contacts in her search for art nouveau treasures. Her grandparents had instituted a "no cell phones on the sales floor" policy since her return, but honestly, it was better this way. To the cameras, it might have looked like she was diligently wiping down the baseboards of the showroom, but she was actually searching for Victoria's ring. It had to have rolled somewhere on the wooden floor, but physics was really playing her for a fool here. She'd searched every square inch of the room's perimeter, and nothing. Then again, for all she knew, her grandparents had found the ring on the floor and hid it in the shop somewhere. She thought returning Collin's relative's ring to him was the least she could do before she told him that it was possible that *her* relative murdered that ring's owner.

Life on Starfall Point was complicated.

Now, as she picked her way along the cold, wet sidewalks of Main Square under her umbrella printed to look like a Van Gogh painting, she smiled down at her phone screen. Collin had been texting her all day, and her lack of responses were making for some interesting escalations from him.

Tile guy tried to convince me to use a terra-cotta color in the bathroom of the Apple Blossom Suite, Collin wrote. But I told him no colors remotely close to the orange family. I told him I have orange trauma.

Later, he added, Tile guy is no longer speaking to me. Julie says she'll handle all tile-related communications from here on out.

Then, I'm going to have to give Julie another raise, aren't I?

Alice laughed. Progress on the suites was running a little faster than the sweeping changes to the "mass-market rooms." The antiques Alice had procured for the suites were waiting in a storage room in the hotel basement. Now Collin just had to fight with the decorator and the work crews to make sure the rooms matched what they found.

Alice typed back, And probably another job title.

Front Desk Manager, Coffee Czar, Tile Comptroller, Person Who Keeps Collin from Losing Valuable Construction Employees, Collin wrote back almost immediately. Also, hey! You finally answered!

That's going to mean at least two more raises, she told him. And yes, some of us are employed by other people. Cranky, unreasonable old people who limit cell phone use during work hours.

Want anything when you get home? he asked. I can ask the kitchen staff to send up a Collin for you. Extra sprinkles.

Alice snorted. The last thing she wanted to eat was a Collin sandwich with sprinkles, and he knew it. Now, covering Collin *the person* with sprinkles just to see what happened? That was a tempting option.

They hadn't kissed since that night in her room. He was just as warm and kind and eager to spend time together, but he was keeping a respectful distance. And it was the sweetest torture. They spent most nights together in the living room at the guesthouse, and he'd had her over for dinner at Forsythia Manor a few times. They talked about their opposing experiences growing up on the island, and books, movies, art. And she wanted to climb the man like a tree. He was just so…climb-able, but she didn't want to do anything to upset the delicate balance they were striking.

They were *friends*. He never made her feel obligated, even as he provided her wages and a roof over her head. But the fact that he was calling the space they shared "home"? (Even if he was technically next door in the manor house.)

Yeah, it was putting her commitment to avoid climbing that tree in danger.

She'd never shared a home with anyone, and felt like it was truly that. And yes, her room was technically in a hotel, but that warm, secure feeling she had when she walked through the door and found Collin waiting for her? That was dangerous. She was going to lose it soon, no matter what happened. She couldn't get too accustomed to it.

But still…the man covered in sprinkles. It was a tempting image.

She wasn't prepared for the voice that intruded in her thoughts.

"I seem to remember a time when I put that smile on your face."

Alice's head snapped up and she nearly let her umbrella fly out of her hand. Clark was standing in front of her, glaring down at her through the rain.

"Clark, I don't want to talk to you," she said, attempting to step around him. He grabbed her arm and dragged her into the alley between two T-shirt shops.

"Well, that's too bad because I want to talk to you," he growled, slinging her against a clapboard wall. "Now, Alice, *sweetie*, I've tried to be patient with you. I let the break-in at my office slide, because I figured it helped cement your place with those other two bitches, convinced them you're on their side. And honestly, I was getting tired of the pretense anyway. But this ignoring-me thing? Using your little coven to keep me at a distance? I'm not gonna tolerate it anymore. I want information, Alice. I need to know what Riley's up to. I need to know how many locks she's found and where she found them. And I want to know why you ran over to Shaddow House the other day in such a hurry. You were *seen*, and she—"

He seemed to stop himself. "Whatever you took over there, I want you to deliver it to my office by the end of the week."

"What?" Alice laughed. "I can't do that. I'm not going to steal from Riley."

He grabbed her arm and shook her like a rag doll. "You're going to do whatever I tell you to do, Alice, or I'm going to tell your little friends what you've been up to, sleeping with me on the sly, feeding me information, setting up times when Kyle and Cole could get close—"

"I *never* did that," Alice seethed, feeling a hot, helpless rage building in her chest. A strange magical awareness was making her skin prickle. She could feel wisps of ghostly energy clinging to Clark.

Was he carrying a haunted item? Maybe he'd spent so much time around attachment objects, helping the Wellings, that the magic stuck to him like static cling?

"Maybe not the last two, but you definitely did the first," he said, smirking. "And in my profession, I've learned that all it takes is a little bit of truth to sell a story."

"No. They won't believe that." She shook him off. Even if she wasn't sure the coven would think the best of her, she had to say it. She couldn't admit defeat so quickly. Pain and power sizzled from her chest to her arms. The tips of her fingers burned. "Those girls are my best friends. They wouldn't believe I would hurt them. They—"

"They know you've been keeping something from them. I overheard the teenage menace and Caroline talking about it at the bar. Whining about how you haven't been around. You've been distant. They think it's your grandparents stressing you out, but we both know that's not it, don't we?" Clark asked.

"I can make them understand," she protested, pushing him away from her. Her palms itched to do *something*. She could feel energy building in the center of her like a lifeline. "I never knowingly did anything to hurt them."

"I could tell them that you're the one who helped Kyle find a way into the house. I could tell them that you and I were the ones who helped Cole kidnap Caroline. They'll believe me. They don't know what has been going on." He was crowding her, pressing her back against the wall, taking up all the air. "You forget that I can be very convincing. Now, you're going to—"

"Get away from me," she growled. She put both hands on Clark's chest and *shoved*, much like the gesture she'd used to ward off Victoria. She felt magic surge inside her, and Clark flew back against the wall, legs flopping and aimless. The boards behind him actually buckled. His head smacked against the wood with a *thud*, and he dropped to the ground like a stringless marionette.

Panting, she looked around the square. Between the cold and the rain, the street was empty. Across the street, the windows at the Starfall Point Theater were dark. She approached Clark's crumpled form cautiously. He squinted up at her, dazed.

This was the most natural her magic had felt in weeks. Even though it had nothing to do with ghosts or haunted objects, this felt *right*. This asshole had tried to hurt her, threaten her. And she was done.

"Stay away from me," she hissed.

She resisted the urge to kick him while he was down, but only barely.

Pulling her rain jacket over her hair, she snagged her umbrella from the ground and bolted from the alley. Shaddow House. She should probably run to Shaddow House. But that wasn't home.

Alice wanted Collin. She wanted her room. She wanted to feel safe. Was she ever going to feel safe on this island again? She should leave. There was no "maybe" anymore. The coven would be better off without her. She could finish up her consultancy for Collin, use what he was paying her to start a new life somewhere else. Finding Victoria's ring would be her last work for the coven.

By the time she reached the guesthouse entrance, tears were streaming down her cheeks, getting lost in the rain. She didn't want to lose the family she'd found. She didn't want to lose this place. But she couldn't stay here any longer.

Her flats slid wildly on the slate tiles as she entered the guest-house. Collin was standing in the kitchen, setting a room-service tray on the counter.

"Alice?" He rushed toward the noise she was making as she struggled out of her wet jacket. "What's wrong?"

She opened her mouth to lie, some smooth, calm story just like all of the other lies she'd told in the last year. It would come easily to her. She would make an excuse and go up to her room, get out of these wet clothes, and for once, be grateful that her sisters couldn't seem to feel her magical distress. But the lie on the tip of her tongue turned into a sob and suddenly, she was hunched in on herself, weeping.

"Oh, sweetheart, what—" Collin was across the room in a flash, his arms wrapped around her. She could feel his chin on top of her head, even as he peeled her out of her wet jacket. His huge hands cradled the back of her head, holding her close.

She didn't want to stand there, crying into his chest, twisting her fingers into his dress shirt just so she could absorb some of the warmth from his body into hers before the shivers shook her bones apart. But there she was, being cradled against him, and she felt her body melt.

"It's going to be OK," he murmured. "Whatever it is, we can fix it."

"You don't know that," she whispered into his shirt. His fingers slipped under her chin to nudge it upward and make her look at him.

"I will help you fix it," he swore.

And in that moment, she believed him with everything in her.

Alice arched up, claiming his mouth. The same itch in her palms that had her throwing Clark across the alley had her tugging Collin closer. She could feel a sort of bubble forming around them, closing them in. Nothing existed outside it, only the pleasure of his touch that hummed through her like a resounding bell. She wanted him and only him, and everything else could just fade away. No noise, no ghosts, no other people.

His lips, wet and parted, followed hers as she moved away to stare at him. She felt like her legs were dropping out from under her. His hands cupped her elbows as if he could sense her knees buckling. Through the wet, cold barrier of her shirt, her nipples chafed against his chest, which didn't help with the knee situation. His eyes were hazy gray, clouded with lust. He wanted her. She grinned. She was not going to stop at a kiss. She wanted him, all of him.

He gave a shaky sort of nod and reached for the buttons of his shirt. She giggled, slapping his hands away so she could tug at his shirtfront. He shrugged and went for the button of her slacks, tugging helplessly at the stubborn wet fabric. She threw her head back and laughed, which only made her dizzy.

Wasn't she just bawling a minute ago?

The strange bubble of "just them" seemed to have burst, but she was too giddy to think much about it. She kicked off her traitorous shoes and they fumbled toward the stairs, a sort of loopy dance of shed clothes and hushed laughter. Outside, the rain beat frantically against the glass, throwing an occasional flash of lightning against the wall. Her wet hair clung to his hands as he pushed it away from her face. His whole body—all rangy, long limbs and broad shoulders—was oriented around her, closing her in, but instead of trapped, she felt protected.

She pushed his shirt from his shoulders as she backed up the stairs, Alice finally at eye level with him from two steps up. She shivered as he dropped her soaked clothes to the floor, and she finally lost the battle with her knees.

Alice slipped to her butt with an "oof." He followed, crouching over her as she laughed, kissing a long trail from her throat to her hip bones. He spent considerable time pressing kisses across the skin of her belly. She threaded her fingers through his thick dark hair and pulled gently, enjoying the way he looked her right in the eyes as he trailed his tongue over the waistband of her pink cotton panties. He tugged them down her legs and threw them over his shoulder, settling between her thighs to kiss and nip until she was moaning with delight.

She didn't even care that the stairs were digging into her back. They gave her better leverage to work under his dramatically taller body. But apparently, Collin minded, because he scooped her up from the floor, carried her upstairs, and spread her across the bed. When he climbed over her, she didn't feel caged in; she felt closer to him, and that in itself was a thrilling sensation.

Kissing him, she hooked her legs around Collin's hips, enjoying her taste on his lips as he fumbled with a square foil packet he'd snagged from his wallet. After protecting them both, his hard length notched against her in the best way. He wasn't even inside her and he was nudging against just the right spots. She scratched his back, making his hips buck.

He licked the hollow of her throat, spread her knees, and drove home. She shrieked with relief and clapped her hand over her mouth. She'd always had to be so quiet with Clark. Her bedroom at the shop butted right against another apartment over the row of Main Street businesses. And her neighbor was a busybody.

"They soundproofed in the nineties," he muttered against her lips. "Be as loud as you want."

She threw her head back and cried, "Yes!"

———————

Alice awoke to clanging and cursing on the stairs. She inhaled sharply, sitting up. The other side of her bed was empty, but Collin had been there just a few minutes ago. Wait, how long had she been out?

Collin nudged the bedroom door open. He'd gone downstairs to fetch their dinner trays, and he was obviously not used to carrying heavy objects in the dark.

"It might be a little cold," he said.

"Doesn't matter. I'm starving," she told him, tucking the sheet over her bare chest. With a dramatic flourish, Collin set the tray across her lap. He whisked the silver dome off her tray and handed her a little ramekin filled with rainbow sprinkles.

"You didn't." She burst out laughing.

"No, it's just a club, extra bacon, and chips," he said. "I can ask the kitchen for something hot, if you need something more substantial."

She pulled him closer by the waistband of his pants and kissed him. "It's perfect."

He shimmied out of his clothes, tossing them aside and sliding under the sheets. He situated his own tray over his legs and pulled blankets around them. They ate in companionable silence. When they were done, she let him curl around her, marveling at the sheer size of him. She felt so small in comparison to the length of his body, but…somehow, still safe. That felt like a rare and lovely thing.

"I know this probably wasn't a good idea, considering that you're technically my employee and I plan on offering you future employment," he told her, tucking his chin over her shoulder. "But I'm not sorry."

She slipped her hands over his. "Me either. What was the future employment?"

"Coordinating historical and educational events for the hotel," he murmured. "It would be an employment alternative, but it's not *just* to get you out from under your grandparents' thumb. That's just a side benefit. You're also the most qualified person on the island. But I'm going to have Julie talk to you about the details, to at least reduce the overall power-dynamic problem a little bit."

"That seems more appropriate," she agreed.

"You were pretty upset earlier," he noted. "And if I'm going to help you fix whatever it is, I'm going to need some details."

Alice took a deep breath. "I've betrayed my friends. And I think I'm going to lose them."

It all came spilling out. Clark, the locks, Kyle, her knocking Clark to near unconsciousness before running to Collin.

"I'm sure it's not as bad as all that," he assured her. "You're a good person, Alice."

She turned to him and he ran his hand down her side. "You don't know that."

"Have you intentionally done anything to hurt Riley or Caroline?"

She shook her head. "No, never."

"Even when Clark asked you to?" he asked.

"*Especially* when Clark asked me to. But I never told them, not even when we broke into his office."

"So, see—" He paused. "You did what?"

"It was mostly to prove a point," she told him. "And the point was Riley could psychically fling a knife at his crotch."

"She can do that?" he asked, grimacing. "Can *you* do that?"

"Not so far," she admitted. "But I think I can fling people, which might be better?"

He waggled his hand back and forth. "So, you just didn't tell them of your suspicions, or when your suspicions were confirmed."

"I told him things about Riley, about Caroline," she said, rolling her head back against his shoulder. "Things about the house. Stuff I thought was harmless. I wasn't *trying* to help him. It was before I knew he was working against us, and I felt bad for him. He'd been wanting to go into the house for so long and I'd been inside. He probably used what I told him to help Kyle break in. Things that he probably used against Riley and Caroline while he was working for the Wellings."

"Before you knew that he was working for the Wellings," he noted.

"But I haven't told them about our...history," she said.

"Has Riley or Caroline told you about all of their previous partners?"

"No," she admitted.

"Are you going to tell them about this?" he asked. "About us?"

"I think they would be even madder about me *not* telling them about this than they would be about me not telling them about Clark," she sighed. "And if he tells them about it, I'm going to lose the only people who have ever loved me for me."

He cupped her jaw in his hand. "Love isn't conditional, not the way Caroline and Riley love you."

"That is not what I've experienced," she told him. "When you're raised to see every mistake as something that can be weighed, measured, cataloged, and then brought up later to wreck your entire relationship... It's hard not to panic when you make them."

"Well, I know a little something about unhealthy relationships," he said. "I'll go with you if you want to go tell them. They're all over at Shaddow House right now."

"How do you know that?" Alice asked.

"Because I got a text while you were asleep, asking if I could bring you over for a coven meeting. 'No excuses accepted.'"

"You're on the group chat?" Alice asked.

"I am now." He held up his phone. "It's mostly nonsensical emoji combinations from Mina, and Josh telling me his theories about, quote, 'what the ceiling ghost is all pissed off about,' which I'm going to need you to explain later. And also a bunch of memes involving witch puns."

"It gets better," she promised. "Josh is just sort of...testing your boundaries. He does that."

She pointed a casual hand at the door. "Are we going to talk about the guy currently standing in the hallway?" she asked.

Collin glanced up and jerked back, ramming his head against the wooden slats of the bed frame. "Ow."

The ghost was barely visible in the dim light. He was a young man in a sort of a Henley work shirt and flat cap. He was tall, with coltishly long arms and legs that he probably would have grown into eventually. Dark shadows under light eyes gave him a melancholy, tired air. He was staring down at them with a wistfulness and seething anger that made Alice's chest hurt. This was a man who had been denied something he wanted, and he'd never gotten over it.

It was a feeling she recognized. Hell, it was a face she recognized—from the photo at the Historical Society. This was Samuel Proctor.

Alice supposed she should be grateful that Samuel was just waving at her, motioning for her to follow, instead of trying to inhabit her brain like Emily had done to Caroline when she'd wanted to communicate a message.

"Shhh," Alice whispered. "Don't startle him."

"Don't startle *him*?" Collin said, throwing his hands toward the door. "Pants. I need my pants."

Samuel's ghost motioned with a hand that was bloodied at the fingertips. Alice whipped off the covers and grabbed the nearest T-shirt.

"The ghost waves to you and you're just going to follow?" Collin said, scrambling to find something that would fit him. "Do you also click on 'You may have already won an iPad' links? OK, seriously, my pants?"

She shushed him, following the ghost out of the room and down the stairs. "Hello, do you need help?"

Samuel didn't respond, so she followed. Collin stumbled after her, trying to fit into a pair of purple seersucker pajama pants she'd thrown in the laundry hamper. Between that and her rain jacket, he was at least partially covered when they left the guesthouse and slipped down the service hallway.

"You realize that while there are no guests, the construction crews are still here, right? They could be awake and see their boss dressed like this," Collin said, motioning to his improvised ensemble. Because of the difference of leg length, her pants were basically capris on him.

"So go back and change," she told him as the ghost silently glided along the hallway.

"I'm not leaving you alone in the dark with a ghost, no matter what I'm wearing," Collin insisted. "Even if it does destroy what little credibility I have with the construction dudes."

"You're very brave," Alice said.

"I don't need your pity," he grumbled, making her snicker.

"Do you need our help?" she called again to the ghost, who ignored her.

Samuel turned and walked through the door to the storage area behind the kitchen. Collin frowned as they approached the locked storage door. He showed her a large ring full of keys in various sizes.

"You located a huge key ring, but not your pants?" Alice asked.

"The keys were out on a table. My pants were harder to locate." He unlocked the door and they entered the darkened room. It looked like…a storage room, with neatly organized shelves stacked with canned goods and staples. Alice made a note to come here if there was ever a severe ice storm or a zombie apocalypse. The ghost seemed to be hovering near the rear wall of the room.

"This would be a lot easier if you would just talk to us," she told the ghost. He gave her one last sad look and melted into the wall.

"Is that normal?" Collin asked.

"Usually, they're a little more talkative," she replied. "What's behind the wall?"

"No idea," he said. "I think the storage area was added when I was a kid. Why did this ghost sort of pointedly ignore us while still acknowledging our existence? The other one acted like she couldn't see me at all."

Wait. Collin was seeing other ghosts at the hotel now? She looked up at him. "Stop. Explain."

"I've been seeing Victoria, running down a hallway." He looked around. "Uh, this hallway, now that I think about it. I had a minor sleepwalking episode the other night where I sort of dreamed I *was* her. And I was being chased."

Her jaw dropped. "You what?"

As if on cue, the shadow-form woman ran out of the guesthouse area as if she was being chased. A dark figure emerged from the orange wall behind her, hands outstretched. The woman's features were less discernible than those of the silver woman they'd met at Shaddow House—like she'd been diluted. And the menacing darkness behind her was hardly discernable at all. But when the ghost stopped in front of Alice, her head turning and her eyes darting around as if she was looking for a way out of a trap, there was a desperation that Alice understood in a way that broke her heart.

"Victoria?" Collin called. But the woman ignored him and continued to run, looking behind her as she bolted for the stairs. Her panicked pants echoed in the long, open space. The shadow chased her and grabbed her hair, throwing her to the floor. Then the figures disappeared like so much mist.

"Like that," Collin said, frowning. "It wasn't like the other ghosts. It's detached. Victoria shouldn't be here if her ghost is 'stored' at Shaddow House, right? It shouldn't be possible for ghosts to be two places at once, right?"

"You're questioning the physics of *ghosts?*" Alice asked.

He pursed his lips. "Good point."

Just then, the woman emerged from the wall again, running down the hall, looking behind her shoulder, as she had just a few minutes before.

"You can't even hear us, can you?" Alice asked loudly. Victoria didn't respond, running away from them without a word.

"It's like she's on a loop," Collin said, wincing when the larger figure snagged Victoria's hair and threw her to the floor. "Maybe she was triggered somehow by the other ghost showing up?"

"I'm not entirely sure what's happening here," she told him. "We should probably go to that coven meeting after all. It will give me a chance to explain myself to everybody. And try to figure out what the hell is going on here."

He slid his fingers through hers. "I'll be right there with you. We'll make them understand."

She stood up on her tippy-toes and kissed him. "Thank you."

"You're welcome," Collin replied.

She pointed at his exposed calves. "But first, you should put on some pants that don't belong to me."

Collin glanced down. "Yep."

Chapter 8
Collin

TO COLLIN'S SURPRISE, THE COVEN–STILL hard to believe he used that word in everyday conversation—was still gathered when they showed up at ten thirty on a weeknight.

"Isn't it a school night?" he asked as they approached the well-lit house.

"Yeah, we've tried keeping the kids out of ghostly matters on school nights and it only blows up in our faces later," Alice said. "Sometimes literally."

It was still a bit of a shock to see ghosts lounging around in the parlor with Alice's friends. Ben and Caroline were tucked into the corner of the sofa, arguing over a very ugly copper candleholder thing on the coffee table. Edison and Riley were making notes on a large rolling dry-erase board while Natalie "the kitchen ghost" stood nearby, wringing her hands over their penmanship. Josh was sprawled on a nearby chair, shoveling jelly beans into his mouth.

"Alice!" Mina bounded up from the parlor sofa and threw herself at Alice, dragging her away. "I knew you couldn't resist the text chain after we added Collin!"

"You added me as bait?" Collin asked, feeling oddly hurt. He glanced toward Plover the butler ghost, who was looking down his long ghostly nose at Collin after he'd greeted Alice warmly. Collin was getting definite, "You're not good enough for my little girl" vibes from him, which was a new experience.

"Not entirely," Josh told him, even while Caroline tried to move the jelly beans away and nudge a bag of almonds toward him. "You're in on the secret, so you might as well help. Also, Riley has the best snack pantry in town. These jelly beans are imported."

"I am not going to be held responsible for him eating that much sugar at this hour," Caroline told Ben.

"It's not like it's going to stunt his growth," Ben said, gesturing at Josh's long legs.

"You're a medical doctor!" Caroline exclaimed.

"Right now, I'm a tired dad who just got off a fifteen-hour shift involving a norovirus outbreak," Ben told her, taking the jelly beans out of Josh's reach. He handed him the almonds. "Son, eat some protein."

"Is there a reason for the meeting?" Alice asked. "Did you find another lock? Did you figure out what the candelabra does?"

The "without me" hung in the air between them, unspoken.

"No," Riley assured her. "We just haven't had the chance to get together recently, what with the kids starting school, Edison being shorthanded at the library, and Ben handling the island's various medical crises. And we wanted you here with us."

"What do you *think* the hideous candle thing does?" Collin asked, before seeing Alice nod shakily. She blew out a breath. Her pale cheeks had gone well past pink into red, and her eyes were growing shiny and wet.

Josh sat up, suddenly very serious. "Alice, you OK?"

"You're going to want to take the kids back home," Collin told Ben.

Mina rose to take Alice's hand. "Anything Alice can say to the coven, she can say in front of us."

Alice blinked rapidly and tears coursed down her cheeks. "It's about my sex life, Josh."

"*And* I'm out," Josh said, standing quickly. "Alice, I love you and respect your sexual autonomy, but you're basically one of my aunts. I don't want to picture whatever you and Collin have been doing in the bedroom. I'm going to the music room."

Collin frowned, watching Josh practically hurl himself down the hall.

"The kids went to private school back in Arizona," Ben told him. "They basically speak like underage college faculty."

"What about Miss Alice's sexual life has upset her so?" Plover asked, crossing to a small table by the door and picking up a silver mail tray. Alice had mentioned that ghosts could interact with their attachment objects…which explained why Plover appeared to be brandishing his in a threatening manner.

"It's not Collin who upset me, Plover," Alice said loudly. "Put the mail tray down before someone gets hurt."

Plover, still glaring, carefully put the tray on the coffee table, where it was still in reach. He pointed two ghostly fingers at his eyes and then pointed them at Collin.

Caroline scooched closer to Alice on the couch, rubbing her back. "If it's not Collin upsetting you, can you tell us what is?"

"Does it have something to do with why you've been avoiding us lately?" Riley asked.

Behind her back, Edison made a sort of head-jerking motion to Ben and Collin. Ben casually rose from the couch and edged toward the atrium room. Collin shook his head. He had hopes that Caroline and Riley would receive this news gracefully, but he wanted to be close, just in case. Ben made a more emphatic gesture. Collin shook his head. Finally, Plover pointed toward the atrium and gave Collin a stern look. Collin rolled his eyes and crept toward the atrium.

Honestly, it was like dating a high-school principal's daughter... if the principal also happened to be a ghost.

"It's really better to let the ladies sort this kind of thing out themselves," Edison told him quietly. "We're support staff, not magical. We may love them, but we're never going to fully understand the bond."

A waterlogged lady ghost burbled from the fountain in agreement.

Ben agreed. "Josh gets it a little more, but he has some magical sensitivity. I also think that has to do with young people being a little more in touch with their emotions these days."

"Well, I'm not going to get so far away that Alice thinks I've left her," Collin insisted. He waited just inside the door to the atrium, so he could still monitor the situation. Now that he wasn't in a complete panic and had a moment to take in the details, he could see that Shaddow House...was a little overdone. Polished hardwood floors, bronze wall sconces, a long ornate red rug that ran from the entryway to the dignified parlor. The walls were real plaster as opposed to drywall, painted a pale yellow that would have given the space a sunny feel in the daylight. The real element of "eye confusion" was the amount of bric-a-brac on every surface. So many colors and media and time periods. He hadn't spent enough time with Alice to know what he was looking at, but he knew there was no theme and no continuity.

Of course, when all your objets d'art were haunted, he supposed that matching was less of a concern.

Alice took a deep breath and in a strong, calm voice announced, "I had a sexual relationship with Clark."

"Oh," Mina said, grimacing. "Oh, that's not good."

Caroline nodded. "OK."

"Like, recently?" Riley asked. "As in, before I came to the island or after?"

"Before and after, but not for very long after," Alice said, relaxing slightly. It redeemed Collin's faith in Alice's friends that they hadn't flown off the handle at her immediately. He took a step back into what was apparently the designated boyfriend corner. "But it started way before. It wasn't so much a relationship as an *arrangement*."

Alice cast a guilty look at Mina, who scoffed. "Am I supposed to clutch my pearls here? My generation invented 'friends with benefits.'"

"No, you didn't," Ben called from the next room. "And please never let me hear that phrase from your lips again."

Mina shrugged.

"Obviously, at the time, Clark had no idea you and I would end up so close. It's just an awful coincidence that I happened to end up in your coven," Alice said.

"Not a huge surprise given the limited dating pool," Caroline admitted.

"But it's over?" Riley clarified.

"I spent less and less time with him, after meeting you. As soon as we found the letterhead fragment in the fireplace, I ended it," Alice told them. "I wasn't sure before that, but once I knew, I refused to 'see' him again. I couldn't put you two in danger, and then the kids got pulled into the coven and I wouldn't even talk to him."

"OK," Caroline said, taking a deep breath. "I'm not mad. I've made some poor sex-based decisions myself over the years. I just need to understand why you didn't tell us. Did you think we wouldn't get that you had a prior relationship with someone who just happened to be working against the coven?"

"Because I lied." Alice's voice cracked in a way that made Collin's heart feel like it was cracking in two. He moved to comfort her, but Edison caught his arm and shook his head. "So many times."

"By omission," Riley agreed. "And that's not great. Don't get me wrong. It really sucks and I'm not happy about it. And we're going to have to talk about that eventually. But more than anything, we were worried about you, Alice. We *are* worried about you. Because Clark is a horrible, *horrible* person and I don't like the idea of you being that close to someone who is bad for you."

"I was afraid," Alice said a voice that made Collin want to rush through the door to comfort her. But he simply hovered, feeling an odd mix of helpless and hopeful. "I didn't want to lose the first real friends I'd had...ever. And then he started asking me to spy on you, give him information. But I wouldn't do it. And I was so ashamed of the lying. I'm so sorry about the lying."

"And you pulled yourself away from us out of some sort of misguided sense of guilt and because somehow, you thought that would hurt us *less*," Mina guessed. Alice nodded. "That was pretty self-defeating, because it hurt us and it hurt you too. We missed you, we were scared, and it just made everything worse. So really... kind of a fail."

Collin's brow rose. He hadn't spent much time with teenagers recently. Had they always been so in touch with their emotions or was this another recent generational development?

Standing nearby, Ben saw Collin's confusion and told him, "They're smarter than me. I tried fighting it. Gave up."

"That's probably why we haven't been able to feel your magic," Riley sighed. "You cut yourself off from us, and your magic followed suit."

"You think I caused this?" Alice asked, sounding something more than miserable for the first time since this heart-wrenching conversation started. She sounded offended. And that was good. Collin figured they could work with offended.

"Not on purpose," Caroline assured her. "But when I was going through my *troubles* with my ghostly pain in the ass Rose, it manifested in weird ways magically. The dreams. The possession. Our power is rooted in emotion. It makes sense."

"Possession?" Collin turned to the other men, who simply shrugged like this was a super-normal thing to say.

"OK, so you've told us," Riley said. "Is there something else?"

"He sort of ambushed me today when I was walking home,"

Alice admitted. "Demanded my cooperation or he would tell you all sorts of lies about how I was helping him—which I never did. But honestly, I think at this point, it might be better if I just left the island. Clark thinks my being near you gives him access, and that makes him dangerous."

"Well, honey, that's just not fucking true," Riley told her, making Mina snort. Plover gasped. "I'll put a dollar in the swear jar, Plover."

"She's right," Caroline said. "Nothing good comes of us splitting up."

"It's one of the first rules of horror movies: stick together," Mina added. "We're stronger. And this sounds like some messed-up programming from your asshole grandparents, telling you that we would never forgive you for something you didn't even do on purpose. Because they're assholes."

Plover cleared his throat.

"I will also put a dollar in the swear jar," Mina told him.

"It's possible that was an idea that I picked up from my childhood," Alice mumbled as Caroline held her close.

"We don't work without you, Alice. And we don't want to," Riley told her, laying her head on Alice's shoulder.

"Would you please open your magic up again?" Mina asked, kneeling in front of Alice and hugging her middle. "It hasn't been the same without you. Even Josh feels it."

"I'll try," Alice promised. "I don't even know how I closed it in the first place."

"Just remember how much we love you, and how much we want you here with us," Caroline said. "No matter what your asshole grandparents told you."

Plover threw up his hands in despair.

"Everybody was cursing. I felt left out," Caroline told him, making Ben snicker.

"What did you do when Clark confronted you?" Riley asked, swiping at Alice's wet cheeks. Even without magic, Collin could practically feel Alice's relief rolling over him like an ocean wave. She'd told them and they hadn't thrown her out of the house. It spoke well of her friends. Collin could see that they were upset, but he could also see their awareness of Alice's fragile state. She couldn't bear their anger right now, so they put her needs first. He wished more people in Alice's life did that.

"I threw him against the wall outside the T-shirt emporium, using my magic," she said, making a shoving gesture with her hands. "I'm not even sure how I did it, considering that he's a living person. Maybe he had a haunted object *on* him? Left a little bit of a dent in the siding. I may owe the owners an apology."

"I approve," Plover told her.

"You did what?" Collin exclaimed. "You didn't tell me that!"

"I was sort of caught up in the moment and the nudity and it slipped my mind," Alice told him. Plover's eyes narrowed at Collin and he picked up the tray.

"Stop it," Mina told him. Plover put the tray aside and bared his teeth in Collin's direction.

"We'll figure this out," Riley swore. "But you can't hold yourself apart from us anymore, OK?"

"We love you," Caroline assured her. "We miss you. We need you. Now stop believing stuff that assholes tell you."

Alice snorted and responded by squeezing them to her in a big group hug. "I love you too. I'm sorry. Not for the sex with Clark part—that was in good faith—but for the lying."

"Also, your grandparents *suck*. Have I mentioned they suck?" Mina asked.

Alice hummed. "Yes, you have."

"You know, we could use this to our advantage," Caroline said.

"Nothing my grandparents do is for our advantage," Alice replied.

"No, she has a point about Clark," Mina insisted. "You could pretend that we don't know about the Clark thing, give him bad information, and keep him busy chasing fake leads all over the island instead of bugging you."

"This is your fault for letting Caroline and Mina live under the same roof," Edison informed Ben. "They're starting to think alike."

"They've always thought alike," Ben retorted.

"I threw him against a wall," Alice reminded them. "I tried to throw him *through* a wall. Magically."

"I approve," Plover said again.

Collin turned to Plover and silently mouthed the words, "Me too." Plover gave him a firm fatherly nod.

"My point is that Clark's not going to want to talk to me, at least not until he removes the shards of wall from his back," Alice told them. "And I doubt very much that he's going to believe anything I tell him."

"Alice, you managed to lie to us and we share magic telepathy with you," Riley noted. "I think he'll believe you."

"Ouch." Alice blinked at her. "That's a little harsh."

"I said we forgive you, not that we would never talk about it again," Riley replied, hugging Alice to her side. "We still have some processing to do."

Alice shrugged. "That's fair, I suppose."

"And we should probably let Collin come in before he wears a hole in the floorboards," Caroline added. "Sir, you are not a subtle eavesdropper."

"Never claimed to be," Collin shot back, making her snort. He considered that a victory.

Collin stood in the Cowslip Suite, watching the construction crew haul in a large crate through the door. Barely.

So far, construction on the hotel was going as well as one could expect.

In the past month, Collin's lawyers had sent some very sternly worded communications to Lawrence and Cynthia, which boiled down to "*lol no*" but in more civil, legal language. He made sure Clark received a copy. Because fuck that guy.

Fortunately, the Cowslip Suite hadn't required much in the way of structural change. It had been stripped down to its original hardwood floors and painted a cheerful yellow to match its namesake. Wide french doors opened to a bathroom that had been tiled in pristine white. The starkness of it would set off the shipping crate's contents to its best advantage. It would be timeless, elegant, and comfortable. The overall design made him think of a Shakespeare quote Alice mentioned—something about how a fairy queen's faithful servant would hang pearls from every cowslip's ear.

Yeah, he had it bad.

"You didn't think about measuring the door before you ordered this, did you?" Hudson Ward, the construction foreman, asked as two of his guys edged the hand truck through the casing with surgical care.

Tall, tanned, with hands the size of frying pans, Hudson was a very talented construction manager Collin had somehow lured from New York to supervise the Duchess renovation. He'd worked on several of the family's business properties over the years, seeming to appear from nowhere. Given the thick Jersey accent and almost-intentionally bland name, there were times Collin wondered if they'd found him through some sort of witness relocation program, but he figured it was rude (and counterproductive) to ask.

Collin admitted, "No, I didn't. I was just so excited to find a company that made these, I put a rush order in... With enough money, you can find basically anything on the internet."

"How ungodly expensive was this damn tub?" Hudson marveled.

Collin scrunched up his face. "That's one of those questions I can't answer without making myself look like a tool."

"Fair enough." Hudson snorted. "Most nonsensical thing I've ever seen."

"I know, isn't it awesome?" Collin said.

Hudson's dark eyes narrowed. "This is about a woman, isn't it?"

Collin nodded. "Yes, it is."

Hudson stared at him for a long moment. "I hope she's a nice girl."

"She's the nicest girl I've ever met," Collin told him solemnly.

Collin helped the crew uncrate the tub and they checked it for damage. It wasn't *exactly* like the treasure they'd seen in the antique catalogue, but it was better because Alice would use it. He knew his girl. She wouldn't be able to relax if she thought her bath was about to flood the whole floor.

His girl.

When exactly had Alice become his girl? He had no clue. Also, he wasn't sure he would say it to her face, because he didn't know how she would feel about being called a "girl."

And yet, she was his girl. Well, maybe it was the other way around. He was hers. Undeniably. She'd left her mark on him, like a tattoo only visible to him, with her stubborn, quiet strength. Even when she thought she was showing weakness, it was because she was trying to depend only on herself, to protect the others from what she considered unforgivable. There was a sort of dignity in that…and he wished she would cut it the hell out.

"Well, it's going to take some time and some skill to install this thing," Hudson told him as they moved the tub into its relative position. "And I want you to know I doubled the waterproofing under the floor for when this thing inevitably breaks. And when it does break, and you need it fixed, I'm charging a twenty percent 'I told you so' fee."

"Understood," Collin said. "Thanks, Hud."

"Your impractical funeral," Hudson replied with a shrug.

Collin's phone buzzed with a text from his pocket. It was from Paige.

I'm going to see you soon.

Why did that seem like a threat?

"Collin?" Alice poked her head in the suite. "Julie told me you were up here. Oh, hello."

"Hudson Ward, this is Alice Seastairs, our furnishings consultant. Alice, this is Hudson, our construction project manager."

"Nice to meet you," Alice said, smiling brightly.

Hudson gave Alice a respectful once-over while shaking her hand. He looked at Collin. "I get it now."

"Would you excuse us, please?" Collin asked, his exasperated huff making Hudson laugh. He made a hand motion and the crew followed him out of the suite.

"What is this?" she gasped. "Is this *the* tub?"

"No, because my insurer wouldn't give us a bond if we installed an extremely old glass bathtub in a guest room," he admitted, making her laugh. "But this is as close as I could get, molded out of Plexiglas and plastic and all sorts of sturdy things that won't hurt guests or my floors or the infrastructure of the building—but looks like the real thing."

"It's so beautiful," she breathed, slipping her arms around his waist.

"You mentioned that cowslips are considered really valuable in fairy lore, and they're used to symbolize something precious found," he murmured. She gave him a warm smile and practically melted against him. "That, combined with what you said about the tub being the bathing place for a fairy queen—I thought it was an appropriate theme."

She leaned her head against his chest. "It matters. That you listened, you remembered."

He cupped the back of her head and kissed her. Suddenly, she pulled away. "Can I be the first one to try it out?"

"I was kind of hoping I could be in there with you when that happens," he purred.

She bit her lip and made what he could only describe as "heart eyes" at him. "I am so looking forward to seeing you trying to fold yourself into that flower tub."

"I live for your amusement, however I can make it happen," Collin told her.

She practically squealed. "You realize that it's going to become a huge booking point, right? Guests in all the other suites are going to be jealous they don't have one."

"We're going to install this one and see if it works. If it does, copies are going in all the other suites too."

"You took my suggestion that seriously?" she asked.

"Of course, I did. I mean, it's not *exactly* true to period and it's not going to be as profound in the other suites without fairy flower connotations, but *oof*—"

She threw herself into his arms and kissed him. "Thank you."

"You're welcome." He smiled at her, bumping her nose with his. "And I think we need to talk about the guy in the doorway again."

She turned and winced at the sight of the same bloodied man who'd been staring at them that night in her room. It was weird, seeing a ghost in the daylight. It made his lanky grayscale form not as scary, he supposed, and less "lurky."

Alice slowly detached herself from Collin. "Oh, hi. Samuel, right?"

He nodded and tried to open his mouth, but only a croak emerged. He huffed in frustration and clutched at his throat.

"OK, OK," she said, approaching him slowly. "Do you have something to show us?"

He nodded and motioned for them to follow.

"Again, with the following ghosts without question," Collin muttered.

Samuel Proctor led them down the sunlit, recently de-oranged hallways. The crews had only primed the walls, waiting until construction was finished to give them the final coat, but they just couldn't stand working inside a tangerine hellscape anymore. It was strange, walking through the hotel with work crews milling about, completely unaware of the ghost in their midst. They couldn't see him because they weren't prepared to, and because Samuel didn't want them to see him. But now, thanks to Collin's connection to Alice, he could see *more*. Not everything, but more.

Samuel led them back to the service hall near the guesthouse, to the kitchen storage. Collin unlocked the door before Samuel could glide to it. He flipped on the light switch. Samuel stopped just short of the brick and stared at them, his lip curling back in seething rage as he pointed to the wall.

Pointing to a wall, Collin said, "I looked at the blueprints and the entrance to the basement used to be behind this wall. But in the seventies, they rerouted staff foot traffic down the hall because the staircase was made of wood and was becoming a hazard."

She followed him as he dashed back out into the hallway, fumbling with the key ring.

"And apparently, someone on the staff tried to store contraband down there and my grandfather wanted the access out in the open," he muttered as he unlocked the door.

"What kind of contraband?" Alice asked.

"I'm not sure, but illegal substances come to mind, considering that one of the previous owners stored a whole bunch of illegal Canadian whiskey down there, 'waiting out' Prohibition. But I suppose anything's possible."

The cold, dry smell of concrete and dust hit them full in the face as they carefully picked their way down the cinder-block steps. Overhead fluorescent light cast a corpse-like green pall over them both. But Samuel, who was waiting for them at the bottom, somehow looked the same.

The basement was walled off into compartments, if for no other reason than to support the structure. It was ten degrees cooler down there, below the Michigan permafrost. And it was relatively clean. For all Robert's faults, at least he was organized. The various storage rooms were meticulously labeled. The Christmas decorations, only used in "low-snow" years, were stacked neatly against their lakeside wall, their cords coiled and tethered. There wasn't anything particularly creepy about the space, aside from the bad lighting and the ghost standing by the far wall, under the restaurant section, staring angrily at the wall.

"The wine cellar?" Collin muttered. It was one of the oldest sections of the hotel, made from rough-hewn stone as opposed to concrete.

"Where the illicit whiskey was kept?" Alice asked.

"No, it's older than that," Collin replied. "It goes back to the original footprint of the hotel." He unlocked the wine cellar door with an old-fashioned skeleton key.

"How big is that key ring?" she marveled. He wiggled his eyebrows.

The wine cellar was carefully lit, so as not to expose the bottles to damaging wavelengths. They were stacked on fluted shelves by vintage and, like the rest of the basement, recently swept and dusted.

"Well, this is kind of disappointing," Alice muttered.

Samuel was standing by the wall left of the door, pointing, looking angry.

Alice frowned. "The room isn't even."

"Sorry, what?" Collin asked.

Alice nodded to the door. "The door isn't centered to the room. The wall is three feet closer to the door on this side than the other."

"Maybe it was a load-bearing wall issue?" he guessed. "There's no architectural rule that doors have to be centered, I suppose."

"All of the other doors down here are," Alice noted, walking out of the room. Collin followed. She was right, of course. The door was off-kilter, and there was no discernible reason for it. But that could have been an issue of stonemasonry, materials, or the whims of an architect.

Samuel didn't follow them out of the room, Collin noticed, just stood inside, glaring at the wall.

Behind them, they heard a female voice pleading, "Please, no."

They turned to see Victoria backing away from the wine cellar door as if the room contained all her nightmares. She looked terrified. All the pink seemed to drain out of Alice's cheeks as she watched Victoria's face contort in dread. She didn't just look scared. She looked *heartbroken*, wretched. And she was staring at the spot where Samuel had just been hovering.

"Victoria?"

The lady ghost didn't respond.

"Why isn't she responding?" Collin asked. "All the ghosts at the house responded."

"Victoria, can you hear me, or is this like…an echo?" Alice asked loudly. "Are you not really here?"

When Victoria didn't respond, Collin turned to the wine cellar. Samuel had disappeared. Were there rumors about him killing Victoria? Had they chased him off the island? If Collin had killed someone, he wouldn't be able to bear to stick around and watch the repeating record of the worst of his sins play out like a bad movie.

Victoria turned on her high-heeled boot and ran, not for the newer staircase they'd used, but for the far side of the basement, to where the original staircase stood. They heard heavier footsteps chasing her, and saw the outline of a thin, long-legged shadow chasing her from the wine cellar, passing them.

"So, an echo." Alice nodded. When Collin just blinked at her, she explained, "She's not really there. She experienced something so traumatic that it left a sort of psychic stain on the location, and we're seeing that play out over and over. The ghosts at the house are *present*. It's like a hologram versus interacting with someone in person."

"Ghosts as people," Collin said, blowing out a breath with a contemplative quirk to his brow. "A whole new world."

"It's strange, but you'll get used to it." She tried not to let the little pat on his shoulder come across as too condescending. "And she seemed afraid of Samuel. Samuel was delivering wine racks the day before he disappeared. The day before Victoria's body was found."

"Well, that's a lot of circumstantial…circumstances," he muttered. "So… What does that mean?"

"I have no idea," Alice said.

"Are we ever going to have a romantic moment without it being interrupted by a ghost?" he asked.

"There's probably a fifty-fifty chance with me, from here on out," she admitted. "Can you live with that?"

He pulled her close, hugging her tight. "Yes, I can."

Chapter 9
Alice

USUALLY, ALICE HATED IT WHEN a ghost sidled into her field of vision, all sneaky and silent, waiting to be seen. It was unnerving, like looking down to see a spider on your arm. But a few nights later, she was thrilled to see Victoria floating into the corner of her visual field.

She itched to be back in the shop, searching for Victoria's ring, but it was her day off. She didn't know what it all meant. Samuel's anger as he was moving through the hotel—it was laced with something darker, sadder. But it had to mean something, that Victoria was backing away from the spot where Samuel was standing, that Samuel had seethed so completely when looking at that wine cellar. Had he killed Victoria in there? Or tried to, before she fled?

It was almost too horrible to contemplate.

Still, it was a balm, being back in Shaddow House, sipping chamomile tea in the sunlit atrium while Eloise splashed in her fountain. Riley wasn't hovering, exactly, but she'd made it clear that she preferred to stay where she could see Alice, knowing Alice was back where she belonged.

Alice had been a fool, trying to stay away, and she knew part of her had been punishing herself even while the people around her assured her she didn't deserve it. She probably would benefit from some therapy.

For now, she was spending time with Riley, reading up on a "repel" spell. It was a combination of intent and hand motions that didn't forcibly move ghosts, but made the witch's space distinctly uncomfortable for the dead. To support Alice's reconnection to the coven, Collin was keeping to the hotel, supervising the construction. The suite floor was coming close to having habitable rooms ready, including the Cowslip Suite and its fairy tub. That only left a few hundred more rooms to do.

Still, progress was progress.

Alice's hand paused over the page of an auction catalogue she'd been perusing when Victoria undulated into sight to her left. Alice was afraid to move, like she was trying to avoid startling a wild bird. She turned her head by increments until she was finally looking directly at the dark-haired woman in the blue lace gown, blood-stained ruffles at her throat. She was perched on the edge of the sofa, a slight smile curving her lips, as if she was waiting for Alice to notice her.

"Hello," she said.

No screaming in the face. That was a good start, Alice supposed.

"Hi," Alice replied. "Er, nice to see you again."

Riley set her book aside but didn't say anything, apparently content to let Alice handle this.

"I'd like to apologize for my outburst," Victoria said quietly. "The longing I felt, being close to his presence after so long, feeling him nearby. It was almost painful, how much I wanted more of it. And I haven't felt pain in a long time."

"I'm so sorry I still haven't found the ring," Alice told her. "It's somewhere in my grandparents' shop. I'm still looking."

Alice could only hope that her grandparents hadn't found it.

"But I'm not sure that's your attachment object," Alice mused. "Since it's outside the house and you're...inside."

"I don't know *what* my attachment object is," Victoria huffed, sounding annoyed. "It makes me a bit of a misfit around here. But it's nice that you're looking for the ring. I did love that ring. And if you're a Proctor, that means you're a relative of his, which is even better. Maybe that's why I could feel his presence on you. His blood runs in your veins."

"Maybe." Alice said, nodding. "Wait, what?"

Riley's jaw dropped with the stunned-thrilled expression of someone watching their favorite telenovela. Victoria smiled and Alice could see a bit of Collin's occasional but profound mischief in her eyes. In that moment, she looked every bit the young girl she was supposed to be.

"Samuel was never supposed to give it to me," she whispered, smiling shyly up at Alice. "It took him a whole year to save for it, working in his father's shop."

Alice's brain was swimming. What was Victoria saying? How had Alice been so wrong?

"I met Samuel because of the mill," Victoria said. "When we were building Forsythia Manor, my father wanted us there, on the building site. We rented a house on the mainland and sailed over every day to see the progress of the house rising. We tried renting Shaddow House and a Zachary Denton practically tossed my father off the porch. Papa wrote his employer a sternly worded letter, which I find very funny now, knowing there was no employer. Anyway, my father thought it was good for us to see the work that went into building something, in overseeing a project like that. From the foundation up, we saw the framework grow, the furnace and pipes, the roof. I would sit there in a camp chair, reading under a parasol. Samuel seemed to be pulling his wagon up to the building site several times a day. He was sweet, sort of silly, shy, just a tall, gangly boy with freckles and ears that were too big for his head. Of course, I also had spots and feet that were far too large for the rest of my body… My feet were large for a longshoreman. I eventually grew into them."

Alice giggled.

"You have his look about you, you know," Victoria told her. "The shape of your mouth when you laugh, the light in his eyes. It's the same."

Alice smiled. It was nice, having someone say something nice about her family. And it came as a relief that Samuel wasn't a murderer. She couldn't wait to tell Collin, even if he'd been pretty understanding about the whole thing.

"He was just a friend," Victoria said. "A good friend, someone I could talk to."

"What happened? How did you end up engaged to Stanford?" Alice asked.

"Stanford was a friend of a family friend," Victoria sighed. "We were connected in that way only those in the *Social Register* could understand. And the autumn that I lost the spots from my face and grew into my unfashionably large feet, he'd somehow found his way into my father's plans for the hotel. He was an architect who had worked on a few high-profile buildings around New York. He was very passionate about his craft, something my father respected, and that whole winter, he was just always *there*. At the Fifth Avenue house, usually around mealtimes, sketching plans, making suggestions. Then he would inevitably be asked to join us for dinner. And I was barely out of the schoolroom. I'd hardly been anywhere. I wasn't allowed to go to a *museum* unaccompanied, and he'd been on a grand tour of the Continent. He knew so much about art and history and the theater, and I was so young. And so foolish."

Riley raised her hand and asked, "Er, how much older was he?"

Victoria didn't seem annoyed that Riley inserted herself into the conversation. She looked embarrassed. If ghosts could blush, Victoria's cheeks would have gone pink. "I had just turned eighteen and he was thirty-two."

"Oh, honey, no," Riley sighed. "That is not OK. And you weren't emotionally prepared to make half of the decisions that were being put on you. If it makes you feel better, that's the sort of behavior that would get him thoroughly shamed on the internet now. Probably put on some watch lists."

"I'm not sure what that means," Victoria replied.

"Things are done very differently now," Alice assured her.

"Good. I like that young lady who spends so much time here." Victoria paused and smiled. "She seemed a little more...energetic than girls of my time, but certain of herself."

Alice and Riley both looked stricken of the idea of Mina being manipulated into an arranged marriage to a man in his thirties.

"I'd just curtsied at my debutante ball when Stanford and his parents approached my father about an engagement," Victoria said. "My father was reluctant, but I was just so sure I would never find someone better than Stanford. Papa insisted on a long engagement, spanning *years*, until I was twenty-one. I think he wanted me to be sure, sweet man that he was."

"He didn't have problems with you marrying someone who worked for a living?" Alice asked.

Victoria shook her head. "Stanford's family were nouveau riche, yes. They made their money in textiles or ceramics or some such thing, but he'd been to the right schools, had the right friends, knew the right people. And my father liked the fact that the Newlin family wasn't afraid of 'getting their hands a little dirty.' He thought families like ours, who'd had means for a few generations, were getting softer. He thought a good match from an *enterprising* family like that would be better for me. And they were all very kind, very accommodating. Fawning, really. It made me a little uncomfortable. My mother had prepared me for a mother-in-law who would tell me I wasn't good enough for her darling boy."

Fawning. That was an interesting choice of words.

Victoria smiled fondly. "And then we returned to Starfall Point that summer and Samuel was all grown up. Just as funny, just as sweet. And so different from what I was used to from Stanford. Warmer, softer. I'd become so accustomed to being instructed by Stanford, to his telling me how to behave, how I should approach situations. I forgot what it was like to just *be*. Samuel and I talked about music and books and instead of telling me how I *should* feel about them, he listened to what I thought. It was the first time I'd been allowed to feel and act like a person my age, not an 'eligible young lady from a fine family.' Samuel was admired not because of what he had or whom he was related to, but because he was so good—good to me, good to other people. And the next summer, he gave me that ring. I had to wear it on a chain around my neck."

She ran a translucent hand along her throat, where Alice noticed a raw red wound under the grayish bruising. It looked like someone had snatched a chain from around her neck, cutting the skin. Not enough to give her a fatal wound, but enough to leave a little blood soaking into her dress.

"V and S," Alice murmured, remembering the inscription. "Stanford" and "Samuel" began with the same letter. She sighed. "Fooled by vague engraving, yet again."

"Would your father's liberal attitudes about hard work have allowed you to marry the son of a casket-maker?" Riley asked.

"Oh, I didn't say that," Victoria admitted. "My family would not have been pleased at all. But I like to think that, eventually, I would have been able to convince them. They would have bought Samuel his own enterprise—a furniture factory in Grand Rapids, most likely. And they would have told their friends that Samuel was the son of a timber baron, heir to a furniture empire, to save face. I hoped he could have lived with that, but I doubt he would have enjoyed it. He loved his family, and wouldn't have appreciated any implication that they were inferior."

"And Stanford?" Alice asked.

"I spent as little time with him as possible," Victoria said, her voice sad. "Honestly, he barely noticed."

"Did you talk to anyone about your doubts?" Riley asked,

and Alice was grateful not to be stuck in this awkward interview alone.

Victoria sat on the lip of Eloise's fountain. Eloise patted Victoria's back as she swam past. Or, at least, she made a patting gesture. Alice wasn't sure how that worked, ghosts touching each other. "My sister knew something was happening, but she was getting so close to her own coming-out and I didn't want to frighten her. My mother? She kept telling me that this was normal, to have second thoughts about Stanford, and that she'd had her doubts about Papa. Which wasn't exactly helpful. I think she was worried about the embarrassment that a broken engagement would mean for her at the Ladies' Charitable Aid Society, the church, her various clubs. And I think she was concerned that if I broke things off with Stanford, I might not make another suitable match. Society mamas would not risk connections between their sons and a lady who had already bolted from the altar once. She kept asking me to wait, not to do anything rash. Meanwhile, she was planning the wedding as if it was inevitable. I told myself fairy stories. I kept pretending that one day, I could introduce them to Samuel as my beau."

"So, it wasn't Samuel?" Alice said, absently gesturing toward her own neck. She already knew the answer, but she wanted final confirmation.

Victoria seemed genuinely offended. "Of course not. I don't remember exactly what happened, but he would never."

"You don't remember?" Alice asked.

"The other ghosts tell me that happens sometimes, that when a death is particularly traumatic, the mind, well, blocks it out, like the blank space in a dream. It's kinder that way, I think," Victoria mused. "And the afterlife has so few kindnesses."

Over their heads, an unctuous black shape slithered along the ceiling. Riley, Alice, and Victoria shuddered in unison.

"Oh, come on," Riley sighed.

The ceiling ghost always brought a feeling of cold, anxious dread into any room it entered. It hovered overhead, dripping down as if reaching toward them. Alice couldn't help but notice it seemed to be shying away from touching her—which she was not going to complain about.

"Speak of the devil," Victoria said, frowning at the ceiling. "Excuse me. I generally make myself scarce when that spirit scuttles about. I find its presence very…unpleasant."

"I do too," Riley told her.

"I'll do my best to find the ring," Alice promised. "I know it's not your attachment object, since you're trapped in here. But—"

Victoria didn't wait for Alice to say goodbye. She simply disappeared in a way that Alice envied.

"You suck," Alice told the ceiling ghost. She grabbed the nearest bowl of herbed salt and threw it up like wedding confetti. The surface of the ceiling ghost hissed like water hitting hot frying oil. It retreated into the heart of the house, behind the basement door, where the scariest things hid.

The salt not absorbed into the ghost scattered across the floor, into the parlor. Alice heard a distinct pinging as it slipped into the heating grates. Alice listened to the tinny noises and nearly dropped her book.

The vents.

Victoria had said her family watched the furnace and the pipes being installed at the hotel.

When her grandparents burst into the shop and called Collin a "hoodlum," Alice had vaguely heard a metallic plink in the midst of her panic. In all her searches of the shop, she hadn't looked in the vents. When she'd first started working at the shop, one of her regular tasks had been lifting the heavy iron grates and vacuuming the shallow pans just beneath the floor. Her grandparents were convinced this was a necessary weekly task because the clover-shaped gaps between the iron bars were wide enough for the odd dust ball or bit of paper to fall through. Apparently, it would be "unseemly" for a customer to look down and see debris, if they happened to crawl along the floor to look down into the vents…? When her grandparents started spending their winters in Florida, Alice had slowly cut back to cleaning the vents every other month or so. And with the disruption of her grandparents' arrival, she hadn't done it in…

"Oh…" Alice whispered when all the cogs in her head clicked into place. "That is not ideal…"

Alice was scurrying again, making record time across the island, considering the wind blowing off the water. Riley hadn't wanted her to go on her own, but while Alice might be able to explain her own presence in the shop to her grandparents, they would *not* appreciate plus-ones.

The shop was dark as she approached and she had to keep telling herself that she wasn't doing anything wrong, entering her workplace-slash-home. She wondered if she would have enough time to claim some of her stuff from her apartment before her grandparents called State Trooper Celia Tyree on her. Alice stood in the same general area of the shop she'd been standing when she'd dropped the ring. She turned, searching the floor for the nearest grate.

"Alice!" Arthur called across the shop. "Oh, how I've missed you. Your grandparents, they're bloody unbearable—pardon my language. They make me want to leave the building for hours at a time just to get away from them, even though it makes me itch, being away from Bessie." He watched as she crawled along the wall of the shop, closest to where she'd been standing when her grandparents had confronted her. "What are you doing creeping around there, love?"

"Hi, Arthur," she whispered. "I'm trying to keep this a sort of stealth maneuver, all right?"

"Oh, sure, sure," he told her. "But still, what are you doing?"

Alice braced herself up on her knees. "I'll explain in just a minute, OK?"

Overhead, security lights clicked on. Apparently, her grandparents had installed motion-sensor lights while she was out.

Perfect.

She sighed, crawling along the wall. The vents leading to the shop's furnace were *ancient*—decorative ironwork with sharp, occasionally rusted edges—nothing that would have been considered child-safe by any standard.

Alice used a small key chain flashlight to peer down into one and then another grate. She thought maybe she saw the glint of gold at the bottom of it, but it was obscured by dust and bits of paper.

She pulled a small tool kit from her purse and loosened the Phillips-head screws that held the cover in place. She grimaced. It had been a while since she'd cleaned out the grates. She ignored the guilt that zipped through her belly, the urge to take a Shop-Vac to every grate in the showroom. That was about to be someone else's problem.

She picked up three quarters, a large black coat button, and a paper clip. It felt like clearing out from under a couch cushion. She searched around with her fingers, reaching into the heating duct, praying she wouldn't feel anything rodent-related. Her fingertips brushed over a rounded shape. She closed her hand around the object and pulled it out into the open.

The ring!

She could feel it, the vibration of ghostly attachment, the heart-break and the hope that had been poured into this object, once upon a time. The weird compulsive tickle to regain the ring since she'd lost it was finally appeased. She practically sank to the floor as the relief spread through her body.

"So. Now you're sneaking into the shop like a thief in the night?" Marilyn asked.

Alice groaned at the sound of her grandmother's voice. The showroom lights clicked on. Apparently, her grandparents had made it across the island in record time. Stupid app notifications.

"What joy is ours," Arthur sighed. "I'm sorry, love. Don't pay attention to anything they say. You're above all their nonsense."

Alice shoved the ring into her jacket pocket and stood up. Her grandparents were standing there in their typical post-dinner attire: fall-friendly cardigans pulled over their day clothes. It was a weird, stuffy affectation that even as a child, Alice realized didn't make her grandparents anything like Mr. Rogers.

"Well, I came by to give you my resignation and I realized I hadn't cleared out the vents in a week or two," Alice lied cheerfully. Because she knew how much cheer annoyed them after five—and they would be so incensed by her quitting, they wouldn't notice the unlikelihood of the vent thing.

"Resignation? Oh, no, you're *fired*," Marilyn barked, while Franklin grumbled, "Don't think you can make up for your lack of attentiveness now. There's no saving your employment with us. It isn't as if we're *unaware* that you've neglected your duties."

Marilyn continued as if her husband hadn't spoken. "We should have fired you properly *weeks ago*, but it was just so shameful, to have people on this godforsaken island know that someone from *our family* was so incompetent that we had to fire her."

"Burn it down, Alice," Arthur yelled. "Their whole damned shop! Give it over to the flames!"

Alice shook her head, careful not to laugh at Arthur's lightning-quick change of heart. It hurt, but not as deeply as she'd expected it to, to hear those words from her grandmother. On some level, Alice had always known that she was expendable to the Proctors—could she really call them her grandparents when they'd fired her? She was disposable. The attachment and grace that most grandparents—still a question mark there—felt toward their second-generation progeny was missing from Marilyn and Franklin. And she was done making excuses for them, now that she'd seen how easily love and acceptance could be offered by people who cared. She'd inadvertently done things that could have resulted in *actual physical harm* to her coven, and they'd forgiven her without a second thought.

If anything, the Proctors' detachment made leaving easier. Alice knew it was inevitable that she was going to have to stop working at Superior Antiques. She would have preferred that it was on her own terms. She'd planned to hand them a resignation notice that Julie had printed off for her in the hotel office. But this was better. If she was fired, she could file for unemployment, if necessary. And, though it wasn't her chief concern, firing their own granddaughter would look pretty bad to the island's population. They were completely unaware of how it was going to affect their business, their welcome among the locals. And it wasn't Alice's job to warn them.

"So, I can't quit? You're firing me?" Alice scoffed, snickering to herself. "Well, that's different."

"What are you laughing at?" Franklin demanded.

"Nothing," Alice said, trying unsuccessfully to keep her lips from twitching.

"We were fools to invest so much in you. There's never been any benefit to us," Marilyn hissed. "From the moment of your birth, you've only brought tragedy and humiliation to our lives."

Well, that one hurt. But honestly, they were just so ridiculous. They were just sad, mean, old people who were probably going to end up alone, and she wasn't going to protect them from that anymore.

"All right, then," Alice said, rubbing absently at her side. It felt like the ring was burning in her pocket. A thought occurred to Alice. What if the ring was *Samuel's* attachment object? If it was, all she would have to do is get the ring to Shaddow House and Samuel and Victoria would be reunited.

A feeling of elation rose in her chest, which felt kind of inappropriate, given the situation.

"We're speaking to you, young lady!" Franklin yelled.

"Yeah, and I'm really losing interest in the conversation," Alice replied. "I'm going to go."

"I suppose you're going to your *friend's* house?" Marilyn sniffed.

"As a matter of fact, yes," Alice said.

"You're not staying with a 'friend,'" Franklin retorted. "You're staying with that *Bancroft* boy."

"Yes, a friend, who offered me a place to stay when you both threw me out," Alice retorted.

"A proper young lady doesn't stay with a *friend* simply because he offered her a bed," her grandmother groused.

Alice rolled her eyes. "A bed at a hotel, where there are hundreds of rooms."

"It's indecent!" Franklin thundered.

Alice threw up her hands. "He's thirty-five years old! So am I, for that matter!"

"It's a matter of family honor," Franklin sniffed.

Huh, more than two sentences from her grandfather in one evening, Alice mused. He must be awfully worked up for that to happen.

"You don't even dislike him," Alice scoffed. "You just like the idea of holding a grudge, of punishing someone. Is it because he could buy you and everything you own, several times over? Is that what really makes you mad?"

Alice didn't wait for the answer.

"Oh, so you're just going to walk away rather than apologize for your behavior?" Marilyn demanded. "After all we've done for you?"

And this was the self-consuming destructive cycle that was a relationship with her grandmother. Marilyn wanted to be able to say whatever she wanted, however she wanted, while feigning a wound whenever Alice finally decided she'd had enough. And the beauty of it was that her coven wasn't running to Alice in response to her emotional turmoil, because Alice wasn't *in* distress. She was just tired and sad and relieved that at the very least, her grandparents weren't pretending anymore.

"Right," Alice scoffed. "I know you want me to grovel at your feet to get my job back, but those days are over. In fact, *I'm* firing *you*!"

Her grandmother gasped, but Alice continued. "That's right, you're both fired. I don't want to be in your precious family any-more. You've done a terrible job of being my caretakers. You're the least caring people I've ever met. So I'm giving the position to people who are way better at it than you."

"How dare you!" Marilyn gasped, actually clutching her pearls.

"Give us back your keys," Franklin demanded, his hand out-stretched imperiously. "Clearly we can't trust you with them."

"Sure," Alice chirped back, dropping them into his palm. "Good luck running this place without me. You have the customer service skills of the average truck stop creep."

"You'll be back!" Marilyn yelled after Alice as she walked out.

"Not freaking likely!" Alice yelled back. She didn't care if members of the Nana Grapevine were camped out on Main Square and heard her.

Damn, that felt good.

Alice strode across the square, rubbing her pocket where the ring rested. Collin was waiting for her at the corner, grinning at her.

"I thought you might be headed this way," he said. "Riley called."

"Yeah, I probably need to start paying you rent," she told him.

"I'm not worried about it," he assured her. Alice glanced over her shoulder and noticed a silvery blur hovering behind them.

Huh.

The silver shape moved past them, up the hill toward Shaddow House. It felt important to follow this indistinct silver wisp, moving with such purpose along the familiar path.

"Um, would you mind if we went…that way?" she asked, nodding toward the ghost's uphill path.

Collin shrugged, appearing completely unfazed. "Sure."

She wondered if the rest of the coven could see the ghost as they approached the porch. The silver shadow had stopped near Gray Fern, seeming to hover, as if watching the others on the porch. The coven was enjoying the early October evening on the porch, with the door propped open so Plover and the other ghosts could talk to them.

She'd done a difficult thing. Yay for her. There was still a ghost at her back. She glanced over her shoulder and saw that the shadowy shape was moving closer, but not fully materialized yet.

"I called an emergency meeting," Riley told her, gesturing to the others. "I also explained Victoria's story on the group text, so Collin knows too."

"You sent a ghost's murder-y origin story over the group text?" Alice marveled. Riley shrugged.

"On an unrelated note, is there a reason Clark was seen digging in the churchyard by a headstone with the name Uriah Albert Dix?" Edison asked, grinning at her.

Despite the absolutely terrible evening she'd had, Alice burst out laughing. "Yes, a few days ago, I went to his law office to drop off a thank-you gift for Norma Oviette and I offered him a calculated fake apology for our 'misunderstanding.' I told him I panicked at the idea of you finding out about our 'arrangement' and wanted to make it up to him. I told him that you suspected Mr. Dix of being a Welling heir and it was possible he had valuable records buried with him. And it took me a long time to find a suitable headstone that would say something like, 'You're a dick.'"

Riley chortled. "Diabolical."

"Any idea why Trooper Celia accused Clark of 'fiddling' with the windows of the Historical Society office?" Caroline asked, smirking as if she couldn't wait for the explanation.

"I may have told him that you thought there was a complete original blueprint of Shaddow House somewhere in the architectural section, stuck between two pages of a Shaddow family Bible."

Riley frowned. "There's no such thing as a complete original blueprint of Shaddow House. Or a Shaddow family Bible. Because there is no Shaddow family."

Alice beamed. "Yes, I know."

"You have a little bit of a vicious streak in you, don't you?" Collin asked.

"I have never pretended otherwise. It's just that it's rarely activated," Alice said, shaking her head. "Do not cross me. Also, I brought this."

She pulled the ring out of her pocket and showed it to the others.

"Aw!" Collin crowed. "You found it!"

Alice dropped the ring into Caroline's hand. "I'm pretty sure it's an attachment object for Samuel. But I wanted to have you check it over before we bring it into the house."

Caroline turned it over in her hand. Alice looked over her shoulder, and the shadow was still moving toward them.

"Aw, Alice's meanness is much more productive than our meanness," Riley sighed. "My meanness is centered around rude pun-based nicknames and aggressive eye contact while singing off-key karaoke of someone's favorite song."

Edison just stared at her.

"You fell in love with the magic part of me, but you also have to deal with the petty everyday me," she protested. "That's the job!"

Edison pinched the bridge of his nose. "You are the person that I have chosen."

"Yeah, and you knew what you were getting into," she countered.

"Yep," Edison let the last "p" sound hang between them, before he started snickering. "Yes, I did."

"You OK, bud?" Ben asked Josh. "This is normally the kind of thing you find hilarious."

Josh didn't answer. He was frowning, his head cocked to the right. "Does anyone hear that? Like a rattling noise?"

"No, but you hear everything before we do," Mina told him. "That could be an old engine driving down a road on the mainland."

"I think it has to be ghost-related for me to hear it before you," Josh mused, still looking a little confused.

The shadow was approaching the fence line, moving with purpose now, but not toward them. It was moving to the right of the house, toward the shared property line with Ben's house, toward the folly.

Riley took the ring from Caroline and studied it. She turned to look through the open front door. "Victoria? Any comment?"

Victoria didn't materialize, but Samuel appeared almost immediately. He was translucent...well, more translucent than usual ghosts. Across the square, the lurking silver shadow that had been following them was still walking toward the house. But Samuel was...right next to Caroline, silently staring at the ring in her hand.

"What the shit?" Josh yelled at the newly arrived ghost. "Give us some warning, man!"

"What is happening?" Riley demanded, her eyes wide as she peered back and forth between the new spectral arrivals.

"You mean this guy, or the weird silvery ghost fog walking toward us?" Mina asked, shrugging. "Yeah, sometimes I see it walking through the yard at night."

"And how long has this been happening?" Riley asked, suddenly far more sober.

"Since we got here and we started seeing ghosts?" Mina said, nodding at Samuel. "This is the first time I've seen this new guy, though."

"We've talked about you not sharing information with us in a timely manner!" Caroline exclaimed, watching the still distant, not-quite-fully-formed ghost shape.

"I thought it was just one of the many ghosts on the island!" Mina cried. "You said the house was warded, so the current ghosts can't leave and new ones can't just walk in!"

Josh nodded. "Otherwise, chaos. If we reported every time we saw a ghost stranger, we would be on the phone with you all day."

"Well, I don't love hearing that," Ben grumbled as the approaching form seemed to gain legs and arms.

"Dude, have you been stalker-lurking around the house this whole time?" Josh asked Samuel, who looked vaguely offended and shook his head.

"I don't want to interrupt this terrifying existential crisis I'm having as a result of *that* information, but that body shape… It's a lot like the figure in the hallway chasing Victoria," Collin commented, nodding at the approaching second ghost, who was still sort of formless and smoky. "Wait, I thought you just said the property was warded for ghosts."

"The wards keep the ghosts in the *house*," Riley told him. "There's nothing to keep them off the lot. It's not like an invisible pet-proof fence."

"Can we get back to Samuel?" Collin asked. "The man is standing right here."

"I'm sorry," Riley said, turning back to Samuel. Alice stepped closer to examine the ring and Samuel became even more transparent. Riley frowned. "Um, Alice, take a step back."

Samuel's form became more solid.

Alice took a step toward him. Samuel became more transparent.

Alice's mouth dropped open. "What the hell?"

Alice walked back to the gate and Samuel became more visible.

"I have a theory," Riley said. "You've become really good at establishing, let's say, 'space bubbles' for yourself recently. What if that includes the ghosts? You're near an object and you're unconsciously casting a sort of bubble around it. The ghost becomes less visible."

"I can't tell if that's a good thing or not," Alice muttered.

Suddenly, they all heard a rattling sound from the area of the folly.

Josh frowned. "What the fu—"

"Nope." Ben held up a hand. "Just because everybody else does it, doesn't mean you can."

Suddenly, Victoria materialized at the open door and yelled, "*Samuel!*"

For the first time since their "screaming introduction," Victoria looked truly happy. She slapped her hands against the invisible barrier as if she could dismantle a centuries-old magical ward through the power of will. Samuel rushed forward, flinging himself at the mystical wall that kept him out of Shaddow House. He beat on the glass with his fists, not making a sound. Alice noticed the wounds on his fingers, the way his nails seemed to be ripped, if not missing; the blackened blood seeping into the cuffs of his shirt.

"Samuel!" Victoria shouted. "Please! Please let me out. I just want to touch him. Please!"

Samuel turned to them, panicked. He seemed to draw breath he didn't need, and made a hoarse croaking noise.

"Umm...not to interrupt this upsetting scene, but have we ever seen that before?" Josh pointed toward the fence. They turned and watched a far less transparent version of a thin, tall man stride through the fence. He was moving toward the folly with purpose.

"Alice, do you think you can control the bubble thing?" Caroline asked.

"I don't know," Alice said, shaking her head. She pictured a microclimate surrounding herself, a force field that protected her from the awful energy of her grandparents, the less genial spirits of the house, Clark's malevolence—and she drew it into herself, as if she didn't need it for now. She wasn't alone. She didn't need the same level of protection.

The approaching guest took on the silver-opacity appearance of most of the Shaddow House ghosts—an older man with a severe expression, wearing the Edwardian version of a power suit. Samuel made another croaking noise, as if he was trying to clear years of cobwebs from his throat.

They looked at Plover, who shook his head. "I don't recall that ghost ever making an appearance before. How odd."

"You bastard!" Samuel suddenly yelled, his voice still gravelly. He chased the older man, screaming at him. But the thin ghost paid him no mind. It was as if Samuel wasn't even there. "I saw you! After you killed me, I saw what you did to her! You murdering sonofabitch! How could you hurt her?"

"What is going on?" Edison asked.

"Stanford?" Victoria's brow wrinkled as she watched the man's progress across the yard. "What is Stanford doing here?"

Stanford didn't appear to hear Samuel's screams. He just kneeled at the base of the folly and appeared to be digging. Victoria watched his crouched figure, an expression of horror dragging at her features.

"Why isn't he listening to me?" Samuel demanded. Stanford stood, laying hands on the wall of the folly, and appeared to be whispering to himself. Samuel yelled directly into Stanford's hazed face. "Answer me!"

"He's not there. He's an echo," Alice told Samuel. "It's like a movie...er, a photograph. You can't get a photograph to talk back to you."

"Samuel?" Victoria whispered. Samuel's head snapped up and he drifted back toward the door. "I followed him...into the basement. I knew it was wrong, whatever Stanford was doing. There was no reason for him to spend so much time in the basement. And he had mortar on his shoes. Stanford never laid a brick in his life. Why would he be putting up masonry in the basement? He was standing by the wine cellar, in front of a freshly laid brick wall, cleaning up tools. He never cleaned anything. And then I saw your handkerchief on the floor, in the corner, dirty and...and there were red spots on it. Your mother embroidered that for you. I knew you wouldn't have thrown it on the floor."

She looked up, her lip quivering. "I knew... I knew what he did... He saw it, in my face. And it was like an entirely different person wearing his face. He'd always been so unaffected, distant, but he was so angry. He didn't even try to explain. He just seemed annoyed that he had another mess to clean up. He chased me up the stairs. He tried to grab my dress from behind, but he caught my necklace instead. My stupid skirts kept getting in the way, and he caught me by the hair... I'd never felt anything like it. So much pain, and the world was spinning, and then everything stopped. I stopped."

"He threw you down the stairs," Samuel said. "I saw the whole thing. I couldn't save you. I'm so sorry."

Because Samuel hadn't killed Victoria. Stanford, who had played the poor, sad fiancé when she was found, had done it. Alice was deeply ashamed. Honestly, she'd seen enough true-crime shows that she should have seen this coming. The spouse-slash-fiancé who mourned a little too much always did it. Stanford had killed poor Victoria with Samuel's blood still metaphorically fresh on his hands. Unaware of the emotional chaos he'd left in his wake, Stanford's echo turned away from the folly and walked unsteadily toward Main Square.

"Take him inside, Riley," Alice whispered. "Please."

Riley nodded and carried the ring through the door. Alice felt the tingle of the Shaddow House magic accepting Samuel's place in the house. Samuel rushed through the door and threw his arms around Victoria, who sobbed into his neck. No beating heart could have stayed cold at the sight of them in each other's arms again, gazing into each other's faces for the sheer relief of it. The reddened skin faded from Victoria's neck and the dried blood seemed to seep back into Samuel's fingertips. It was as if being together was undoing the emotional and physical damage that their deaths had wrought.

Alice's brow rose. Well, that was new.

"He told me you were hurt," Samuel murmured. "That you'd insisted on seeing the new phase of the building, and then he hit me over the head with a shovel. I woke up with my feet in a bucket of dried mortar. He was bricking me in, stone by stone, whistling a happy tune. He was already halfway done."

"Oh, man, full-on *Cask of Amontillado*'d you?" Josh marveled. "That sucks."

Ben stared at his son, who shrugged. "I told you I'm doing the American Lit reading."

"Please continue," Ben told Samuel.

"I screamed at him to stop, but he ignored me, like he did just now," Samuel said, glaring toward the wall where Stanford had been digging outside. "I screamed until I lost my voice. I screamed until it felt like there wasn't any air in the awful little hole he'd built for me. I screamed and scratched at the wall until everything went gray."

"I heard your voice," he whispered, turning to her. "Even in death, I saw what he did to you. I saw him pull the chain from your neck. I'm so sorry I couldn't do anything to stop it."

"You didn't have a body," Victoria reminded him, rubbing the back of her hand against Samuel's cheek. "I understand how that works now. There was nothing you could have done."

"Do you remember what happened afterward?" Riley asked. "That might help us figure out your attachment object."

Victoria shook her head. "Everything was gray, like Samuel said. I could see vague shapes, but I couldn't feel anything around me, hear anything. Nothing felt real," she sighed. "I wanted the letters Samuel wrote me. I wanted proof that I'd been loved, that what we felt was real. That *I* had been real. He wrote me such beautiful letters."

Samuel ducked his face into Victoria's hair. Alice wondered how that worked, ghosts touching, but now she could see. If they wanted to touch, they could touch each other, and there was a comfort in that.

"I'd asked my maid to hold the letters, if anything should

happen to me," Victoria said. "Tildy had more access to my room than anyone else in the household. And I didn't want my family to see things that were so…personal."

Samuel's eyes went wide. "Oh, right."

"I think Tildy left my parents' service shortly after my body was found," Victoria said. "She left my letters in a rosewood box I'd kept my less important jewelry in—birthstone rings, my first earrings, and my silver baby spoon and such. And then I was here. Being dead leaves one with blank spots in one's memory."

"It's possible that box is being used as a bookend in the shelves," Edison admitted, pointing to the house's library. "I found it in Nora's office. I couldn't open it and it was the perfect size to hold island history separate from island legends."

Everybody seemed to be staring at Edison. He cringed. "Sorry."

"It's OK. The indignity keeps me from making jokes about Victoria being born with a literal silver spoon," Riley told him. She offered Victoria an apologetic smile. "Inappropriate humor is how I cope."

"There was a tiny silver fork too. It was a gift set from my godparents, but a little excessive," Victoria assured her.

"So, Stanford snatched your engagement ring, but he didn't take the Sun Fire?" Alice asked. "They found the ruby near the bod… you. Sorry, that's so awkward."

Victoria took this in stride, merely snuggling into Samuel's side. "I don't think he meant to break the chain. I think he just grabbed at whatever he could reach. I don't even know what happened to it after."

"What do you think he was burying at the base of the folly?"

Riley asked. "Maybe he was trying to cover up evidence? Someone could have found it later. Also, I don't like murderers digging at my foundation, for the record."

"One of my cousins found the ring. He was working at the hotel, trying to keep up with deliveries and such after I 'disappeared.'" Samuel said, shaking his head. "Cousin Dell was one of the few people I'd shown the ring to, before I gave it to Victoria. It never sat well with him, that I would just disappear. He knew I would never just walk off the job. It wasn't in my nature."

"And also, people thought you were guilty of murder," Caroline noted. "I feel like the whole island owes you an apology cake, or a banner, or something."

Samuel shrugged. "Dell spent what time he could sneaking away, snooping around the hotel. He found the ring in the corner of the stairs, where Victoria…fell."

"Well, Dell must have tucked it away in the back of a drawer for safekeeping," Alice said.

"I didn't spend time at his place if I could help it." Samuel shrugged. "I never much cared for Dell's wife. So, I wandered away from the ring whenever I could, went back to the hotel. Even though it was uncomfortable, being away from the ring. It made me itch and ache.

"But the hotel was the last place I had seen my Victoria. Over the years, I guess I got confused, not really existing properly in either place, and I couldn't find the ring again and everything just became a gray mess."

"I'm so sorry, Samuel," Alice told him.

"That still doesn't explain why Stanford was digging," Caroline noted.

"Still do not like that," Riley added.

"Since he wasn't at all responsive to Samuel, I'm guessing it's an echo haunting, like Victoria running from what we now know to be Stanford in the halls at the hotel." Alice paused and looked at Victoria. "You aren't in two places at once, right?"

Victoria shook her head. "No, frankly, I'm horrified to know any piece of me is trapped in the hotel with Stanford."

"Pardon me. An echo haunting?" Mina asked, raising her hand.

Riley said, "According to Plover's assigned reading, which I am only now getting around to, now that I'm not chasing Aunt Nora's 'witchy character building assignments' around the house."

She paused to give Plover a pointed look. He shrugged his insubstantial shoulders. "Your Aunt Nora believed the ruse was an essential part of your magical development."

"Still hurts my feelings," Riley told him. "Victoria left a psychic imprint on the hotel when she died a violent death there. If you think about it, most ghosts that regular, non-magical people see are probably echo hauntings. That much emotion, the trauma, a ghost wouldn't have to choose to be seen. They're just *there*."

"And she just keeps repeating it over and over again, even if there's no one there to see it?" Ben asked.

"Well, it's not really *her*, but in a way, yes," Riley said.

Edison shivered. "That's rather awful."

"Especially when you consider the orange," Alice noted.

"Oh, wait, does that mean that Samuel has *seen* Victoria's echo running around the hotel, doing the same thing, for all of these years?" Mina asked, a horrified expression on her face. "Not able to talk to her or be seen by her or..."

Mina—who once threw a rock at a ghost who was terrorizing her, following up by calling said ghost a "lying old bitch"—was on the verge of tears. Josh put his arm around her and awkwardly patted her shoulder. "It's OK, Meanie. They're together now."

"I tried to avoid the hallways whenever possible," Samuel admitted. He nodded at Collin and Alice. "I heard the staff whisper about hearing strange noises in the hall, shadowy figures. But you two, you're the first ones to *see* her in decades. That's how I knew I could reach out to you, show you what you needed to see."

"And now you're here," Riley said. "Plover can put you through the new ghost orientation. And after you've adjusted to the initial shock of your reunion, you can decide whether you two want to stay here, together, or if you want to move on to whatever's next, also together. Completely your decision. You're welcome here if you want to stay—"

Riley stopped her sentence short as the ceiling ghost slithered its way into the foyer, cutting Alice a wide swathe to hover over Samuel.

"It would appear the ceiling ghost feels the need to posture for the newest addition," Plover huffed.

"He did the same thing when I moved in," Natalie called from the kitchen door. "It was gross then too!"

Alice did not want Samuel and Victoria's reunion marred by the ceiling ghost being the ceiling ghost. She did not like the way it was lurking over them.

"No, no," Alice told it. "Not today."

She stepped forward and was thrilled when the ceiling ghost retreated. For once, she was the menace. She was the threat, and it was a heady feeling. She imagined that same space bubble surrounding her stretching upward, pushing the ceiling ghost back. She grinned sharply at this new development. Yes. She could work with this.

Meanwhile, Riley grabbed one of the many bowls of salt stashed around the house and slung it upward, careful not to throw it in the direction of the rest of the coven. The salt hit the ceiling ghost, forcing it to dissipate and retreat.

"That never stops being fun," Mina said, shaking her head.

Chapter 10
Alice

WEIRDLY, COLLIN WAS NO LONGER comfortable with Alice sleeping alone in the hotel's guesthouse, what with the rampant murder echoes and the previously undiscovered bricked-in corpses and all. Not to mention whatever Clark or her thwarted grandparents might try to come up with to get her back into the shop. Alice figured this was a reasonable response and did not put up much of a fuss.

Also, he was going to have to figure out a quiet way to get Samuel's body out of his wine cellar. His to-do list had grown infinitely more weird since Alice came into his life.

Moving her suitcase from the guesthouse as well just seemed like a logical step. And while Alice appreciated the courtesy of Collin depositing her things in the sumptuous guest room in Forsythia Manor, she had no intention of sleeping there.

"You know, you're the first girl I've really had up here," he said, waving a hand around the spacious primary bedroom with its elaborately carved four-poster and sweeping view of the moonlit lake. He rubbed the back of his neck. "I mean, as an adult."

"Do you feel sort of naughty?" she asked.

"Well, my grandparents smiling at us... It doesn't help." He gestured toward the framed photo of an older couple, beaming down at them serenely. He nodded to another photo, a young couple, both dark-haired and suntanned. They were smiling at each other, instead of at the camera. "And my parents. We can just turn those around."

She giggled as he reached over to do just that, and caught his hand.

"The ring is interesting," she said, nodding to the cushion-cut solitaire on Collin's grandmother's finger and then his mother's. "Same stones. Different settings. Two carats on the diamond?"

"You can tell that?" Collin grinned at her. "What am I saying? Of course you can. I normally keep this in a safe at my apartment back home, but it made sense to have it here."

He pulled out a small cherrywood box from his dresser drawer. It was neatly organized, filled with cuff links, earrings, wedding bands—the ring from the photos. The piece was indeed a stunner, a perfectly clear two carats flanked by two small rectangular emeralds. The dresser contained a whole collection of important family jewelry pieces...unsecured, in a drawer. Alice wasn't even sure if the front door had been locked when they walked in—and while Starfall Pointers prided themselves in providing a friendly atmosphere, they also didn't believe in that "town so small that no one locks their doors" nonsense.

"This was my grandmother's ring, but reset for my mother," he said, handing it to her. "Grandma Marty wanted Mom to have a fresh start, fresh stories."

"That's sweet," she told him.

He nodded. "I think I would do the same thing for the woman I want to marry, carry on the tradition."

Alice tried not to think about the sort of woman Collin would give this ring to. She focused on the beauty of the piece for just a moment. The only reason she didn't spend a prolonged, awkward amount of time studying the gorgeous gemstone was that she didn't want to look like some sort of jewelry ghoul.

"This is valuable and should be in a vault," she told him, handing it back quickly. "All of this should be in a vault. And maybe guarded by a dragon."

"I know. I just like having it somewhere I can see it," he said. "I left it here in the house for so long. I like knowing I can just walk across a room and open the door and bam, there it is. Also, my dragon access is limited."

"I don't believe you should let that stop you," she said, placing her hand on his chest. He wrapped his long, warm fingers around hers and pressed it even closer to his heart. He bent his head to kiss her and she could almost feel the soft brush of his lips against hers when—

"I've been engaged," he suddenly blurted out. "More than once."

"Oh." Alice's chin seemed to retreat into her body for a second. "OK."

"To the same woman," he added, his face going beet red.

"Oh." The way she said "oh" changed. She couldn't help it. "It sounds like there's probably a story there."

She pulled him over to the bed, where they sat on the thick down-filled duvet. She held his hand as he explained, "This is

embarrassing, but I figure, the more you know about my history...
Forewarned is forearmed, you know?"

"Trust me, engagement stories in my coven tend to be pretty
horrific, so my bar is pretty high," she told him. "Did anybody die
in a boating accident?"

"No!" Collin blanched. "No one died in any sort of accident. I
mean, no one died in an intentional, murder-y manner either."

"OK, then," she said.

"Who died in a boating accident?" Collin asked.

"I'll explain later," Alice promised.

"Weirdly, I feel a little better now. So, I mentioned Paige before,
my girlfriend during my 'irresponsible douche' phase? Her family
has been close with my family for years. We've known each other
since grade school, always being thrown together at parties and
dinners. My parents didn't discourage it because they thought she
was a good influence on me, but her parents were *insistent* about
us spending time together. They saw it as a joining of two financial 'dynasties.' And after my parents passed, it was nice to have
that consistency, a connection to something that I knew my parents
would approve of. And Paige, she saw me do some of the most self-
destructive, stupid things humanly possible, and she stuck around.
I thought that meant something. I thought it meant she had to love
me, that she would love me through anything. Who smiles and
holds a guy's hand as he has his ass stitched up because he drove a
Vespa through a department-store window if she doesn't love him?"
Collin asked.

Alice marveled, "Wow."

"At nineteen, I asked her to marry me in a fit of drunken

'romantic' idiocy on the street in Rome, with a ring I bought from a souvenir cart," Collin sighed.

"That's kind of sweet," she said.

He shook his head. "We were too young. It was not the dream proposal she wanted, and her family wasn't pleased with the timing. We were still in school, after all, and they didn't want any rumors circulating about us 'having' to get married. And yes, families in our social climate are still quaint enough to be concerned with the appearance of that sort of thing."

"You've met my grandparents," she reminded him. "Trust me, I get the 'concerned with appearances' thing."

"So, they talked us into delaying the engagement at least until after graduation, which made sense," Collin sighed. "At the time, I was hurt. I thought I was going to get a family, be part of something again. Paige panicked, I think, probably from the very idea of marrying an idiot who proposed to her with a ten-dollar ring from a tourist cart. She broke things off, started dating other people. And after thinking about it for a while, I was kind of relieved. But then, her junior year, her boyfriend cheated on her with one of her best friends and she came running back to me, and that was another eighteen months of dating."

He rubbed his free hand over his face. "A lot of our friends were getting engaged around graduation. I felt bad, watching her smile get a little tighter every time someone else made an announcement. And I thought, why not? She was *an appropriate choice*, something I'd been told all my life was important. Besides, it wasn't as if I'd found someone I thought I would be happier with—which I know sounds fucking terrible. I thought... This is what my parents would have wanted for me: settling down, being responsible, making a life. I was still in occasional contact with Lawrence and Cynthia back then and I wasn't smart enough to see why they would be pushing me toward that idea—because, somehow, they thought there was money in it for them. Maybe Paige's family would give them a finder's fee? Anyway, I bought what I considered to be a respectable ring and proposed over dinner very publicly in one of her favorite restaurants." He pinched the bridge of his nose. "I even phoned in a tip to a society gossip column that I was planning to propose because I knew she would love that sort of thing."

Alice wasn't sure how to process *any* of this, but was careful to keep her expression neutral. Paige and her parents sounded like pieces of work, taking advantage of a young man who needed help and guidance, and not guidance toward sharing community property with Paige. Even now, Collin sounded so lost and uncertain, and guilty. And she knew what it was like, to twist guilt and what passed for love into bonds made of barbed wire. She knew their sharp weight better than anyone else. "And that one didn't take?"

"This is starting to sound pathetic. No, it probably sounded pathetic a couple of minutes ago." He shook his head. "Let's just say I see a lot of my own situation in Victoria and her unhappy engagement. This time, Paige didn't like the ring. The stone was the wrong shape and the wrong sort of band or something. And she didn't like the proposal. She wanted something all of her friends could see in person."

"You have a perfectly lovely ring in that drawer," she told him, pointing toward his dresser.

Collin hesitated. "It wasn't Paige's style. She wouldn't wear it, even if it was an heirloom. She likes, uh, contemporary designs.

"It occurred to me that if Paige really wanted to marry me, she would say yes, and we could figure out the jewelry and logistics later, so I stopped proposing," he said. "Not out of anger or anything, but… I told you about the treatment process. I did a lot of therapy, got sober, stopped talking to my aunt and uncle, went back to school to get my MBA. I actually paid attention in class, which was a novel experience."

"Oh, that hurts my soul," she told him, making him laugh.

He threw up his hands. "I never said I was perfect. I was starting to have doubts about whether we were good for each other, not in a relationship context, but just health-wise." He sighed. "I'm not even sure she ever loved me, not really. I mean, she's fond of me. She enjoys spending time with me. But I think she sees me as an investment. She's put too much time in to quit now, if that makes sense."

Alice shuddered. "That's a little gross."

"I don't think she's a bad person. She's just not good for me," he said.

"Are you sure about the 'bad person' part?" she replied. When he opened his mouth to object, she added, "I'm just saying my grandparents use the same word, 'investment,' and they're not great."

"Anyway, last year she showed up at my door with a ring she'd selected herself, telling me that she'd set up an engagement photo session to go with the announcement she'd already sent the *Times*."

"Well, that's bold!" she gasped.

"She said we'd waited long enough," he said, pursing her lips.

"She wouldn't 'accept any excuses this time,' as if she wasn't the one who turned me down a few years ago."

"So, you let her down easy?" she asked. "Or you let yourself down easy…out of your apartment on a ladder made of knotted bedding? Because I'm picturing the second one."

"I told her I wasn't ready," he said. "And I wasn't sure that I was ever going to be ready. I realize now that gave her hope—because I didn't flat-out say that I was *never* going to be ready—and that was cruel."

"It can be difficult, ending a complicated relationship," she told him. "Obviously, that is a concept I'm familiar with on several fronts."

"You used magic to throw your 'complicated relationship' through a wall," he deadpanned.

"Well, I don't recommend that," she said. "It was satisfying, but it has only made things *more* complicated… Is that part of the reason you're here on the island? To avoid this woman?"

"No, I'd always planned on being here," he told her. "But I can't say that the isolation was a con in the pro-con consideration columns. My feelings for Paige are complicated, and it's better for me to work through them when she's not around."

Did that mean that he was so drawn to Paige that he couldn't think straight when she was present? Alice wondered. And where did that leave Collin and Alice? Had she thrown herself in with another emotionally unavailable man? Only this time, instead of unintentionally acting as a saboteur for Clark, she was acting as some sort of relationship surrogate to help Collin process his feelings for someone else? Maybe her grandparents were right. The only thing she attracted in life was tragedy.

Because this was starting to feel pretty tragic.

"I think Paige and I kind of used each other as an excuse not to have to commit to people or move forward with relationships. We could focus on our careers, which was good. But we also always circle back to each other in a way that isn't healthy," he said.

"Why do you think that is?" Alice asked.

"I have spent a lot of time talking to various therapists, trying to figure that out." He sighed. "That's my big secret. I'm covertly a fucking mess. I just cover it up with passable manners and nice suits."

She reached for his hand and squeezed it. Yes, she liked the seemingly perfect man she instinctively wanted to rumple, but this was better. This man was human, not quite as intimidating. Infinitely more climb-able.

"Well, you're not alone in that. I've clearly got my issues," she told him. "And those suits aren't just nice, they're fantastic."

"Thank you," he replied, kissing her forehead. "For not running from the room screaming."

"Well, you have accepted my house full of ghosts and weird friends," she said.

"I like your weird friends," he told her. "Dead people and all."

Several days later, kneeling in the dark, digging at the base of the Shaddow House folly, Alice was grateful that Caroline had turned off the security cameras. This was not something she wanted recorded for posterity.

How could grown adults be so bad at digging?

"Caroline, I swear, you haphazardly throw dirt in my face one more time, I'm telling everybody that the 'homemade house rolls' your mom serves at the Rose pop out of a can," Riley sputtered, wiping a spadeful of dirt from her cheeks.

"My mom's homemade house rolls *do* pop out of a can," Caroline said, shrugging.

"Yes, so people will believe it!" Riley exclaimed, pausing to spit dirt particles onto the grass. "Dang your devil-may-care shoveling!"

Alice snickered. It was nice, spending time with just the coven in the autumn moonlight—even if the magic they were working involved landscaping. Ben and Edison knew better than to involve themselves in shovel-witchcraft. Collin was having dinner with the construction team to try to foster goodwill before the crews realized they were stuck on the island when the snow hit, which was due any minute. And frankly, Alice needed a little time with the coven to process what Collin had told her about his ex.

Alice couldn't judge past poor relationship decisions, but she couldn't help but wonder how "current" Collin's feelings for Paige were. At best, it sounded like unresolved business. And Alice had spent enough time around ghosts to know how dangerous that could be.

"Just want to point out, we could be helping," Josh called from a lawn chair near the gazebo. Mina sat nearby, reading her precalculus textbook by flashlight.

"You have school tomorrow," Caroline reminded them. "Your dad was willing to let you watch us look for whatever thing creepy Stanford was burying here, but he didn't want you to wear yourselves out before Mina's precalc test."

"That was before we knew you lacked the hand-eye coordination to operate a shovel," Alice retorted.

"I've had a long day!" Caroline cried, waving her shovel at the moat they'd dug around the rounded stone curve. "We've hired a new cook at the Rose, and she and my mom are having an epic power struggle over, well, everything—including the rolls that pop out of a can."

"Wow." Riley winced. "I'm sorry I brought that up. But I'm glad that your parents hired a new cook to give your mom a break. I know how they feel about hiring nonfamily members."

Caroline leaned against her shovel and caught her breath. "It was under threat of something very unpleasant to my dad."

"As in violence?" Alice asked.

Caroline shook her head. "No, as in having to pay one of us overtime."

Riley pursed her lips. "That would do it."

"Have we considered that maybe Stanford wasn't 'digging'?" Mina asked absently, turning her book page. "It's not like we saw a shovel."

"Does anybody hear the rattling noise?" Josh asked, cocking his head, staring over Alice's shoulder. She turned her head and saw a tall gray shape in the distance, approaching Shaddow House's gate.

"Do you think Stanford's coming back?" Caroline asked, squinting at the swiftly moving shape. "Maybe we can watch a little more closely this time."

Alice watched as the shape came nearer to the fence, walking up to the gate and opening it. "I don't think Stanford used the gate."

"Aw, dammit, it's Clark," Riley sighed. "I thought we'd agreed he would leave us alone and, in return, I wouldn't throw knives at his crotch with my brain."

"You did what, now?" Josh asked.

"She didn't hit him," Caroline assured the kids. Behind Caroline's back, Riley turned to them and measured "I came this close" with her thumb and forefinger. The kids snickered, making Caroline whip her head toward Riley.

Alice sighed. "It's possible this is my fault. I provoked him with that story about a possible Welling heir burying family heirlooms in the 'haunted cave' on the east coast of the island."

"The cave that floods regularly?" Caroline asked.

Alice nodded, biting her lip. "I heard the Coast Guard had to come rescue him."

"Good, he deserves it," Mina told her as Clark approached. "Dick."

"Nice mouth. Your influence, I'm assuming, Caroline?" Clark sniped.

"I think you need to ask yourself, if Riley can throw a knife at your crotch, what could a teenage witch with rampant hormones, a loose grip on her temper, and spotty magical control do?" Mina asked, smiling sweetly.

"You don't have spotty magical control," Josh whispered out of the side of his mouth.

Mina's smile turned ice cold. "He doesn't know that for sure."

"Clark, I thought I made it clear that you weren't welcome on the property," Riley told him.

"And I thought I made it clear that I plan on helping the Wellings do whatever it takes to undermine you," Clark shot back.

He smiled, and his features looked eerily skeletal in the blue-white moonlight. "It's a wonder, Alice, how you manage to keep in their good graces, despite everything you've done."

He looked surprised when she laughed in his face. "Oh, give it a rest, Clark. I told them, and no, they weren't happy about it. But instead of rejecting me, they forgave me, and they encouraged me to screw with you for the last couple of weeks. Because they love me a lot more than you could understand. You didn't break me. You didn't break us. Like Riley said, you really, really suck as a supervillain."

"And you're a lousy lay," Caroline added. "I'm guessing. I never found out for myself. You know my rule. No locals."

"He was an adequate lay," Alice corrected her, spotting a shudder from Josh. "Sorry kids, cover your ears."

Clark's responding sneer was razor sharp. "And you were—"

But before Clark could deliver what Alice was sure would be a pretty vile insult, his entire body seemed to buckle. Tendrils of dark ectoplasmic smoke rose through the front of his dress shirt and began to *wriggle.*

Alice shrieked and stumbled back into Riley, who caught her around the waist. Caroline leaped in front of the kids, shovel in hand, ready to defend. Clark flopped to the ground like a marionette whose strings had been cut.

"WHAT THE FUCK!" the coven yelled collectively. Even the kids. No one had the presence of mind to chastise them. Alice would feel bad about that after she processed the emotional trauma of watching *something* emerge from Clark's chest.

A small, dark transparent shape rose through the barrier of his shirt. It wasn't quite an animal, nor a ghost. It was like an eerie, furious combination of the two—a tiny, rodent-shaped, pocket-sized ghost surrounded by trails of dark smoke. It turned its flat, catlike face to the group and bared a mouth full of gleaming fangs, rowed and hooked.

Screaming, the women took another step back, their arms thrown protectively across each other. The kids joined them, curving their hands around the trio's shoulders, forming a line. The little monster took a run at them, but seemed to bounce off a ring of light that surrounded them. It seemed very insulted by this development and ran at the protective barrier again and again.

Alice knew, somehow, that the light was something that she was making, but she had no idea how it was happening. She'd never tried to repel ghosts from *other* people. But these were *her* people, and she wasn't about to let whatever that was touch them.

She glanced down. Clark was dead. He'd been standing there one moment, ready to say something horrible, and the next, he was lying on the ground, *dead*. No blood, no marks, just dead. How was this happening?

"Alice, is this you?" Riley asked.

"I'm not sure how. I just know I don't want that thing coming near us. And apparently the magic is doing what I ask, which is nice."

"Well, keep it up." Caroline told her, baring her teeth when the little demon-hamster-thing tried to run at Josh. "I will punt you clear across the island, you little…whatever you are!"

The little monster bared its teeth right back and retreated to Clark's chest, watching, waiting, staring up at them like a shark calculating how to bite through a diver's cage.

"Oh, don't be that way," a soft voice cooed as a person stepped out from behind a bare lilac tree. "Chester's such a well-behaved creature, when I tell him to be."

A pair of orthopedically correct shoes stepped into view. Margaret Flanders smiled coldly as "Chester" skittered off Clark's body and scrambled up to sit on her shoulder.

"Margaret?" Riley marveled. "You... Are you the Welling heir?"

"I did not see that coming," Caroline said, shaking her head.

Alice asked, "Is that why you quit volunteering at the library?"

Mina gave her an incredulous look. Alice shrugged. "My brain snags on insignificant details in a crisis."

"I never liked her," Riley replied, never taking her eyes off the older woman. "Oh, no, someone should check on Edison."

"Don't bother," Margaret huffed as Chester hissed at them. "It's not to my advantage to target Edison without you *knowing* I can target Edison. It's annoying, really. After all this time taking his orders, listening to him whine, I was looking forward to a nice creative payback. Though, I suppose there's still time for Chester here to turn his special brand of pressure to Edison's circulatory system, stop his heart, turn his insides to a nonfunctional soup like he did to Clark's. He can make it look like poor Edison finally succumbed to all his stress and anxiety and had himself a massive coronary event. So young, so tragic, after he finally found his second chance at love."

"You touch him and I will *end you*," Riley growled.

"And now, you know." Margaret smiled as if Riley hadn't spoken, but there was none of the unassuming, sweet-old-lady warmth she'd feigned for years. The reptilian sharpness of it made a shiver run down Alice's back.

"Chester here is what you might call an adaptation of the family magic. I've been working on it for years, like previous generations of Wellings, and only just figured out the process—combining magic and ghostly energy and sheer *force of will* to make something entirely new. Ghosts have always been able to hurt the living, but how to maintain absolute control? It was a breakthrough, inspired by necessity—as all magic has been for my family since your family *stole* what we made," Margaret seethed. "You took *everything* from us—"

"By kicking you out of a group project that you tried to hijack with secret supernatural time bombs?" Riley countered. "The amount of planning that went into making and hiding the locks borders on supervillain territory."

Margaret looked annoyed at being interrupted or possibly by being reminded that her family had played a role in its own catastrophe. All their attempts to control the ghosts of Shaddow House with their hidden lock system had never gotten them the power they wanted. Instead, it relegated them to a lonely secret world filled with lies, twisted schemes, and festering resentments. Chester hissed and growled at the coven, swiping his long, sharp-clawed fingers at the circle. He chittered in frustration every time he was deflected.

"Creating him took quite a lot out of me, and then there was even more of a time investment to train him, make him civil," Margaret said, scratching under Chester's chin. "As you can now see, he does whatever I tell him to, hurts whomever I tell him to. It's undetectable, untraceable. It's the achievement of several lifetimes."

"Oh, man, I'm going to have to explain another body on my property," Riley huffed. "Celia is not going to believe this was natural causes."

Alice wondered how she was able to keep her cool under these circumstances, but Riley had always been an accomplished compartmentalizer.

"Why reveal yourself now?" Riley asked.

"Because I know how close you are to the last of the locks. Honestly, I'm just getting bored, using all these intermediaries, the games," Margaret told her, sounding bored. "And to be even more frank, it's getting really expensive. You girls have proven worthy adversaries, far more so than that joke Nora or your mother."

"Don't talk about my mother," Riley warned her testily.

"But I'm a senior citizen, you know. I'm on a fixed income. I only have so much time left. I wanted to clear the field, so to speak," Margaret simpered, her smile razor thin. "Simplify matters."

"And Clark was causing problems for you?" Caroline asked.

Alice looked down at Clark, and it was as if she'd finally processed that the man that—while she loathed him more than a little—she had once shared intimacies with was dead. Nausea rolled up her throat, threatening the delicate control she held over the protective circle. She swallowed with an audible *gulp*. She did not want to be trapped in a magic circle with vomit.

"The little prick was demanding *another* retainer," Margaret seethed, losing her grip on her temper. She kicked Clark in the ribs. "For his silence."

It was truly disconcerting to hear such profane language coming from the mouth of the woman who once played Mother Goose at the library's story hour every week. Between that and the corpse-kicking, this was an eye-opening evening in terms of Margaret's character.

"It's going to be really hard to explain his death as a non-murder if you leave kick marks on him," Riley said. "And we will sell you out to anyone with any semblance of authority. Mina can work up tears at the drop of a hat. She and Josh can be sympathetic *and* convincing."

Margaret's face shifted to that of an actual human being, eyes wide and pooled with tears, mouth turned down in a distressed frown. "Oh, well, I was just passing by and saw poor Clark on the ground. The poor thing must have had a heart attack, so unusual for someone his age, but with the workload he took on, who knows what sort of strain he put on his system?"

Margaret followed this by whipping out a lace-edged hankie and dabbing delicately at the corners of her eyes.

"Damn, she is good," Caroline mused quietly.

"You've been warned," Margaret told them, her tone flint-hard again. "I'm bored and impatient, which is not good for you, in combination with my little pet here. I'm clearing extraneous frustrations from my life. That means that you're out of your league. I'm going to find a way into that castle of yours."

"But if you're able to make Chester, why even bother?" Josh asked. "I thought that's what you wanted. Shouldn't you be happy?"

"You don't even know what the locks do, the supernatural wealth that's inside Shaddow House—do you, you stupid boy?" Margaret scoffed, drawing angry hisses from Caroline and Mina. "I'll be happy when I finally get what my family is owed, what I'm owed. And your stolen empire will crumble to the ground."

"To be fair, we stole it back after your family tried to bury *supernatural time bombs* in it," Riley told her. Margaret sneered.

"We could tell everybody you're a murderous ghost-hamster-wrangler," Mina noted.

"Oh, of course you could, sweetheart," Margaret cooed. "But who would believe you?"

Realizing Margaret was correct, Mina grumbled quietly to herself. With that, Margaret sauntered off, with Chester turned on her shoulder, making deeply unpleasant faces at them.

"I should feel bad for him, but he was such a dick," Mina said, staring down at Clark's prone form.

"My dad is right. Children are desensitized to violence," Riley muttered as Caroline put her arms around the kids.

Mina pulled a disgruntled face. "Ghost violence. It barely counts."

When the rest of them stared at her in horror, she flung her arms out and cried, "He hurt Alice!"

"Kids, go call your dad, tell him we're going to need him to declare somebody dead," Caroline told them.

"We should probably open with, 'Hi, we're fine,'" Mina said. Caroline nodded. "Sure."

Mina took Josh's elbow. "Also, I recognize that you're probably trying to get us away from the dead body."

But Josh was watching Margaret's retreating back, a heartbroken expression on his face. "Chester's so mad. He's just rage...no name, no story."

Mina immediately shifted from her usual sarcasm to concern for her brother and his more daunting gift. "What, like the ceiling ghost?"

Josh shook his head. "Worse. It's like one of those bad mash-ups of songs that don't match, when the producer is trying too hard? It's a bunch of different ghosts, all their negative traits, all their pain. Their voices crash over each other until it's just noise. Do you think that's what Margaret meant by 'creating' him? That she made him out of a bunch of different ghosts? Could she do that?"

"I don't know," Riley admitted. "She said it was a magical adaptation, so witchcraft was definitely involved in building him. But she had to build him out of something, right? And her family has a long history of trying to harness power from ghosts. It all sounds like a witchcraft attempt at Frankenstein-ing to me." She shook her head. "But first: phone, Dad, doctor, death certificate."

"Right," Josh replied, still staring into the distance.

"And what are we supposed to do?" Mina was muttering as they walked away. "Just pretend that we *don't know* that Margaret is heir to an evil dynasty and the proud owner of a murder hamster? That we saw her murder someone? Also, Chester? Could she have picked a creepier name?"

Celia did, in fact, believe that Clark collapsed of a heart attack—with Ben's expert medical opinion backing up their story. Because honestly, Ben couldn't come up with an explanation of Clark's demise other than, "It looks like something reached into his chest and squeezed his heart until it exploded."

Which was accurate.

Technically.

Celia, however, had lots of questions about why and how Clark had his "heart explosion" on Riley's lawn, none of which Riley could answer to Celia's satisfaction. She was particularly interested in why grown-ass women were outside digging in flower beds at night so late in the year.

"You know, I shared this island with your aunt for almost ten years and never once set foot on this property," Celia was saying when Collin suddenly burst through the gate and bolted toward Alice like a semitruck intent on hugging.

"Gah!" she yelped as he caught her under the arms and lifted her up. "I'm fine."

"Some of the construction guys said that Celia was over here because someone died at Shaddow House," he said, his face pressed against her neck as he guided her to wrap her legs around his waist.

"I'm fine," she assured him, trying to keep her voice calm, even as she melted against him in relief. He'd come for her. He was worried about her. "Clark had a heart attack."

"Good," he muttered, making Celia's brows wing up into her auburn pixie cut. He gave her a long, flat look, and she went back to her clipboard of paperwork.

"Look, I know that Clark wasn't a particularly...cuddly local figure," Celia said to Ben. "But I have to make sure this is an official and complete report. Do you have any reason to believe that this was anything other than a heart attack?"

"Nothing that immediately jumps out at me," Ben said.

"And does anyone here know of any reason someone might have to hurt Clark?"

Mina opened her mouth, but Riley held up her hand. "No."

"Did you need Alice for anything else?" Collin asked. "Statements or signatures or anything official?"

"No," Celia told him, bemused. "I have her statement. Alice, I'll drop by the shop if I have any follow-up questions. Wait, I heard you don't work at the shop anymore."

"She's working at the hotel," Collin replied.

Celia's brows somehow rose even higher. "Really?"

"I'm staying at Forsythia Manor," Alice told her as Collin slung her over his shoulder.

Celia grinned. "Really?"

"Mind your business, Celia," Caroline told her. "Don't you have enough to handle right now?"

"Fine, I'll just get it out of the Nana Grapevine later anyway," she grumped, scribbling on her clipboard.

"I'm taking Alice home," Collin told the group.

"See you later, sweetie," Caroline told her. "Get some rest. It's been a long night."

But Collin was already carrying her toward the street.

"My legs work just fine," Alice reminded him as she waved to the others.

"It gives me something to do with my hands," he told her. "When I thought you were hurt—"

"But I'm fine," she told him again. She was fully aware that someone was going to see Collin carrying her down the street, and by the morning, the Nana Grapevine would be on fire with news that either Collin and Alice had eloped, or they had a terrible row and he was seen carrying her, caveman style, back to the hotel.

"Clark didn't have a heart attack, did he?" he asked.

She leaned back so she could see his face. "No. It was decidedly supernatural causes."

"They can do that?" Collin asked.

"Ghosts? Sure. It's just that most of them aren't strong enough and have no desire to hurt the living. Or they just haven't figured out how yet," she said as they passed the hotel, toward Forsythia Manor.

Collin shuddered. "That's terrifying."

"And yet, the world keeps on spinning and the living are just fine," she reminded him.

"You're pretty unflappable, aren't you?"

"Me?" Alice laughed. "No, I'm flapped pretty much full-time."

"Well, you'd never know it—" He stopped talking. He stopped moving. He stood on his front walkway, silent, while she was pointed toward the hotel. His hand fell away from Alice's rear. His voice sounded hollow as he gulped, "Paige?"

Chapter 11
Collin

HOW WAS FINDING OUT THAT his kind-of girlfriend's ex was ghost-murdered the *least* awkward part of his night?

Collin had been so relieved after running to Shaddow House to find Alice healthy and whole. He'd slung her over his shoulder and carried her home to Forsythia Manor because it felt like the only secure way for her to get there. He no longer trusted the ground to carry her. That was normal, right?

He was so caught up in the moment, carrying her to his home, admiring how the moonlight caressed the curves of her face, when he heard a light knocking sound. The sound drew his attention to his front door, where, to his surprise and horror, Paige was standing in the doorway, and he felt his smile melt right off.

"Paige?" He carefully placed Alice on her feet. "W-what are you doing here?"

She was as polished and presentable as always, wearing a long, dark, tailored silk coat over a designer dress and pumps more suitable for a cocktail party than walking around lakeside. Wait, how the hell did she even get here? The ferries had stopped running hours before. Collin registered that she had several sleek black suitcases on the porch behind her.

How long had Paige been out here? And how long was she planning to stay?

"Collin," she crooned, drawing his name out into something just short of insulting.

She kissed both of his cheeks, surrounding him in a cloud of her signature amber-heavy perfume, but he managed to collect enough brain cells to step out of range when she tried to kiss his mouth. She frowned at him, and then her eyes zeroed in on Alice, as if she'd just realized that there was another person standing there.

"I'm going to need those bags delivered to my room," Paige said, flicking her fingers toward the door of Forsythia Manor. Alice snorted in response, looking more bemused than offended.

"Alice doesn't work here," Collin told her. "What are you doing here, Paige?"

She reached up to run her fingers along his shirt collar, smoothing it out. "I told you I would see you soon."

Collin frowned. Paige did say that. He should have listened. He should have known that she wouldn't be content to be ignored when she knew where he was. But somehow, he'd let himself get distracted by his contentment, and now Paige was right on his doorstep, paralyzing him from the brain down.

Collin wanted to brush her fingers away. He didn't want her touching him, not in front of Alice, not ever. But he couldn't be aggressive with Paige, couldn't reject her outright. Not because he was afraid for himself, but for Alice. Paige had gone after other women before—waitresses, salespeople, hotel clerks—getting them

fired for giving Collin "too much attention." And that was for gestures a lot less friendly than having Alice thrown over his shoulder.
Hell, Paige had managed to get an airline attendant fired mid-flight
for offering Collin extra pretzels. (Paige's dad was part-owner of
the airline.)

Plus, Paige couldn't have Alice fired, so what would she do to
hurt her? Would it involve Alice's grandparents? Collin couldn't let
that happen. And Alice seemed to be noticing his lack of reaction,
which was draining all the contentment out of her face. He felt
pinned. He wasn't ready to see Paige. The shame of what she'd
seen from him over the years—the partying, the stupid adolescent
stunts, the ways he'd disappointed her over the years with the failed
engagements—felt like a stone weight on his chest, drowning him in
regret. And to have Alice see him going through this, how he wasn't
able to tell Paige to just *leave*... He wasn't fighting. He wasn't flying.
He was frozen, and it was humiliating.

"Did your assistant twist her ankle?" Paige asked, frowning
at Alice. "That would be the only reasonable explanation I could
fathom for you carrying her around."

Alice's chin retreated back at the insult, and Collin couldn't
blame her. This wasn't a good start to an introduction. He knew
there was a good heart under all of Paige's posturing, but she wasn't
really helping him in terms of convincing Alice she was a benevolent
nonentity from his past.

"This isn't my assistant," he told Paige. "This is Alice Seastairs.
She runs an antique shop here on the island."

Like her mother before her, Paige had mastered the art of bend-
ing her facial features into a facsimile of a smile without expressing

any actual warmth or approval. "How quaint. Did you injure your ankle moving furniture?"

Alice stared at Paige as if she didn't understand the language she was speaking. So, of course, Paige repeated herself, louder and more slowly. "Did. You. Hurt. Your. Ankle?"

"Why are you talking to her like that?" Collin asked, letting his annoyance show in his tone. He cleared his throat.

"Well, I can't imagine what other reason you might have for carrying your assistant up the front walk of your family home," Paige said, still smiling, but not.

"She's not my assistant. Her name is Alice. I wish you would have called," Collin said, stepping away from Paige.

"I did call," Paige reminded him. "And I'd like to have this conversation away from...whoever this is."

"Alice Seastairs. I've told you three times now," Collin told her again. "Alice, would you please go inside so I can talk to Paige for a moment?"

"Why don't you just send her away and *we* can talk inside?" Paige demanded, slipping her hands around his arm.

"No," Collin told her, shrugging her off.

Paige's lip curled back as her eyes narrowed at Alice. "Why not?"

Shit. Shit. Shitshitshitshit.

"Renovations," Collin blurted out. "We're having the manor house and the hotel renovated. Everything's a mess. Where are you planning to stay?"

Alice's eyebrow rose and she got a decidedly Mina-ish expression on her face. He deserved that.

"With you, of course," Paige cried. "Why would I stay anywhere else?"

"Because I didn't invite you," Collin reminded her.

Paige's nostrils flared just the tiniest bit, making Collin's stomach drop. That was what had happened right before the flight attendant was fired. Mid-flight.

"Be careful, Collin," she warned him, glancing at Alice. "You wouldn't want to make me feel unwelcome."

"How did you even get here?" Collin asked.

"I chartered a boat," Paige told him. "And then I sent it back, because I assumed that you would have accommodations waiting for me."

"That doesn't mean you just—" He sighed. "Look, I can put you up in the hotel's guesthouse for a night or two."

"Guesthouse!" Paige exclaimed just as Alice asked, "A night or *two*?"

Apparently, she'd been pushed to her limit and found her voice.

"Don't be silly," Paige insisted. "I'll just stay with you. If you're comfortable in the manor house, I'll be comfortable here too."

"No," Collin said. "That won't work for me. Give me a minute, and I'll show you where you can stay."

Collin reached out to Alice and opened the door for her. Paige frowned after him, but she seemed so shocked by the fact that he'd told her no, she stayed rooted to the spot. He hurried Alice through the door. She opened her mouth to speak and stopped, and opened her mouth again, only to close it again. Then she nodded toward his ex. "That's Paige? She is...exactly what I expected."

"Alice, I know this is not a good time," Collin started.

"Is there a good time for your ex-fiancée—who seems to think she might still be your fiancée—to show up unannounced?" she asked. "And you're going to let her stay in the guesthouse? Please tell me you'll at least put her in a different room than the one I was in."

"Well, I don't want her staying in the manor house with us," he said. "Trust me when I say this is the best option."

"You could put her on a boat and send her back across the lake," Alice noted.

"At night?" Collin threw his hands at the darkened window. "I may not want her in my house, but I don't want her dead in a boating accident."

Alice winced at that. "OK, that's a good point, I suppose. I think I'm going to just go upstairs and grab my stuff. I can stay with Caroline or Riley or...something. I'll figure it out. I have options. It was just that before, you offered, and I wanted to be close to you."

"And I want you close," he insisted. "I don't want you to leave. Look, I know this is awkward—"

"No, no, having you witness my grandparents melting down and talking to me like they only do in private? That was awkward. This is... I don't know what this is, but I'm not staying anywhere near that woman. She gives me the creeps. I don't like how she talks to you. I don't like how she looks at you. I really don't like how she looks at me. And I've stared down howling dead people," Alice said.

"She's just known me forever," Collin assured her. "It gives her a certain air of forceful intimacy."

It sounded so pathetic, even as the words came out of his mouth. He didn't know how to feel about Paige being there. He felt a loyalty to her. He couldn't just send her out into the waters of Lake Huron in the dark without another thought. But he didn't want her around. How did he explain it to Alice, the complex emotional knots he'd tied himself into with this woman?

Alice frowned. "From what you've told me, I'm assuming she acts like she's carrying around a little notebook with all your mistakes in it, so she can wave them in front of your face, just in case you forget. Trust me, I know the type."

"It's not that bad," he insisted.

She arched her coppery brows.

"OK, it's not great. It takes some negotiating. You have to give her a little bit of what she wants so she feels like she's won, and then she doesn't get an attendant fired in the middle of a flight to Japan!" Collin said.

"That's not how negotiating works!" Alice cried.

"I know, I just— Don't go anywhere," he told her, backing out the door before Paige decided to come through the front door. "I want to talk when I get back. There are things I need to say. But I'm just too...flapped right now."

Collin rushed out of the manor house before she could answer. Paige was *not happy* to be escorted to the guesthouse, given the way she kept telling him to just take her back to the manor house, insisting that she didn't mind a little construction dust.

"What is this place?" Paige demanded as he unlocked the front door. "Why haven't you told me about it before?"

She sounded offended that there were Bancroft family secrets she wasn't privy to, like the family didn't have the right to them. Like she was *more* than that family, now that they were mostly gone.

"It's a space that's available to special guests. If you need anything, I can get it for you in the morning," Collin told her.

He was almost to the door when he heard her say, "We need to talk."

"About what?" Collin asked.

"Collin." She sighed, pouting and pulling at his jacket. "It's time. Our families expect us to get married. They expected us to get married *years* ago. We've put them off for long enough. I was just talking to Lawrence and Cynthia the other day, and they were telling me how concerned they are about you out here all alone. They think you've taken on too much, and you know what happens when you feel overwhelmed. I would just hate for you to damage your family legacy with your self-destructive tendencies."

He swallowed heavily. She would bring that up. The drunken scenes. The stupid stunts. The time he got arrested for taking a cow into a bespoke tailor shop in Mallorca, because he thought it needed a dinner jacket. It made sense at the time. Alice said she didn't care about his checkered past—not even when the Jet Ski story came up—but Paige would lay it all out for her, in far more unflattering detail than a Google search would accomplish.

"I think you should just forget about running the hotel and come back to the city," Paige said. "Just sign the hotel over to Lawrence and Cynthia. They need a project. Why not just let them take their rightful place and you can find something else you want to do?"

"This is what I want to do," Collin told her hoarsely.

"You're only saying that because of some childhood dream," she insisted. "You think you're honoring your family's memory, or something. But this isn't going to bring your parents back. You need to just let this go."

"Let go of the same family you're sure would want me to marry you?" Collin asked.

"Yes, because *I'm* good for you, Collin. You need me to guide you. Look at what you do when I'm not around," Paige told him.

She gestured to the guesthouse, like it was wrong, something to be ashamed of.

"Stop," he said softly.

"And what was that ridiculous *scene* in front of your assistant?" she demanded. "Just another sign that you're well on the way to another catastrophe. It's only a matter of time."

"She's not my—what does Alice have to do with anything?" Collin asked.

"Why is *she* still at your house? Why does *she* get to go inside this construction war zone, when I don't?" Paige demanded.

"She's an antiques expert. She's helping me pick out appropriate pieces for the house," Collin said.

She rolled her eyes. "At ten o'clock at night?"

"Our meeting ran late." Why was he making excuses? He didn't owe her an explanation. How did she always do this to him? Stupefy him with embarrassment and regret and head games.

"Paige, you and I aren't together anymore. You don't have the right to show up here and act like we're still a couple," Collin said.

"I don't have the *right*? After giving you years of my life, I don't have the *right* to have a simple conversation with you?" she hissed. "A conversation, let me remind you, that we could've had by phone had you bothered to pick up more than once."

"Forgive me, that came out wrong," he insisted. "Listen, there are things we need to talk about, but I really don't have the time or the energy right now. We'll talk in the morning, OK? And then we'll charter a boat to take you back to the mainland."

"The mainland?" she scoffed. "Is that really what you call it? Like this is a real island?"

"It's a landmass surrounded by water," he noted.

She gave a dismissive roll of her eyes. "But it's hardly Saint Barts, is it?"

"I'll see you in the morning," he told her, closing the door behind him with a decisive slam. He'd hoped Alice would be there when he walked inside the manor house. But she was gone, having left a little note that said, "Shaddow House." No "dear" and no signature, just those two words.

Meaning she'd walked alone back to Shaddow House, in the dark, with a murderous ghost pet on the loose, rather than stay with Collin.

Shiiiiiit.

Collin did not sleep well, even after Alice very thoughtfully texted him that she'd arrived safely at Shaddow House, with an additional confirmation text from Riley. Because, as Riley noted, In the unlikely event Margaret managed to kidnap Alice, she probably wouldn't be able to get both of our phones to fake a text.

How had Collin's life gotten to the point that this all seemed reasonable?

And while grateful for the peace of mind, Collin was not cheered by Alice's text responses when he informed her that Paige was secured at the guesthouse. She'd texted, K. Not even an *OK*, but a *K*.

That was bad. Alice hadn't even participated in the text chain where Riley begrudgingly caught him up on the events of the evening before. Collin had to pretend that everything was normal. That he and every person in Alice's coven weren't under some sort of supernatural threat from a menacing grandma, lurking somewhere on the island. Then there was putting on a show of appropriate mourning for a "beloved" local like Clark, even if Collin was relieved that threat was removed from Alice's life. And damned if Collin didn't have a videoconference scheduled with his marketing team for the spring relaunch first thing this morning. It was the sort of meeting that a responsible adult would not skip because his sort-of girlfriend was mad at him.

Of course, said sort-of girlfriend's coven didn't know about the videoconference, so they felt free to interrupt it by walking in en masse, Julie at their heels.

"I tried to explain about the meeting. But...um, the teenager scares me?" Julie told him before dashing back out the door.

"It's fine. We were wrapping up anyway," Collin said, waving to his New York team before they signed off. He closed the video program and his laptop with a decisive snap. He did not want to accidentally leave a video window open and expose his marketing gurus to ghost talk.

Also, Alice was not with the group. He did not want to think about what that meant.

"What did I do?" Mina asked, watching as Julie booked it down the hall. Josh shrugged.

"I told you, all adults are afraid that teenage girls will figure out their secret fears and weaknesses, then exploit them," Caroline explained.

Mina replied, "Well, yeah, but we have to have a reason to deploy our primary weapon. We don't just go around mocking people willy-nilly."

"That has not been my experience," Josh told her.

"All right, all right." Riley huffed. "Hi, Collin. We come bearing not gifts, but protective...items."

There was a businesslike briskness to her tone, like she was there to conduct an audit, not pull a box full of really weird holiday decorations out of her bag.

"Are those glass Christmas ornaments...filled with salt?" he asked.

"And herbs," Riley told him. "Think of them as ghost hand grenades. You have to throw them at the ground close to that awful Chester thing. The Denton journals are really unhelpful regarding what sort of magic Margaret might have used to put him together. I guess because it's unprecedented magic, which is terrifying."

"I'm still having a hard time wrapping my head around the Story Time lady being an evil sorceress," Collin said, shaking his head. "I remember her big purple Mother Goose hat from when I was a kid."

"I don't know if I would call her a *sorceress*," Josh said. "More of an evil fairy-tale poisoned-candy-house vibe—"

"Josh," Mina said, shushing her brother. "We agreed, no friendly chat with Collin."

"We don't know that he did anything wrong," Josh insisted

quietly, as if Collin couldn't hear them. "Bro code dictates that I give Collin the benefit of the doubt, even if I want to staple his stupid tie to his desk for upsetting Alice."

"Wait, wait, is Alice OK?" Collin asked. "She wasn't in a *great* mood when I saw her last, but…"

He'd never had four people with magical powers glare at him simultaneously. It wasn't an experience he wanted to repeat.

At his left, his desk phone rang.

"She says she's OK, which we all know is bullshit, because that's what she said when Clark and her grandparents were—" Riley shook her head and didn't finish the thought. "No, she's not OK."

"And that's on you," Caroline told him as the phone continued to ring.

"Oh, we're just going there?" Josh said, glancing between the others. "I thought we—all right. Women change conversational lanes quickly. No, dude, she's not OK! She's upset and hurt!"

"She's pretending she's OK," Mina told him. "She's acting like everything is normal and we don't have a ghost-wielding grandma out to get us or that her boyfriend isn't wearing his own ass as a hat."

"Easy," Riley warned him.

"Thank you," Collin replied.

Riley shrugged. "Collin wouldn't wear his ass as a hat. A fancy ascot sort of thing, maybe."

Collin was lost. Were they using magic on him right now? Some sort of confusion spell? He picked up the phone and answered rudely, "What?"

"I'll try not to be offended by the greeting, since you're clearly under duress," Julie said through the receiver. "I'm sorry to interrupt, but Lori from housekeeping has a question."

"Can't you take care of it?" Collin asked. "I'm a little busy at the moment."

"I really think it's something you're going to want to weigh in on," Julie replied.

"Julie, I trust your judgment. You're a pro. You know this hotel better than anybody. Whatever you and Lori think is appropriate," Collin told her. "You've got this."

He hung up and Caroline immediately asked, "Did you really let your ex stay in the guesthouse? After you told Alice that she's a destructive and manipulative influence in your life?"

"I don't think that's how I phrased it, exactly," Collin protested.

"The ex you've proposed to multiple times?" Riley added. "Giving her the impression that you might panic and propose at any given moment?"

"Well, it was *technically* multiple times, yeah, but—" Collin said.

"Trust me, don't 'yeah, but' them," Josh told Collin, shaking his head. "They don't like it."

"Paige just showed up in the middle of the night!" Collin exclaimed. "With no way of getting her back off the island. What was I supposed to do, build her a boat out of cardboard and wish her the best?"

"Find some other place for her to stay?" Caroline suggested.

"Tell her to figure it out for herself, since she put herself in the situation?" Riley countered.

"You're stupid rich!" Josh exclaimed. "Summon your helicopter or hovercraft or whatever, and tell her it's a one-way ride." Josh glanced at Mina. "Nothing to add?"

Mina shook her head. "No, that was a good one. That's our new suggestion. Collin, summon your hovercraft and export the source of Alice's hurt from the island."

"It's complicated with Paige," Collin said, making all three ladies in the room cringe. "I know, I know how that sounds!"

"What?" Josh asked.

Caroline turned to the boy who was her stepson in all but legal papers, and reached up to cradle his face. "I want you to promise me, when you get older and you are a bright, beautiful man capable of epic affection, you will never utter the words, 'It's complicated' unless it's in reference to the inner workings of a hadron collider."

"Or international politics," Riley added.

"Or how Caroline's brothers manage to burn coffee *every time* they make it," Mina groaned.

"It's not complicated," Riley told Collin. "It's just difficult. You and Paige have a lot of history and hurt. Telling her that you've moved on is going to suck. And you don't want to do it because she is most likely going to have a negative reaction, and that makes you feel like the bad guy. Nobody likes feeling like the bad guy."

"You don't—" Collin began and then pursed his lips. "That is fair."

"And I'm sorry, but we don't have time for you to procrastinate over having awkward conversations with your ex. We have a crazed ghost-hamster-wielding grandma to contend with," Caroline said.

"So, in the nicest of terms available," Mina said, "figure your shit out."

"That was the nicest of terms?" Collin asked dryly.

All four answered, "Yes." In unison. It was unnerving.

Chapter 12
Alice

PAIGE LAGRAVENESSE WAS THE STUFF of teenage nightmares: flawless, pearlescent cream skin that seemed illuminated by some invisible lighting director assigned by a cruel universe; smooth, bobbed black hair that probably never frizzed; wide blue eyes lined by naturally sooty lashes granted by that same hateful universe. And everything in her wardrobe seemed to have been assembled by fairies, the mean-spirited kind who made poisonous spinning wheels.

And she was staying in the guesthouse, just a few hundred yards away from Collin's front door. Alice was fully aware that proximity wasn't the real problem here. Paige wasn't even the problem, really. The problem was Collin's seeming inability to make declarative statements to Paige. Why was he being so wishy-washy? Did he still have feelings for Paige? Even if he didn't, was this something Alice was willing to put up with long term? The Ghosts of Possessive and Intimidating Girlfriends Past?

She had enough ghosts in her life...like the ceiling ghost, who appeared to be trying to hide in the far corner of the foyer, watching her as she read.

Ew.

But considering that the ghost wasn't doing anything but watching, she didn't want to try to confront it alone. If it moved any closer, however, she had several of Riley's ornaments sitting next to her mug of chamomile tea.

Every once in a while, Alice would get a glimpse of Victoria and Samuel dancing through the atrium or chasing each other like children, laughing. They never materialized for very long around the ceiling ghost's unnerving presence, not that Alice blamed them. Still, it was nice, seeing Victoria happily reunited with the man she loved, getting the freedom to love him openly in the unrestrained, joyous way of young people. Collin said he saw his own situation reflected in Victoria's unhappy engagement. Maybe that was why he was behaving so oddly about Paige?

"Would you like me to speak to Mr. Bancroft, Miss Alice?" Plover asked, tugging Alice's attention away from a book on protective magic. She was curled up on her favorite chaise, near Eloise's fountain under the pale light of the atrium windows. Riley was betting on the Christmas-ornament plan, but she thought they could use silver to boost it against…whatever Chester was. Alice knew the coven hadn't really gone out to "grocery shop"—they'd been far too agreeable about Alice lingering in the house to safeguard it. She knew they were going to Collin's, probably to threaten him, but honestly, she couldn't stop them from doing that if they wanted. And if Collin couldn't handle a tiny little threat from her coven, he wasn't going to last in her life long enough for her to worry about Paige anyway.

If she had been in love with Collin, she would have taken

Caroline up on her offer to force-feed Alice ice cream and watch movies about women who find their power or new love or set fire to things—sometimes all at once. And apparently, there would be cocktails involved. Caroline insisted it was a "friendship imperative."

Alice wasn't in love with Collin, but she'd developed feelings for him. She was teetering on the edge of love, but something had told her to stop and slow down; she felt like she couldn't trust someone who seemed to give affection and acceptance so easily. Obviously, this was it. Collin came with baggage well beyond Alice's angry grandparents and last romantic entanglement. Because his baggage was *current*.

"Miss Alice," Plover said again. "Would you like me to speak to Collin?"

"Wouldn't that require me dragging him into the house?" Alice asked.

"I believe Joshua and Miss Mina would aid in the effort," Plover noted, arching his brow.

"I don't know. I'm not mad, I'm hurt. He put her first. He thought about her feelings and her comfort before he thought about me. Because it was easier or more convenient or—whatever. I've had too much of that in my life," Alice said. "I want someone who will put me first, think about me and what I need before calculating how giving me what I need will weigh against everybody else's needs. Is that unreasonable?"

"I don't know," Plover admitted. "I've never been through a 'breakup' before. I'm not even sure that's what this is or how to help you through it."

"You're doing great," she assured him. "But honestly, I think worrying about our ghost issues would be a nice change from worrying about whatever I have going on with Collin."

Plover demurred. "Of course, Miss. But if I may…"

"Yes?" She turned toward a firm knock at the front door. As she moved, Alice's eyes landed on the folly through the atrium glass.

"I've watched enough living relationships to know when a man regrets the loss of a woman and when he simply regrets her. I don't believe he regrets the loss of this former friend of his. Not from the way he looks at you. As much as it pains me to admit it, he is quite smitten with you. No one else holds his heart."

She stood and walked to the door, salt-filled ornament in hand. And as much as Alice appreciated this fatherly advice, something Mina said when they were digging outside the folly was sticking in Alice's mind. *What if Stanford hadn't been digging?*

The ceiling ghost seemed to note her movement and slithered away toward the dining room. That suited Alice just fine.

Finding her grandparents standing on the other side of the door, staring at it as if they could open it through the sheer force of their angry stares? That, she hadn't been prepared for.

Franklin and Marilyn were looking a little worse for wear—with dark circles under their eyes and dust smudges on their normally immaculate clothes. Apparently, running their own store, even during the glacially slow season, did not agree with them. They were missing their sunny Florida climes and the ease of having someone else do all the work.

"Oh, what the hell!" she huffed. "What are you doing here?"

"Such a short time away from the home we graciously provided for you, and you've already taken on the manners of a fishwife," Marilyn Proctor drawled.

"Oh, yes, you can tell I'm really roughing it," Alice said, closing the door quickly behind her so they couldn't get a look inside Shaddow House—for no other reason than that she knew it would annoy them.

"Honestly, Alice, this is shameful," Marilyn told her. "Have some pride in the name we've given you. I know that you're not particularly well regarded for your judgment, but this is beyond the pale. Just admit that you've made a mistake and—"

As if summoned by magic, the rest of her coven trooped up the walk, grocery bags in hand. Hmm, maybe they had gone grocery shopping.

"Mr. and Mrs. Proctor?" Riley said, smiling with a cold civility that sent a shiver down Alice's spine. She'd only seen that smile around Clark...and Edison's mom.

"Yes, hello, Miss Denton. We'd like to speak to Alice. May we come in?" Marilyn asked.

"No," Riley told her cheerfully. "You're not welcome in the house. You can speak to Alice when she's ready, out on the porch."

Marilyn laid a hand across her collarbone. "How rude."

Riley smiled sweetly as she opened the front door. She also kept it mostly closed so the Proctors couldn't see inside. "No, rude would be telling you to fuck off directly into the lake. This is just mildly discourteous."

Franklin gasped. "Now, see here, young lady!"

Plover pressed his transparent face against the barely open door to grumble, "I am sorely tempted to appear to both of them so I might also request they 'fuck off directly into the lake,' but I would not put additional pressure on you, Miss Alice, giving them knowledge of the afterlife."

Alice nodded, trying very hard not to laugh. This whole scene was worth it just to hear Plover say "fuck."

"It's no wonder that Nora's niece turned out to be so crass. The whole family has gone rotten over the years," Franklin intoned, sounding very put upon. "Speaking of which."

He turned his attention to Alice. "We understand your 'dalliance' with Collin Bancroft is at an end. You were seen slinking across the island last night, dragging your suitcase behind you. And while we're not surprised, we're not here to tell you, 'I told you so.'"

"Telling someone you're not going to say 'I told you so' still counts as 'I told you so,'" Alice observed.

"We're willing to accept your apology, if you offer it—sincerely—right now," Marilyn told her.

"Apologize?" Alice laughed loudly, with just enough of an edge to make them both take a step back. Good.

"Yes, are you so stupid that you don't understand the meaning of the word 'apology'?" Marilyn demanded.

Over their shoulders, she saw Caroline rolling her eyes and making...frankly, a truly obscene gesture that she probably shouldn't be making in front of the kids. And somehow, the profane, irreverent hilarity of it disrupted Alice's thought cycle enough for her to examine Marilyn's words carefully.

Alice Seastairs wasn't stupid. That was a ridiculous statement. People on the island didn't think she was stupid. People came to her with questions about their antiques. They came to her with history questions. They asked her for book recommendations in the library's nonfiction section.

People trusted her word.

It was like a needle, poking a hole in their ridiculous rants, even if it was only in Alice's head. Her grandparents had lived in an echo chamber for so long, isolated from the rest of Starfall Point, bouncing their opinions off only each other—on how things were on the island, who Alice was, how they were perceived by the locals. And with no one around to tell the Proctors they were wrong, their opinions became cemented in their own minds. But just because they believed it to be true, didn't mean it was so.

And the thought was so ridiculous, it made Alice giggle. She clapped a hand over her mouth and it turned into a snort. Apparently, that was too much for Marilyn.

"If you don't come back to work for us in the *family* shop, where you belong, we will never forgive you," she announced in a shrill tone that had Josh wincing.

"You seem to have mistaken me for someone who gives a fuck," Alice shot back. And while the words felt alien and "too big" coming out of her mouth, she knew she needed to say them. Well, maybe not those *exact* words, but she wasn't going to let her grandparents silence her anymore. The days of timid, long-suffering Alice were over.

"I cannot believe you are speaking to us this way, after all we've done for you," Franklin told her.

Alice moved closer to her coven, the warmth of them, the power humming along her nerves. "Right. You raised me, the child of your own daughter. Congratulations. Do you want a medal? A cookie?"

"We could have left you to the system," Marilyn hissed.

At that, Riley put her hand on Alice's shoulder, while Alice replied, "Yeah, and I can see how that could have been awful, living in foster care. But I also would have had some chance of being raised by nice, caring non-assholes, in comparison to the one hundred percent certainty of assholes I encountered with you."

Speaking to them like this, it felt like poison was being released from her bloodstream. It was a warm flush that hurt, but it needed to be purged from her. Her grandmother didn't seem to appreciate this.

"How dare you! Do you know how much we *invested* in raising you?" Marilyn demanded.

Alice cried, "Well, why don't you do me a favor? Come up with a list of expenses from across the years, write it all in your little ledger, roll it up, and shove it up your tightly clenched ass."

Riley watched as Alice made several extremely descriptive hand gestures of her own, communicating her instructions. She snickered. "Dang."

"I'd always wondered what it would look like when Alice finally tapped into all the repressed rage," Caroline muttered, nodding. "This is pretty much what I pictured."

Marilyn's face went paper-white as she struggled to find a response. "Alice, we at least raised you not to speak that way in front of *children*."

"The *children* agree with her. Shove it up your ass, lady," Mina told her.

"Mina," Caroline said, smothering a laugh.

"What? She sucks," Mina insisted.

Josh nodded. "Mina and I have been trained by life to recognize sucky adults. Trust me, they both suck."

"Young lady," Mr. Proctor barked. "Remove yourself from the premises. I have no patience for children like you, you poorly raised hooligan."

Caroline turned on him. "Oh, zip it, Frank, you do suck. And don't talk to my kid that way."

"You're her mother?" He sniffed derisively. "Little wonder."

"Oh, OK, now you're getting hurt," Mina said, rolling up her sweater sleeves as she stalked toward him.

Caroline caught her around the waist. "No, no. You're reaching the age when you can be charged as an adult."

"You're right. I'll wait until there are no witnesses," Mina seethed.

"That was not at all the point I was trying to communicate to you," Caroline told her, hugging her tight. "But thank you."

"I really hate that the first time you've referred to me as your kid is in relation to that dipshit," Mina told her.

Caroline hugged Mina and Josh close as Franklin gasped in indignation. Caroline ignored him, patting Mina's back while saying, "I know. Me too."

"I'm asking you politely to remove yourself from *my premises*," Riley told the Proctors. "Because you don't have the right to tell anyone here to leave. Alice is welcome to stay here as long as she likes. I am not humoring her."

"Alice, for the last time, come back to the shop," Marilyn told her. "At this point, we won't hold a grudge. But after this, there will be no coming back."

Alice stared at them, long and hard.

No more of this. No more placating people who never bothered protecting her. No more being afraid.

"Fuck off," Alice told them. "Into the lake."

She had to pretend that she didn't hear Plover cheering for her as she walked back into Shaddow House.

Distraction was just what Alice needed to keep her from interrogating the others about what they told Collin during the "grocery trip." They didn't offer information, and she figured it was better not to ask, which was how she found herself outside at dusk while everybody else was inside making dinner. She was crouched by the folly's base, thinking about what Mina said.

What if Stanford hadn't been digging?

All the stones at the base of the folly looked the same except one of them, at the farthest corner of the house. It was cold, which was normal in Michigan at this time of year, but this was a different kind of cold. Angry cold, the sort of bitterness you could feel through the skin.

She picked up a rock from the flowerbed border and gently knocked it against the stones. They all sounded the same, *plink plink plink* over and over, except for the rock that was colder than the others. It was deeper, more open. *Plonk plonk plonk.*

Oh, dear.

Alice stood, ready to run back inside and alert the others, only to find Paige standing behind her in that stupid luxurious winter coat. "*Gah!*"

They really needed to find a way to ward the property against the living.

"What are you *doing?*" Paige asked. Alice began to construct a lie about nighttime gardening as an island pastime, but Paige interrupted her. "Never mind, I don't care."

Alice stared at her, silent.

"Well?" Paige threw up her hands.

"I assumed you were about to say something condescending and terrible, so I might as well wait," Alice replied.

"Everybody on this stupid little island thinks they're so clever," Paige sighed, sounding bored. "Just like you all think you know Collin *so well.*"

Alice shook her head. "No, actually, we only met recently."

Paige frowned. "I thought you grew up on the island."

Alice didn't explain herself because she didn't want to. Sphinxlike silence seemed to be the only appropriate reward for this…well, bullshit. Everything Paige was saying was bullshit. And Alice had been handling bullshit for years. She'd dealt with customers like Paige before—bored and frustrated and looking for some joy in life, and bewildered when they couldn't find it.

"You know he doesn't belong here, right?" Paige finally said. "He could literally live anywhere. Work anywhere. He doesn't even *have to work.* He only does it because he thinks it makes him a better person."

Alice nodded. "OK."

Frustrated by her lack of reaction, Paige doubled down. "So, you can see why I don't want him wasting his life here in this backwater, wasting himself on the people here. People like you, who don't understand him, who don't know what sort of person he is, what he needs."

Alice stared at Paige, long and hard. "Look, Peyton."

"Paige."

"Whatever," Alice said, returning the same sickly smile that Paige had given to her. "You're not going to come between me and Collin by trying to make me feel like I'm not good enough for him. I don't think I'm good enough for him. But I also don't think *you're* good enough for him. That's the difference between us. Well, one of them. I also think you're shallow and patronizing—two more traits we don't share."

"It doesn't matter," Paige snapped. "I'm what his family wanted for him. And he's always going to go back to that starting point because he doesn't know what else to do. Why do you think he keeps coming back to me? Because he knows it's inevitable. He may fight it, but he knows how this story ends. He's disappointed his family in a lot of ways, but he won't leave this undone."

Alice took a deep breath, even as her hand itched to respond with magic or a good smack or *something* that Paige deeply deserved. "It's truly offensive, the way you oversimplify him. You're not doing either of you any credit."

"Then why do I have this?" Paige asked, pulling out her phone. She showed Alice the screen, which featured a photo of Paige's immaculately manicured hand wearing a sizable diamond—*the* diamond engagement ring from Collin's parents' photo. Paige was wearing his mother's ring.

"He's having it sized, of course," Paige said, her tone confidential. "His mother's fingers were a little bigger than mine, so I couldn't just wear it around the island. I wouldn't want to lose it, after he trusted me with such a valuable family heirloom."

And while Alice's first instinct was to despair, to picture Collin proposing to this woman, she knew... Collin had told her the ring wasn't Paige's style. He was reluctant to give it to her years before, so he'd bought her a big flashy ring for that last attempt. He'd told Alice he pictured himself resetting the stones for his future wife.

Fresh start, fresh stories.

Collin wasn't engaged to this woman, no matter what Paige said, but the real problem was the background of the photo. Yes, Paige's hand was the perfect model for an absolutely gorgeous heirloom ring. And behind it, barely in focus, was the tub in the Cowslip Suite, filled with bubbles.

"Where were you when this photo was taken?" Alice asked, careful to keep her tone indifferent.

"Oh, I don't know," Paige huffed, sounding bored, despite the catlike smile spreading on her lips. "One of the new suites upstairs at the hotel. Collin moved me there earlier today. It took a little fussing from the housekeeping staff, but he knows how I like things."

"You're staying in the Cowslip Suite?" Alice asked.

Paige rolled her eyes. "Yes, of course. I couldn't stay in that ridiculous grubby guesthouse. He had perfectly good suites right there. Why would I stay in some dinky little room? I wouldn't stand for it. I'm his fiancée, after all."

Alice focused on breathing steadily through her nose, not letting her hurt show. And still, Paige was talking.

"For a second-rate hotel, it's not a terrible room," she admitted, sounding sincere. "Honestly, I was surprised. Particularly in the en suite. I took a little swim in the tub this morning to wash the ick of that moldy guest room off me."

"Y-you used the tub?" Alice asked.

"It's the only thing that makes the suite remotely interesting," Paige drawled. "Normally, I don't go in for that sort of drama, but it has a certain quaint charm."

Alice was boiling inside, even while she tried to keep her face still. The ring story? That wasn't Collin's fault. Paige was clearly lying, trying to get to her. But this? He'd let her into the Cowslip Suite, *their* suite? Alice hadn't even seen it all put together yet with bedding and the special antiques she'd selected, and Paige had already taken a swim in *her* fucking tub? The tub of her dreams? Collin knew how much that tub meant to her. He'd heard her wax poetic about it, and he knew Alice didn't wax poetic about much. He'd taken something that was special to Alice and handed it to Paige as if it was nothing, an afterthought. She might be his employee, but this made her *feel* like she didn't matter. He made something Alice loved feel less valuable by treating it like it was nothing. Would he have even told her about Paige's "occupancy"? Or would he have pretended that it never happened and let Alice think she was the first to use the tub?

Hell, she might be less mad if he *was* engaged to Paige.

Later, she was going to take Caroline up on that offer of a non-stop, all-you-can-eat ice cream buffet. But for right now, she was going to escape this situation with a little dignity.

"I don't believe that you're engaged, because Collin would never give you his mother's ring," she told Paige. "He knows you wouldn't appreciate it, so I suggest that if you still have it, you put it back where you found it before I call the cops and you spend a couple of nights in our little one-cell jail."

"Who are you to tell me what I'm going to do with what's mine?" Paige seethed, grabbing Alice's arm. For a moment, Alice considered using the same sort of magic on Paige that had repelled Clark. She could feel her magic simmering under the surface of her skin, waiting to erupt. With the rage bubbling inside her, she could probably make every wall sconce on this floor explode. But as satisfying as that might be, she wouldn't expose her coven to that sort of danger. Wantonly harming a person—or light fixtures—had to be against some sort of magical law. So instead, using strength born of moving furniture around for a living, she peeled Paige's fingers from her sleeve, one by one.

"I'm Alice Seastairs. And I'm tired of your bullshit," she told her, walking around the house to the porch. As she walked up the steps, she called, "Also, your quote-unquote 'Cartier' bracelet's a fake. Cartier doesn't work in gold plate."

Hours later, the coven stood at the base of the folly with Caroline and Edison. Holding pickaxes. In the dark.

Alice wanted to yell at Collin. She wanted to rage at the thoughtlessness, the deception. But honestly, she had more important things to worry about than tub-based infidelity. And it was probably a good thing to stay away from Collin at this moment when she was holding a pickaxe.

"Honey, you know I offered anything you needed to process

your Collin feelings, but you reached the angry, destructive phase really quickly," Riley told her.

"Alice, I don't know if it's the best idea for us to be standing out here in the open like this, even if we are well armed," Caroline said, nodding at the pickaxes Alice had found in Ben's garden shed. "I don't like that Margaret hasn't been seen on the island since Clark's death. She told her son Jeff that she had a medical appointment in Charlevoix, but that seems unlikely. It just seems weird for her to be so quiet after she's threatened us so effectively."

"I'm still reeling from the whole thing," Edison admitted as Riley kissed his cheek. "I knew it was possible that the Welling heir was someone we knew on the island, but Margaret? It just...hurts, knowing that she could have used me as an avenue to hurt you. Who knows what bit of information she picked up from me that she used against you? It's insidious!"

"I know how that feels, Edison," Alice told him, patting his shoulder.

Edison nodded. "Although, now that I think about it, she did seem to take her authority as head library volunteer far too seriously."

"And look, this isn't about Collin," Alice told Riley. "Well, not entirely about Collin. I've been thinking about something Mina said. What if Stanford wasn't *digging* at the base of the folly? Plover said the folly was added around 1900. Maybe Stanford was putting something *in* the folly during its construction. What's inside?"

"As far as I know, it's a spiral staircase that flows upward into the ceiling," Riley told them. "The journals haven't been super helpful."

"That tracks," Caroline said. "How would we even get inside? There's no door."

"No, there is not," Riley agreed. "But I do hear rattling from behind the bricks, sort of like when I found the first lock behind the wall. But that was more of a cold, emanating energy thing—like a magical conversation I couldn't get out of fast enough."

"So we make a door," Alice suggested, brandishing the pickaxe.

"I don't know how I feel about this," Riley said. "That seems a little more serious than the average renovation. It sort of feels like we're attacking the house."

Alice paused and nodded. "Also, I'm kind of getting the feeling that this thing, which is most likely a lock, is really, really excited about the possibility of us letting it out. And when scary things get excited, it's time to take a step back and maybe reexamine our plan."

"Yeah, what if the house protects itself and retaliates?" Caroline asked. "We've never done anything that could be seen as acting directly against it before."

"That is…not an unreasonable concern," Alice admitted.

"Do we have dynamite?" Caroline asked.

"Right, because there's no way *that* could go wrong." Edison snorted. When he caught the contemplative look on Riley's face, he barked, "No dynamite! I should not have to explain to you the many ways that would put you in danger!"

"Fine," Riley sighed. "But I should do it. Maybe the house wouldn't take it so personally if it's from me." Riley picked up the pickaxe. "You guys stand back."

Riley swung the axe and the point struck between two stones, pulverizing the mortar between them. She paused, as if she was waiting for something to blow up or hit her in the face. When Shaddow House didn't smack her back, she swung the pickaxe again and again. The others joined in, careful not to hit each other as they broke the folly open like a stubborn egg. Dust burped from the gaping wound in the tower wall, making them cough and collectively wave hands in front of their faces. The air felt colder somehow, and at the window, the ceiling ghost hurled itself at the glass, angrily shaking it.

"Well, that can't be good," Riley observed.

"Should we reach inside?" Alice asked.

"Not that I'm trying to guilt you guys when we're choosing volunteers to reach into the mystery hole," Caroline told them. "But I just want to point out I took one for the team when I got repeatedly possessed earlier this year."

"Technically, we all got possessed," Alice reminded her.

"Eh," Caroline said, waggling her hand. "It was more satellite possession for you two."

"I'll do it," Riley sighed. "My house, my ghosts, my hand risk."

She crouched, putting her face near the opening. She clicked on her flashlight. "Please don't be another evil hamster thing."

Alice winced as Riley extended her entire upper body into the mystery hole. She wriggled around, clearly searching the floor of the tower.

"It is indeed a plain old metal spiral staircase...going directly into the ceiling," Riley said, her voice muffled. "That is consistent with the rest of the house."

Alice was poised, ready to drag Riley out of the tower by her feet if necessary. Suddenly, this all seemed like a terrible plan. Her friend could be bisected at the waist because Alice got a feeling about a mystery hole.

"And there is nothing on the floor," Riley added.

Alice took a step back. The brick that had felt cold to her was just a few stones away from Riley's opening. "Hey, Riley, you see anything to your left?"

Riley's lower half turned on its side. "Um, yeah. One of the bricks looks different than the others. Can you hand me the pickaxe?"

"You're going to take a pickaxe into the mystery hole?" Caroline asked. "This doesn't strike you as ill-advised?"

A couple of loud, sharp *thunks* later, Riley yelled, "Ow! Shit!"

Alice sprang into action, pulling on Riley's ankles.

"No! No, I'm fine!" Riley yelled, kicking gently at Alice's hands. "No blood or anything! I just banged my elbow."

"Yeah, you might want to get out of there soon, Riles, because Plover appears to be having a small paternal ghost meltdown," Caroline said, nodding at the window where Plover seemed to be yelling accusations of incompetence at Edison.

There were a few more *thunks* before Riley shouted, "Got it!"

She scrambled out of the mystery hole and held up an object formed from copper loops. She was staring at it with a combination of horror and wonder.

It was a lock. Dusty and covered in a patina of green, but it was *the* lock.

"What the fuck…" Alice breathed. When Caroline sent her a startled look, she shrugged. "The occasion calls for it."

"She's right," Edison said. "This is the moment for celebratory profanity."

"Did we actually do this? We found it!" Riley laughed, holding the lock out for Caroline and Alice to see. "Honestly, take this from me, because I forgot how creepy it is to hold these with your bare hands."

Edison approached with a cotton bag. Riley dropped the lock inside.

"We did it," Alice gasped, nodding. "I can't believe we did it."

"I couldn't have done it without you," Riley told Caroline and Alice, throwing her arms around them. "Thank you."

"Yeah, suck it, previous generations of Dentons!" Caroline crowed.

"Too far," Alice told her. "What now?"

"No clue!" Riley exclaimed. "But let's get it inside before Margaret feels some sort of disturbance with her evil Welling powers."

Edison hustled the bag toward the door. Caroline and Riley helped Alice gather the pickaxes. It seemed like a bad idea to leave them lying around unattended.

"I'm just sorry Mina and Josh missed it," Riley said.

"Eh, Ben's stuck at the clinic," Caroline told them. "Plus, Mom's trying to give the kids extra hours at the bar."

"They're not allowed to serve alcohol," Alice noted. "They're underage."

"They are allowed to clear tables and wash dishes," Caroline replied. "And it's football season. There's plenty to wash."

Alice shuddered. "Oof, that adult-responsibility thing is off to a brisk start."

"Ah, it's good for them, in judicious quantities. And Mom is thrilled to have them around," Caroline said. "Oh, speak of the devil. Hey, sweetie, where's your brother?"

Alice turned to see Mina running up the sidewalk, hopping over the fence with an agility that only belonged to the young. She looked absolutely stricken as she threw herself into Caroline's arms. "Josh is gone."

Chapter 13
Collin

COLLIN BANCROFT WAS NOT A fool.

He could be a bit of an ass on occasion, but he was no fool. He knew it wasn't a good sign that Alice hadn't returned any of his texts that day—not even the dancing furniture GIFs, and she *loved* those. He knew it was a worse sign that Paige was nowhere to be seen all day. Not calling him. Not texting him. Not lurking in his office demanding room service and a massage from a spa staff that wasn't currently employed.

Where the hell had she *been* all day?

What could Paige possibly find to occupy herself on Starfall Point? The most exciting thing to happen in the last month was one of the Perkins ferry line's oldest boats sinking after a hundredth-anniversary celebration for the company. Fortunately, no one was hurt, so the sunken ruin, just a few yards from the shoreline, was more of a sad irony than a tragedy.

He was certain Paige hadn't had anything to do with it.

For the most part.

Also, he wasn't particularly proud of using the dancing furniture GIFs.

Collin had buried himself in work all day—legitimate and time-sensitive work—not because he was hiding from her but because he was trying to prevent himself from texting Alice on repeat. He'd only spent a little time with Mina and Josh, but he distinctly remembered them saying something about more than five texts in a day as coming across as "desperate" and "creepy."

Twenty would probably get him some sort of restraining order.

A knock at the door sounded just before Julie poked her head inside.

"What are you still doing here?" she asked. "It's late, like the-paint-crew-have-already-gone-to-bed late."

"Eh, just going over the website redesign the marketing people put together for us." Collin sighed. "I still don't know about centering the rebrand around brick red. It's a little too close to the previous orange incarnation. But it goes with the roof, which is sort of a signature feature of the hotel, so what are you going to do?"

"You're worried about color schemes? It's not that you're avoiding that fancy-coated, four-hundred-dollar haircut in the Cowslip Suite, is it?" Julie asked. "Because she hasn't been around all day."

"It's not strictly because I'm avoiding her," Collin began, holding up one finger in a "wait a minute" gesture. "She's in the what, now?"

"She's in the Cowslip Suite," Julie said. "We moved her there this morning. The suite floors aren't ready for anyone to stay in them, much less someone high-maintenance. The paint is barely dry. We don't have bedding or towels in there. We had to assemble a bed specifically for her, and one of the plain reproductions, not an antique. Haircut was *not* pleased."

Collin blew out a long breath. He'd fast-tracked the Cowslip Suite because he wanted Alice to see it all together. He wanted her to be the first one to see it. And Paige was sleeping there?

Julie winced. "Yeah, from your expression, I'm assuming that Haircut has something to do with why Alice sent me an email that says"—she stopped to check her phone screen—"'Thank you for your proposal of employment, but I will not be accepting any offer made to me by Collin Bancroft, personally or professionally. He is aware of my reasons.'"

"Wait? What?" Collin stood. "When did Alice send that? And what about Paige? Julie, what in the hell happened?"

Julie held her own hands up, speaking very calmly when she said, "I will remind you that when you hired me, it was under the condition that you would not yell at me or make me feel disrespected. I had enough of that from Robert. In fact, there's a clause in my new contract that states that making me feel disrespected results in a generous severance, and I get to take the fancy coffeemaker with me."

She pointed at his coffee bar.

With intent.

"I'm sorry," Collin told her. "Go back. Explain."

"The Haircut—" Julie began.

"Please stop calling her that," Collin asked.

"No," Julie replied. "When I tried to call you, it was because Haircut came storming into my office, demanding VIP treatment. She said it was shameful that she was 'sloughed off to some damp, smelly guest room' when we had 'perfectly good suites available' and demanded an immediate upgrade."

"But she's not even a paying guest. There are no paying guests, so there's nothing to upgrade," he insisted. "I'm the one who sloughed her off to the 'damp, smelly guest room,' which I find a little offensive, by the way."

"I tried explaining that to her, but she was insistent that you wouldn't want her staying there. I tried explaining that the paint was barely dry in the Cowslip Suite, that we hadn't even moved in furniture. She just snapped those long, bony fingers at me and told me to make it happen. By the time I got the room sort-of-furnished and Lori from housekeeping was putting sheets on the bed, Haircut was stripped down in the tub, taking bubble bath selfies and treating us like we were the intrusive assholes for being there."

"*That's* the question Lori from housekeeping had?" Collin cried.

Julie threw her hands up and yelled, "Yes!"

Collin gaped at her. "Why didn't you tell me?"

"I *called* you," Julie reminded him very slowly. "And I told you I thought it was something you should weigh in on. You sloughed *me* off and told me to do whatever I thought was appropriate."

"You thought putting her in a suite we've barely finished renovating appropriate?"

"More appropriate than an entitled city-idiot having a tantrum in the lobby, distracting the crews with her shrill promises to have me fired?" Julie nodded. "Yes."

Collin groaned and scraped his hand over his face. "She can't have you fired."

"I know," Julie scoffed. "Only I can get me fired. And during the years I worked with Robert, I came up with far more interesting plans to get fired than responding appropriately to your girlfriend having a tantrum."

"She's not my girlfriend. She's barely even a friend," he shot back. And in that moment, he realized he meant it. What did Paige bring to his life? Shame, old wounds, her inability to let him move on to new patterns. They'd built a relationship on old connections that just weren't relevant anymore. He'd made his mistakes right with her over the years. He'd apologized and meant it. He'd tried to break free of this cycle of commitment and breakup. It was not his fault that she was unwilling to let go. He'd spent years trying to remind himself that she was a good person only because he couldn't believe that he would spend so much time and effort to keep a bad person in his life.

"Well, good, because she's not as nice or as smart as Alice," Julie said. "And her haircut is terrible and overpriced."

"Let the haircut go," he told her.

"No," Julie told him. "And you're probably going to need to tell *her* that she's not your girlfriend because she seems to think you're engaged. Or engaged to be engaged. Some form of engaged. She was flashing around a big ol' rock."

"Oh, no," he sighed. "Not again."

"Again?" Julie cried. "She's done this before?"

"Yes." Collin squinched his eyes shut. "Sort of. Some variation of it."

"I know you're my boss and all, but…buddy." Julie huffed out a laugh, shaking her head and flopping into his club chair.

"I know," he sighed. "There's a lot of history there."

"I don't care if there's a Magna Carta there," Julie told him. "You want to talk about Alice's email now?"

"Yes…?"

The door burst open and while Collin was relieved to see it was Alice charging into the office, the thunderous look on her face was enough to send an ominous chill down Collin's spine.

"Hi, Julie," she said with sincere friendliness. Because Alice was too good a person to be rude to innocent bystanders. "Would you mind if I talked to Collin for a minute?"

"No problem," Julie replied, standing quickly. "I think you two need to talk. And I need to go…that way."

Julie made for the door. Collin couldn't have envied her more. Alice was remarkably still for someone who appeared to be seething.

It occurred to Collin that this was the first time she'd been in his office. Normally, they'd held their meetings somewhere else in the building so she could get a feel for what sort of pieces he would need in each space. It made him a little sad that she was so angry at him that she wasn't going to enjoy this space, so full of his family history and weird little artifacts they'd collected over the years. But clearly, that wasn't something he could point out now.

Collin began, "Alice…"

"No, no," she said, holding up her hands. "I get to talk now. Have you seen Josh?"

"Josh?" Collin stared at her. "No. Why would I see Josh?"

Alice's hands began to shake. "Because apparently, he went outside the Rose to drop some garbage in the dumpster, and, according to Caroline's brother, some 'hot brunette in expensive clothes' came up and asked Josh to help her get her suitcase unstuck from a sewer grate behind one of the T-shirt shops. Josh was frustratingly easy to lure, despite his whole treatise on internet safety. Wally was 'super jealous of the kid,' because Wally is an idiot. And then, according to Gerda over at the snow-globe emporium, Josh was seen walking toward the hotel with the same attractive brunette, lugging a huge suitcase. So how about I stop talking and you help me find my friend? Because I'm assuming the brunette is Paige. And if she's done something to intentionally put Josh into Margaret's hands, I'm going to do something very, *very* bad. I don't care how she's connected to you."

"Wait, none of this makes sense," Collin said. "Why would Paige be luring Josh anywhere?"

"I don't know, but I would very much like to talk to her about it," Alice told him. "Then I would like to search your building thoroughly, every damned room, even the Cowslip Suite—which we will be talking about later, by the way. Also, you're lucky it's me here right now and not Caroline. She's at Shaddow House, being forcibly restrained. By Mina. Who is also being forcibly restrained. By Riley. It's a whole tangle. I'm only here talking to you because I didn't want to see your hotel razed."

"This is ridiculous," Collin protested, pulling up the security feed from the last few hours. He'd set the filters to search for "person moving" around the exterior doors. And while several segments popped up featuring members of the paint crew taking their breaks, around seven, there was footage of Paige and Josh, lugging a large black suitcase into the north-wing entrance—which someone had helpfully propped open.

"Dammit," he huffed, turning his screen around so she could see. "This is not ridiculous. This is very easily explained, because Paige apparently lured Josh into the north wing."

Alice gave him a withering look. He never wanted her to give him that look again, so he simply stood up, shrugged on his coat, and gestured for her to follow him out the door. He pulled out his phone and dialed Paige's number. She didn't pick up, so he left a terse voicemail. "I don't know where you are, but you need to call me back right now."

"The north-wing entrance is the fastest way to get to the basement," Collin said as they moved quickly out of the office. Collin took her down a shortcut, a service staircase that led to the hallway Victoria's echo haunted nightly. In fact, the shadow was currently chasing her directly toward them as they opened the door.

"Oh." Alice shuddered, showing some emotion other than anger for the first time since entering his office. The shadow Stanford overtook Victoria's echo and threw her to the ground. "That is awful."

"Yeah," he muttered, texting Paige, telling her to call him immediately.

"I am trying really hard to focus on anything besides how upset I am at you right now," she told him. "I am not used to being angry with someone I care about. I don't like it. It's a bad feeling, like I've swallowed a battery coated in coagulated fish grease. That's on fire."

Collin began, "I'm so sorr—"

"No," she said. "The time for that will come later. Now, we focus on finding Josh and getting him back to his dad and Mina and Caroline. Margaret's done this kind of thing before."

"Really?" Collin asked.

"Yeah, fortunately, she's not great at it," Alice told her as they approached the basement door. They were silent as they descended the stairs. In the distance, Collin could hear a buzzing noise. He had the worst possible thought that they were about to enter some sort of power-tool-based torture scenario.

But when they reached the bottom of the stairs, the basement was just...the basement. It was as orderly and dusty as it had been the last time they'd visited. But now, there was a folding chair near the wine cellar.

And it was empty.

"No," Alice moaned, running closer to the chair, which was surrounded by several discarded strips of silver duct tape. A cell phone, encased in black "destruction proof" plastic, buzzed in the corner of the basement, and it was starting to feel like it was mocking them.

"This is Josh's phone." Alice picked up the phone and turned the screen toward Collin so he could see a picture of Mina sprawled on sand. Apparently, Josh's home screen was a picture of his sister just after she'd tripped face-first on a beach somewhere.

"Josh never goes anywhere without his phone," Alice said, her voice shaky. "If he was separated from his phone..."

Collin picked up one of the loose silver strips from the floor. "Have these been...chewed on?"

He held up a piece of tape that looked like it had been gnawed on by a tiny land-borne Great White...or an evil little ghost hamster named Chester. What little blood that was left in Alice's face drained out of it. Collin could almost smell the reactive magic gathering inside her, ozone and the unsettling scent of burning paper. It seemed to run along her skin, like a shimmer of static.

That was new.

"I need to get back to the house," she insisted, dashing for the stairs. Somehow, she was bolting upstairs while *simultaneously* texting. Collin didn't question it. He simply ran after her, his long legs easily allowing him to catch up with her as she bolted down the hallway. She seemed angry and terrified and anxious all at once, and he felt very sorry for Josh's captors, when the coven tracked them down. If that included Paige? Well, she was a big girl and she would have to accept the magical consequences.

"If you want to show me you're sorry, you can hire me a lawyer," Alice told him as she ran. "And pay for it. I'm going to need one. Because I'm going to *murder* your *fiancée*."

How did she manage to sound so threatening as she ran like a freaking Olympian?

Collin groaned. "She told you we were engaged, didn't she? Alice, I wouldn't do that...again."

"Not now," she growled. "Oh, fuck it, yes, it's going to be now, because the terror I feel for Josh right now is outweighing how pissed off I am at you. And have I mentioned the battery coated in coagulated fish grease? That's on fire?"

"OK, you're mad. I can work with mad," Collin told her. "Alice, I am not engaged to Paige."

"And that's great," Alice told him. "You managed to be on the same island for a whole day without accidentally getting engaged to her. But you *did* put her in the Cowslip Suite. With *my tub*. She used my tub before I did."

"I didn't know she was going to stay in the Cowslip Suite," Collin said. "There was a—let's call it an administrative error. She bullied the staff until they gave her a preview."

"And she used my tub," Alice repeated. "I know it's not the point, but I find myself really, really annoyed by it."

"I was surprised by that too. Paige is more of a shower person." She glared at him. He raised his hands. "Not the point. I know I keep using the word 'complicated' but—"

"Yes, and it makes me think you don't understand the word. Your situation is not 'complicated.' You act like she's some immovable object in your life, like you have no option but to let her near you. She's just a person," she told him. "And as long as you think of her as a mystical element you can't defeat, you're never going to be free of her. I wonder if you want to be, honestly." She stopped running and turned on him, panting. "You two, you figure out whatever is going on between you, but leave me out of it."

"Look, I'm not saying you're wrong," he told her, wrapping his fingers around her upper arms. "And I get that you're upset."

"I'm not upset," she insisted, shaking off his gentle grip. "I'm *hurt*. It came down to protecting something that you assured me was mine, and you chose to give it to her—even indirectly. She has a hold on you that I don't understand, and I really don't need to, I suppose. I don't want to spend our time together fighting it. My relationships with my grandparents, with Clark, they've all been struggles. I don't want to take on another fight." She darted toward Shaddow House. "Except for Paige. I'm willing to fight Paige. Physically. With punching."

Chapter 14
Alice

ALICE HAD ALWAYS CONSIDERED HERSELF good at compartmen-
talizing. It was why she thought she was the best choice to go to
Collin and demand to search the hotel for Josh. Currently, Edison
and Riley were at Shaddow House, trying to coach Ben and his
family through their first kidnapping.

Well, it was their second kidnapping, technically, considering
what had happened to Caroline.

But seeing that tape torn on the cold cement floor, all the little
walls dividing her panic about Josh from her seething indignation
over the tub violation came crashing down and she felt everything
all at once. Maybe it was good for her, Alice thought, as she and
Collin bolted around the corner.

Nope. Feeling really, really mad at Collin while also admiring
how his long legs seemed to eat up the pavement? That was just
confusing. It was not good for her. Also, her calves were starting
to cramp.

Just as they ran into the yard, Alice heard repeated *thunks*
at the back of the Shaddow House. She and Collin practically

hockey-slid into the backyard to find Margaret standing in front of the reading gazebo, wearing a hunter-green wool coat, her arms raised. Inside the house, the ugly ceremonial candelabra was smashing against one of the rear windows near the kitchen, as if trying to escape.

"Oh...no," Alice said, shoving Collin behind her. She didn't know what Margaret could do to him, exactly, but between the two of them, Alice was the only one who could fight magic with magic. She was very relieved when the rest of the coven came pouring out of the back door. Plover was left standing in the kitchen doorway with Natalie and Eloise.

"Margaret, this is not the behavior of a reasonable senior citizen!" Riley yelled.

"I was really hoping you would be out trying to find your annoying little teenage friend," Margaret sighed, not bothering to drop her arms. She sounded *bored* and annoyed that the coven was interrupting her repeatedly bashing the candelabra against the window through some magical means. Alice suspected Margaret's Welling magic had something to do with it, but she didn't have time to think too much about it.

It was impressive, really, that the window was holding up to this abuse.

"Should I go get...somebody?" Collin asked Alice. "Or a weapon...or something?"

It was flattering that he was asking her, but unless Collin had some sort of paranormal enforcement unit's information saved in his phone, she wasn't sure what he could do.

"Give us back our young man, right now!" Plover thundered.

"Wait, *all of you* were still in the house?" Margaret huffed. "Don't any of you care about Todd?"

"It's *Josh*," Ben barked. "Margaret, *where is my son?*"

"We knew we would just have to wait for you to show up," Caroline growled. "Where. Is. He?"

"Well, I thought I laid an obvious enough trail to make you follow him to the hotel. Maybe to find his lifeless body in the basement. Who knows?" Margaret shrugged. "Chester's a little more unpredictable than I thought he would be."

That was enough to make Mina attempt to launch herself off the back porch. Fortunately, Edison caught her around the waist and kept her earthbound.

"Margaret, please," Edison implored. "We worked together for years. I know you. This isn't you."

But Mina was having none of it. "I don't care that you're an old lady. If you don't tell me where my brother is, I will end—" Ben clapped a hand over his daughter's mouth to prevent a threat that might escalate the situation beyond repair. The only muffled words that came through were "hot poker" and "badger" and "fluffernutter."

Even Collin took a step back on that one.

Alice tried to reassure Ben. "We looked in the hotel basement. Josh wasn't there. Neither was her creepy little murder-pet."

Margaret's head whipped toward Alice. "Impossible."

"No blood, no signs of a struggle," Alice added. "It was like he just walked away. It's entirely possible that he's fine."

"It's equally possible that Chester wanted to take him somewhere private and is munching on his entrails as we speak," Margaret countered.

Riley took a deep breath, her eyes locked on Alice and Caroline, who gave her a shaky nod. All of their work. All of their effort. What did it mean now?

Edison shook his head. "Riley, no."

Riley disappeared inside the house and walked back out with the candelabra in hand. Alice felt the magical wards shift as Riley exited the kitchen door, like the clicking of gears. Mina's lip trembled, "Riley."

"What good is this without Josh?" Riley demanded. "Our family is worth more than the house or anything in it. We can work around the greater good issue later, when we know he's OK. Besides, the locks are in a safe in the house. We have that much bargaining power left, at least."

Margaret waggled her fingers, summoning the candelabra from Riley's hand to land at her feet in the dirt.

"Finally," Margaret panted. "*Finally.*"

Her smile equal parts gleeful and mad, she raised her arms. Alice's gut churned as the sound of metal ricocheting around the house filled her ears. The wards weren't as strong as they'd been before Riley actively chose to give Margaret a piece of her family's history back. The unspoken contract of that choice had weakened their position—deteriorated it so much that the first lock came rocketing out of the kitchen door like a bullet. Ben flung himself over Mina and Caroline, covering their heads with his hands as more locks came flying out of the kitchen door.

"Well...shit," Riley marveled as the big copper objet d'art elegantly assembled itself, each lock cupped in its little indentation on the loops. Alice could feel the magic around Shaddow House shifting; the pleasant tension that was always present in her chest whenever she walked through its doors was starting to unravel. And apparently, Riley's safe was toast.

This was bad.

"You didn't know what would happen once the set was complete, did you?" Margaret asked, her grin making her face look skeletal. "It's more than the sum of its parts. Each lock serves a different magical purpose, doing its own little trick, but when they're combined..."

She paused to wave a hand over the locks, making a few of them rotate in their little containment cups. Slowly, ghosts began crawling out of the open door behind Plover, like ants swarming out of a hill, slithering along the surface of the house. And none of them were familiar faces Alice recognized from her days in Shaddow House. Haggard, bloodied, radiating angry confusion—these were the ghosts that lurked in the shadows, watching, making the hairs of her arms stand up when she realized the outline of a person standing in the corner wasn't her imagination. Alice shivered, stepping back, moving Collin with her.

"All of you, stick around. No sense in running off to terrorize the locals just yet," Margaret told them, her triumphant smile sickly sweet and more than slightly mad. "You're going to want to see this."

To Alice's surprise, the ghosts did exactly what they were told, perching on the roof as if to watch how it all unfolded. Dozens more were gathering at the kitchen door, creating a sort of gray, misty traffic jam as they all tried to escape at once. Plover was at the front, shoving at them, shouting for them to stay where they were.

"What is happening?" Edison asked.

"The magic is crumbling," Riley whispered. "*Margaret's* holding the ghosts here, all of them.*"

"Oh, sure, the locks can make ghosts do whatever I tell them to," Margaret told them, sounding bored. "Like this."

She turned her wrist, making one of the locks spin in its cup. She looked around, as if choosing a teammate for dodgeball, and made a beckoning gesture with her fingertips. A clown ghost emerged from the swirling misty chaos near the kitchen door, smiling broadly at Mina.

"Oh, hell, no," Mina said, turning and planting her feet.

Alice stared in horror as the clown ghost drew close to Mina in the creepiest way possible.

"Is that a clown ghost?" Collin whisper-hissed. "*Why is there a clown ghost?*"

Ben and Caroline attempted to throw themselves into the ghost's path, but he didn't seem to notice at all. Caroline even made the "repel" hand gesture as Riley dashed back into the kitchen, yelling, "I'm getting the salt bombs!"

"Let me try something!" Alice yelled, raising her hands.

"What are you doing?" Collin asked, sounding panicked. "Is it going to make the clown ghost come closer?"

Alice made a hand gesture based on the "repel" spell, but intended a different outcome. She imagined an invisible bubble around the clown ghost, sealing him away where he couldn't hurt anyone she cared about—or, at least, would stop creeping Collin out so badly. She pushed her right hand forward, picturing the bubble floating *through* the kitchen door. The clown disappeared into the churning spirit chaos.

Margaret looked irritated but didn't seem to realize it was Alice who had interrupted the undead fisticuffs. "I always forget you have *some* grasp of magic. Do you know what it's been like for me, listening to Edison talk about you all day long, knowing what you and your little friends were, while he bored me with lies about paint swatches and bookshelves? It's been *so frustrating*. Helpful in the long run, really, gleaning all that information about your schedules and your habits, to add to what Clark was telling me. But it was so excruciating to put on an interested, neutral face while he blathered on. To know that I was so much more suited for his job but was obligated to *not* kill him because I needed his information? It was *galling*."

"Well, that hurts my feelings more than I expected," Edison muttered.

Margaret stooped to pick up the lock they'd found in the folly, the one covered in a green coat of age. "I suppose you don't know what this one does."

"It's not the whole 'Wellings want to use the locks to turn ghosts into assassins' thing, right?" Caroline said, Mina tucked firmly behind her. "I never really bought that theory."

"The Denton family's vision was so limited, believing the locks only had one use. Your magic is a joke, a parlor trick." Margaret continued talking as if Caroline hadn't even spoken. "My family had to go underground, humoring rich idiots like the Bancrofts. And then we had to change gears, pretend to be nothing. Sweet, guileless blue-collar folk who would blend in on this godforsaken island, even as we used our wealth to fund our search for the locks. For years, I worked against your bitch aunt—"

"Watch it," Riley told her, even as the most grotesque spirits—most likely Plover's "basement ghosts"—crept closer from their rooftop perches like a murder of crows waiting for their chance to plunge.

Margaret continued. "—sowing discord on that ridiculous Nana Grapevine, letting people think the worst of Nora, but she was such a goody-goody that the worst anyone could say was that she was aloof. You, though—oh, you and your faithless mother provided far more fodder. People on this island will believe anything. And all that time, I was hiding what I could do. I had this magic inside me." Margaret lifted one of the locks from its cup, the green-patinaed specimen they'd found in the folly.

"This is the prize gem of the collection. Each of the locks serves a different purpose, hones some aspect of the Welling magic, but this one, this was what we were planning on, drawing the suckers into our 'communication center.'"

"So *not* ghost assassins," Caroline said. "I knew it."

"Oh, no, ghost assassins would have been one of the many services we offered," Margaret replied, holding the green lock out in her palm like bait. "Once we booted your idiot predecessors out of the house and claimed our rightful place. But this little beauty would have allowed us to do *this*. Uncle Stanford!"

"Uncle?" Riley turned to the door just in time to see the ceiling ghost sail through the door—no longer bound by the wards. The dark, viscous surface melted away and from the murk emerged a thin, pale, sharp-featured man in a high-collared shirt and suit. He landed on his well-shod feet next to Margaret, beaming at her like an old friend.

The ceiling ghost was Stanford Newlin, Victoria's former fiancé.

"That, I did not expect," Natalie called from the doorway.

"What the hell?" Alice exchanged glances with her covenmates, and so many pieces fell into place. The way Victoria seemed so uncomfortable whenever the ceiling ghost was nearby. The way it hovered near the locks, seeming displeased whenever they made progress.

"Yes, one of the locks allows you to let ghosts through the wards at will. Or hadn't you figured that out yet?" Margaret simpered. She patted where Stanford's insubstantial arm should have been. "Uncle Stanford was the Welling heir. Until my grandmother took over for him."

"Designing the Duchess gave me access to the best families on the island," Stanford told them, his voice raspy from disuse. "We'd changed the family name a few times by then. Not that the Dentons would give me the time of day. Their detachment from the town allowed me to sow discontent among the yokels, about how the Shaddows—and, by extension, the Dentons—were snobs who thought they were too good to talk to anybody. I'd hoped marriage to that silly twit Victoria would give me a permanent hold here, the ability to undermine the Dentons and take back our legacy. But I suppose you know how that turned out."

"You're a murdering asshole?" Riley suggested. "Oh, no, this means Victoria's been stuck inside the house this whole time with the guy who killed her?"

"Oh…no," Collin sighed. "That's so awful."

"She wasn't aware," Stanford said. The basement ghosts seemed thrilled by Stanford's appearance, like they were members of his fan club. That…really told Alice all she needed to know.

"I took on that amorphous form so she wouldn't run when she saw me, warn others, give the Dentons some clue they might be able to follow to my identity. It's such a relief, dropping the ruse, even if I did enjoy keeping an eye on her. I like to think that eventually, I could have won her over again."

"Riley's right," Collin told the ghost. "You are an asshole."

This was good, Alice supposed. Caroline once said it was important in a crisis to keep the villain talking, stalling them so... what? She glanced up at the ghosts lining the roofline like crows. What was the coven going to do? Call Celia? There was no backup. There was no weapon against the combined locks. They only had themselves.

"I knew my time on the island was short," Stanford replied. "I knew I couldn't explain lingering on the island much past the completion of the hotel, particularly with Forsythe asking when I was planning to move on to my next project. So I took long walks around the island at night, waiting for the opportunity to take my lock to the house, to influence the others. I failed in a spectacular fashion. I don't want to go into it, but somehow, the brick closed *over* it."

"I'm telling you, the house is alive," Caroline whispered to Riley, who shrugged.

"Nothing I did could get the lock back and I suppose that the shock of it all, after so much recent manual labor..." Stanford sighed and made a helpless gesture.

"Heart attack on the way back to the hotel?" Edison guessed.

Stanford nodded. "I felt a horrific pressure in my chest and then I woke up in Shaddow House itself. I couldn't get out, couldn't interact with any object around me, much less the haunted ones. I was trapped. It was awful. I suppose some part of me remained in the hotel too. It was my greatest creation. It's really rather tragic."

"Yeah, just imagine how much worse it would be if your fiancée pushed you down the stairs and then you were stuck in a house with her for a hundred years?" Riley deadpanned, making Stanford give her an undead frown.

"A note telling my grandmother where the lock was hidden would have been helpful," Margaret told him.

"I didn't have time," Stanford snapped. "It's called unfinished business for a reason. The house was my attachment object. It's a bit poetic, if you think about it."

"What does Jeff know about any of this?" Alice asked. "He's always been so...nice and normal."

"Nothing," Margaret insisted. "Jeff doesn't have the—well, my generation would have called it 'gumption'—for this sort of thing. And honestly, the effort would have been wasted on him. He's never shown the slightest magical ability. He gets that from his father's side. Useless, really. I'm the last hope for my family."

Even after being raised by the Proctors, it was shocking to hear a mother talking about her son that way. Poor Jeff.

Margaret sniffed, as if she didn't like being reminded of Jeff's place in all this. "Enough of this waltzing down Memory Lane. It's time for you idiots to see what this masterpiece does."

Margaret raised her arms, and all the locks twisted at once.

"Oh, I have waited my entire life and after for this," Stanford crooned.

The candelabra began to spin, grinding into the cold dirt and sending clods of it flying. Overhead, the now-familiar void split the sky. The silence seemed to overtake the earthbound ambient noise, swallowing it up. Unlike before, they could see shapes moving inside that black endless space, not quite bodies, not quite smoke.

"Once the other locks opened this doorway into the next world, this piece"—she paused to stroke the candelabra—"would allow our family to call forth any spirit a client asked for."

Stanford put his hand on Margaret's shoulder, smiling like a proud papa.

"Bullshit," Mina called. Stanford frowned at her and Mina snarled at him. "Oh, correct my language, you evil dickhead, I dare you."

"I'll bet you want me to call forward your poor dead mama, don't you, Riley, dear?" Margaret cooed. "Or maybe even your dear Aunt Nora. Maybe *she* could help."

Her simpering tone set Riley's teeth on edge—visibly, to Alice.

"I suppose that would be too distracting for you," Margaret said. "How about someone you have a little less emotional attachment to?"

Margaret moved her hands, a little bit like the basic movements of the Denton system, but more aggressive, like she was expressing her displeasure in heavy traffic. A figure in the depths of the void moved forward, became more solid. He landed on the ground in a ghostly heap.

"Whoa," Riley marveled.

"See?" Margaret huffed, watching dark-purple magic swirling around her fingers like smoke. That was a skill none of them had mastered yet. "Thank you. That's all I'm looking for, some respect for my family's craft. A little cowering would be nice."

"Cole?" Caroline cried as the former construction foreman stood, looking pretty healthy and whole, all things considered. Alice supposed it helped that he'd had the life squeezed out of his heart. It didn't leave any marks.

"Hi," he said, his expression chagrined. "Uh, ladies, good to see you again."

"No," Caroline shot back, shaking her head. "Too soon."

"Oh, great, it's the other guy who kidnapped a member of my family," Ben muttered. "Also, could we get back to *where is my son?*"

"Yeah, I've had a lot of time to think about it, and I owe you an apology," Cole said. "I was wrong to kidnap you and try to get your ghost grandma to kill you. That's on me. My bad."

Alice stared at Cole and wondered at the summation of a murder attempt as "my bad."

"Well, I'm sorry I basically let my ghostly grandma kill you out of boredom," Caroline admitted. "Her boredom, not mine. And then you got sucked into this afterlife vacuum thing, which seems kind of scary."

"It isn't so bad, really," Cole sighed. "Peaceful, quiet. Like taking a deep nap that you fade in and out of."

"Well, that's weirdly comforting. At least we didn't shove Bobby Carlucci into some hell dimension," Alice said.

"Really, you're worried about Bobby now?" Riley asked.

"He was a gross catcaller, but I'm not sure he deserved hell," Alice muttered, shrugging.

"I can bring him forth too," Margaret offered, only to have everybody but Ben and Mina shout, "*No!*"

"Eh, Bobby's not so bad," Cole said, only to have Margaret make a gesture that resulted in him flying upward into the void.

Margaret smiled. "I am never going to get tired of this feeling. The power. Knowing that you're watching my every move, dreading my every decision. It's just so delicious. I know it can't last forever. Well, it can't last longer than tonight, really, because I'm going to kill you all, but I'm old enough to know when to savor a moment."

"Really?" Stanford asked. "You don't think leaving the bodies of seven people behind one of the most famous homes on the island will attract some attention?"

"We have all sorts of things that can explain weird occurrences now," Margaret told him. "Carbon monoxide, electrocution, mass food poisoning. And people will accept those explanations because they just want to move on to the next weird thing that happens in the news cycle. It'll simply be another strange footnote in the Shaddow House history, and I'll have the locks, and I really won't care."

"That seems like a limited perspective," Stanford told her, sounding disappointed.

"Fine, I'll only kill half of them," Margaret sighed. "No one will believe the other half anyway."

"And how are you planning on going about that?" Stanford demanded. Margaret gave him a pointed look. "Oh, *I'm* supposed to snuff out the lives of three or more people?"

"Well, I was going to have Chester do it, but he's not responding when I call!" Margaret explained, sounding a bit like a petulant teenager.

"Yes, it's almost like creating a weird Frankenstein monster out of ghost energy is a *bad* idea," Mina muttered.

"Who's Chester?" Stanford asked.

A chittering echo in the distance caught Alice's attention. She saw a small, dark shape darting around the corner. Was it a rabbit... or a rat?

Or an evil hamster?

"Oh, no." Alice shoved Collin out of the path of the oncoming ghost hamster. She might have been upset with him, but she didn't want him to die an evil ghost-hamster death. That seemed to be emotional progress.

Unfortunately, Collin refused to be protected by her. He shielded her with his body, stepping in front of her, facing the direction where she was staring in horror. In the process, she tripped over his feet and they both landed on the freezing-cold ground with a *thump*.

Collin cradled her body, covering it with his own, protecting her head with his huge hands. Behind them, the basement ghosts were hiss-whispering among themselves, buzzing with excitement about the thrill to come.

That was ominous.

"What?" Collin demanded, searching around for the hidden danger. "What's happening? What's coming? What do you need me to do?"

He looked down at her like he was counting her essential body parts again. He'd chosen her...over himself. He didn't know what the threat was, or where it was coming from, but he'd thrown himself in front of her with his own body.

She did not know how to process this.

While she appreciated his concern, this was not the best position from which to fight an oncoming evil ghost hamster. As soon as Collin realized what was running by, he scrambled back, carrying Alice with him. "Gah!"

But Chester just streaked past them on the ground. He slid to a stop in front of Margaret and bared his little shark teeth. Alice heard Ben breathe out, "No…"

"Chester," Margaret cooed. "Oh, sweetie, you took a while but you got the job done. I'm sure you did, didn't you? That's my good boy. Oh, was that big, dumb, gangly boy mean to you?"

To everybody's surprise, Chester hissed at Margaret and snapped at her hand, sinking his teeth into her finger. Even if they were transparent ghost teeth, it looked painful.

"Chester, what are you *doing?*" Margaret cried, shaking her hand.

A young voice sounded from the depths of the night. "Chester doesn't want to work for you anymore." The collar of his peacoat was pulled up like some adolescent TV vampire, and Alice thought maybe Josh knew exactly how cool he looked as he stepped into a shaft of moonlight and said, "Chester works for me now."

"Josh!" Ben yelled. He almost bolted toward his son, but Edison gently took his arm and shook his head. As much as they all shared the relief that Josh was all right, this sort of distraction was exactly what Margaret needed to do something bloody and terrible.

"You specifically waited for a moment like this so you could make a dramatic entrance, didn't you?" Mina asked, her eyes shiny with happy tears. "You enormous jerk."

Ben nodded, similarly teary. "I'm pretty sure he popped the collar on his coat too."

Josh shrugged, grinning like the much-beloved smart-ass he was. "How many opportunities like this am I going to get?"

Caroline was just wiping her cheeks. "I'm going to hug the hell out of you, kid. Just prepare for it. And then we're going to have a long remedial talk about stranger danger."

Josh sighed and dropped his head. "I know."

"Has *everyone* forgotten the point here?" Margaret demanded, gesturing up to the void. "I'm standing here with a portal to the afterlife open like a gaping chest wound and you're talking about *hugging*? Can I get a little attention, please?"

"Coming across as a little needy, Maggie," Josh noted. "Be a little gracious about other people getting attention. Were you an only child?"

"Now, you listen here." Margaret took a threatening step toward him, but before she could reach Josh, Chester snapped at her again. He was like a tiny protective dragon, guarding his treasure. And that treasure was Josh.

"Now, Chester," Margaret barked. "You listen to me. I'm in control here. I *made* you. And I want you to hurt every single person here except me, do you understand?"

Margaret pulled out a little silver charm, shaped a little bit like the locks. She used it to gesture at Josh. Chester sat on his back haunches and licked his fore...paw? They were going to have to create a whole new anatomical language to deal with ghostly murder-pets.

"Impressive," Stanford told her.

"What's happening?" Margaret seethed. "Why isn't he obeying?"

"I talked to him," Josh said. "You left me in a basement with a seething ball of rage, hoping he would hurt me. Because he doesn't speak in a language you understand, the language of a wounded person who feels alone and helpless. The language of an anxious teenager. But it's amazing what sort of loyalty you can secure when you just listen and treat someone like they matter."

Riley burst out laughing at the angry expression on Margaret's face.

"That was your big move, wasn't it?" Riley asked, shaking her head. "Chester the evil hamster—"

Chester turned and hissed angrily at Riley, who cringed.

"Sorry, buddy, we'll become friends later," Riley promised Chester. "Chester was your nuclear option. The big, bad weapon. And you just got outplayed by a teenager. A teenager with an unusual degree of emotional intelligence, but a *teenager*. That has got to *sting*!"

Riley probably could have enjoyed this less, Alice mused, but she'd had a long year.

"Enough of this!" Stanford yelled. "We've waited long enough. Avenge your family, Margaret! End them!"

"Chester, heel!" Margaret barked. Stanford took a running start at Riley.

Behind her, Alice saw a tall, dark shape step slowly out of the gloom of the kitchen door. Plover was on the move, breaking through the shredded wards and stepping in front of Riley. When Stanford reached her, he burst into a sort of dust cloud against the shield that Plover's love provided. Stanford re-formed just in time for Alice to cast the same "containment bubble" spell she'd used earlier, encapsulating him like an angry ghost pill.

Alice moved, her hands like a conductor, manipulating the bubble back toward the void as she and Collin moved to the porch. Stanford was beating angrily at the bubble's walls, his screams silenced. He became the ceiling ghost again, formless and empty, filling the bubble entirely like ink.

Alice gathered all the strength of her magic, thinking back to every harsh word that had ever been said to her, every rejection, every hurt. She extended her hand and pushed that ball of Welling rage into the void.

Margaret growled in frustration. "Do you think that's it? That you've won?"

"Well, it doesn't feel like losing." Josh sauntered toward the porch with all the charisma a teenage boy could hope for—right up until the moment that Ben and Mina smothered him with hugs and kisses. Alice thought that he deserved the moment.

"You're sure of your control over Chester?" Alice asked Josh.

He nodded. "As anyone can be of the friendship with a tiny pocket ghost you've trauma-bonded with during an abduction."

"OK." Alice nodded. "I think we should let Chester determine Margaret's fate."

"Wait, Chester gets to decide this?" Riley asked.

"Do you want to be the one to kill Jeff Flanders's mom?" Caroline asked.

"No," Riley sighed. "It just seems risky."

"Trust me, Chester's going to vote thumbs-down," Josh told

her. "Margaret's 'training' methods were pretty awful. Also, she named him Chester."

"When Margaret loses control of the locks, however that happens, we're going to have to deal with the ghosts that escaped the wards," Riley reminded them.

"Oh." Mina glanced up at the ghosts hunched on the roofline, who appeared to be waiting for their chance to flit away. "Right."

"Everybody ready?" Riley asked.

"Ready," Josh and Alice said together. Caroline and Mina simply rolled their shoulders and nodded.

"Chester!" Josh called. The little form turned into the darkness, chirping inquisitively. "What we talked about? Make the choice."

"Oh, please," Margaret scoffed. "Chester might be a little angry now but—"

Margaret was cut off when Chester jumped at her, landing squarely on her chest. Alice averted her eyes. Even if she didn't want Margaret to walk away from this, she didn't want to watch Chester do whatever it was he was made for.

"I don't quite trust Chester," Riley muttered as she, Caroline, and Mina drew a protective circle around them and Edison and Ben shook salt around them all, including Plover.

"Is there something I can do?" Collin asked.

Alice shook her head. "Just be here."

With Collin's hand on her shoulder, Alice gave one last final shove, ensuring Stanford would not return from the depths of the void. Meanwhile, Margaret...

Well, the tension of the Welling locks had disappeared entirely, because Margaret was gone. Chester chirped happily and skittered up to the protection circle. He nearly bounced off the line, making a disappointed noise.

"Sorry, buddy, it's not personal," Josh said. "It's for all ghosts right now."

Chester swept his paw at Plover, who was inside the circle. Josh nodded. "OK, good point."

"We need to step out anyway and get a handle on that." Riley nodded at the Welling candelabra. The ghosts on the roof were growing restless, a few of them carefully moving as if they were going to make a break for it.

"Great," Caroline sighed, cracking her neck. They stepped out of the circle, leaving Ben, Collin, and Edison in the circle with Plover. As they dashed to the candelabra, Chester skittered up Josh's leg, taking hold of his collar, riding there like a parrot. Josh grinned and scratched behind Chester's ears.

All the locks were apparently exactly where they were supposed to be on the candelabra, to best serve their purpose. Keeping a watchful eye on the freed ghosts, the coven formed a circle around the locks. Each put a hand on the next witch's shoulder, joining their free hands in the center.

Something that felt like a cold hand of fear slid up Alice's back. She shivered. It was like previous interactions with the locks' magic, but more intense, and frankly, a little gropey.

"It's a conversation," Riley said, even while she shuddered. "Just a really loud one, between our magic and the locks. We're asking the locks to give their loyalty over to us, because we need to shove all those ghosts back into the house before they can, you know, wreak havoc on the island and its innocent citizens."

"Couldn't we just shove them into the void?" Mina asked.

"I think we would have to push them all at once," Riley said. "We couldn't keep Plover or Natalie or the ghosts who aren't ready to go yet."

"It would be cruel." Alice nodded, breathing deeply. Somewhere, in her magic, she asked that fearful pressure to move away and if it would mind if she used it to control the army of ghosts currently looking down on them from higher ground.

After a moment, the hand slipped away from her spine and seemed to join the coven's combined energy in the center. The candelabra spun in the dirt and the locks turned, like a dead bolt in Alice's chest. She breathed out in unison with the others. They turned their heads to the house and as one, moved their hands up. The rooftop ghosts, even those who were trying to move away from the house, snapped to attention. The wards were back in place.

"Listen up!" Riley yelled. "All of you, except Plover and Chester, please return to the house."

The ghosts didn't move. Chester chirruped, as if pleased to be included.

"Please don't make me force you," Riley sighed. "I'd like to maintain the spirit of cooperation in the house, so to speak. I appreciate that some of you want to move on eventually or want to find a way to resolve your business. And we can work with that. But leaving now? We can't just let you out all at once. It would be chaos."

Alice watched as the creepier specimens, the basement ghosts, were sucked into the house as if a vacuum was pulling them inside. As for the rest, there was some resistance, but eventually, like a stream of water, the ghosts trickled back toward the kitchen door.

A precious few stepped toward Riley. A World War II soldier in a U.S. Navy uniform seemed to speak for the group when he asked, "What if we don't want to go back inside?"

"I think I just went over it," Riley said. "The basement ghosts didn't get a choice. That's just common sense. And I appreciate that you want to go out into the world, but—"

"No, look, we appreciate that you kept us for as long as you did," another ghost, wearing a short-order cook's apron and paper hat, told them as he nodded to the void. "But we think it's time for us to move on. Just protect my toaster, will ya? It's a good one."

"*You're* the toaster ghost!" Riley cried. "I've been stuck with a 1950s toaster I haven't been able to use for fear I'd lose a finger!"

The toaster ghost protested, "I'd never really—"

Riley held up a finger with a griddle-shaped scar.

The toaster ghost rubbed at the back of his neck. "Sorry. I just love that toaster. It was my ma's."

"If you choose to move along, I will treat it with kid gloves," Riley promised. "Which I will wear. While making toast."

He grinned. "Thank you."

"All right, move along with my best wishes, if that's what you want," Riley said as the spirits moved toward the void. "I hope you enjoyed your stay in Shaddow House."

The coven waited as ten or so ghosts faded into the empty space. The others dutifully filed back into the house until Plover and Chester were the only ghosts left outside. Natalie waved wordlessly from inside the kitchen.

The coven closed the void overhead with a final gesture. Chester hummed happily from Josh's shoulder, nuzzling against his cheek.

Alice shuddered as Chester's sharp fangs came dangerously close to Josh's neck. But the awful little thing seemed completely enamored of him.

Josh turned to his father. "Dad, can I keep him?"

"As happy as I am that you're safe, that's going to be a hard pass, son," Ben told him from the circle.

"This is just like that time you asked for a ferret at the mall, with no prep work," Mina told him, shaking her head. "No strategy at all."

Edison scraped a foot across the salt line, allowing Plover to step out of the circle. "I believe it would be better if...Chester...stayed here at the house where I can keep an eye on him, Joshua."

Chester made a sad little peep and nuzzled Josh's cheek.

"I promise to take good care of Chester," Riley said, looking very uncertain of the whole enterprise. "You just have to, you know, promise not to reach into my chest and stop my heart."

Chester made what sounded like an agreeable rumble.

"I guess," Josh sighed. "But I'll come see you every day, OK? I'm right next door."

"Also, both of you are getting a whole new edition of the stranger-danger talk," Ben told his kids. "Clearly, I was not thorough enough."

Josh threw his hands up. "You gave me the stranger-danger talk, not the 'hot lady asking for help with her luggage' talk."

"Well, you should both prepare for many, *many* amendments to the stranger-danger talk," Ben told him.

"So, you're outside," Riley said, beaming at Plover. "How does it feel?"

"Uncomfortable," he replied. "I am so very proud of you, my dear. All of you. You've managed what generations of Dentons before you never could have imagined."

"And we figured out who's attached to the toaster," Riley said, even as she blinked past pleased and tired tears. "The kitchen is safe for toast."

She discreetly wiped her cheek as Edison wrapped an arm around her. She peered down at Margaret's body, peaceful and still. It looked like she'd just decided to take an evening's nap on the grass.

"We're going to have to move her body," Riley told them. "Celia is never going to believe this."

"We're interfering with crime scenes now?" Caroline asked.

"We didn't commit a crime," Riley insisted. "We're just harboring a killer ghost hamster."

Chester made an indignant peep from Josh's shoulder.

"It's a thin distinction, but it's there," Riley replied.

"Sorry, your theory about the ceiling ghost being a poltergeist was wrong," Mina told Josh, putting her arm around his waist. She was careful to avoid Chester, who was sniffing at her, curious.

"I don't know," Josh said. "His attachment object was the house, so in a way… OK, yeah, we probably should have figured it out a while ago."

"Well, we were kind of distracted," Mina told him. Josh hummed. "Come on. Dad says we're probably going to need to move Margaret into our yard. We're going to tell Celia she probably felt ill and tried to drop by the house to ask for help. We're going to need your upper-body strength."

"Of all our family bonding experiences, this is the most traumatizing," Josh muttered.

Alice turned to Collin, who appeared to be leaning against the gazebo railing, breathing deeply. She was still upset with him, but the business with Paige seemed so distant now, unimportant. He'd let another woman use her tub. And yes, they were going to have to have a lot of conversations about healthy boundaries and learning to say "no," but for right now, she was really grateful to have someone in her life who would throw himself in front of an oncoming evil hamster for her. Even if the hamster turned out to be mostly OK.

When directed appropriately.

"So... This is my life," she told Collin. "Evil house pets. And haunted antiques. Occasionally covering up suspicious deaths. Ghost butler-dads who are going to think you're not good enough for me, despite the fact that you're ridiculously well-off and own all the things."

"She's right," Plover said. "I don't think you're good enough for her."

Alice snickered and Collin hugged her. She wasn't ready for a kiss just yet, but that would come. It just felt nice to be held.

"It's a very interesting life, and I would like to be part of it," Collin whispered into her hair. "And I know I've messed up and we're going to have to have a lot of talks about it, but I think I can begin to make it up to you with eight little words."

She leaned back to look up at him. "What's that?"

Collin grinned at her. "I'm going to have another stained-glass tub built."

Chapter 15
Collin

TWO DAYS LATER, JULIE WAS waiting for him outside the Cowslip Suite with a grim but determined look on her face. In fact, she had an entire housekeeping squadron waiting with her, all with grim but determined looks on their faces.

"Good morning, ladies. I don't need backup for this." Collin inclined his head to the trio of housekeepers, each dressed in comfortable brick-red winter-weight scrubs they'd all agreed upon for "non-occupation dates."

"No, but I promised the ladies here that when the Haircut eventually got herself ejected from the hotel, they would be allowed to be part of the process," Julie said.

"You knew that Paige would eventually get herself ejected from the hotel?" Collin asked.

"Yes, and that we would be allowed to be part of the process," Hester Murphy, one of the older housekeepers on staff, repeated. "Miss LaGravenesse has not made friends here. Not like Alice."

Collin considered that for a moment. Paige had been uncharacteristically quiet while he and the coven recovered from their confrontation with Margaret, explained to Celia how yet another body had ended up near Shaddow House, explained to poor Jeff what had happened to his mother. Fortunately, Celia and Jeff were inclined to believe Ben's medically qualified assurances that Margaret had died of a heart attack. Jeff seemed more embarrassed that his mother was lurking around Ben's place. He'd chalked it up to her trying to get a look inside Gray Fern or Shaddow House.

Collin had been distracted by helping their friends negotiate these real-world, non-magical problems. He'd almost forgotten that Paige was still around. Clearly, Paige hadn't been on her best behavior in her boredom.

"Understood," Collin said, raising his hand to knock on the door. "Ladies, if we could move about this as quickly and quietly as possible, I would appreciate it. I'm not asking you to protect her dignity... Just try not to throw any physical punches."

"Understood," Hester replied, echoing his tone. She turned to her coworkers. "Plan C, girls."

"Plan C?" Collin asked as he knocked on the door. "How many plans were there?"

"You think this is the first time they've had to do this?" Julie asked him.

Collin shrugged. He hadn't told Alice that he was planning to remove Paige today. He knew that at this point, Alice didn't want words from him. She wanted action, and that was fair. He'd been too indirect in his interactions with Paige. He'd tried to be kind, but all he'd done was give Paige a vague hope that maybe someday... And now he was paying for that lack of clarity and, well, his cowardice. Alice was paying for it too, and if he wanted any sort of future with her, he was going to have to make things very clear.

"What do you think you're doing?" Paige shrieked as Julie and the housekeeping squad marched into the room as a unit. As he looked around the sparsely furnished space with its barely dried (not orange) paint, he wondered why Paige had bothered. She would have had more comforts in the guesthouse. Here Paige had no decorations, no place to sit, not even a nightstand. The bed didn't have a headboard, just a hastily constructed frame and a mattress. It had been a misguided flex, Paige trying to show Alice that she could get Collin to do whatever she wanted. And she'd paid for it with days in a room without so much as a closet bar to hang her precious clothes.

"Your stay with the Duchess Hotel is at an end, ma'am," Julie told her with no small amount of professional glee. The housekeepers had already located her suitcases and began unpacking the drawers of the tall, fluted maple dresser Alice had chosen for the room. "The staff will help you pack up, and your transportation will be ready shortly."

"What are you talking about?" Paige demanded. "Collin, what is going on?"

"You're leaving, Paige," Collin told her. "Right after you return my mother's engagement ring, which is to say, right now."

"What? Why?" Paige huffed. "I just got here. And we have so much to talk about."

Somehow, the housekeepers managed to sweep the bedroom *and* the bathroom of Paige's belongings before Collin could even reply. "You're no longer welcome here."

"Since when? My family has *always* been welcome on your

properties, you know that. You wouldn't turn away a LaGravenesse. You wouldn't *dare*—where are you going with my things?" she yelled at the housekeeping staff as they carried her bags out the door.

Julie smiled sweetly as she walked out after them. "Thank you for staying at the Duchess. Now, please get the hell out and never darken our doors again."

"I'll have you fired, you little bitch!" Paige yelled. But Julie had already left the room.

"No, you won't have her fired," he barked at her. "Your days of terrorizing people in my name are over. You've gone too far now, Paige. We won't even talk about manipulating my staff into putting you into this room far before it was ready for occupancy, and putting what I'm trying to do here in danger. That's just window dressing on the bullshit you've been trying to pull. You put that boy Josh—someone I care about—in danger."

"Oh, please," she scoffed. "A little old lady wanted to talk to him about breaking one of her windows. He and his doctor daddy had been dodging her."

"Bullshit," Collin replied.

"Seriously, I was just trying to protect your image here, locally," she insisted. "Being a part of the commun—"

"Bullshit," Collin said again.

"Fine, *fine*," Paige grunted. "I was down at that piddly little bakery, *trying* to find something gluten-free, and that old woman heard me complaining on my phone about the mousy little frump you've got shacked up with you. She asked me for a favor, and in return, she would make sure Alex or whatever her name is would leave you alone. Big deal. I just asked a kid to help me carry a bag to the hotel. It's not like I gave him drugs or something. Why are you being so *dramatic*?"

"If I had any idea that you *knew* your actions would put Josh in danger, the police couldn't help you. Because I would let Mina have five minutes with you," Collin told her. "As it is, I can only suspect that you were trying to mess with Alice. Now, you've intruded on my hospitality and my life long enough. I want you gone. Now."

"Oh, Collin, don't be silly," she giggled, stroking his shirtfront. "You've said this kind of thing before, and you've never meant it."

He removed her hands from his shirt and pushed them away. "I assure you I am being very serious. I have called my helicopter. I only call my helicopter when I'm serious."

As if on cue, he could hear the beat of rotors in the distance. Whatever he was paying Julie, it was not enough.

Paige rolled her eyes, and she strode toward the door.

"Paige," he called at her. She turned, an expression that was simultaneously smug and hopeful on the face he'd once adored. He held out his palm. "My mother's ring?"

"Why?" she demanded. "We both know I'm going to end up with it eventually anyway. I'll just take it to my jeweler and have it sized."

"Paige," he said again, his hand still out. "Now."

She huffed out a sigh as she dug a ring box out of her purse and handed it to him. Collin opened the box to make sure she'd actually returned his mother's ring and not some other bauble. To her credit, it was there. "Thank you."

"After all these years, you think you can just end things?" Paige demanded as she followed him out of the suite. "You *know*

NEVER BEEN WITCHED 335

we're supposed to end up together. I've let you run around and have your freedom, your fun, but your family and mine have expectations—and it's time we met them. I know who you are, Collin—who you *really* are. Not this polished-prince act you're putting on for the yokels, but the real you and the stupidity you're capable of. Do you think that sweet little schoolmarm is going to put up with the bullshit I've seen from you? She has no *idea* what you're capable of."

"I'm not that person anymore," Collin said.

"I've heard that from you before too," she shot back, following him down the hall. "Tell me a new one. Look, we belong together, because I'm the one who will accept you, love you, no matter what. I've put too much time and effort into—"

"You *don't love me.* I *don't love you*," he told her. "You've been a friend to me over the years. I don't know what we are now, but I know we're not friends. We don't really want each other. We just don't want to let go of the idea of each other. But it's time. What you did was really dangerous and could have gotten Josh killed."

"You're exaggerating," Paige's voice was strident, bouncing off the lobby ceiling in an eerie mockery of Victoria's final agonies in the hotel hall. "Don't do this, Collin. Please, I love you!"

He exited the lobby to the left, toward the helipad, which was simply a nice, stable, flat piece of un-landscaped lawn that served as a landing space for high-profile guests and Medivac flights alike.

"If I thought that was true," Collin said, pausing at the door to the west lawn, "I would be so sad for you. But it's not true, you know that. You don't love me. We're both just scared of what we are without this lie to fall back on. I'm trying to figure that out for myself. And it's time you did the same."

"Don't you spout that therapy crap at me," Paige seethed. "I know *who you are*, Collin Bancroft. And I know what a disappointment you are to everybody who knows you."

Collin opened the door to find Paige's suitcases at the edge of the helipad where the Bancroft Enterprises helicopter was waiting. "Paige, get your ass on the helicopter. Then find your own flight home. Don't come back."

"Whatever." Paige slid her sunglasses onto her face. "This place is a dump anyway."

"So, you won't miss it, then," a sweet voice announced from beside the door. Alice was standing there, all insincere smiles with enough of an edge to make something in Collin's gut shiver. "I watched your suitcases for you," Alice said. "Fly safe."

"As if I want to come back to this godforsaken hellhole," Paige snapped, pulling her bag toward the waiting pilot. "You'll be calling me in two weeks, Collin, bored out of your skull!"

Collin waved her off, even as she struggled to get her bags off the hotel porch and carry them to the helipad.

"Julie texted you about the 'ejection' happening this morning, didn't she?" he asked Alice.

"No. Julie texted me to schedule a meeting with the hotel's prospective historical marketing coordinator," Alice said, gesturing at herself. "She just happened to mention this morning's ejection because she likes me more than Paige."

Collin grinned at her. "You're still not accepting my very generous offer?"

"Not officially," Alice told him. "I like keeping you in suspense. Besides, the more I put you off, the more generous you're likely to become."

Collin laughed. He would wait until Alice was ready to take a job from the hotel. It would get Alice out of her grandparents' orbit and employment, and that was all Collin wanted for her.

"OK, you've convinced me to pull the ultimate card," he replied. "Unlimited Collin sandwich."

"No deal." Alice's disgusted expression made him laugh. "I can't believe you actually summoned a helicopter to boot her off the island."

"And last night, my lawyers sent a letter explaining to my aunt and uncle why they are not legally entitled to anything I own," he said. "It was written in very simple yet scary-sounding language so they would understand."

"That should not be as sexy as it is. I mean, I feel guilty that I can be swayed by this sort of flashy consumerism. But... When you decide to do something, you get it done. And I appreciate that."

He smoothed her hair back from her face where the wind had dislodged it. Things were going to be tentative between them for a while, and that was OK. They had fallen rather fast for each other, and they needed to find a more even, "not in the midst of a witch-slash-ghost crisis" keel. But they were going to try, and that mattered.

"She actually threw her bag at the feet of the man who was supposed to fly her out of here," Alice observed as Paige pitched a tantrum on the helipad. The pilot had been warned to expect this and had been instructed to leave any bag Paige tossed on the ground...right there, on the ground.

Collin sighed. He was going to have to give the pilot hazard pay. "You seem to be in a good mood, considering your recent heroics," he said.

"All in the line of duty of your local witch-slash-ghost-wrangler," she said, grinning at him.

"You are the coolest girl I will ever meet," Collin told her.

"Well, sure. Do you know any other witch-slash-ghost-wranglers?" Alice asked.

Collin laughed. "I do not, but is there a reason for your particularly good mood? Other than the promise of a new fairy-queen tub?" Alice absolutely beamed as Paige climbed into the helicopter. He bumped her gently with his hip. "OK, there's something special behind that smile."

"Well, it's possible—given our newfound ability to bring ghosts out of Shaddow House—that I sneaked a button into one of the tiny, basically useless pockets on the exterior of Paige's suitcase. You did say she basically lives out of that suitcase, right?"

"It's her favorite Vuitton. She's had it since college." Collin chuckled, walking with Alice off the veranda, toward the manor house. "Paige travels most of the year, yes, but that button is significant because…"

"It came from the toque of a French boulanger," she told him. "His name was Xavier."

"I assuming Xavier is haunting said button?" Collin asked.

"Yes, and one of the side effects of said haunting is that the ghost always smells like bread. The most delicious, crusty, proper French baguettes you could possibly imagine. Because this man loved bread so much, he clung to the button of his uniform he wore when he made it. Because he couldn't imagine moving on to a dimension where he wasn't sure bread existed," she told him. "And he will make Paige smell that delicious bread, but she won't be able to eat it, because the bread doesn't exist. And because the button is so small, she'll never find it, and she'll certainly never think that's where the smell is coming from. So, unless she gets rid of the suitcase she loves, she will smell the inaccessible, ephemeral bread. It's like a carb-based curse."

He nodded. "I am beginning to fall deeply in love with you, but you might be evil."

Alice shrugged as he led her through the front door of Forsythia Manor. "It was Plover's idea. Xavier's missed the outside world. He craved a bit of travel."

"This is why you love that ghostly man," he observed.

"Yes, it is," she said, stopping in her tracks at the sight of a large wooden armoire in his parlor. "What's this?"

Arthur popped up from behind the cabinet and shouted, "Alice! I've missed you!"

"Arthur!" she cried. She ran forward, but seemed to realize she couldn't hug a ghost, so she simply gave Bessie the cabinet an affectionate pat.

"I bought Arthur's armoire," Collin said. "Well, I had Julie buy Arthur's armoire, a few days ago. I know how much it means to you, and how much you hated leaving him behind with the Proctors."

"Bessie and I have been very comfortable here. I like this one much better than your grandparents," Arthur assured her, pointing to Collin. "Now, he says you won't be joining us right away."

She glanced at Collin. "He's right. We're not ready for that yet, but I'll be nearby, renting somewhere. And I'll come by to visit often."

"And if you miss her too much, I can always move you and Bessie over to her place," Collin promised Arthur. "No rush, no pressure."

"I appreciate that," she told him. "And I appreciate you rescuing Arthur from my grandparents."

"They are no more pleasant than they were when you left," Arthur told her. "Now, go on, Alice, give the boy a kiss for all he's done. He's had a busy morning."

"You have had a very busy morning," Alice told Collin, slipping her arms around his waist. "And I appreciate everything you're doing to try to make me more comfortable."

"I want our weird, awesome life together, whatever form that takes," Collin replied, kissing her long and slow.

She laughed, bumping her forehead against his. What he had with Alice wasn't love yet, but it was something good, something solid—something he could build on.

Epilogue
Plover

SEVERAL MONTHS LATER...

IT WAS A FUNNY THING, to see one's purpose fulfilled.

Plover stood at the window overlooking Shaddow House, admiring the way the moonlight shimmered on the thick blanket of snow.

There was a lovely sense of rebirth in an early Michigan snowstorm. The world was new once more.

For years, Plover thought he didn't know how to handle anything new. And yet, the universe insisted on throwing these new things at him. Like Miss Riley.

For *decades*, Plover had watched the Denton family try and fail to recover the locks. But it took an unknown Denton—raised away from the family, the house, the magic—to crack the puzzle. Riley did things in her own way, instinctive and unorthodox, relying on non-Dentons, which had only been done a few times in the family's history. But despite all the obstacles, she had managed it.

Centuries of Denton effort, ending in a confrontation with an "evil hamster" and a library volunteer. Plover had not seen that coming. It had quite the effect on Edison, knowing that he'd harbored Riley's nemesis at his workplace for years, and Plover understood his need to mourn someone he'd thought was his friend.

But now, the moon was brighter, the wind crisper—not that he could feel either, but somehow, he got the impression. He tilted his transparent face toward the bright, full moon. It was...pleasant.

Plover wasn't certain how he felt, now that the coven had decided not to destroy the locks for the time being. But his ladies, and young Joshua, seemed to have a plan, and since his days of living, Plover's role was not to question his employers, but to trust in their plans. And with his family?

He'd learned to trust them implicitly.

Plover turned to see Miss Mina sitting in one of the lounges, poring over college catalogues, while Josh was sprawled across the couch in that boneless way of his. The young people had brought a sense of life and joy that had been missing from the house for the better part of three generations.

How deliciously odd it was for an old, deceased man to only find a family after death, but here he was, the patriarch of a large, loving, extended-kin group of choice. He only wished his beloved Nora was here to be a part of it.

"The whole family went on a campus tour," Mina was telling Miss Alice. "We saw the freshman dorm." She paused to shudder. "Super haunted. At least two ghosts per floor."

"Well, you're more prepared for that than most underclassmen," Alice said as Riley unlocked the basement door. Collin dropped a kiss on Alice's forehead as he passed her. She beamed up at him.

Plover still wasn't sure if the young man was good enough for Alice, but she seemed to love him completely—even if she wasn't aware of it herself—so he would abide.

Mina swore, "I am salting *everything*."

"I signed you up for a monthly salt delivery for your graduation present. Salts from around the world!" Riley told her from the basement stairs, making Mina laugh. "Surprise!"

The unspoken part was that the entire group was all grateful Miss Mina was going to be able to leave the island to attend school. For a while, there was some concern that the magic would choose Mina or Josh as its new Steward, in the same way Miss Riley had been selected without her assent. Riley had taken some short trips without the customary discomfort Dentons experienced while traveling away from Starfall Point. For now, it appeared that Shaddow House was loosening its grip on all of them.

The ladies came up from the basement door, hauling the candelabra and the small wooden trunk they'd used to store the locks. It seemed more dignified than a cardboard moving box.

Plover joined Miss Natalie, watching the coven set up their ritual space in the atrium. It seemed wisest to do this in the most open space in the house, even if it was surrounded by glass. It might have been more advisable to do this outside, but it seemed like the sort of thing that would attract attention, opening a giant hole into the beyond.

Josh and Mina sprinkled a large circle of herbed salt near Miss Eloise's fountain. Eloise eyed it suspiciously.

"Don't worry, sweetie, you don't have to leave until you feel like it's time," Riley assured her.

"Still feels weird that we're not destroying these things," Caroline muttered as they arranged the locks on the pedestal. It didn't feel hostile any longer. It didn't feel *positive*, but neutrality was probably the best thing they could ask for right now. "For all we know, Jeff is going to come looking for them."

"I really don't think so," Riley said. "He seemed completely in shock when I stopped by to offer my condolences. There wasn't a hint of dastardly plotting or threats. And if Jeff does come for them, he's in for a fight. We're stronger now. We know who he is. Besides, we might as well put the locks to some good use, considering all the problems they've caused."

Plover and Natalie joined the "associates" of the coven outside the circle. It was to be a clandestine nighttime gathering, as most workings of the coven needed to be. Their dress wasn't exactly ceremonial—jeans and sweaters—but there was an air of gravity. The candelabra sat in the center of the circle, the locks arranged carefully on their cups. They raised their hands, making a series of gestures that reminded Plover of an orchestra conductor. Overhead, a swirling vortex of empty black opened, like a wound in the air flowing up from the copper coils. It was still, so very silent, and the sight of it filled Plover with a dreadful longing. There was something waiting for him inside that void.

Behind the coven, a haze of ghostly mist started to gather—so many spirits, dozens of them, were drawn to the void. Ghosts that Plover hadn't seen in years were edging forward, curious expressions on their silvery faces. Eloise, however, swam to the far end of the fountain and stayed as far away from the empty space as possible.

"Anyone who *wants to* move on, you're more than welcome. I

understand that maybe you didn't, uh, feel ready to walk into the light the first time it appeared—well, when you died, and you didn't know how to get it back in the time since, but here's your chance. We've enjoyed hosting you here at Shaddow House, but don't feel the need to stick around on our account." Riley looked at her sisters, cringing. "I really should have prepared a speech or something."

"No, it's fine," Alice assured her, motioning for the ghosts to release their hold on this world. "It's sincere."

"Are you sure about waiting to 'evict' our more hostile guests?" Caroline asked.

"This is a lot for one night," Riley said. "We need to leave something for tomorrow."

"We're shoving the clown ghost through, though, right?" Mina asked. "Whether he wants to go or not?"

Riley nodded sharply. "Oh, yeah. It's all part of my anti-clown-ghost initiative."

The figures surrounding them solidified and multiplied, edging forward toward the void. They reached for it and seemed to sag in relief as the void accepted them. They floated upward in droves, like embers from a bonfire winking out into the ether.

"Weird. It's like I can feel their connection to their house fading away," Riley murmured, cracking her neck as if the effort exhausted her.

Josh stared up into the void. "It's like there's more space in my head, less noise."

Mina opened her mouth as if to make a joke, but Ben raised his hand and told her, "Don't."

Mina pinched her lips shut and contained herself.

"I feel something approaching," Caroline said, frowning. "It feels like someone walking up to the front door."

"She's asking for permission," Josh agreed, tilting his head as if listening. "Which is a nice change of pace."

"She kind of looks like..." Riley peered into the darkness and suddenly her mouth dropped open. "Aunt Nora?"

Plover's head snapped up. A distant shape came into focus within the void. Plover saw a handsome woman, her iron-gray hair swept back from her face in a neat chignon, and if his heart still beat, it would have stopped still. She was just as elegant and lovely as he remembered her—all high cheekbones and gray eyes that only he knew as laughing and playful. She was in a dress in peridot green that brought out the fathomless depths of her eyes. It had always been his favorite.

"Bert," Nora Denton whispered, reaching out as she materialized in front of him. "I miss you."

"Oh, Nora." Plover blinked, as he was warding off tears he couldn't physically shed. "I have missed you so very much. You left me here without you."

Nora moved her fingers gently down Plover's cheek. It was warmth and love and everything he'd missed in both planes of existence. "I didn't mean to."

"I know," he said, pressing his hand against hers. To feel her touch, finally. It was a balm to his soul he'd never thought possible.

"You seem tired," Nora said. "We're not supposed to get tired."

"In the words of the children, 'I've had a lot going on,'" Plover said.

"But you're not ready to leave," Nora said, shaking her head.

"The young ladies have completed their primary task, but they still need me," Plover said.

"For supervision," Mina muttered.

"For guidance," Plover told her, a gentle note of chastisement in his tone. He turned to Nora. "I can't leave them just yet."

"I understand," Nora promised. "I never could have moved on, seen what I've seen, if I hadn't known you were here to protect Riley."

"Your name is Bert?" Josh asked.

"That's what you got out of that?" Mina asked.

"I'm trying so hard to break the tension," he replied.

"It's short for 'Filbert,'" Nora told them.

"Really? *Filbert* Plover?" Riley gasped. Plover nodded.

"I am sorry for setting this burden on your shoulders, sweetheart," Nora told Riley. "I kept waiting for the magic to appoint a new Steward, new helpmates for me, a coven. But it never happened. Seeing what you've accomplished now, I suppose that it was because you were meant to be here to do this. And I'm grateful for it. You did what generations of us couldn't."

"I didn't do it alone," Riley noted.

Nora turned to smile at the others in the circle. "Yes. It's been very interesting, looking in on all of you from time to time."

"You haven't been able to see...everything, though, right?" Edison asked, scratching the back of his neck.

"Like most spirits, I looked away when it was appropriate," Nora said dryly.

"Thank you," Edison whispered, looking at the floor while Collin and Ben laughed at him.

"I think you'll find that with your coven looking after things for you, you'll be able to travel a bit more freely," Nora told Riley. "But you'll always need to come back to Shaddow House."

"It's home now," Riley said, shrugging. "It's nice to have some flexibility, but I don't mind."

"And I think you'll find with the locks, you can call me forth any time you need to talk," Nora said. "I believe that was the point of the locks, once assembled."

"We think so too." Riley said. "But my mother?"

"She's already moved out of my reach," Nora said. "Whatever comes beyond the beyond. The afterlife has many layers and facets. But I have a sense we'll see her again at some point in our journeys. Time is very different here." She turned to Plover. "And I will see you soon."

Nora leaned close and kissed Plover fiercely. It was the first kiss they'd ever shared as equal creatures, and it would have to last him for a long time. He felt her, in his whole being, and he was grateful for it.

He vaguely heard Josh say, "This is unsettling."

"Josh?" Ben said.

"Yeah, Dad?" Josh asked.

Ben told his beloved son, "Shut up."

Josh nodded. "Yep."

When Nora finally, reluctantly, pulled away, she gave Plover a knowing smile. "I'll be waiting."

"I'll see you soon," Plover promised. With her hand on his cheek, she faded into nothing.

"That was very sweet," Alice told him as Collin slipped his arm around her. "I'm glad you got to see her."

"Should we close it?" Caroline asked, nodding up at the void.

"I would prefer not to stare directly into my own existential dread," Edison told them.

"One more thing," Mina said, making a hard pull motion that drew a short, squatty shape in a disheveled red-and-white striped suit toward the circle. Jingles the Clown, with his off-putting red-and-white makeup and oversize pants, had frightened his last Denton witch.

That was one spirit that Plover would certainly not miss.

"We're melting your creepy stork statue," Mina told him as she forced Jingles through the shrinking ring of shadow energy. "Only a clown would be attached to a bronze stork playing a saxophone. Gah."

"Feel better?" Josh asked.

Mina pursed her lips. "Yes, I do."

The witches closed the circle and swept up the salt. Plover stood, staring up at the space where the void once hovered. Mina was correct, as usual. The house, with all its nooks and bric-a-brac, felt more spacious somehow, and Plover's shoulders felt less burdened. Still, there were simply too many spirits sealed inside Shaddow House—well, resealed, to put it more accurately—for him to retire now.

Besides, what would a retired ghost do?

Shaddow House was no longer a trap for ghosts who posed a threat to the living; it was a haven for those who didn't. His ladies (and Josh) needed him to act as a liaison between those spirits and the coven. His love, his Nora, was waiting for him on the other side, but the time for that would come. That was the benefit of the afterlife.

The dead had nothing but time.

"I declare this meeting of the Shaddow House Ghost and Friday Night Euchre Club adjourned," Riley announced.

"Still not the name," Caroline told her.

"It's the name if I say it's the name," Riley shot back.

"I think we have to vote on these things," Alice said.

"I'm on your side, Riley. I think it's an awesome name," Josh told her.

Mina snorted. "You're saying that because you're trying to get more imported jelly beans."

"Two things can be true at the same time," Josh replied primly.

"We can have custom club shirts made," Riley said, clapping excitedly while she hopped up and down. Edison chuckled and hugged her close.

"No custom shirts," Caroline told her.

"With little ghosts embroidered on them!" Riley added.

"Will it have my name embroidered over my heart?" Alice asked. "Like a bowling shirt?"

"Don't you start with this!" Caroline cried.

Plover smiled to himself. The coven was certainly going to make that time interesting.

While Plover stepped in to de-escalate the custom shirt debate, several floors down, in the secret basement level, the brass lock on a single red door slipped open. The door swung free and a cold, howling wind swept out and hovered over the bare floor. With a hiss of discontent, it spiraled up toward the stone foundation of Shaddow House.

Read on for an excerpt of

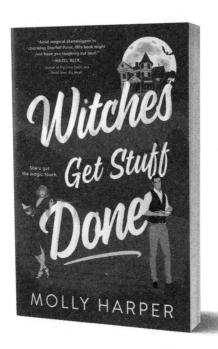

Chapter 1
Riley

RILEY EVERETT WISHED SHE HAD the internal fortitude to admire Starfall Point as it rose in the watery distance. Unfortunately, she'd thrown up everything in her body over the rail of the island's mid-morning ferry. She had no fortitude left, internal or external.

The Loyal Retriever cut through the choppy blue waters of Lake Huron with a surgical grace that should have been reassuring. Instead, Riley was anxiety-sweating through the newly purchased cargo jacket necessary to protect her from the brisk early May wind.

Brisk. Wind. In. *May.*

Her Floridian brain simply couldn't comprehend those words being strung together.

Maybe it was only brisk to Riley? Maybe she was cold because she was used to the soul-melting heat of Orlando? Maybe it didn't matter because she felt like she was going to throw up again.

Wisps from her chin-length cap of dark gold hair clung to her clammy cheeks as her stomach attempted to turn itself inside out like a possessed balloon animal. And the worst part was there was nowhere to hide. She'd dashed for the ferry's bathrooms just after the *Retriever* left the dock, only to find one marked with an OUT OF ORDER sign and the other locked tight. She'd had to hang over the railing to be sick, much to the gleeful horror of the school group standing nearby.

It might have been easier if she'd been able to sit inside, away from the sight of the churning waves, but all the seats inside the ferry cabin were taken by semi-elderly tourists in some sort of discount group. It seemed early in the season to brave the chill and the wind, even if the island was considered one of the most picturesque spots in Michigan. She supposed that's why there was a discount.

Riley was left to sit on a peeling blue bench built into the exterior of the main cabin, which seemed to magnify every pitch and roll of the boat by the power of ten. And it was very difficult not to resent the group of eight-to-ten-year-olds standing at what Riley considered to be an ill-advised distance from the railing in their bright yellow Sunnyside Day Camp windbreakers. They were whooping and screaming with every dip of the hull like they were riding some epic roller coaster headed straight to Hades. Oh, to be young and not have the taste of regurgitated breakfast burrito coating one's mouth.

"Is she gonna do it again?" one kid asked, shoving handfuls of rainbow fruit snacks in his face. His obvious half-agonizing, half-hopeful state, made Riley think of untold Jane Austen adaptations involving evil zombie children.

"It's another ten minutes to the island. I'll bet she'll go one more time, at least," the boy's little buddy, all ferret features and spiky auburn hair, said as he eyed Riley intently.

Were all "up north" kids so morbidly interested in public pukers, or was Riley a special case?

She had never been this nauseated in all her thirty-three years. Hell, she'd worked as a cocktail waitress on a half-derelict cruise ship during the hurricane-plagued off-season and had never been this sick. Maybe her motion sickness was lake-specific? Or could her "boat anxiety" just be regular anxiety? She *was* traveling to meet her heretofore unknown, long-lost elderly aunt after a lifetime without any relatives besides her parents. Riley couldn't help but feel she was sailing into some sort of trap. Didn't half of the women featured on true crime podcasts end up murdered because they answered messages from strangers? Hell, she was pretty sure this was how a lot of 1970s horror movies started.

Maybe she should just forget this whole thing. She could open her phone for the first time all day and email her aunt, who hadn't responded to any of her messages in the previous few days, and tell her, "Sorry, I came down with a sudden case of 'not wanting to die in your clearly demon-based world domination plot,'" and run back to Florida like her ass was on fire. Elderly people rarely checked their emails, right? She could get as far as Tennessee before Aunt Nora figured out Riley had ditched her.

Of course, an abrupt turnaround would mean she'd have to get back on the boat almost immediately after landing on Starfall, and Riley wasn't sure she would survive that.

Much like her emotional state, the *Retriever* pitched wildly into the waves, throwing Riley's weight against the cabin wall. Her stomach gave another watery twist. Riley groaned, clapping her hand over her mouth.

A desperate and awful pressure rippled up her throat, like some sort of digestive earthquake. With the schoolkids milling around between Riley and the nearest trash can, she had no alternative but to run to the railing again. She wrapped her arms around the rust-roughened metal, lest she get thrown headfirst into the water while she gagged. The schoolkids' excited noises changed very quickly to a chorus of disgusted *"ew!"*s in stereo.

"She's gonna barf again!" Fruit Snacks yelled.

"Nope, she's thrown up so much that she can't throw up anymore!" Ferret Face hooted. "My uncle Max calls it the 'dry heaves.' Mom says that's why I'm not allowed to drink anything from his fridge."

Riley's realized Fruit Snacks was holding up his cell phone as if he was recording her. Oh, shit. She was going to end up on some sort of horrible "Best Boat Barf Fails" compilation video.

In a day filled with emotional punches to the chin, this was the final indignity.

Riley breathed deep and immediately regretted it as the smell of exhaust and dead-fish-slash-lake water filled her nostrils. Right. If she'd learned anything over the years, it was when to strategically retreat. Relinquishing her hold on the rail, Riley stumbled towards the little alcove containing the bathroom doors. She rattled the knob, which was still locked and immobile.

"Oh, come on!" she yelled, feeling her stomach lurch again. She banged her fist on the door, every impact with the sturdy metal biting her chilled skin. "There are *other people* out here who need the bathroom! *Wrap it up!*"

"Won't do you any good," a tall, willowy woman with a bright shock of strawberry-blond hair sighed to Riley's left. Hunkered against the OUT OF ORDER door, the redhead was dressed in a prim dove-gray suit that made her fair skin look slightly sallow and didn't quite look up to the task of protecting her from the cold. Riley was pretty certain there was a tinge of blue under the woman's work-appropriate nude lip gloss. Her eyes narrowed at the closed bathroom door. "I've been locked out of the bathroom for most of the ride, and the situation is too damn close to desperate." She flinched, as if she'd just heard the words coming out of her mouth. "Please, pardon my language. I'm Alice Seastairs."

"Riley Everett," she said, nodding to Alice, who seemed genuinely distressed by her use of a fairly minor curse word. To lower the social stakes, Riley offered, "My mom used to tell me that some people think that they're the center of the universe. And then she would rattle on about 'mainlander assholes' and end up ignoring me for the rest of the day."

Alice snorted and then blanched again, covering her mouth with a slim, elegant hand. Now that Riley had cursed at a higher level, she seemed to relax a bit. "Well, your mother sounds like an interesting person."

"She was," Riley nodded as she felt another prickle of cold sweat flush her cheeks. She groaned, leaning against the wall behind her. Though she wasn't looking up at Alice, Riley could pinpoint the moment that her new acquaintance started feeling sorry for her. Riley's mother, Ellen, had died a few months before. Riley touched on the subject so rarely that she hadn't quite grasped the art of not dropping it on people like that.

Hank Everett felt the loss of his beloved wife so deeply, he was rarely able to talk about her, not even with Riley. That was why his insistence that she accept Nora's invitation had shocked her—particularly after his response to Nora's message was, "Well, your mom always said she was an only child, and an orphan. But maybe you should look into it."

Riley had been living with Hank for *months*, helping him cope with the loss, and suddenly, he was strong enough—hell, *eager*—to send her away? Didn't most fathers make it their goal in life to keep their daughters off *Dateline*? Then again, maybe Hank thought Riley would use up all her questions and conversations about Ellen with this over-helpful stranger, and he would never have to relive those painful memories.

Leaning against the wall and bracing her hands on her knees, Riley felt Alice pat her shoulder. When a thrum of electric discomfort shot through her, ricocheting into her chest, she thought maybe it came from the act of discussing her mother with a stranger. She wondered what Ellen Everett would think of Riley traveling all the way to the Upper Peninsula of Michigan to meet her aunt Nora. Probably not much, considering Ellen had never told Riley that Nora or Starfall Point even existed. Maybe that was contributing to Riley's sense of unease? Knowing that her mother hadn't wanted her to know about this part of Ellen's life, her history?

Riley's relationship with her mother had always been distant, something she'd attributed to her parents having Riley later in life and not being used to her generation's insistent communication. Now, she wondered if Ellen just didn't trust her to handle the family history.

Could it really be so bad? Starfall Point had looked so

charming in the photos—aggressively quaint houses, fudge shops, and island-wide garden shows. Riley had found one website claiming the town had a negative crime rate, as in the good deeds done there outstripped the bad, but Riley couldn't confirm such a thing existed.

Riley realized she'd been silent for so long, Alice probably thought she was either going to throw up again or start crying. She wasn't sure which Alice would consider preferable. She looked up to find Alice holding out a can of ginger ale. "Try this. I don't normally take the ferry myself, so I never know how I'm going to handle the motion. I always get one at the dock, just in case... Not to be indelicate, but I didn't want to put more pressure on my bladder."

"Thanks," Riley sighed. Cracking it open, she drank down the cold, sugary bubbles and was grateful. She noticed Alice squirm in discomfort as Riley glugged down most of the can and realized the other woman was probably thinking of the inevitable consequences of consuming liquids.

"Hey, there are people out here, waiting!" Riley yelled, pounding her fist on the bathroom door again, her hand stinging at the repeated angry impact. But her bravado seemed to drop through the bottom of her stomach as the boat tipped over a particularly high swell. She braced her arm against the wall and clutched her middle. "Sorry, Alice, the bathroom hog seems impervious."

"Oh, I think I like you very much," Alice told her. "I also think I might be slightly afraid of you."

"That seems like a reasonable response," she whimpered in return.

"They say staring at the horizon helps," Alice told her gently. "Look, there's Starfall."

Slowly, Riley poked her head out of the alcove to see a coastal postcard come to life. Storybook houses formed a sort of wall at the front of the island's craggy stone hills with tiers of similar buildings rising behind them. Dabs of bold color dotted the houses' front porches in the form of hanging flower baskets. But her eye was drawn high on the point where Shaddow House stood, as if the rest of the island was meant to sit at its feet. The house where Aunt Nora had lived and worked for decades looked metastasized, like it was originally built as a quaint Victorian family home with a turret tower and rather theatrical front porch, then grew unbidden into its current disarray of random additions and chimneys. The robin's-egg-blue siding stood out from the pale grays and yellows typical of the other houses. The dreamy color seemed at odds with its somewhat ominous name.

For just a moment, a strange dark gray mist seemed to shroud the house between blinks of the eye. Riley shook her head, fluttering her eyelashes rapidly and downing the rest of her soda. Maybe she was sicker than she thought?

"I've lived here for most of my life, and I'll never get used to the way it just seems to rise out of the water like that," Alice sighed, smiling gently. "Like some friendly sea creature."

"Oh, you grew up here?" Another strange thrum bolted through Riley, a bit of sadness. She'd thought maybe Alice was an outsider too, and that they would both approach the island as strangers to it. But now she was alone again.

Alice nodded, her smile faltering a bit. "I moved here when

I was nine. I spent a lot of time roaming around unsupervised, until my grandparents decided it was time for me to work in the family antiques store. I probably know every inch of the island, except Shaddow House, of course. It's never been open to anyone, tourists or locals, for that matter. The family prefers their privacy. They don't want a bunch of fudgies traipsing through their rooms. And honestly, I can't blame them. Sorry, I tend to overshare when I feel that my internal organs are in danger of bursting."

Riley hummed in sympathy. She couldn't imagine what her aunt Nora did at Shaddow House if she wasn't organizing tours. Maybe she was something like an estate manager or a housekeeper? That seemed like a lot of work for a woman who was sixty-eight years old. Also, she was very curious as to what a "fudgie" could be, but she was afraid to ask.

Alice shrugged. "People tend to act like public places are disposable when they're on vacation. Or if they start to take a privilege for granted. Or if it's a day ending in Y."

For the first time in a while, Riley grinned. She hadn't connected with another person in so long; she didn't want this peculiar kinship to be over so soon. Maybe if she asked her aunt nicely, Riley could sneak Alice in on a special *private* tour of Shaddow House? But she didn't want to make any promises or set Alice up for disappointment. For all she knew, Aunt Nora was going to hand Riley a box of Ellen's old CDs and softball trophies, then boot her back onto the ferry.

And then Riley realized that she'd neglected to mention that she was Nora's niece, and now it felt like the moment had passed. It would be weird to bring it up now, right? After Alice had made comments about Riley's family, wouldn't that make Alice feel uncomfortable? Great. She used to be a lot better at this, the "talking to people" thing. Hell, she used to work as a telemarketer. People hated to talk to telemarketers, but somehow, she'd managed to make a living at it even while *she* hated it.

"Starfall Point, docking in five minutes," a cheerful recorded voice announced over the PA system. "Feel free to gather your belongings, but please don't stand near the gangways. You'll be enjoying our beautiful island before you know it. Thank you for choosing *The Loyal Retriever* on the Perkins Ferry Line, the *finest and oldest* family-run ferry service operating on Starfall Point."

"Maybe I can get off this boat without having to relieve myself off the side," Alice muttered, making Riley snort. She liked Alice's strangely formal way of speaking and wondered if it was a result of living on the island. She raised her hand to beat on the door, hollering again in Alice's defense, when suddenly, the door opened. A slumped form appeared in the doorway, and Riley's fist froze in midair.

All yelling stopped. Riley was stunned silent by what was possibly the most beautiful man she'd ever seen. He had black hair cut short around a long, angular face and eyes so dark blue, they rivaled the waters around them. His jawline was so ridiculously sharp, she was afraid to touch it—not that she thought he would be open to any such thing, anyway. But he was as pale as she was, possibly paler, with a sickly gray ring standing pale around his mouth.

"Could you please stop banging on the door?" he rasped, his lips going somehow even more ghostly.

Acknowledgments

I can never say enough "thank-yous" to my wonder of an agent, Natanya Wheeler, and the endlessly kind and "editorially generous" Rose Hilliard, for their unflagging support as I took us all through my unhinged version of an antique store. Thank you to Jocelyn Travis and the rest of the Sourcebooks Casablanca team for their enthusiastic and unwavering support. There is no Starfall magic without you. And then, there's Jeanette Battista, Caroline Johnson, Lish McBride, Chelsea Mueller, and Kristen Simmons; I will always appreciate you for reminding me to be nice to myself, drink water, sleep—all that responsible adult stuff. Thanks to my family for not blinking when they found cryptic story notes I'd left around the house, such as, "sprinkles, nothing but sprinkles" and "haunted narwhal." And finally, much gratitude to Judith Miller for her invaluable books, *Collectibles and Antique Handbook and Price Guide (2021–2022)* and *Furniture: World Styles from Classical to Contemporary.*

About the Author

Molly Harper is the *USA Today* bestselling author of more than forty paranormal romance, contemporary romance, women's fiction, and young adult titles. A lifelong romance reader, she graduated with a Master of Fine Arts from Seton Hill University, focusing on writing popular fiction. She lived in Kentucky for most of her life before recently moving to Michigan with her family...and she's still figuring out how to choose outerwear and play complicated winter card games.

Website: mollyharper.com
Instagram: @mollyharperauth